**Anthology of
Hindi Short Stories**

The sculpture reproduced on the endpaper depicts a scene where three soothsayers are interpreting to King Suddhodana the dream of Queen Maya, mother of Lord Buddha. Below them is seated a scribe recording the interpretation. This is perhaps the earliest available pictorial record of the art of writing in India.

From Nagarjunakonda, 2nd century A.D.

Courtesy : National Museum, New Delhi

Anthology of Hindi Short Stories

Compiled by
Bhisham Sahni

Translated from the Hindi by
Jai Ratan

Sahitya Akademi

Anthology of Hindi Short Stories: English translation by Jai Ratan of *Hindi Kahani Sanghrah*, compiled by Bhisham Sahni. Sahitya Akademi, New Delhi (2009) Rs. 150

Sahitya Akademi

Head Office
Rabindra Bhawan, 35, Ferozeshah Road, New Delhi-110 001

Sales Office
Swati, Mandir Marg, New Delhi-110 001

Regional Offices
172, Mumbai Marathi Grantha Sangrahalaya Marg, Dadar, Mumbai-400 014

Central College Campus, Dr. B.R. Ambedkar Veedhi, Bangalore-560 001

Jeevan Tara Building, 4th Floor, 23-A/44X, Diamond Harbour Road, Kolkata-700 053

Chennai Office
Main Guna Building Complex (second floor) 443(304), Anna Salai, Teynampet, Chennai-600 018

© Sahitya Akademi

First Published: 1993
Reprint: 1996, 2009

E-mail: sahityaakademisales@vsnl.net

Rupees One Fifty

ISBN: 81-7201-527-5

Printed at: Swastik Offset, Naveen Shahdara, Delhi 110 032

Contents

Introduction *Bhisham Sahni*	1
The Queen of Hearts *Phaneshwar Nath 'Renu'*	20
Lord of the Rubble *Mohan Rakesh*	34
Two Faiths *Amritlal Nagar*	46
The Soul of Bhola Ram *Hari Shankar Parsai*	67
Before Daybreak *Amrit Rai*	74
The Midday Meal *Amarkant*	86
Wang Chu *Bhisham Sahni*	94
Lost Directions *Kamleshwar*	117
Where Lakshmi is Imprisoned *Rajendra Yadav*	134
The Cherry Tree *Ram Kumar*	160
The Swan Flies Alone *Markandaya*	171
The Miller of Kosi *Shekhar Joshi*	186
My Enemy *Krishan Baldev Vaid*	197

Exorcism *Shailesh Matiyani*	207
Nanho *Shivprasad Singh*	226
The Encircling Clouds *Krishna Sobti*	242
Birds *Nirmal Verma*	262
Trishanku *Mannu Bhandari*	297
Return *Usha Priyamvada*	317
The Paperweight *Giriraj Kishore*	329
The Parrot *Hridayesh*	340
Hell-Bound *Shaani*	352
The Road *Ram Darash Mishra*	369
The Gong *Gyanranjan*	376
Encounter *Mudrarakshash*	389
Disturbance *Ramakant*	405
The Splinter *Govind Mishra*	413
Go Your Way, Baba! *Kashinath Singh*	420
Cake *Asghar Wajahat*	436
The Return of the Assassins *Mithileshwar*	453
Contributors	467

Introduction

I accepted this assignment of the Sahitya Akademi with great enthusiasm; as I have an abiding interest in the art of the short story. I felt I had had close professional links with the writers and the literary creations of my own generation as well as with the generation that followed mine. Added to this was the fact of my own close involvement with the various movements that had arisen from time to time in the sphere of the short story. My task would be interesting as well as easy, I thought. It was just a question of bringing together a couple of dozen stories. Given my own scholastic and creative labours of thirty to thirty-five years, surely I could assemble some twenty-five stories.

But the task was not as easy as I had presumed. Problems cropped up from the word 'go'. The first question that arose was: should I draw up a list of authors or a list of outstanding stories? When I started drawing up a list of authors it became longer and longer. Not twenty-five but fifty names contended for inclusion, not because so and so was my friend, or that so and so thought like me and therefore deserved a place, or that so and so was hostile and if I did not include him he would accuse me of favouritism, or that so and so, though not considered to have made the grade in the eyes of the readers, had done so in mine, etc. Not for these reasons did the list grow long, but because during the last thirty-five years, undoubtedly significant work has/been and is being done in the field of short fiction. More writers than ever before are seriously concerned with this art and are enriching our literature with their work.

What was I to do? Whom should I retain, whom exclude?

I decided upon a master list of outstanding stories. It would be easier to finally select twenty-five stories from this master list.

Now another question stared me in the face. Was I expected merely to select twenty-five unparalleled stories or stories that were also representative of their age? Without being a literary masterpiece a story may be significant even if it is not a literary masterpiece. It may give a new direction to the art of story writing, give it a new perspective, so to say. It may be a commendable effort in the task of breaking new ground, possess a freshness of tone, give the sense of being a trendsetter. It may suggest a breaking of boundaries, may give the feel that the writer's sensibility was struggling to capture some vibration in the environment.

And then, what if the outstanding stories happened to be about urban life only? People might well ask whether all writers had deserted the village! And what if all the outstanding stories had the same tone? All with high-sounding intensity. Or all didactic and moralistic? People would ask if the founts of romance and humour had dried up in the Hindi short story.

I concluded finally, that I was required to put together representative stories which reflected the trends of their times. In addition to high literary merit, they ought to provide glimpses of the multi-faceted and many-hued development of the short story.

But this was also none too easy a task. It did not seem right to me to first classify stories into stories of city life, of rural life, domestic life, of women's life, etc. Or into stories of humour, of the middle class, the lower middle class, existentialist stories, socially conscious stories, stories representative of particular literary movements, stories of Muslim or Hindu milieus etc. This would make my task mundane and mechanical, which I did not like.

Another problem: should I select stories only by writers who were primarily known as short story writers and had made their mark in literature basically through this genre? Or was I free to include writers whose main contribution did not lie in the field of the short story, but in other artistic or cultural fields, but had in passing happened to write some good stories? Some writers are essentially poets, or painters or journalists; what was to be done with their stories? Or with the stories of those, who, on their entry into the literary field, worked full tilt for some years, wrote many stories, and then gradually moved into other fields such as publishing or journalism? For that matter there was Guleriji who had left behind a host of literary descendents, who had fired just a couple of arrows in the field of the short story, but those arrows had made their mark. What was to be done with the stories of such writers?

The question was not whether to include them or not. The question was whose stories should be removed from the list in order to make room for their stories? Should priority be given to those who had devoted years to the art of the short story genre, had refined it, chiselled and shaped it, and had made it their main medium of expression, or to those who had in passing produced a couple of memorable stories, and then, getting bored, had turned to other fields?

And then there were some others such as Ramnarain Shukla, Ibrahim Sharif, Raj Kamal who had met an untimely death, those who were just coming into their own when the pen fell from their hands. These writers might have influenced the course of the short story writing, but they had certainly contributed to it.

Sinking deeper and deeper into the morass of selection, I began to wonder whether my own selection could be called impartial. I myself claim to be a story writer. What kind of a writer is one who finds the same stories outstanding that others do? If all stories evoked the same response, why indeed, the stormy disputes and denunciations that are so much more marked in the domain of the story than in other branches of literature? Where was the guarantee that my selection would be impartial and objective? I have my own preferences and these could come in the way. Various controversies are going on among us about form and content in the story, about its aims, about its structure, about the relationship between the author and the reader, about the writer's sense of commitment. I have my own views on these questions, and even while trying not to inflict views on others could I avoid doing so? So on and so forth. There were hordes of such questions that made my task difficult.

In a way I am offering an argument in my defence, by dwelling on all this. I was really hamstrung by the fact that in an anthology of a specified length it was just not possible to include all the representative stories I had in mind. Some stories had to be left out, for one reason or another. But if this collection succeeds even to some extent in providing a glimpse of the post-independence short story, if it helps us feel the pulse of our times, I shall consider it a worthwhile effort.

Story writing is not a conscious activity in the sense that the writer makes a conscious effort to communicate to the reader a sense of the times by using the medium of the story. A story worth the name is never written with that kind of deliberation. It is the story writer's sensibility that determines the direction of the story, not the writer's theories or hard and fast convictions. To my mind, the form of the story too, is not anything separate or distinct, that can be used as a wrap or a guise, that can be used for its own sake. The emotions rising in the writer's mind bring with them their own forms of expression. Form and content are one. It is not that the emotions comes first and then to give shape to it, the writer, with a calm, deliberate mind chooses a framework in which to fit the emotion, its theme and substance. Just as the line comes whole, to the poet, complete with emotion, word, and rhythm, the story too, from its very first line, finds its own form or mode of expression, feels its way to it, and shapes itself as it goes along. In saying this, I do not in any way minimize the writer's judgment, logic, values or structuring of form. All these are significant, but only after absorption into the writer's sensibility, and expressed as organically one with it.

The writer's sensibility, through its network of predispositions absorbs its environment, lives and breathes in it. Therefore, a story written in a particular period of time cannot but be coloured by that time and its atmosphere. The stories written before independence and those written 20 or 25 years later are bound to be different, considered from this premiss. In the development of the story we do not come across milestones or stages, we cannot state categorically that after a particular event the story changed its form and substance, or that the hold of traditional values and beliefs abruptly slackened. That is never how it happens. No matter how strongly a writer denounces tradition it stays in some form or other intermixed with or latent in the changed environment. But with changing times its impact begins to slacken. And we begin to sense a new vision, a new grasp. For instance, in my childhood, Mother India was often imagined as a woman in chains, and in accordance with this image literature came to be marked by voices singing of sacrifice and of an idealised freedom.

> Pluck me, O gardener,
> Cast me in that path
> Which heroes tread
> As they go to give up their lives
> for the motherland.

But such verses gradually lost their force after Independence. Times changed. Life became more complicated more tense. It is not without reason that an ironical vision emerged in post-independence literature, a satirical vision that exposed the contradictions in society and expressed dissatisfaction.

Thus the literature of each period is coloured by its atmosphere; we feel in it a peculiar pulse of life. It is, of course, true, that we do not savour the pleasures of literature period-wise. Were it so, we would only read stories written in our own time. However, it does often happen, that older readers do not very much care for stories written by younger writers. They have got so habituated to the literature that influenced them in their youth that they cannot appreciate later writing. These later writers, do not fit into the value system and assumptions to which they are accustomed. That, however is a different matter. In spite of differences, the literature of one period is not altogether different from that of another. The depth of human sensibility that permeates all good writing links the literatures of one period with that of another. This humanity enables literature to transcend time, prevents it from ageing despite the passing of centuries. This humanity makes literature relevant in time as well as free of time. The literature that is most relevant to its time, becomes, on the strength of this humanity, meaningful for other times too. But when the wellsprings of humanity begin to dry up in a literature, it grows irrelevant even in its own time, let alone later times.

After Independence a great many changes took place in our social context, on a material level, and also on the emotional and mental levels. Before Independence, a whole generation was emotionally involved with the freedom struggle and lakhs of people were active in it. After Independence these lakhs of people suddenly became inactive. The affairs of the country began to be run by the government, the bureaucracy, the police and the army. This was to some extent inevitable, but it deeply hurt the sense of a collective endeavour. Overnight those who had been involved in the freedom struggle were marginalised as mere spectators. That sense of connection with every process in the country, of personal contribution to a collective efforts, of regarding every national gain as one's own gain, began to cool in ardour. A gulf opened up between the establishment and the people, a gulf which gradually widened.

Moreover, it is one thing to fight for freedom and quite another to play the chessboard of politics. A particular type of human being emerged in the country who had rarely been seen before—cunning, pragmatic, a manipulator, one who pushed others aside to make his way forward, one whose field of action was political manouvering. The selfless patriot of the pre-Independence days was replaced by the manipulator. Society swarmed with these aggressive, bossy and monopolistic people who collect amenities for themselves and their kin, who elbow their way to the head of the queue for everything, from a licence for trade to a bed in the hospital. This gave a rude jolt to our image of a patriot. Opportunism grew in national life, and the ordinary person felt that this was not the freedom we had dreamed of.

Admittedly, after Independence, the pre-Independence situation had to change. To fight for freedom is one thing, but to sustain it, strengthen it, to run the administration and build new bases of national life were not tasks that could be accomplished overnight. Possibly, we were getting over-eager and impatient. To construct big dams, establish factories, to extract the ore from the bowels of the earth, to develop agriculture and industry are time-consuming jobs. The poverty of thousands of years could not vanish in a day as if by magic. But behind these strivings there was no sense of collective endeavour. And daily life was becoming more difficult. No palpable change for the better was discernible in the system.

The complexities of life grew. Inequalities grew. Contradictions and disparities in social life grew. The common people's struggle for existence became more intense, with the escalating prices and increasing unemployment. The effect of all this could not but be felt in our social life and our perceptions. In literature the voices of dissent and doubt began to be heard. In some case the disillusionment was so strong that life came to be seen as meaningless, and belief in traditional values seemed to dwindle. Yet the human voice of literature remained. This was a time when many movements known by different names sprang up in the field of the story, reaching their climax in the movement of the non-story, in which not only were moral values negated, but attempts to break down the form and structure of the story were also made.

The writer, in his own life, could not escape the effect of these pervasive changes. The metropolitan cities became centres of literary and cultural activity. The call of the city became irresistible to writers, most of whom had graduated from universities. Soon Delhi and Bombay became the chief centres of the literary upsurge. Here there were renowned magazines, there was the radio, there were publishers and far greater professional facilities and prospects. Many writers took to metropolitan life. It goes without saying that there is a difference, in terms of an experienced sphere between those living in the metropolis and those living in small towns or villages. A writer entrenched in the rural milieu has deep ties with his environment. The village in its entirety forms his/her field of vision—the quality of human relationships within it, the changing colours of nature, even the ways of life of animals are the breeding ground of his/her creativity. Such writers feel the pulse beat of all of rural life. It is not so in the city. Here one is a stranger to one's own shadow. The inhabitants of the city are mostly the middle classes and one characteristic of the middle class is that they are not free mixers, and usually limit their concerns to themselves and their own affairs.

As a result of this there grew a preponderance of short stories depicting middle class life. The story's links with small town life weakened. Bearing in mind the fact that the bulk of the country's population lives in villages, and that the impact of their lives is not much felt in stories, the range of the short story has certainly shrunk. However, being a generally a city dweller, the writer developed a surer grasp of urban middle class life. City life too was getting more complex, with more stresses and strains. The joint family system was beginning to crack. After all a whole clan could not be contained in a two-room flat. Due to economic strains women began going out in search of jobs which told on family life in various ways. New dimensions of women's personalities began to emerge. New situations arose, bringing with them new problems such as the stifling effects of city life, changing values in the context of changing human relationships, growing professionalism and an individualistic vision.

The writer assimilates experience from a material environment. Even if unconsciously, the writer's sensibility grasps those invisible hurts which connect one event to another. From the maternal context arises the atmosphere, the spirit of the times which the writer's sensibility catches.

Despite many incongruities and contradictions the life of our country after Independence retained a certain dynamism as many new challenges emerged. There were three wars, many movements, strikes and public demonstrations. In the agricultural, industrial and other sectors things were on the move on a massive scale. Things never stagnated. The times were rife with discontent, agitation, struggle, competition, and such an atmosphere is undoubtedly conducive to creativity. The movements that took place in the field of story writing were the results of this ferment, even if some were motivated by professional considerations. The prevailing temper, however, was one of genuine ferment. The short story broke new grounds, tried new experiments both in language and style. Didactic stories were left far behind, the kind of story based on a narrator's recounting of an episode emerged with a new insonance. Diversity flourished. Some found lyricism a suitable mode of expression, others took to satire, hollow sentimentalism more or less disappeared from the story. The hold of realism became stronger and the definition of realism also underwent a change. By realism was not meant literal depiction of an event but a grasp of the factors, the conflicts latent in the material context; the tendency to confront life directly gathered strength, while any form of escapism, of evasion of the ugly facets of life grew increasingly outmoded.

It cannot of course be said categorically that the Hindi short story took a new turn after 1947. Such clearcut lines cannot be drawn in literary history. But one can say with some certainty that while old practices gradually faded out, new trends made themselves felt, and gradually the short story began to break new grounds and develop new dimensions.

There is no doubt that didactisism was on the wane; It had been on the decline even earlier but had now begun to exasperate the reader. That a story should be written merely to illustrate a moral maxim-such a conception of story writing was definitely out of favour. This, however, did not mean that the Hindi short story had ceased to be purposeful or concerned with moral values. Purposiveness remained, but now it entered the warp and woof of the story; to fit it into a preconceived framework was considered wrong. The earlier framework of the story had started to break. The tendency to provide a moral to the story, to simplify life, and see it in black and white terms, was definitely being sloughed off by the story. Now the tendency was to come in direct contact with life, to take cognizance of its complexities, to submerge oneself in it, and to liberate oneself from preconceptions.

Gradually, moral platitudes ceased to be the focus of the short story. The story now moved into the sphere of 'human situation'. This shift in emphasis widened the scope of the story and also enhanced its aesthetics. The contradictions in human relationships, the dilemmas created by changing contexts, the inner tensions of characters, new pressures and new problems became the raw material for the story. The story presented itself as a more authentic and living genre. In short, the story had come to life as never before.

It is true that the pressure towards an idealistic vision had been a part of our tradition down the ages. This meant that human values were sustained in our literature but it also meant that our grasp on the realities of life never grew very strong. But now, definitely, the writer's vision had shifted somewhat from abstract ideals and principles to a greater concentration on the realities of life.

In the meanwhile we went through a spell in which stories of disenchantment came to be written, that is, stories about loss of faith, in these beliefs, expectations and hopes which had served as guideposts to us. In these stories emphasis was laid on the darker aspects of life, on the distortions to which human nature is subject, on the smallness, dwarfishness and helplessness of the human being. This was partly the result of the influence of a particular kind of Western literature—of a kind of realism wherein the writer saw futility and meaninglessness as the prevailing reality of existence. But the real basis of these stories was not so much the dilemmas of life, as of a certain mind-set which wanted to see life in these terms. All said and done, however, the anti-idealist stance was the high watermark of the short story in this period. But this phase was short-lived and the Hindi story soon regained its equilibrium.

Another kind of diversity also entered the Hindi short story. The Hindi speaking region is vast, embracing seven states of the Indian Union. And one comes across Hindi writers in almost all parts of the country. It is also an interesting truth that non-Hindi speaking writers have perhaps contributed more to Hindi literature than the Hindi speaking ones. The short story written in Rajasthan and the one written in Bihar have each their own distinct colour although both are in Hindi. One has the flavour of Rajasthani, and the other, of Bhojpuri. The proverbs, sayings, jokes, modes of humour, and customs are distinct. This has enriched the vocabulary of Hindi and has increased the diversity of the Hindi short story.

Before Independence, English was the medium of our contact with Western thought and literature. And there is no doubt that generations of our intelligentsia have been deeply influenced by English literature. The short story as we know it today is a gift of the West. After Independence this contact grew wider. American, French, Russian, Latin American, African and other literatures began to reach us through translation and the influence of foreign literatures grew.

The Second World War in Europe came to an end in 1944, and after it disenchantment was the key-note of the literature that began to be written in Western Europe thereafter. In fact the existential temper gained ascendency in Western literature on the wings of this disenchantment. Undoubtedly this temper was strengthened by the horrors of war and the complexities of the post-war era.

Since in our country too, a mood of doubt had begun to grow around 1950, it began to be felt that the conditions in our own country and those in Europe were not so far apart. This attitude, accordingly, began to find expression in our literature. Existential stories began to be written here too.

Existential literature did, undoubtedly shake up the sensibility of Indian writers, but it could not find the conditions for growth here, conditions which are created by authentic life experience. We were no doubt deeply moved at the intellectual level but the experiences of which these stories were the products in Western Europe were not experiences through which we had passed. In addition, the impact of 200 years of industrial life on their society was not part of our life, at least not in that form. A perspective cultivated merely through intellectual excitement, and lacking the solidity of actual experience cannot take one far. We did not have the experience of two hundred years of industrial growth, nor did we have the experience of the acute contradictions of a capitalistic system. In spite of the problems coming in the wake of Independence our country was a struggling country. We were just entering the industrial age. Our traditional ways of life—caste, community and kin networks, the joint family, indigenous collective business practices—had shown no signs of cracking up. They had only begun to feel the stress of changing conditions. The pace of life in our country was not what it was in Europe; not that kind of competitiveness or that kind of individualism. Our people managed to survive by sharing each others joys and sorrows, nor had we lost all hope in the future. We had not developed the sense of groping in a dark blind alley from which there is no way out. Hence to try to transfer the mentality of citizen of post-war Europe to the Indian situation amounted to gross reductionism. It is difficult for us in our country to conceive of the human condition in the same way as it is conceived of in Europe. A citizen of our country will not be able to understand directionlessness, especially a citizen who is struggling at some level or other, and is still deeply connected with traditional assumptions and values.

If this trend failed to change the course of the Hindi short story it was because it was not linked with either our experience or with our tradition. Conditions here were different. The endeavour to forcibly fit this trend into the Indian context proved unsuccessful. But we cannot say the same of Europe's literature of the past. The literature of the 19th century had proved very popular in our country and had contributed substantially to the development of our own literature. Dickens, Victor Hugo, Tolstoy and others had deeply influenced us because there is a close similarity between difficulties of life in the society of the Europe of that time and our own society. Consequently, even if we had appropriated the mental outlook of the Europe of that time our own experience would have created a base for our appropriation. From this point of view the literature of the socialist countries is closer to our life experience.

Nonetheless, this literary phase had a definite role in the development of the Hindi short story. In the stories written under its influence, events were relegated to the background and the emotions produced by situations were brought to the fore. The mental state of a person placed in a particular situation was analysed in minute details with a subtle pen. A lyrical quality came to mark the story. For that matter, the effects and counter effects of concrete events are not essential to poetry.

The story became more inward looking. The direct cognizance of life was no longer its cardinal aim, but the subtle depiction of emotions set in train by events. The hidden powers of language emerged, and the portrayal of a mentality centred on the self acquired importance. One can see these features in Nirmal Verma's stories, as also in those of Govind Mishra, Mrinal Pande and Raji Seth.

If we traverse the ground covered by the Hindi story from the beginning, when it shook itself free of the influence of the occult and detective thriller and descended to the terrain of realities, up to today, we find the story becoming increasingly society-oriented. The development of this humanist society-orientedness has passed through many stages. There was a time when didactic stories were the rule, with a moral tagged on. Then came a phase when, stepping out of the confines of the individual and the family, the story entered the larger domain of society and the individual came to represent a collectivity, a group, and the depiction of events too came to have a larger relevance, related not only to personal life but to the collective objectives and aims of society as a whole. Then came another phase when the incongruities and disparities within society and the forces at work behind them on the social and economic planes became the themes of the story, when the story became problem-centred, and when society was no longer seen as a single unit but as the theatre of the struggles between various classes for their own benefits. Here the characters were not merely individuals, but represented their class.

In this manner, new facets kept being added to socially oriented realism. And this process still continues.

The story has neither lost its ground nor shifted away from its larger humanist perspective. The urge to come face to face with life has, if anything become more pronounced by which it has gained not only the solid ground of experience but also a greater authenticity.

One question relating to ideology has cropped up again in relation to the short story. This question is in a way inevitable because various ways of thinking have from time to time, arisen like powerful waves, whether the existential, socialist or any other. Here we are not concerned with this debate but no writer has ever been free of ideology. Every writer has his or her own vision of life—inherited patterns, life-experiences, reading and study, values and assumptions all contribute to the making of this vision. While presenting an image of life the story also induces readers, to think and gives them a perspective on life. No story can be conceived without the bedrock of thought, yet, a story is primarily a story, thought comes assimilated with it, and it is the evidence of the narrative that imparts plausibility to the thought contained in it. Ideology becomes fruitful only when it comes as an inalienable part of the writer's vision, and total creative personality. A story cannot be exploited as a vehicle for a brand of thought, nor can a story ever prove the truth of a particular ideology. If ideology is evident in Premchand's stories, his stories are also formally grounded, bearing the stamp of authenticity and deep emotion. But where he seems to give primacy to a way of thinking the stories fail to satisfy. Of course, it sometimes happens that the emotions of the writer are so profound and authentic that we cannot but be moved by the writer's intense feeling.

When we come to think of it, the various movements in the short story have each been agitated by this question of ideology. Some philosophy or vision of life animated each one, and its protagonists expected the writer to see and judge life from the perspective they thought was correct. No movement was free or empty of ideology, much less living in a state of vacuity. Many writers who were closely associated with these movements have emphasised the importance of a 'vision of life' in their writings:

> The new story is not the communication of some isolated or concentrated moments of life, but the story of those dormant or hidden values and meanings of life which make themselves felt at may levels. Today the selection of the narrative viewpoint is of the utmost significance, and therefore, the importance of situations loaded with meaning has naturally increased.
>
> —Kamleshwar
> *Introduction to the New Story*

Similarly, according to Maheep Singh, 'Awareness' is a point-of-view, whereby life is lived as well as understood:

> The word 'aware' evokes a special way of looking at reality, at the environment, and of life—a way that stresses human consciousness and activity. In other words, the writers of awareness stories wish to see human beings in their fullness, from their unconscious and subconscious being to their conscious being. The conscious self is taken to be the decisive element in the building of personality.
>
> —Rajiv Saxena
> *Sachetan Kahani:*
> *The New Boundaries of Literature*

But all said and done, a story speaks for itself, with its own voice. A story that spontaneously illuminates its latent vision, it is not in need of explication.

Undoubtedly, in its evolution the Hindi short story has become multi-faceted. It is true, that from the point of view of theme, the Hindi short story is still tied to the apron strings of city life, especially the life of the metropolis. Comparatively speaking, there is still a paucity of stories based on rural and small town life. Many other spheres of life also remain almost untouched such as, industrial life, life on the high seas and so on. And this fact underlines the point that in prose the writer can write with some authority only about those aspects of life which are a part of his or her own area of experience. One may be able to write poetry without much concrete experience, but not fiction. Of course we can make an effort to gain experience of an area of life, enough experience to write a story. But such efforts demand another effort, for which the Hindi short story writer is not yet usually prepared. Who would leave behind the amenities of city life and go to live amongst miners or agricultural labourers? The writer does this either from some inner urge, some inner compulsion or out of sheer economic necessity. The Hindi writer is a member of the middle classes, accustomed to urban life, timid and easily frightened.

The Hindi short story has undoubtedly gained in depth but not so much in range. Sometimes one feels that the sphere of experience in the short story is shrinking. Before Independence there was a plethora of stories in Hindi with a Muslim context. Premchand himself has written several such stories. He knew well the Muslim way of life. After Independence the Hindi writer has seldom tried his hand at such stories, a shortcoming which had begun to jar. Fortunately, many fine Muslim writers themselves have made good this shortcoming by writing in Hindi. Among them are the late Ibrahim Shareef, the late Badiuzaman, Alam Shah Khan, Meherunisa Parvez, late Rahi Masoom Raza, Gulsher Khan Shaani, Asghar Wajahat, Abdul Bismillah and others. We have come to know about the special problems and travails of writers. They have played a great role not only in enriching Hindi literature but also in increasing mutual understanding in national life, bringing people closer to each other, and truly strengthening a composite culture.

In the same manner there has been in the last two decades a great increase in the number of women writers whose writings occupy a special place in the Hindi short story. New names are constantly coming up. We cannot name them all—they are just too many. For the past many years we have been familiar with the names of Krishna Sobti, Mannu Bhandari, Usha Priyamvada, Shivani, Mamta Kalia. Along with them we now have Dipti Khandelwal, Manjul Bhagat, Mridula Garg, Nirupma Sevti, Indu Bali, Mrinal Pande, Raji Seth, Suryabala, Namita Singh—all names to be reckoned with.

Every generation lives under the happy illusion that it is unique among all generations and is unparalleled in achievement. After its exit, it will be curtain down, it thinks. But the truth is that even while it is holding the stage, other writers invade the arena and fill the stage so fast that the older writers feel that their generation lacks standing room. This is the situation in the short story today. The writers of the fifties, the sixties and the seventies jam-pack the literary scene today. It is said that in the Hindi short story a generation matures every decade, and a movement begins to make waves every ten years and this situation seems peculiar to the Hindi story. There are several writers of whom it is difficult to say to which generation they belong. But their contributions have certainly enriched the Hindi short story, for example, Ramakant, Shekhar Joshi, S.R. Yatri, Ravindra Kalia, Mudrarakshas, Maheep Singh, Himanshu Joshi, Ganga Prasad Vimal, Kamtanath, Jagdamba Prasad Gupt, Ramdas Dixit, Ramesh Bakshi, Dharmendra Gupt, Ramesh Upadhayay, Madhukar Singh, Yogesh Gupt, Satish Jamali, Satyen Kumar, Balaram, Dhirendra Asthana, Ramesh Batra, Israel. The list seems endless.

Conditions today are harder for the younger writer. The main problem is one of getting published. It takes years to break into print in established journals whose number is very small. If one gets published in small magazines one will catch the eyes of only a few. The little magazines have rendered commendable service in keeping younger writers from losing heart. But in spite of these difficulties many new younger writers keep appearing on the literary scene and are playing an influential role.

The Hindi short story thus has passed through many stages in its evolution. On the one hand it has maintained its links with the humanist tradition of Indian literature, and on the other, it confronts contemporary life and conveys the feel and pulse of modernity. Most important, it has grown ever more deeply connected with life. Maybe thematically it has not acquired range, but it has definitely acquired intensity and depth. The story is still the most popular genre in Hindi literature, and perhaps it is for this reason that writers of diverse temperament and tendency have adopted this form. No matter that in its course it has often tilted in one direction or another, losing its equilibrium. It still has not lost its hold on the substance of life. And that is why it is still alive and kicking. Undoubtedly it will continue to enrich our country's literature in the years to come.

BHISHAM SAHNI

Phaneshwar Nath 'Renu'

The Queen of Hearts

'Birju's mother, aren't you coming to the dance?'

Birju's mother had just boiled sweet potatoes and was sulking in the courtyard. Seven year old Birju, who had received slaps instead of sweet potatoes from her, writhed in the courtyard, coating his body with dust in the process. Champia too was in for trouble. Gone since afternoon, when half the courtyard was still sunlit, to buy jaggery from the grocerwoman, she was not back yet, at lighting-up hour. 'Just let her come back, the foot-loose wanton!' The goat had got the mange and leapt wildly every now and again. Birju's mother stepped out, ready to unleash her anger on the goat. Those bunches of chilli in flower! Who else but the goat could have breakfasted on them? She had just picked up a clod of earth to fling at the goat when she heard her neighbour Makhni aunt call out to her: 'Birju's mother! Not going to see the dance?'

'Birju's mother can go only when she has no hearth to blow on and no cooking to mess about with.'

The scalding words, soaked in the lava of anger, pierced Aunt. Birju's mother threw back the clod of earth on the ground, her anger vented. The poor goat, driven mad with the ticks cried A-ha, Aay...aay...hr...r...r...!

From where he lay Birju struck the goat with a stick. Birju's mother wanted to beat to boy with the same stick but stopped when she heard ripples of laughter from the women standing under the acacia tree, waiting to draw water.

'You wait!' she growled at Birju. 'Your father has taught you to be very free with your hands! Swiping at everyone! Just wait!'

Aunt Makhni, putting down her pitcher from her waist, cried out for justice to her companions. 'Look at this mother of Birju! Ever since she sold four maunds of jute her feet don't touch the ground! Judge for yourself. For a whole week before the fair she has been shooting off her mouth in every lane and by-lane, 'Birju's father has promised to take me in the bullock cart to the dance at Balrampur. We have our own bullocks, a thousand carts can be had for the asking'...So what did I do wrong if I went to remind her that. All those going to the fair are ready and waiting, having done with the kitchen. Well, burn my tongue! Why did I go there? Do you know what Birju's mother said?'

Aunt Makhni twisted her lips to one side of her toothless mouth and parodied: 'B ..i ..r ..j ..u ..'s mo .. ther ca .. an go whe .. n she has no h .. e .. a .. r .. t .. h to blow into and no coo .. k .. i .. n .. g to mess about with.'

Jangi's daughter-in-law is not afraid of Birju's mother. Full-throatedly she says, 'If you too had flirted with the Settlement Officer in a bright print sari and given him *bhanta* plants, he would have earmarked a few bighas of fertile land in your name too. Then you would have ten maunds of good quality jute stored in your house. Enough to buy two bullocks. Then they would have blown into your hearth and taken over the cooking from you.'

Jangi's daughter-in-law is bold of speech. Brought up in the vicinity of the railway station, it's just three months since she came as a sparkling new bride and has already had triumphant skirmishes with all the quarrelsome mothers-in-law in the Kurma Colony. Her father-in-law Jangi is a notorious dacoit, marked by the police. Her husband, Rangi, is a renowned *lathi* wielder of the Kurma community. That is why she swaggers around tossing her horns!

Jungi's daughter-in-law's full-throated remarks whizzed into Birju's mother's yard, like stones from a catapult. Birju's mother had a sharp retort ready but she held her tongue. Why fling a stone at a heap of dung?

Swallowing her anger, Birju's mother called out to her daughter, 'Champia,' 'Champia-a-a-a, I'll wring your neck today and shove you into the hearth! Getting to be a wanton. City brides crooning theatre and film songs have flooded this village. You slut, you must be sitting somewhere I earning to sing 'Baje muralia'. Champia-a-a-a...'

Relishing Birju's mother's tirade, Jangi's daughter-in-law secured her water pitcher at her waist and swaying her hips said,' Come, sisters, let's go. This colony is the preserve of the Queen of Hearts, red and fiery. Don't you see electric lights flame and flare here two quarters of the day and four quarters of the night?'

They all burst out laughing.

'Devil's grandmother?' Makhni Aunt let fall an affectionate expletive through her broken row of teeth.

Birju's mother felt as if someone had blinded her eyes with the dazzling light of a torch. Flaming and flaring electric lights! Three years ago, after the Survey Camp had left, the envious village women had spread a story that the electric light glared and glowered all night in Champia's mother's yard. In Champia's mother's yard were now heard the beats of iron shod boots like the clacking of horse shoes!

Let them burn with envy! Burn more! Let the women burn black like baked brinjals at the sight of silvery jute drying in her courtyard, and golden paddy heaped in her barn.

Licking off her fingers some jaggery that had spilt out of the pot, Champia came in, was slapped by her mother, and screamed: 'Why do you beat me? The grocer woman takes her own time. Oh, ...'

'Don't talk rubbish! So that woman didn't serve you soon? But there are other shops. Was it raining pearls in that shop that you took root there? Speak up or I'll kick you in the neck and smash it, you hussy, if I ever hear you singing that Krishna song! Goes to learn dirty tricks from the slatterns around the station...' She stopped to gauge if her voice had carried to Jangi's hut.

Birju had risen to his feet, forgetting the slaps he had received. Brushing the dust from his clothes, he greedily stared at the pot from which wet jaggery oozed. If he had gone with his sister to the shop, surely she would have allowed him a lick. The lure of the sweet potatoes had held him back. And look what he had got in place of sweet potatoes!

'Ma, ma, give me a fingertip's breadth of jaggery,' implored Birju, spreading out his palms, 'Give me, ma, just a little bit!'

'Why just a bit? I'll throw the whole pot in the backyard, then you can to lick it. No sweet potato *rotis* will be made in this house. Slobber away all you like!'

Birju's mother placed a plateful of sweet potatoes before the weeping Champia. 'Sit down and peel them, or I'll ...' Ten-year-old Champia knows that while she is peeling the sweet potatoes her mother will shake her by the hair at least a dozen times, pick holes in her work and shower her with abuses... 'Why do you spread your legs like that? Shameless girl!' Champia knows her mother's temper.

Birju cajoled, 'Ma, shall I also peel the potatoes?'

'No,' his mother said angrily. You will eat three for every one you peel. Go and fetch the frying pan from Sidhu's mother. The woman borrows it for an hour and keeps it for ever. Go on, get moving.'

With a hangdog expression, Birju paused in the yard to cast a covert look at the jaggery and sweet potatoes. Champia stole a glance at her mother from behind her screen of scruffy hair and quickly tossed a sweet potato to him. He made off with it.

'The sun-god has set. It is lighting-up time. And no cart yet.'

'Ma, nobody in the Koyri colony is willing to lend his cart.' Champa spoke up. 'Father told me: Tell Ma to be ready. I'll ask for a cart from Mianjaan of the Maldahiya's colony, he said.'

Birju's mother's face fell like an umbrella folding up when its spokes cave in suddenly. No one in their own Koyri colony was prepared to lend his cart. Why should Mianjaan of the Maldahiyas oblige them then? They had fallen between two stools. Why peel sweet potatoes? Put the thing away. This man show them the dance? This man give them a joy ride in a cart? No way—much chance they had of a cart or a dance! Who had set out on foot must have reached there long ago!

Birju came back, wearing the iron frying pan on his head. 'Look, didia, military helmet. It will take ten lathi blows and no harm done!'

Champia refused to be drawn out. She sat silent, without even a hint of a smile on her face. Birju understood that his mother was still angry.

Birju's mother chased the goat out of the hut, muttering, 'You devil, tomorrow I'll hand you over to Panchkori butcher. Sniffing at everything. Champia, tie up the goat and take the bell off its neck. Tinkling away all the time. The sound is hateful!'

The word 'tinkling' reminded Birju of the bullock carts going along the road. In the Babu's colony carts were all on their way to the dance... The tinkling of bells on the bullocks' necks, did you hear....

'Keep your mouth shut!' Champia said, as she, removed the bell from the goat's neck.

'Champia, douse the fire with water. When your father comes tell him to fly to the dance in his flying machine. I'm not interested in going to any dance. And don't wake me up. I've got a headache.'

Sitting on the threshold, Birju whispered to Champia, 'Didi, will there be a flying machine at the dance?'

Wrapping herself in a patchwork quilt, Champia sat down on a mat and signalled to Birju to sit quietly beside her. The poor boy would be in for another beating otherwise.

Birju snuggled beside her under the quilt, with his knees drawn up to his chin. He had learnt to sit like this during the cold winter months. Putting his mouth to Champia's ear he whispered, 'Aren't we going to the dance? Not a bird is left in the village. Everybody has gone.'

Champia had now lost all hope of going to the dance. The evening star had set. Father had still not come with the cart. For a whole month, mother had been saying she would make sweet *rotis* to carry to the Balrampur dance, Champia would wear her printed sari and Birju his pants. And they would sit in a bullock cart....

A tear glistened on Champi's eyelashes. Birju was also near crying. In his heart he vowed an offering of a brinjal to the genie living in the tamarind tree—the first brinjal of the season, from the plant he had himself tended. 'Please, Jinn Baba, send father soon with the bullock cart.'

Birju's mother was lying on the mat, tossing and turning. She was thinking, 'Never, never nurse hopes in advance. God always dashes them. The first thing she has to ask God was for which lapse he was punishing her like this. To the best of her knowledge she had kept all the vows made to all the gods and ancestors, all the vows taken in the hope of getting land when the survey was going on. Oh, of course, the vow of *rot* for Mahavirji! That was still not fulfilled! Forgive the oversight, Mahavir Baba! Birju's mother will double the offering!'

Jangi's daughter-in-law's words kept stabbing at her—glaring and glowering electric light indeed! Daughter-in-law of thieves and scavengers—why would she not burn with envy? A mere five bighas of land Birju's father had managed to get and the women of the village had their eyes gritty with envy! The jute growing on the five bighas of land made all the villagers' hearts burst. The young jute plants are exploding out of the earth like monsoon clouds that come in masses. But could they bear the darts of so many eyes? Where there should have been fifteen maunds of jute only ten tipped the scale on Rabbi Bhagat's weighbridge. What was there to be jealous of? Birju's father had explained to each man in the Kurma colony, 'You will slog as labourers all your life. Survey time is here. Hold fast to your lathi and stake a claim for two or four bighas of land.' But not a single man among them dared to so much as cough against the Settlement Officer. Had Birju's father not suffered for his daring? The zamindar had snarled at him like a circus leopard. His eldest son had threatened to set their hut on fire. In the end, the landlord had sent his youngest son, who addressed Birju's mother as aunt. The child had said, 'Father bought this land in my name to provide for my education.' A hundred other things he had said. A chit of a child but could charm the skin off you. A true landlord's son...'

'Champia, has Birju gone to sleep? Birju, come in, son. And you too, Champia. Just let that man come home today...'

Champia went inside with Birju.

'Put out the lamp. If father calls don't answer. And let down the screen.'

A fine man he is! Oh, a fine man indeed! The cheek of it! If Birju's mother had not nagged him day and night, the land would never have been theirs. Every evening he had come back and flopped down holding his head:' Birju's mother, I can do without this land. Better to be a labourer all one's life.'

Birju's mother had her answer ready. With much thought and weighing of words she would say, 'All right, forget it. You just don't have it in you. Wife and land are for the strong, not the weak.'

She loses her temper very easily with Birju's father. And her anger keeps mounting. It is her bad luck that such an idiot of a husband has fallen to her lot. What comforts and pleasures had this man ever given her? This man she had tied herself to? Like a blinkered bullock at the oil mill she had toiled all her life and had her husband ever even bought her a paisa worth of sweets to eat. He had pocketed all the money he had got from selling the jute to Bhagat and had marched off to buy bullocks! Did he let her have even a glimpse of the currency notes? Just got the bullocks and began bragging throughout the village: 'Birju's mother will go to the dance in a bullock cart.'

Then she got angry with herself. She was as bad as he! May her tongue be singed! At what ungodly hour had the desire to go in a cart to see the dance form in her head and escape her mouth? God knows from morning to noon today she must have blabbed eighteen times about going to the dance in a cart. Now go, go and see the dance! What a dance! Stretched under a patchwork quilt and dreaming of a silken shawl. Tomorrow morning when she went to fetch water from the well the tongue-wagging females would titter and snigger at her. Jealous of her they were! Yes even god, the bastard! Mother of two and yet slim as ever. Husband at her beck and call. Puts coconut oil in her hair. And has her own land. Was there any woman around with even a cubit of land? Why would they not burn with jealousy? Three acres of paddy land she has. May it escape the evil eye cast by all these people!

The jingle of bullock bells sounded from outside. All the three perked up and listened intently.

'Our bullocks, aren't they, Champia?'

'Yes.' Champia and Birju spoke together.

'Quiet,' Birju's mother whispered. 'Maybe there's a cart too. Don't you hear a creaking?'

'Yes', both spoke again.

'Quiet! I don't think it's a cart. Peep through the hole in the screen, Champia. Quietly. And run back.'

Champia went, soundlessly as a cat. 'Yes, Ma, there's a cart too.'

Birju got up excitedly, but his mother caught his hand and forced him back on to the mat: 'Don't you say a word.'

Champia too crept back under the quilt.

They heard the sound of the bullocks being unharnessed. Birju's father spoke to them firmly: 'Yes, yes, we are home. You were so anxious to reach home weren't you?'

Birju's mother guessed at once that he had partaken of opium in the Maldahia colony. His voice sounded so metallic.

'Champia-a' her father called from outside. 'Give the bullocks some grass...Champia-a-a'.

No response from inside. Champia's father came into the yard and saw no light in the house, neither lamp, nor fire in the hearth. What was the matter? Had they taken off on foot to the dance?

Birju's throat tingled. He tried hard to suppress a cough but once it started there was no stopping it for five minutes.

'Birju! Son Biraj Mohan!' Birju's father called in a caressing voice. 'Has your mother gone to sleep in anger? But people are still on their way there.'

Birju's mother wanted to tell him in a no-nonsense voice that she was not going to the dance and he should return the cart.

'Champia-a, why don't you get up? Here, take this sheaf of paddy.' He stuck a small bunch of paddy into the door of the hut. 'Light the lamp.'

Birju's mother got up and came to the door of the hut. 'Why bring the cart at midnight? The show must be over by now.'

Then she saw the stalks of paddy in the dim light of the lamp and her anger vanished. The fresh greenness of the stalks cooled her eyes and soaked into every fibre of her body.

'The dance couldn't even have started. Just now the Balrampur Babu's Company car has gone to fetch the Collector Saheb from Mohanpur hotel bungalow. This is the last dance of the season. Stick the paddy stalks into the screen. It's paddy from our fields.'

'From our own fields?' Birju's mother lit up with joy. 'Has the paddy ripened?'

'It will take just another ten days or so. When the grains turn red the green stalks bend with the weight. I was going to the Maldiah colony when I happened to look at our crop and was dazzled. It's the truth I'm telling you, my hand shook when I plucked the first five stalks.'

Birju took a grain from a stalk and put it in his mouth. 'You monkey!' his mother scolded him mock-seriously. 'With you scourges around what rules and rites can we keep up?'

'What's the matter? Why are you scolding?'

'Don't you see he has bitten into the new grain before the new grain ceremony?'

'Oh, these rules are not for children. They are little birds, fledglings. It's just the two of us who shouldn't taste the grain before the ceremony.'

Champia also bit into two grains of rice. 'O, Ma, what sweet rice!'

'And has a fragrance too, hasn't it, Didi?' Birju helped himself to some more.

'Made the *rotis*?' Birju's father smiled at his wife.

'No,' Birju's mother said, standing on her dignity. 'There was no knowing if we were going. Make *rotis* in that mood?'

'Wah, how funny you people are! If you own a bullock why wouldn't you get a cart? After all, Cart owners too need bullocks at times, don't they? It is give and take. I'll show those Koyari colony people when that time comes! Hurry now, make the *rotis*.'

'Won't we get late?'

'You are an expert—You make a basketful of *rotis* in a jiffy. How long will five *rotis* take?'

Smiles now played openly on Birju's mother's lips. From the corner of her eye she saw Birju's father devouring her with his gaze. If Champia and Birju had not been there he would have bared his heart to her. Champia and Birju exchanged glances and their faces glowed. So like mother, losing her temper for nothing!

'Champia, just go to the cowshed and call out for Aunt Makhni.'

'Hey Aunt, Aunt! Are you there? Ma is calling you?'

Aunt Makhni did not reply, though they could hear her muttering. 'What is she calling out to Aunt for now? In the whole colony it's only Aunt who is without a hearth to blow into and cooking to do!'

'Oh, Aunt,' Birju's mother laughed. 'Don't take offence at what I said! Look at me—with my hearth-and-cooking fellow who comes home at midnight, cart and all! Come over, aunt. I don't know how to make sweet *rotis*.'

Aunt came along sputtering and coughing. 'That's just why I was asking you in the afternoon if you were going to the dance. If you had told me I would have lit my stove and left it here.'

Birju's mother showed Mausi her own stove and said, 'There's neither grain nor seed in the house, Mausi. Only some pots and pans and that goat outside. I'll keep tobacco for you to last you through the night. You have your hookah with you, haven't you, aunt?'

If aunt got tobacco she could stay awake not one night, but five nights in succession. In the dark she measured the tobacco with her hands. Aha, Birju's mother was generous with tobacco! Not like that grocer woman, God's mercy on her. The other night she had left a lump of tobacco the size of an opium pill or the size of a pea, and had gone off to the Gulab Bagh fair, telling Aunt that a boxful of tobacco was kept for her.

Birju's mother lit the fire. Champia mashed the sweet potatoes and made them into small balls. Birju placed the iron frying pan upside down over his head and began showing off. 'An army helmet! Whack! Give it ten lathi blows and nothing will happen.'

All laughed aloud. Laughing, Birju's mother said, 'Three fat sweet potatoes are lying on the shelf. Champi, give them to him. The poor child has been asking for them the whole evening...'

'He's no poor child, Ma. He's clever,' Champia opened up. 'You don't know, do you, why his jaws were working under the quilt?'

'Hee! Hee!'

Birju spoke through his broken milk teeth, 'Polished off five sweet potatoes in the black market, I did. Ha, ha, ha!'

They all laughed again. To keep Aunt in good humour, Birju's mother consulted her 'I've a fistful of jaggery to spare. Shall I add it to the sweet potatoes?'

'But sweet potatoes are sweet themselves, silly,' Aunt said, fondly. 'Why waste so much jaggery on them?'

By the time the two bullocks had eaten their fodder and were licking each other, Birju's mother was ready. Champia put on her printed sari, and Birju, for lack of a button to his pants, tied a jute string to hold it up.

Coming out of her courtyard Birju's mother looked towards the village trying to hear what was going on there. 'No, no they must all have gone. Why should those going on foot wait all this while?'

A full moon overhead. Today, for the first time Birju's mother had worn a real silver pendant on her forehead. What is happening to Birju's father? Why doesn't he harness the bullocks? He stands there gazing at her, as if she were the Queen of Hearts at the dance...

As Birju's mother got into the cart a strange thrill coursed through her body. Holding on to the bamboo pole for support, she said, 'There's still a lot of room in the cart. Take the road to the right.'

The bullocks broke into a run and when the wheels creaked, Birju could not hold himself back. 'Father, make the cart fly like an aeroplane.'

When the cart passed Jangi's back door, Birju's mother said, 'Just ask Jangi if his daughter-in-law has left for the dance.'

The cart stopped and the sound of crying was heard from the hut.

Birju's father asked: 'O brother Jangi, who is weeping in your courtyard?'

Jangi had built a fire and was warming himself. 'Don't ask me,' he said. 'Rangi has not returned from Balrampur yet. How can his wife go to the dance? She has been sitting here waiting for all this while and all the women of the village have gone.'

'Oh, you belle of the railway station, why do you cry?' Birju's mother called out. 'Come along. Get dressed and come. Plenty of room in the cart. Poor girl! Come along quick.'

Radha's daughter Sunri called out from the neighbouring hut: 'Aunt, is there room in the cart? Can I go too?' On the other side of the bamboo grove is Larenya Khava's hut. His wife too, hadn't gone to the dance. She came along too, a heavy artificial gold anklet on one ankle.

'Come along, come along, all those who are left behind.' Jungi's daughter-in-law, Larenya's wife and Radhu's daughter Sunri come together up to the cart. One of the bullocks kicked out a hind leg. 'Wretch!' Birju's father swore mightily at the animal. 'Want to lame the daughter-in-law?'

All burst out laughing. Birju's father glimpsed the two daughters-in-law sitting with lowered heads behind their veils. They reminded him of the drooping stalks of grain in his field.

Jangi's daughter-in-law had come as a bride just three months ago the smell of mustard oil and vermilion still rose from her wedding sari. Birju's mother was reminded of the day she had come to her in-laws' house. She took out three sweet *rotis* from her bundle and said, 'Here, eat one each. You can drink water at the government well in Simraha.'

The cart left the village and skirted the paddy fields. The full moon above, the full moon of the month of *Kartik*! The fragrance of falling paddy flowers in the fields. In the bamboo bush milk-white flowers have just bloomed.

Jangi's daughter-in-law lighted a leaf cigarette and passed it on to Birju's mother. Suddenly Birju's mother remembered that Champia, Sunri, Larenya's wife and Jangi's daughter-in-law were the four in this village, who knew how to sing film songs. Wonderful!

The cart leaves a trail through the paddy fields. All around is a rustling of paddy like the rustling of wedding night saris. Moonlight gleams on Birju's mother's pendant.

'All right, Champia, sing a film song for us. Don't feel shy, go on. If you forget a line your teacher is by your side!'

The two daughters-in-law did not, but Champia and Sunri cleared their throats.

Birju's father prodded the bullocks, 'Come on brothers, faster! Sing, Champia, or I'll tell the bullocks to slow down.'

Jungi's daughter-in-law brought her veil near Champia's ear and whispered something. Champia began in a soft, low voice, 'Ah, moonbeams of the moon...'

Birju's mother sitting with Birju in her lap, felt a strong urge to join the singing. She looked at Jangi's daughter-in-law who had also started humming in a low voice. A sweet girl really. A characteristic fragrance was wafted from her first night sari. What she said was right, after all. Birju's mother is the Queen of Hearts. Nothing wrong with being called that. Yes, she is indeed the Queen of Hearts!

Birju's mother focussed both eyes on the tip of her nose, and tried to catch a glimpse of her beauty the shimmering border of her red said, the moon-shaped pendant on her forehead... right now, Birju's mother has nothing left to desire. She begins to feel drowsy!

Mohan Rakesh

Lord of the Rubble

They had come to Amritsar from Lahore after seven years and a half. The Indo-Pak hockey math was just a pretext. More than the match they wanted to see the buildings and the bazaars which had become alien to them seven and a half years ago. Bunches of Muslims were to be seen sauntering along the roads, looking as eagerly at everything, as if this was no ordinary city but a place endowed with some very special attraction.

Passing through the narrow alleys in the bazaars, they reminded one another, at things with they had which been so familiar: 'Look, Fatehdeena, how the candy shops in sweets Bazaar have dwindled in number! Do you remember the corner shop where Sukhi used to sell parched gram? It's no longer there. Its place has been taken by that betel leaf seller. And, Khan Saheb, isn't this the Salt market? It's here that they dye clothes in bulk. And those dyer women! So spicy indeed— each one of them!'

It was after a very long time that plumed turbans and red fez caps were seen in the bazaars. Among the visitors from Lahore a good many were old inhabitants of Amritsar who had been forced to leave the city at the time of partition. The inevitable changes that had come about in the course of seven and a half years aroused their surprise and sometimes gave them a stab of pain: 'Good heavens, how they have widened

Jaimal Singh lane! Did all the houses on this side burn down? Hakim Asif Ali used to have his shop here, remember? Now a cobbler has entrenched himself in his place.'

And, occasionally, one could also hear observations such as,' Wali, this mosque is still standing here in tact. How come they haven't they made it into a *gurdwara*?'

Wherever the Pakistani groups passed people eyed them long and with curiosity. Even now some people viewed these Muslims with suspicion and stepped out of their path. But there were others who came forward and hugged them warmly. They would ask the visitors 'What's Lahore like these days? Is the Anarkali as crowded as before? Is it true that they have completely re-built Shah Alami Gate Bazaar? Krishan Nagar hasn't changed much, has it? Was Rishwatpura really constructed from money raised by bribes? They say *burqa* is no longer in vogue in Pakistan. Is it so?' The questions had such a ring of personal involvement that it would seem Lahore was not just a city but a personal relative, a friend to thousands of people who were eager to find out how it was doing. That day these visitors from Lahore were the guests of the whole city and the locals were unaccountably happy to meet them and talk with them.

Bazaar Bansan was a kind of neglected market in Amritsar, mostly inhabited by poor Muslims, before the partition. Most of the shops here sold bamboo poles and wooden material. All those shops had burned down in one huge conflagration: That was the most devastating fire of Amritsar city of and for sometime it was feared that it would spread and burn down the whole city. Flames had already lapped up some neighbouring areas. Somehow the fire was brought under control, but while it raged it burnt to ashes several Hindu and Muslim houses.

In the course of seven and a half years many of these buildings had been restored, but one could still see the piles of rubble lying in between the new buildings. The heaps of rubble presented a strange sight in the midst of those new buildings.

That day too, as usual, there was not much activity in Bazaar Bansan. Most of the people who had been living there had perished in the fire and those who had managed to get away could not muster enough courage to return.

Only a thin, wasted-looking Muslim returned that day to that scene of devastation. At the sight of the new and the burnt-out buildings, he seemed to feel that he had strayed into a maze. His feet rose to enter the lane to his left but he hesitated. He could not believe that this was the lane he wanted to enter. Near the mouth of the lane some children were playing *kiri kiri*. Further down two women were brawling and flinging abuses at each other at the top of their voices.

'Everything else has changed but not ways of speaking,' the old man said to himself in a low voice, and stood still, leaning on his walking stick. His knees stuck out of his pajamas, and his *sherwani* which ended above his knees was patched in several places.

A child came out of the lane crying. 'Come here, son,' the old man said in a soothing voice. 'Come, I'll give you sweets.' Putting his hand in his pocket, he started to search for something for the child. The child kept quiet for a moment and then twisting his mouth, again started crying. A girl of sixteen or seventeen came running from inside the lane and holding the child's arm dragged him back into the lane. Still crying, the child struggled to free his arm. Lifting him in her arms, she held him close, kissed him, and said: 'Stop crying, my prince. If you cry that Muslim will take you away. Keep quiet my good little boy. Keep quiet!'

The old Muslim had taken out a coin to offer to the child but now he returned it to his pocket. Lifting his cap, he scratched his head and put the cap under his arm. His throat was parched and his knees shook slightly. He leaned against the front plank of a closed shop in the lane and put his cap on again. At the mouth of the lane, where they had once stacked long wooden beams, now stood a three-storied house. Two well fed kites sat motionless on the electric wire above the lane. Near the electric pole was a small patch of sunlight. The old man stood for a while, watching the flying specks of dust in the sun light. 'Oh Lord of all!' The words fell from his lips.

A young man came along, twirling a key-chain, and stopped on seeing the old man. 'Why are you standing here, Mianji? Is anything the matter?'

A faint tremor ran down the old man's chest and arms. He brushed his tongue over his lips and looking attentively at the young man said, 'Son, aren't you Manori?'

The young man stopped shaking his key-chain, and closed his fist over it. 'How do you know my name?' he asked, giving the old man a surprised look.

'Son, seven-and-a-half years ago you were so high' the old man tried to smile.

'Have you come from Pakistan today?' Manori asked.

'Yes, We used to live in this lane,' the old man said. 'My son, Chiraghdin was tailor to you folks. Just six months before the partition we had built our new house here.'

'Oh, Ghani Mian?' Recognition shot through Manori.

'Yes, son, I'm your Ghani Mian. I cannot meet Chiragh and his wife and children but I said to myself that I would have one look at my house.'

The old man took off his cap and moved his hand over his head, trying to hold back his tears.

'But hadn't you left here long before?' Manori's voice was filled with sympathy.

'Yes, son, it was my misfortune that I left earlier all by myself. If I had only stayed back with them I too would have...' He stopped short, realizing that it was not right to say such things. But he could not hold back his tears.

'Let be, Ghani Mian. The past is dead and gone. Why recall it?' Manori held the old man by his arm. 'Come, I'll show you your old house,' he said.

The news had gone round that a Muslim was standing outside the lane and had been about to abduct Ramdasi's son. The child's sister had saved him just in time, dragging him back, or else the Muslim would have decamped with the child. Hearing the news the women sitting in the lane picked up their tuffets and disappeared into their houses. They called out to their children, who were playing in the lane to come indoors. When Manori entered the lane with Ghani, it was deserted except for a solitary hawker and Rakha the wrestler, who as usual lay sprawled asleep under the peepul tree next to the well. Of course, faces peeped out from behind windows and doors. Seeing Ghani they exchanged remarks with one another in whispers. Although his beard had turned grey, they had recognised Chiraghdin's father, Abdul Ghani.

'That used to be your house,' said Manori pointing to a heap of rubble in the distance. Ghani stopped in his stride and looked with lost eyes at the debris. He had long ago resigned himself to the death of Chiragh and his wife and children. But he was not prepared for the shock of seeing his house in this shape. His mouth turned drier and his knees shook even more than before. 'That rubble?' he asked incredulously.

Manori saw Ghani's face changing colour. Supporting him by the arm firmly, he said in a steady voice, 'Your house was burnt down in those days.'

Leaning on his walking stick, Ghani somehow managed to reach the heap of rubble. Most of the rubble was now mud from which burnt or broken bricks stuck out here and there. Anything made of iron or wood had been pilfered long ago. Miraculously, a burnt door frame had escaped although it was jutting out of the rubble. Further back, there were two charred almirahs slowly blanching under their dark surfaces. 'Is this all that is left of my house?' Ghani asked, seeing the rubble from close up. His knees seemed to give way and he sat down holding on to the burnt door frame. After a while his head also came to rest against the door frame, and a moan escaped his lips: 'Oh, my Chiragh Deena!'

For seven and a half years the charred frame had stood there somehow, protruding from the rubble but its wood had badly crumbled. At the touch of Ghani's head fragments fell from it and were scattered around. Some fell on Ghani's cap and hair. With the slivers a worm also fell down and began to wriggle about, seven or eight inches away from Ghani's feet, on a brick path near the open drain. It raised its head to look for a hole and finding none, struck its head on the ground now and again in disappointment.

Now there were several more faces peering out of the windows. They were whispering among themselves, fearing something would definitely happen today. Now that Chiragh's father Ghani was here, the secrets of seven years ago were bound to unfold themselves. Maybe the rubble itself would tell Ghani the whole story.

It would tell him that on the evening of that day Chiragh was in the room upstairs eating his dinner when wrestler Rakha asked him to come down for a moment as he had something important to tell him. Rakha was the king of the alley in those days. Even the Hindus lived in awe of him and Chiragh after all was a Mulsim. Putting down the morsel he was about to eat. Chiragh came downstairs while his wife, Zubeida and two daughters, Kishwar and Sultana, looked down through the windows. Chiragh had just emerged into the lane from his porch when Rakha grabbed him by his collar, felled him to the ground and sat down on his chest. Chiragh caught Rakkha's hand that was holding a knife and cried, 'No, Rakkha Pahalwan, don't kill me...don't. Oh, won't someone save me? Zubeida! Save me!'

And upstairs, Zubeida, Kishwar and Sultana screamed in despair. Zubeida ran down screaming, while Rakkha's cronies caught hold of Chiragh's flailing arms. Rakkha drove his knees hard onto Chiragh's thighs and cried, 'What're you screaming for, you sister fucker? I'm giving you Pakistan. Here, take it.' And before Zubeida, Kishwar and Sultana could reach him, Chiragh had already been despatched to Pakistan.

The windows of the houses around closed. Those who had witnessed the scene bolted their doors from inside, absolving themselves of any responsibility. Even behind closed doors they could hear Zubeida and her daughters screaming far into the night. Rakkha and his cronies despatched them too to Pakistan that same night but by a longer route. Their bodies were later found; not in Chiragh's house but floating in the canal.

Chiragh's house continued to be ransacked for two days. When it had been completely looted someone set fire to it. Rakkha swore that he would bury alive the man who had set the fire going, for he had decided to kill Chiragh in order to take this house for himself. He had even bought ritual offerings for the ceremony to purify the house. But he failed to find out who the arsonist was so he could not carry out his threat to bury him alive. For seven and a half years now, Rakkha Pahalwan had been regarding this rubble as his private estate. He would not allow anyone to tie a cow or buffalo here nor any vendor to put up a make-shift kiosk near the rubble. Without his permission one could not remove even a brick from the rubble.

People expected that the whole story would reach Ghani's ears somehow or other. One look at the rubble and he would surely read the story on his own.

Ghani scratched earth from the rubble with his nails, poured it over himself and hugged the door frame, crying, 'Speak Chiragh Deena, speak to me. Where have you gone?, Oh, Kishwar, Oh, Sultana, Oh, my children, why have you left Ghani behind, Oh, Oh!' Slivers of wood rained down from the crumbling doorway.

Lord of the Rubble

Someone woke up Rakkha Pahalwan sleeping under the peepul tree, or perhaps he woke up on his own. When he learnt that Abdul Ghani had come from Pakistan and was sitting on the debris of his house, phlegm rose from his throat that made him cough and he spat on the well's parapet. He looked at the pile of rubble and a growl rose from his chest as from a pair of bellows. His lower lip flared out.

'Ghani is sitting on his rubble,' Rakkha's henchman, Lachcha Pahalwan told him, sitting down by his side.

'How does it belong to him? It's mine,' Rakkha said in a voice hoarse with phlegm.

'But he is sitting there,' Lachcha said in a meaningful voice.

'Let him sit there for all I care. You get me the pipe.' He spread out his legs and stroked his naked thighs.

'If Manori tells him...' Lachcha said, with the same meaningful look. He got up to fetch the pipe.

'Why would Manori invite trouble?'

Lachcha went away.

Dry peepul leaves lay scattered around the well. Rakkha kept picking them up and crushing them between his palms. When Lachcha came back with the pipe and offered it to Rakkha after putting the filter cloth under it, Rakkha took a long pull at the pipe and said: 'Has anyone else been talking to Ghani?'

'No.'

'Here,' Coughing, he handed back the pipe to Lachcha.

Lachcha saw Manori returning, holding Ghani by the arm. Squatting, Lachcha took a quick, short pull at the pipe while his eyes darted from Rakkha's face to Ghani's in the distance.

Now Manori was walking a step ahead of Ghani, holding his arm as though he wanted Ghani to walk past the well without noticing Rakkha. But Rakkha was sitting with his legs sprawled as if asking to be taken notice of. Ghani had seen him from a long way off. As he came near the well he spread out his arms, 'Rakkha Pahalwan!'

Raising his head, **Rakkha** narrowed his eyes and gazed at Ghani. A lump seemed to form in his threat but he did not speak.

'Rakkha Pahalwan, haven't you recognised me?' Ghani lowered his arms. 'I'm Ghani—Abdul Ghani, Chiragh Din's father.'

Pahalwan looked him over suspiciously, from head to foot. Abdul Ghani's eyes had brightened up on seeing Rakkha Pahalwan and under his white heard his wrinkles had fanned out in joy. Rakkha's lower lip trembled and he said in a booming voice: 'What news, Ghania?'

Ghani was about to stretch out his arms again but finding no response they fell of their own accord. Supporting himself against the trunk of the tree he sat down on the parapet of the well.

The whispers in the windows above intensified. Now that the two were facing each other things were sure to come to a head. They might even start abusing one another. Rakkha couldn't have his way with the old man any more. Now the times had changed. Lord of the rubble indeed! What braggadacio! The rubble was neither his nor Ghani's. It was government property. And this fiend would not allow anyone even to tie a cow there.

And Manori was a coward. Why didn't he tell Ghani that it was Rakkha who had murdered his family—Chiragh Din, his wife and children. Rakkha was not a man but a bull and like a bull he roamed about bellowing without let or hindrance. How thin and wizened poor Ghani looked, his head gone all white!

Sitting down on the edge of the well, Ghani said, 'Just see, Pahalwan, I left a bustling home behind me and to say I have come all this way to see this mud. That's all that is left of a whole household. Honestly, Rakkha, I don't have the heart to tear myself away even from this keep of mud.' Tears rose to his eyes.

The wrestler folded his out-spread legs, picked up his shoulder cloth from the wall of the well and flung it on his shoulder. Lachcha held out the pipe to him and he took long pulls at it.

'Tell me, Rakkha, how did all this happen?' Ghani said in an insistent tone, holding back his tears. 'All of you were near him. All of you loved one another like brothers. If he wanted to, couldn't he have taken shelter with one of you? Didn't he have that much sense?'

'It happened, that's all, 'Rakkha said, his voice sounding unnaturally hollow even to himself. Thick saliva glued his lips. From under his moustache sweat dripped on to his lips. A heavy weight seemed to press down on his forehead and his spine asked for support.

'How are things in Pakistan?' he asked in the same hollow voice. The veins in his neck had become taut. He wiped the sweat under his armpits with his shoulder cloth and sucking the thick saliva from his throat he spat it out in the lane.

'What can I tell you, Rakkha? Ghani pressed down on the knob of his walking stick with both hands. 'If you ask how things are with me, only God knows. If my Chiragh had been with me it would have been a different story, Rakkha. How often did I plead with him to leave and go with me. But he was adamant. He said he couldn't go, leaving a newly constructed house behind. He said this was his own locality, his own lane, and there was nothing to be afraid of. It did not occur to that innocent pigeon that even if his own lane was safe, danger could stalk it from outside. Four people laid down their lives to protect one house! Rakkha, he had great faith in you. He used to say that as long as Rakkha was around, no one could do him any harm. But when death stalked him even his Rakkha could not stop it.'

Rakkha tried to straighten up because his spine was now beginning to hurt him. He was feeling a great stress in his groin. Something seemed to be bottling up his breath in his entrails. His entire body was drenched in perspiration and the soles of his feet tingled. Every few minutes sparklers seemed to rain down on him from above and float past his eyes. The distance between his lips and his tongue seemed to be increasing. He wiped the corners of his lips with his shoulder cloth and the words, 'Oh, God, the True One, Only you exist, only you, only you,' escaped his lips.

Ghani saw that the wrestler's lips had gone dry and the circles under his eyes had deepened. He put his hand on his shoulder. 'Rakkha, don't take it to heart now. What had to happen happened. The dead cannot come back to life. May God stand by the virtuous and forgive all sinners! If my Chiragh is no longer here, at least all of you are still here. I am comforted that someone of the days gone by is still living. Having seen you I have seen Chiragh. May Allah keep all of you healthy. May you live long and see great happiness!' Leaning on his walking stick, Ghani rose to his feet. Walking away, he said, 'Rakkha, keep me in your memory!'

A feeble sound of assent rose from Rakkha's throat. Holding his shoulder cloth between his hands, he folded his hands in salutation. Looking walking round the lane wistfully, Ghani slowly walked away.

The whispering in the windows continued for a while. Once out of the lane Manori would surely divulge everything to Ghani. How Rakkha's throat went dry in Ghani's presence! Lost face as he had, how could he now prevent people from tying their cattle at the rubble? Poor Zubeida! What a good woman she was. How soft spoken with everyone! And here was this fiend, Rakkha with neither home nor hearth to call his own. How could he have any feelings for mothers or sisters?

After a while the women started coming out into the lane and the children resumed their game of *gulli danda*. Two teenage girls started squabbling and then fell upon each other.

Rakkha sat long into the evening by the well, coughing and dragging at the pipe Numerous passers-by asked him, 'Rakkha Shah, we hear Ghani Khan had come from Pakistan today?'

'Yes, he came,' Rakkha had the same reply for everyone.

'So what happened?'

'Nothing happened. He went away.'

As night approached, Rakkha, as usual, came out of the lane and sat down on the front plank fo the corner shop. Every night he would accost the passers-by and give them tips about the local stock exchange or the secrets of good health and nostrums which served as short-cut remedies for various chronic diseases. But that night he narrated to Lachcha the story of a pilgrimage to Vaishnav Devi he had made fifteen years ago. After parting from Lachcha as he entered the lane he saw Loku Pandit's buffalo tied on the rubble plot. As he did daily, began to drive it away—tut; tut! After driving it away he sat down on the door frame for a short breather. The lane was deserted and since there were no street lights it grew dark in the evening. At the edge of the rubble heap there was a drain in which scummy water flowed, gurgling as it went. A medley of sounds rising from the rubble merged into the stillness of the night... chic...chic...chic...chir...chir...r...ri.ri...ri..

A crow appeared from nowhere and sat down on the door frame, scattering wood scantlings when it flapped its wings. A dog which was sleeping in a corner woke up and started barking at the crow. The crow sat there, undecided whether to stay or fly away and ultimately flew away flapping its wings and perched on the branch of the peepul tree near the well. After the crow had flown away, the dog advanced a few steps and resumed its barking facing the wrestler. The wrestler tried to shoo the dog away in a lazy, ponderous voice 'Get away, dum, dum, dum.' 'Wow, wow, wow, wow!' 'Get away! ...Get away!...dur...dur...dur...' But the dog drew nearer and continued to bark. The wrestler picked up a clod of earth and threw it at the dog. The dog retreated a step or two but did not stop barking. The wrestler abused the dog and then slowly rose from the door frame and walking up to the well again, lay down on the parapet. After the wrestler moved away, the dog entered the lane and facing the well, again started barking. It kept barking till it saw that nothing and no one was stirring in the lane. Flapping its ears, it returned to the rubble heap, where it lay down in a corner and set up a low, continuous growl.

Amritlal Nagar

Two Faiths

'Where are you, wife of Inder?' Pandit Devdhar's wife called out, crossing the courtyard and towards the dark and rickety staircase.

Inder's wife was in the room upstairs, stitching a child's frock on her machine.

'Come in, Aunt, I'm here,' she said. Stopping her machine, she came to the door.

Devdhar's wife worked her way up the stairs, pressing her hands on her knees for support. By the time she reached the top, she was panting so hard that she sank back against the wall.

Holding the end of her sari between her fingers, Inder's wife stepped forward and bent seven times at the feet of her husband's aunt.

'May you live long, may you bathe in milk, may you have many sons,' the old woman blessed her. She paused for breath and then with renewed vigour blessed her again: 'Daughter-in-law, I pray for you day and night. If your firstborn had been living you would today be thinking of getting a bride for him.' She sighed deeply. 'May Rama help. May the sage Markandaya help. May all the seven joys of life be yours, child.'

Inder's wife's face shone with gratitude and devotion making her eyelids droop. Helping her old aunt to rise to her feet, she coaxed her into the room: 'Come inside, aunt.'

'Yes, my little queen, my limbs want a little rest. First let me get back my breath. It's my age, child. I've become too weak to climb or descend the stairs. But there's nothing I can do about it, child.'

Inder's wife led the old woman into the room. Seeing a child's frock on the machine the old woman gave Inder's wife an inquiring look. 'This frock..?' she asked.

'It's for the milk-woman's child,' Inder's wife said, a smile on her face. 'A son has been born to her after four daughters. It's an auspicious occasion for the poor woman.'

'What compassion you have in your heart child. May God grant all your heart's desires. It always gladdens my heart to see you and Inder. May both of you live long! Look at my Bhola and Tribhuvan and their wives. Like man like wife. Why should I blame girls of other families alone?'

'Aunt, has anything new happened?'

'*Arre*, anything can happen in a family which changes the ways of life it has inherited. I say, child, our sins have come home to roost.'

Aunt gazed into vacancy, denying Inder's wife the cue to something 'new'. Inder's wife was left guessing—she was sure that something untoward had happened. Inder too had said that uncle was looking rather lost these days.

'Did elder brother-in-law's bitch again stray into the kitchen...?' She had guessed right. Pandit Devdhar's oldest son, Dr Bhola Shanker Bhatt kept a purebred Scottish dog, Juliet, whose daughter was the culprit. This time she had surpassed herself.

In Panditji's back garden was a private meditation chamber built by his forefathers. The back garden was within the compound wall and there stood a small temple erected on a high platform. In the temple there was a handmade picture of a sage resting on an elaborately carved but decaying sandalwood platform. One could enter the temple only in a squatting posture and through a narrow aperture. The meditation chamber was inside the temple, to the right. It too could be entered only by squeezing the body through an alcove-like opening.

Within was a rare marble image of the goddess Saraswati which was kept covered with a piece of silk drenched in oil. Only the divine face was left uncovered for worshippers. A lamp was always kept burning in front of the image. The sanctum was wide enough for only one person at a time to sit cross-legged before the image and long enough for a person to make a full prostration.

A sage had given this image and a sacred *mantra* of the goddess Saraswati to Pandit Devdhar Bhatt's great grandfather. It was said that it was as a result of his worship of the goddess of learning that he had earned great merit, wealth and fame. He was highly respected in royal courts. Panditji's grandfather and father were also renowned figures, who, although they did not get the *mantra* from their ancestors, yet received devotion and gifts from wealthy men. They could not get the *mantra* because by the rule of inheritance, the oldest son Dharnidhar got it. But he died in the prime of his youth of sudden heart failure. Pandit Devdhar was a staunch devotee of the ancestral goddess Saraswati. At the same time he had also been a life-long worshipper of the goddess Jagdamba.

One morning, in keeping with his daily routine, Panditji entered the temple after returning from the Ganga and found it had been utilized as a maternity ward by Bhola Shanker's bitch. His anger flared sky-high at the sight. His sons and he fought a pitched battle of words with Bhola's sons and their wives and took a vow that he would never enter their house nor eat the food cooked in it. He just lay in the courtyard near the well adjacent to the temple. For the last four days he had eaten nothing. To eat food bought from the market was out of the question. Was he eating at Inder's house? This was what his wife had come to find out. But when Inder's wife told her that Panditji had not been eating with them, she was petrified. That her sixty-eight year old husband who rose at three every morning, walked two miles to the Ganga for his bath, kept up his whole routine, praying and performing rituals and reading the Gita till noon, had not put a grain of food into his mouth—the bare thought of it made her blood freeze.

'Aunt, I never knew this, just got to know now from you. Under has not said a word about it to anyone, as far as I know. It would have reached my ears if he had.'

'Your uncle is a sage, my child, an ascetic. If it were not for his temper he would have been a realised soul, without a parallel on this earth. What can I do, I've done my duty. You have to more with the times. How can you fight your own children?'

'How long will uncle go on without food? And he is getting on in years.'

'That's what I too say, my child. But the stubborn man that he is, what effect can I have on him? When it becomes too much to bear I sit in a corner and weep.' Aunt's voice grew choked. 'If I can only depart before he does, it will be my salvation. What more is in store for me I don't know.' Aunt burst into tears.

'Don't cry, Aunt. Don't worry. I didn't know all these days. But now I'll make all arrangements for Uncle's food.'

When Dr Inder Dutt Sharma returned from the university and was having his tea, his wife told him the whole story. Inder Dutt was stunned. Tea, which was dear to him as a sweetheart, seemed tasteless suddenly, like an abandoned wife. He knew how stubborn his uncle could be. He could quietly die, fasting, with nobody the wiser for it—Indradutt knew that very well. Noticing his troubled look, his wife said, 'Make him stay on for food today. I shall follow all the rules of purity while cooking for him.'

'But will he agree? He's one of those who would rather see the sun or moon fail than break his vow.'

'Ask him and see.'

'Of course, I will. But I know what he'll say. How long can he carry on like this?' Bhola ought not to be so callous.'

'What can Bhola do? He can't keep track of the bitch all the time. Each man has his fancy, all said and done uncle needn't make an issue of it.'

'We can't judge Uncle.'

'Suppose it had happened to you?'

'I would have put up with it, somehow.'

'Easier said than done. Uncle wants everybody to live just as in the past. Tuft and sacred thread, rules of pollution, veiled face, no visits to the cinema—can go on with all this nonsense?'

'I don't think Uncle ever...'

'He may overlook all this. But he doesn't like it.'

'All right. But you also do not like many of the things I do, just as I don't like many of your habits. It cuts both ways.'

'What habits?'

'I am not complaining. I'm only giving examples. No two persons think alike and if they do, it's very rare. Yet don't they get on with each other? Bhola's self-important ways are rubbing off on Tribhuvan too. He behaves as if he was not born of his parents. Uncle may be orthodox and stubborn but he is not one who should be treated with such neglect. These people cook garlic, onions, eggs and fish in the house just to insult him. Even so, Uncle only set up a separate kitchen for himself. He didn't quarrel with or rebuke anyone, did he?'

Normally gentle and soft-spoken, Inder Dutt grew excited. It pained him to know that Uncle had been without food for four days. He had always respected him greatly. The whole world respects him. For the past many months, at his insistence, Uncle had been spending two or three hours with him every evening. Uncle would talk about the Bhagat or the Ramayana or some Puranic narrative. Panditji would talk in his own way and through him, Inder Dutt seemed to see a picture of ancient Indian society and its development, and felt a new interest in it. Sometimes, when in his element, Pandit Devdhar would reminisce entertainingly about the interesting ways of the wealthy men and landlords with whom he was connected. 'As Panditji delved into these as a family priest reminiscences they often evoked Inder Dutt's memories of childhood and youth; glimpses of the past of then neighborhood would come before him. Expanding his own knowledge through Panditji's experiences, Inder Dutt had come to have not just respect but affection for Panditji.

Inder Dutt's wife too had regard for Panditji. But she had developed a suppressed complaint too against him ever since he had begun to visit them. She had no time for herself with her husband now, either for a game of carrom or dice, a chat on domestic matters or for exchanging ideas about the ongoing reconstruction of her parental house. Besides, she was fairly taken with her younger sister-in-law, Tribhuvan's wife, and under her influence had become lukewarm towards Phoophaji's old fashioned ways. So when Inder Dutt said that Uncle had set up a separate kitchen ever since his children had taken to eating meat and fish but he had not rebuked them, she could not help remarking, 'But the old man has completely cut himself off from his family,' she said. 'He does not speak even to his grandchildren. Whom could he go to complain to?'

'That's where you are mistaken in your understanding of Uncle,' Inder Dutt had said. 'His love is silent. I have realised this from my own experience.' Just as hot blasts of wind break in through chinks even when the door is closed, Inder Dutt's agitation broke the surface of his normally calm bearing.

Perceiving his train of thought, Inder Dutt's wife adjusted her perception in tune with his thinking. 'I do understand Uncle,' she said in a mellow voice. 'A learned man like him has no place in that house. He can love only people like you. Rest assured, he will break his fast today.'

'Do you think so?' Inder Dutt gave his wife a sceptical look; his voice sounded sad.

'Love is stronger than custom.' With wifely skill and sweet assurance she assuaged her husband's anxiety and concern, yet she could not persuade him to drink his tea or eat anything.

Dr Inder Dutt Sharma was too mentally upset to remain cooped up in the house. Uncle generally came at about six or half-past six. Inder Dutt had a feeling that he would come today too. But he also suffered doubts. Perhaps Uncle was too weak to walk. He decided that he would himself go and bring him over, although he knew that at this time he would be busy with his evening rituals and bath. Pandit Devdhar's house was not far away. Instead of entering it by the front door, Inder Dutt went by a back lane and entered the house through the back garden. Uncle was reciting the *Ganga Lehri* and his sweet voice filtered through the compound wall like the fragrance of flowers.

> O mother, renouncing all my worldly wealth and kingdom like a blade of grass I have sought refuge along the river bank where its soothing waters flow frolicking and gambolling.
>
> Drinking deep its nectar-like water I get satiety akin to bliss of human birth.
>
> It is so rewarding like ultimate salvation.

Inder Dutt stood at the door listening. Tears came to his eyes. He felt as if this was the last time he would hear this voice. A time would come, would soon come, when this sweet voice would be stilled for ever. What devotion there was in the voice, what vigour. Who could tell, by listening to it, Pandit Devdhar was angry or hurt, or that he had been without food for four days? Such a man, such a father was being hurt by the Bhola Tribhuvan combine.

Driven by his intensely aroused emotion, Inder Dutt changed his mind. He would not disturb Uncle in this moment of surrender, he decided. He was reciting the *Ganga Lehri* now which meant that he had either just had his bath or was on his way to the river. After that he would do the *sandhya*. For the next couple of hours his routine was cut out for him.

Inder Dutt went back through the lane by which he had

come. He would spend the time with his Aunt, he thought.

'Amma!'

'Yes, wife of Bhola.' She was sitting in her room, against the door, chin resting upon her drawn-up knees, arms around them, deep in thought. Hearing her elder daughter-in-law's voice her drooping spirits suddenly revived. But yes, the long spell of silence had filled her suppliant voice with poignancy.

The smugness on the older daughter-in-law's face was complemented by the swelling fat around her waist, and her voice had a touch of hauteur:

'He has sent me to find out what exactly is on father's mind. What does he want?'

'Bahu, he doesn't want anything.'

'Then why has he gone on this hunger strike?'

In an even more controlled voice, Pandit Devdhar's wife said, 'You know his temperament, Bahurani.'

'This is no answer, Amma. Will he kill himself?' Why should one be so adamant? Pious, learned, a fountain of wisdom, he should know better. Doesn't a dog too have life given by the same God?' The daughter-in-law's anger was mounting and her mother-in-law listened in silence.

'This is not the way parents should behave. It's enmity against children—what else? As it is, he has long ago stopped talking with everyone in the house.'

'But he never was a great one for talking, bahu. You have seen him all these years. Bhola and Tribhuvan have known it always.'

'But he is totally at ease at Inder Bhaisaheb's place, he talks a lot there.'

'Inder is highly educated, you see. And he is interested in the same things.'

'Of course, of course, all of us are idiots—a degraded lot not worthy of his notice. Far from talking to us, even to look at sinners like us would pollute him.'

'Child, getting angry won't help. We old ones are half-way to the pyre. Let me depart in his lifetime, seeing all of you safe and well. This is my prayer to Baba Vishwanath day and night. I've no life left in me.'

She started sobbing. Inder Dutt had stolen into the courtyard and had been listening to them for some time. He could not restrain himself any longer. 'Aunt!' he called out.

Aunt quickly wiped her tears at the sight of him. 'Come, child,' she said sweetly.

Bhola's wife adjusted the *sari* over her head and with a formal smile, folded her hands to her older brother-in-law.

Coming into the room Inder Dutt touched his aunt's feet and proceeded to sit on the floor by her side.

Aunt looked at him in confusion. 'What's this? Sit on the bed.'

'No, I feel quite comfortable sitting by your side.'

'Wait, I'll get you a mat.'

As Aunt got up, Inder Dutt gently pulled her down again. 'How are you, Susheela?' he asked, addressing Bhola's wife. 'And how is Manorama?'

'Everyone's all right.'

'And the children?'

'They are fine. You and sister-in-law never care to call on us although you live so close by.'

'But I always enquire about all of you. As for visiting...'

'I know you don't have the time. But what about sister-in-law? She has all the time in the world. No children, no chores...'

'There's construction work going on in their house,' Aunt intervened on behalf of Inder Dutt. 'So how can the poor thing leave the house?'

Bhola's wife widened her eyes as if recalling a faint memory. 'Yes, of course. Which part of the house are you getting renovated, brother?'

'The whole house is being reconstructed. There won't be a finer house in the neighbourhood once the job is done.' Aunt spoke in a voice of suppressed animation, with the desire to cut her daughter-in-law to size. She had not wanted to speak in that tone but her wounded feelings got the better of her. Bhola's wife's eyes glinted and she plastered her double chin against her throat to show the effect of Aunt's words on her. 'But they live in the rear portion don't they?' she said in an insinuating tone.

'Yes, the rear portion—that's where were born, Jeejaji, myself and brother. There was also another brother. My father, uncle and so many others—I don't remember how many—were all born in that part of the house.'

'But that's the worst part of the house. How do you manage to live there?'

'Where our forefathers were born is heaven for us. Ancestors are the gods of the earth.'

His sister-in-law did not say anything more. She adjusted the *palla* over her head and looked away while Inder Dutt fell to talking with Aunt. After a while she went away, leaving aunt and nephew to their tete-a-tete. There was a short silence after she left and then both launched on a speech together. Aunt fell back, yielding place to Inder Dutt.

'I hear Uncle has...'

'Don't worry about him, son. Will he ever listen to anybody?'

'But how long can he continue like this?'

'As long as he can.' Aunt's voice rose and fell with her tears. 'Whatever is written in my destiny.' She could speak no more and she began wiping away her tears.

'Tell me the truth, Aunt. Have you been eating?'

'Yes, every day.' She hid her eyes behind her *palla*. Inder Dutt felt that she was lying.

'You come to my house this minute, Aunt. Uncle will come there as usual but today I mean to take him with me. Otherwise I'll start a fast too.'

'Do as you like. I have no control over anyone.' Tears flooded her eyes that were still veiled by her *palla*.

'No, Aunt. Either Uncle must break his fast today or...'

'How do you do, brother?' Bhola said coming into the room. Seeing his mother crying he grew tense. Though she tried to hide her feelings, her eyes freshly bathed in tears gave her away. Bhola's expression hardened further. Turning his face away and plonking his heavy body down on the bed, he asked his cousin, 'Is your house ready?'

'It's almost ready. It'll be complete before the rains set in.'

'I hear it's a beautiful plan you have drawn up. You must have taken great pains over it.'

Inder Dutt did not reply.

'I'm also thinking of getting a bungalow built for myself. We can't manage in this house any longer.'

Inder Dutt remained silent. After a pause Bhola said, 'Have you seen Dad's latest drama? He spends a lot of time with you these days. Complaining against us, I suppose?'

'You should know better than I do that Uncle has never been given to backbiting and carrying tales.' Though apparently calm, there was an edge to Inder Dutt's voice.

'Maybe. But be fair. What kind of learning and knowledge is this that teaches disgust for dumb creatures? And against one's daughters and daughters-in-law, even against grandchildren? Tell me, sir, which scripture teaches us this?' Bhola's animus burst open like a sewer when the stopper is removed from its outlet.

Inder Dutt replied in a calm resolute voice, 'You are looking at the whole thing in the wrong light, Bhola. Complicated domestic problems are never settled this way.'

'What wrong light, sir? I'm only telling you what's true and fair. It takes two hands to clap.'

'But you are clapping with one hand, by beating your hand on the ground.'

'What do you mean? I don't follow you.'

'You are fighting with yourself and doing yourself harm in the process, Bhola. It's not necessary to go along with all of

Uncle's beliefs. But he is worthy of our respect all the same. He represents the generation before ours through interaction with which that we develop. You see his shortcomings all right and so you should, but, remember also that if we gloss over his virtues it can do more harm than good to you and me and the whole of the new generation.'

Bhola frowned as he took out a gold cigarette case from his pocket and said, 'I thought, brother, that the study of history and so on would have knocked a lot of wisdom into your head.' This observation seemed to give him great satisfaction. Having dismissed Inder Dutt's erudition as not worth a farthing Bhola seemed to rise to the seventh heaven: 'The pious fraudulence of our older generations have caused enough suffering to our country and to the Hindu society in particular. Things are not what they were forty or fifty years ago when 'Father is God, father is dharma' was rammed down our throats by these people so that they could bully us into submission. I tell you, you are out of date, you may be committed, yes, but keep your commitment to yourself. The new generation is not prepared to submit to your tyranny.'

'If you won't submit to other's tyranny why should anyone submit to yours?'

'In what way am I being tyrannical, sir?'

'You are always out to foist your false reformism on others?'

'Tell me, what I have done?'

'You deliberately provoke Uncle, Bhola. Let me say this clearly. You and Tribhuvan provoke Uncle,' Inder Dutt said in a steady voice.

'I'm not used to listening to such rubbish. Look, sir, we like to eat meat and therefore we eat it and shall continue eating it. Let's see what you can do about it.'

'I'm not going to do anything Bhola Shankerji. Eat with pleasure. I don't think Uncle has ever objected to it. He does not eat meat because his heritage and thinking are different— why do you want to impose your views and your thinking on him? As for segregating his kitchen or being angry with you, you can't by any stretch of imagination call this being tyrannical. He doesn't like it, that's all.'

'But why doesn't he like it, I ask? I hobnob with a great many professors and other intellectuals. In Vedic times Brahmins and sages even ate beef.' Bhola jerked his neck and the flabby flesh on his face quivered while his cigarette burnt between his fingers.

Inder Dutt said, 'That's right, they did. Rama, Krishna, Arjuna, Indra all ate well and drank well. But by saying that you can not obliterate the later culture which changed with the times and in the wake of Vaishnavism became nearly countrywide.'

'Fine, so our new culture is also becoming countrywide.'

'I don't deny that.'

'Then why is father opposing us?'

'Bhola, we can't sit in judgement over Uncle. Not because we are not capable of doing so, but because now he has not the time left to fall in line with us. In his last days he cannot have the urge to change his habits.'

'But why does he lack the urge, I ask?'

'You are being unfair, brother. He belongs to a bygone age over which we have no control. We can only mould the present and the future. We have to accept the values and faith of the past as appropriate to it. We can't tinker with them—can we? Hear me out first and then speak. I was saying we should dwell on the virtues of our ancestors so that we can carry them forward into the future. True, we have to understand their shortcomings and limitations also so that we can reach new horizons. But to foist our reformist zeal on them is tantamount to tyranny.'

'And what they do is not tyranny?'

'If it is tyranny you certainly must oppose it tooth and nail. But not with hatred. He is a very close relation of yours—your father. You must show him some respect, sympathy and understanding.'

Inder Dutt was sitting cross-legged and talking very calmly.

Bhola's face swung between irritation and disdain-filled swagger, the smoke from his cigarette swathing his face.

'So you mean we should stop eating meat?' he flared.

'My friend, it would be seemly if you had indulged your taste for meat and fish outside the house at least during the life-time of your father and mother. Not to act by stealth but to show them respect. This would have raised your standing in the family. Anyway right now, your quarrel is not over this. It is over your...'

'...Over my Juliet. She goes into his room and recently had pups in his Saraswati temple. So you would wreak vengeance on a dumb animal, sir? Is this your humanism?'

'I want to know why you have kept this pet? You should have shown some concern for your parents' feelings.'

'Where does the question of feelings come in, brother?' Bhola got up and began pacing up and down. Going to the end of the room he turned and said, 'It's my hobby and I have a right to indulge it. It's not a bad hobby, either, brother. Other parents participate in their children's pleasures. It's my bad luck that...'

'Bhola, you think only about your pleasures. You have not given a moment's thought to the patience and forbearance with which your father has been putting up with your doings.'

'Forbearance? What forbearance? He has been abusing us day and night.'

'And so in revenge you set your bitch upon him!'

'If he is so finicky about purity let him put up a wall on his side of the house. We shall do as we like. And now we shall do it with a vengeance.'

'So you are spoiling for a fight? This is no way of coming to an understanding.'

'I declare openly that father and I can't come to any understanding, Tribhuvan is with me on this. If father cannot see eye to eye with our progressive outlook then we have no place in our house for him.'

'Bhola!' Aunt, who had been sitting silent all along, said in a trembling voice, her hand stretched out in entreaty. 'Son, never say that to him even by mistake. I fall at your feet.'

'I will say it to him...I'll say to him a thousand times over. Now it's open war between us. He can't stand the way our children dress, he can't stand their having a good time—endure us. I kick at his pieties, his god and his religious tomes. Religion indeed—my foot!'

Tears came to mother's eyes and she bowed her head. Inder Dutt boiled over at the extent of Bhola's rudeness. He tried to keep his voice calm but a bitter laugh escaped his lips. He said, 'Bhola, if this behaviour of yours is a sample of your 'progressive' outlook and if this is what makes a man educated and fashionable, then I shall say, Bhola, that you and your men of the new age are barbarians or in fact worse. Your new age is neither new nor old. Not only are your ideas far from new; they are only the stale remains of British slavery. And your culture is not better than the hollow pride of wealthy feudal lords. Your ideas are not human, but demonic.' Inder Dutt was naturally excited.

'Keep your humanity to yourself,' Bhola said, 'I know hypocrites when I see them. And I keep them at arm's length.'

Bhola Shanker got up in a rage and stormed out of the room. Reaching the door, he looked back and said to his mother, 'Amma, explain to father that his threats of fasting will cut no ice with me. If the worst comes to the worst he will die. Let him. But I won't let him die in my house to die in. Let him go to the banks of the Ganga. There's no place for him under my roof.'

'But this house does not belong only to you.'

'We shall settle that in the court, if it comes to that. But I have nothing to do with him henceforth.'

Bhola Shanker was gone. His mother wept silently. Inder

Dutt sat there looking greatly agitated. When a man has very little of something, when he acquires even a little of it, it seems a great deal to him. All this excitement and anger seemed vastly important to Inder Dutt. He sat brooding for a while and then he suddenly grasped Aunt's hand and said, 'You and Uncle must come and stay with me. My house is also yours.'

'Son, don't tell your uncle the things Bhola has said.'

'No, I won't.'

'And somehow or other make your uncle give up his fast, son. You'll be blessed for it. I'll bless you all my life.'

'That is what I came for. You must come with me too. Your face tells me that you too...'

'Don't worry about me.'

'Yes, it's you and Uncle who will soon have to start worrying about me. I won't eat until the two of you have eaten. I am firm about my vow.'

His aunt grew anxious. Then she said cajolingly: 'Look, son Inder, you are my son too, just little Bhola and Tribhuvan. Your house is mine, just as this is. Today you must somehow make your uncle eat. As soon as I hear he has broken his fast, I too will worship god and eat, I swear by you. But I'll eat in this house. I don't want to hurt anyone, son. What to do, I am helpless before your uncle's anger. He hurts himself, true, but he also hurts the children. The times are evil, son.'

Inder Dutt heard his aunt out.

For a moment Aunt was lost in thought. Then she said in a soft voice, 'Look, Bhaiyya Inder, I have the same affection for you as I have for Bhola and Tribhuvan; I make no difference between you and them. Their house is as much mine as yours. Today somehow prevail upon your uncle to eat his food. As soon as he breaks his fast, I swear by you, I shall also partake of food, regarding it as divine food. But I must eat under this very house. Son, one shouldn't do anything to hurt one's feelings. How tell you, son, your uncle gets so worked up that I can't have my way with him. He suffers silently and makes his children also suffer with him. Oh, how miserable they feel! It's the age of *Kalyug*. Nobody can stop it from running its course, Bhaiyya.'

For sometime Inder Dutt watched Aunt in silence as she struggled to get over her feeling.

As was his practice, Pandit Devdhar Bhatt came to his nephew's house at dusk and called out, 'Inder Dutt!'

'Welcome, Uncle'. Inder Dutt was standing near the railing and watched Panditji walking in, making a staccato sound with his wooden sandals, on the damp brick-laid floor of the courtyard. His ash-smeared face glowed and his body covered with a shawl printed with the name of Shiva seemed to emit an other-worldly radiance. The house seemed to undergo a change with his presence. Inder felt this every day but this evening seemed special. Uncle's four-day fast seemed to have lent an extra charisma to his personality in Inder's eyes. Today Inder Dutt was feeling extra-emotional about his Uncle. Inder felt there was no trace of exhaustion or hunger on Uncle's face. He did look a little wan but his spirit seemed undimmed. Inder Dutt was deeply moved by this.

Panditji sat down on a wooden stool while Inder Dutt sat on a tuffet, facing him. The construction work had put the drawing room to sixes-and-sevens and he was embarrassed about receiving visitors in this tumble-down room. With Uncle, of course, he felt no embarrassment. He turned the fan in Uncle's direction. For some time they sat silent and then Uncle broke the silence: 'I'm told you have just been to my house.'

"Yes, I have.'

'Your aunt told me. She also told me that you held out some juvenile threat on my account.' Pandit Devdhar removed his neck-cloth and placed it on the stool by his side. He sat erect, cross-legged, his erect, composed bearing spiritualising his pale face and enhancing its fairness.

Inder Dutt said in a careful tone, weighing each word, 'My

obstinacy is not for self-satisfaction. It is my humble contribution to the obstinacy of my elders.'

'It's no use Inder. My conduct is governed by my own rules.'

'Well, I can have my rules too.'

'Sure, you are free to act as you like.'

'Then, if I have decided to go on fast there is nothing wrong in it.'

'You are weighing me down under your affection. I fast to purify my soul. The defilement of the temple of my forefathers is the result of some sin of mine. I must wash the temple of Saraswati clean with the Ganga of my inner being. Take back your vow, son.'

Silence again reigned in the room. Only the whirring of the fan created waves in the silence.

Inder Dutt said in a calm voice, 'May I ask you one thing? If the presence of a dog can defile a temple then the idea of the omnipresence of God is false. Why should one presence of his be regarded as pure and another as impure?'

Pandit Devdhar was silent. Then he said in a grave voice, 'The Hindu religion is very profound. You had better not get involved in its intricacies.'

'Uncle, I will not get involved in these intricacies. I am only voicing a thought. If Lord Rama moved by love, could eat the berries tasted by Shabri and if Hindus have faith in this breaking of rules, then untouchability should be thrown overboard. Yudhister refused to enter Heaven unless his dog was allowed to accompany him. Don't these stories reveal the greatness of the Hindu religion? Do not great ideas, great feelings inspire them? Why then do you uphold an orthodox touch-me-not ritualism which is ever afraid of pollution? Don't we dwarf ourselves by binding ourselves in these orthodoxies?'

Panditji heard Inder Dutt in silence. Inder Dutt feared he had gone too far, that his uncle would take offence so he at once added, 'I'm of course worked up at the moment. But what I am asking is purely in a spirit of enquiry.'

Panditji said, 'In our religion right conduct is held in the highest esteem. Manusmriti says right conduct is the supreme dharma. As is the conduct, so will be the thought. Do you think the concept of pure conduct is wrong?'

'No, not at all.'

'Then why do you wish to corrupt my conduct?'

'I would never dare to even dream of doing do such a thing. But I would still say, with all respect to you that your insistence on forms of conduct does not producing any fresh stimulus for thought in our age. So I feel these forms have no value. I am not being disrespectful, Uncle, but I do truly feel that the world is forging ahead and your view of things is holding up the momentum of change... But let us not talk of that for the moment. My fervent request to you just now is only that you should break your fast.'

Panditji smiled. Inder felt hopeful.

'All right I'll eat but on one condition,' Panditji said.

'I'm at your command.'

'You will have to abide by all that is the old ways of life, regulations, rites and rituals. For, these rules which have no value for you, mean everything to me. I value them more than my life.'

Inder Dutt was stunned. He had never thought that his uncle would tie him down with such an impossible condition.

'For how long will I have to abide by these rules?' he asked.

'All your life.'

Inder Dutt was in a quandary. How could he bind his intelligence with rules in which he had no faith, which, in his view, bound people in superstitions, which were blots on the Indian culture? He had seen these fasts, rules, sacrifices, miracles and false beliefs of Hinduism result in heinous atrocities on society. A man earned a reputation for spirituality through the crudest masochism and led the country to ruin. Brahminism, based on leading a 'pure' harsh life, had for centuries ground down the women and the so-called low castes of this country, kept them enslaved, and this continued even today. Possibly, at a time when human consciousness was just beginning to grow, this so-called pure conduct had lit the lamp of thought in darkness, for centuries now this moth-eaten ritualism had made an average Indian a slave, a superstitious fatalist, a believer in false gods and goddesses, in alluring but impossible fantasies. It had undermined the average Indian's self-confidence and broken the country's backbone. The Upanishads had tried to counter this stagnation and so had humanism, Yoga, the Gita, the Buddhists, and the medieval Sant movement. Today's scientific era had proved its emptiness and dug its grave. This stagnant religiosity could never make India great. The greatness of India lay in its philosophy of action, its profound sense of universal humanity, the liberal vision of Valmiki and Vyasa. Ancient Indian philosophy, schools of logic, literature, sculpture, and music could never be the products of this stagnant religiosity. And yet this stagnation had held the country in its vice-like grip for ages. Because of his disgust of it, the new Indians of today had thrown overboard the whole body of tradition without critical scrutiny and had become devoid of principles, commitment and action. No, he could never accept Uncle's religion, never. But what about Uncle's fast? When will Aunt get to eat? What irony! The moral responsibility for two people's deaths would rest on him.

Seeing him silent, Pandit Devdhar asked, 'So will you be serving me food?'

'I am in a quandary...'

'State in clear terms whether you will accept my ways?'

'Uncle, you are asking too much. You are asking me to surrender my beliefs. I don't consider your brand of religion the right thing for today. I do not consider it mine.'

'I like your frankness. You have your own dharma, so you should recognise mine. I cannot give up my religion. Although being in your company for sometime has taught me that my religion my times are on the way out, are going to become extinct, yet I will stay by it to my last breath. May God bless you. May you be happy. I shall go now.'

'But my decision to fast is firm, Uncle. I swear with my hand on your feet.'

'Let go of my feet, son. These feet have already become immobile. And immobility will depart only with my final departure, not before. Anyway, think about your fast tomorrow. Give it a second thought.'

Panditji uttered the last sentence in such a way that it gave a severe jolt to Inder Dutt. But he was forced into silence. Uncle was about to leave, a fearful storm raged in his mind. He felt defeated. What would he tell Aunt? And how was it all going to end? Should be agree to Uncle's condition? But why should he? Uncle was so staunch in his beliefs that it impressed him tremendously. But still how could he accept those beliefs?

Pandit Devdhar stopped near the staircase. Inder Dutt was close at his heels. Turning round Pandit Devdhar said, 'I don't have faith in your beliefs. But I do see something of their authenticity. One thing more. I wish to know, do you think that Bhola's or Tribhuvan's beliefs are the authentic expression of the present age or any other age?'

'No, not at all. They have no beliefs at all.'

'May you be blessed, son. Fight this hollow faith born of the intoxication of wealth as I did. You fight in your own way, son by your own faith. But fight you must. This way of life which is devoid of philosophy, faith or commitment and only flaunts its arrogance bodes ill for the universe. Fight it. Do I have your word for it?'

'I give you my word.' Inder Dutt bent low and touched Uncle's feet.

The staccato beat of his wooden sandals descended the stairs, went across the courtyard and receded into the distance. Inder Dutt came in and fell down on his bed like a felled tree. Of its own volition the new age was bidding goodbye to the old. But what powerful attachment there was ever at the moment of parting and what ruthless conduct too!

Hari Shankar Parsai

The Soul of Bhola Ram

Such a thing had never happened before.

For aeons Dharamraj, the god of death, had been assigning places to the dead in Heaven or Hell on the basis of their merit acquired through action or through good 'contacts,' that is, devotion, karma during their sojourn on Earth. But nothing like this had happened before.

In front of him sat Chitragupta, wiping his spectacles again and again, and wetting his fingers with his saliva as he turned the pages of his Register. He carefully ran his eyes over each page but couldn't spot the mistake. At last in irritation he banged shut the Register so hard that a fly was trapped in its pages. Flicking the insect away he said, 'Maharaj, my record is correct in every detail. Bholaram's soul left his body five days ago. It set out for our world under the vigilance of our messenger yet it has not yet reached here.'

'And the messenger of Death? Where's he now?' Dharamraj asked.

'Maharaj, he too is absconding. There's no trace of him anywhere.'

Just then the portals of the great hall opened and the messenger of Death came in, looking utterly distraught. His normally ugly face looked still more ugly from fear, fatigue and anxiety.

'You, where were you all these days?' Chitragupta almost jumped out of his seat when he saw the messenger. 'And where's Bholaram's soul?'

The messenger of Death folded his hands in supplication, 'Merciful One, I don't know how to tell you. Until today I've never been caught napping. But Bholaram's soul has given me the slip. Five days ago when his soul left his body, I caught it and set out for our world. At the outskirts of the city just as I got ready to ride an air current he got out of my grip and disappeared I do not know where. I have spent five days ransacking the entire universe but I have failed to track him down.'

His explanation greatly annoyed Dharamraj. 'Idiot!' he said in anger, 'your hair has turned grey escorting souls and yet you have been diddled by the soul of an ordinary old man.'

Bowing his head abjectly, the messenger said, 'O King, I was exceedingly careful, leaving nothing to chance. Even eminent lawyers have not been able to hoodwink me in this game. But this time some miracle has taken place.'

Chitragupta said, 'O King, there is a widespread racket on earth these days. People send gifts of fruit to their friends and the railway people pilfer them en route. Railway officials remove socks from parcels of hosiery goods and wear them. Whole bogeys detached from goods trains and diverted to other destinations. And the funniest thing of all, the leaders of political parties kidnap their opponents in rival parties and lock them up elsewhere. Could it be that some rival with a score to settle has spirited away Bholaram's soul to harm him even after death?'

Dharamraj gave Chitragupta an ironic look and said, 'It's time you retired. Your brain seems to have addled. Tell me, could anybody stand to gain anything from a down-and-out man like Bholaram?'

At this point, the sage Narad, out on his usual peregrinations, happened to come in. Seeing Dharamraj lost in thought he said, 'What's the matter, Dharamraj? You look worried. Are you still groping for a solution to the problem of lack of residential space in Hell?'

'That problem was solved long ago, venerable sage. In the last few years a lot of clever craftsmen have descended on Hell. Some of them are building contractors who had fleeced their clients and put up worthless buildings. There are engineers too who joined hands with these contractors and ate up the funds of India's Five Year Plans. There are overseers who marked non-existent labourers present on their rolls and gobbled the money. All these gentlemen have constructed many buildings in Hell in record time. That problem has been solved to our satisfaction. At the moment we are worried about a man called Bholaram who died five days ago. This messenger went to take possession of his soul, but it slipped through his fingers on the way. He has searched high and low over the Universe but he has not been able to trace the soul. If things start happening in this manner the distinction between evil and good will vanish.'

Narad asked, 'Did he have any arrears of income-tax? It is just possible the income tax people have detained him.'

Chitragupta countered: 'He could have paid income-tax only if he had an income. He was starving.'

'An interesting case,' Narad said. 'Well, give me his name and address. I shall go down to Earth.'

Chitragupta consulted his Register. 'The man, Bholaram by name, was a resident of Jabalpur city, where he lived with his family colony in Dhampur in a one-and-a-half roomed tumble-down house by the side of a drain. He had a wife, two sons and a daughter. Age, around sixty years. He was a government servant and had retired from service five years ago. He had not paid his house rent for the last one year and the landlord was therefore threatening him with eviction. But meanwhile Bholaram had left the world. Today is the fifth day of ten his death. Quite possibly, the landlord, if he is true to type, has evicted Bholaram's family by now. So you may have a hard time locating the family.'

The joint crying of Bholaram's wife and daughter helped Narad identify the house.

Going up to the door, he cried, 'Narain! Narain!'

The girl looked at him and said, 'Maharaj, move on further.'

'I'm not asking for alms,' Narad replied, 'I want to make some enquiries about Bholaram. Send your mother out, daughter.'

Bholaram's wife came to the door. 'Maa, what was the nature of Bholaram's disease?' Narad asked her.

'What can I say? It was the disease of poverty. He retired from service five years ago but he did not get even a paisa of his pension money. Every few days he would send a petition to the government but either there was no reply or there was the stock reply that the matter of his pension was receiving due attention. In these five years we have sold off all my jewellery to buy food. Then the utensils. And then there was nothing left to sell. We just starved. Worry and hunger ate into him and brought about his end.'

'What can you do, Maa? This was his life span.'

'Don't say that, Maharaj. He could have had a longer span. If some fifty or sixty rupees a month had come to him as pension he could have taken up some other job. But what could be done? Five years passed after release from service and not a paisa in hand.'

Narad had no time to listen to tales of woe. He came to the point. 'Maa, tell me, did he have any special attachment for anyone that took his mind off things?'

'Maharaj, one has attachment only for one's family and children.'

'No, it can be outside the family too. Some lady...'

The woman growled at Narad. 'Don't talk rot, Maharaj,' she said. 'You are a sadhu, not a loafer. All his life he did not so much as glance at another woman.'

Narad laughed. 'Yes, yes, you may be right. This illusion is the basis of conjugal happiness. Well, mother, I must be going now.'

Bholaram's wife said, 'Maharaj, you are a sage, a self-realised man. Can't you do something to get my husband's blocked pension? My children will be saved from starving.'

Narad felt sorry for the woman. He said, 'Nobody cares for sages these days. And I don't have any establishment here to impress people. Nobody will listen to me. Still, I'll to my best for you.'

Narad went to the office which dealt with pension cases.

Entering the first room he talked about Bholaram's case to a man sitting behind a desk. The clerk listened intently to Narad and when he had finished, said, 'Bholaram did send numerous petitions, but he didn't put any weight on them so they flew away.'

Narad said, 'Brother, I see so many paperweights on your table. Why didn't you use one of these to keep the petition from flying?'

The clerk laughed. 'You are a sage. You don't know the ways of the world. Petitions are not made secure by paperweights. Anyway, you had better go and talk to the clerk in the next room.'

Narad went to the adjoining room where the clerk sent him to a third, who in turn sent him to a fourth, and he on to a fifth. In this manner, after Narad had danced attendance on about thirty clerks and officers, a peon accosted him and said, 'Maharaj, why have you involved yourself in this mess? Even if you keep running around in this office for a whole year nothing will come of it. You go straight to the Big Boss. If you make him happy your job is as good as done.'

Narad entered the room of the Big Boss. His peon was dozing at the door no one barred Narad's way. The Boss frowned. 'You should have sent your visiting card first,' he said. 'Do you think this is a temple that you barge in headlong? You should at least have sent in a slip.'

'How could I?' Narad said, 'Your peon was dozing.

'All right, state the purpose of your visit,' the Saheb said in a commanding voice.

Narad explained the case of Bholaram's pension.

'You are an other worldly man,' the sahib said. 'You don't know the rules and regulations of offices. It is Bholaram who was at fault. A government office is also like a temple. Here too one has to make offerings and give aims. You appear to be Bholaram's friend or well-wisher. Bholaram's petitions keeps flying away. Put some weight on them.'

'Again the same business of weights!' Narad said to himself.

'This is a question of government money,' the Big Boss said. 'Pension cases travel to scores of offices. Delay is inevitable. The same thing has to be recorded twenty times in twenty different places. It is only then that the case is fully confirmed. The cost of the stationery alone is almost as much as the pension. The matter can of course be expedited but...' he paused.

Narad said, 'But...?'

The Big Boss gave a cunning smile. 'But we must have the weight' he said. Can't you understand such a simple thing? This beautiful musical instrument of yours can well serve as a weight to keep Bholaram's petition in place. My daughter is learning music. I'll give her your instrument. Sadhus' instruments play better than ordinary ones. If my daughter picks up music fast, her marriage will not be delayed for long.'

Fearing the appropriation of his *veena*, Narad lost his nerve for a moment. But he quickly regained his poise and placed his *veena* on the Saheb's table. 'Here it is,' he said in a gracious tone. 'Let your daughter make good use of it. But kindly give orders for Bholaram's pension right now.'

Pleased, the Big Boss offered Narad a chair to sit on. Depositing the *veena* in a corner of the room he rang the bell.

'Bring Bholaram's pension file from the head clerk,' he said to the peon as he came in.

The Soul of Bhola Ram

The peon soon came back with the file. It was a thick file, loaded with about 150 petitions and other papers relating to the case.

The Saheb examined the name on the file and then he looked up at Narad. 'What name did you say?' he asked to make doubly sure that it was the correct file. Narad thought the Saheb was a bit hard of hearing 'Bholaram!' he said loudly.

Suddenly a voice rose from within the file. 'Who is calling me?' it said. 'Is it the postman? Have my pension papers come?'

The Saheb fell off his chair in a fright. Narad looked up, startled. But the next instant he got the hang of the affair.

'Bholaram? Are you Bholaram's soul?' he asked.

'Yes,' the voice replied.

'I'm Narad,' the sage said. 'I've come to fetch you. Come, they are waiting for you in Heaven.'

'No, I'm not going,' the voice said, 'I'm entangled in this mass of petitions. I'm very busy here. I can't leave my petitions.'

Amrit Rai

Before Daybreak

Morning. Singly or in pairs, or in small groups, those who love to bathe in the Ganga are returning from its shores. They stop at the vegetable and fruit shops on Dasashwamedh Ghat over their morning purchases. The shops are well-stocked and bedecked like brides. The tea stall owners are handing out cups of thickly brewed tea the colour of catechu while the betel leaf sellers too are doing brisk business. A Bengali newspaper vendor is hawking *Jugantar* and *Ananda Bazaar*. All faces, all voices and clothes exude a magical freshness. The golden sunshine of morning spreads out, colouring springtime with its hue of health and vigour. At this moment, S.N. Dey's Chemists Pharmacy and the whole range of Ayurvedic medicine shops around looked pleasant to Indubhushan. But a moment's thought is enough to make Indubhushan alive to the fact that this special glow of spring is transitory, a thing of an hour or two. Soon one must return to the daily routine, with its cycle of health and illness.

Indubhushan heard someone calling out. 'Well, sir, how are you?'

Unaware that the call was addressed to him, he kept walking slowly towards the ghat, lost in his own thoughts.

Finding Indubhushan deaf to his call, the fairly well-built, wheat-coloured middle-aged man of shortish stature whose fat had started running loose, caught up with Indubhushan and barred his way. 'How are you,' he said. 'I called you but you did not hear me.' In one hand he held a bag with some bunches of spinach and a couple of brinjals and in the other a baby fish weighing about a quarter seer or a little more.

Indubhushan failed to recognize him. From his general appearance and from the mole under his left eye, Indubhusan faintly recalled having seen the man somewhere before. But exactly when and where he just couldn't remember. Before he could get over his bewilderment and say something, the man who was himself feeling embarrassed, smiled and said, 'You have not recognized me. I'm your neighbour. My house is in the same block as yours.'

Now Indubhushan gradually remembered all the details. Just the other day this Bengali gentleman had shifted to that yellow house at the end of the lane. It couldn't be more than a week ago. He and his three daughters.

'Yes, now I remember, Bengali Babu. Forgive me, it took me some time. I have not met you before, that's why. I hope you have settled down in your house by now? It's a nice house—looks nice from outside.'

'Yes, quite nice in its own way, I agree. We are not a big family anyway.'

'Just your three daughters and you?'

In reply the man gave a funny smile and glancing around said, 'Yes, no one else at all. And your name, sir?'

'Indubhushan. And yours?'

'Beni Madhav Bose.'

After a pause the Bengali said,' I thought one must get acquainted with one's neighbours. I hope you have not taken offence?'

Slim and fair, Indubhushan had just crossed the age of adolescence at which a young man is generally hungry for closeness with a young girl, when he feels the need for a partner with whom he can share the strange stirrings of a newly found youth. Perhaps that was the reason why he had felt a little excited on meeting Beni Madhav. Coming in or going out of his house, he had often seen the three girls standing at the window of their house.

It was a Sunday morning. Indubhusan was reclining in a deck chair in his courtyard, reading a book of stories.

He had just finished reading a story and he closed the book, and lay still looking into space. The heroine of the story had committed suicide by taking arsenic and her pale, sad face was haunting his mind. 'I could not live. That's why I am dying,' were her last words.

Indu's young mind was unable to understand why the girl had taken poison. Was arsenic the only way out for her? Why did she take it into her head to die? Why couldn't she say, 'I scorn such a society...' Courage? But she had the courage to take arsenic!

His mind was filled with impotent rage at the heroine's suicide. Impotent, because in some corner of his mind lurked the feeling that it was easier to talk of scorning society than actually to scorn it.

He was still debating the issue when he saw Beni Madhav Babu at the gate. The same dhoti, the same dirty-looking full-sleeves shirt which must have been white at one time. He walked with the uncertainty of a man entering a strange house for the first time. After walking in through the gate he looked around warily when Indhbhushan got up from his chair and greeted him, 'Come Bose Babu, how have you strayed this way today?'

Beni Madhav responded from where he stood, 'Thank you, thank you, are you well?'

Indu's healthy, fresh face was the best answer to this formal courtesy. Offering Bose Babu a chair, Indu said, 'I'm perfectly well, but you look a little pulled down.'

'Well, you know how it is, Indu Babu...You know what my life is.'

Sensing that Bose wanted a word of sympathy, Indu said, 'I know your life is a hard grind. How old would your eldest daughter be, Bose Babu?'

Beni Madhav did not quite understand the significance of this question but he saw in a flash that he must cultivate this young man and that he must not let this opportunity go by.

He looked right and left and then said in a very low voice as if disclosing a secret, 'The girl you are alluding to, Indu Babu—her age is twenty years. Her name is Madhavi. The next girl is called Putul. She is eighteen years of age. And Hashi—she is still a child.' To cover up his embarrassment Beni Madhav gave a hollow laugh.

Indu was not expecting such a detailed reply. He had only made a casual enquiry, out of sympathy for Beni Madhav, thinking that he might be worried about his eldest daughter's marriage. But Beni Babu had come out with his complete genealogical tree. Indu found this unduly intimate. He sat silent for some time and then begged leave of his visitor, saying that he had to go somewhere. He pushed back his chair.

Beni Madhav felt a little upset at Indu's abrupt decision to leave. He hadn't even paved the ground for a meaningful exchange and this man was raring to go. The words remained stuck in his throat like a fish-bone. Taking his clue from Indu Babu, he too rose from his chair. But he lingered for a while, with his eyes turned away. Indu realised that Beni Madhav had something to say.

'Anything I can do for you, Bose Babu?' Indu asked.

A drowning man clutches at a straw. Sometimes it is easier to come straight to the point than to beat about the bush. Cautiously looking around him he said in a low voice in his accented Hindi, 'Can you lend me ten rupees? I'll return it in ten days or at the most in a fortnight. Today I'm in dire need...'

Without a word Indu went in and came out holding a ten rupee note in his hand. He gave the note to Beni Madhav, folded his hands in greeting, and returned instantly to his room. The very thought of the ingratiating smile that the tenner would spread on his wretched face sickened him.

But no sooner had he gone in than he came out again. He wanted to tell Beni Madhav in passing that he should discourage his daughters from standing at the window because in the city... Surely, Beni Babu, you know what it is like in the city...

But Beni Babu had already gone out of the gate by the time Indu came out. He didn't think it right to call him back. He would tell him some other time he thought.

Many days passed.

It was twilight. Indu was returning home late from college. He had spent more time than usual in the library.

His house was about a hundred yards or so away from the main road and he had to go along an uneven, unpaved path. Beni Madhav's yellow house was situated at the end of this unpaved lane. Putul was standing at the door. 'Indu Babu!' she called out to him.

Indu hesitated for a moment before walking towards her.

'Indu Babu, why don't you ever visit us?' she gave a faint smile.

Apparently, Bose Babu must have talked freely about him to his daughters. He was not displeased.

'One must wait for a suitable opportunity,' he said. 'Actually I have often thought of dropping in.'

Putul was affected by Indu's smile. 'Please come in,' she said.

'Not now,' he said. 'They must be waiting for me at home. If possible I'll come an hour or so later.'

'But you must come,' Putul again smiled.

Indu walked away, feeling lighthearted.

When we entered their house one had to pass through a vestibule which was plunged in darkness. A tumble-down chair was resting in a corner. Not finding Beni Madhav there,

Indu as unwilling to proceed further. The vestibule opened onto a courtyard which was very damp. A dim lantern was burning in it, emitting dull reddish rays. An overhead iron grill served as a roof for the courtyard. Some clothes were drying on a clothes line—a red bordered sari, two petticoats, two or three blouses. Indu now lacked courage to proceed further. Stepping into the courtyard he called out in a loud voice, 'Bose Babu, are you in?'

Madhavi happened to be downstairs. 'This way, Indu Babu,' she said on hearing Indu's voice.

'Is Beni Madhav Babu not at home?' he asked her.

'He has gone somewhere,' Madhavi replied. 'He should be back presently. Please come up.' She called out to Putul, 'Putul, your Indu Babu has come.'

Putul was already coming down. 'Come, Indu Babu,' she said.

Indu answered her with a smile. 'I'll come another time,' he said and prepared to go. But Putul stepped forward and caught his hand and pulled him towards her. 'You must come up, Indu Babu. Baba will be here any moment.'

Indu's feet still refused to move forward. Putul pouted, expressing displeasure. 'What are you afraid of, Indu Babu?' she asked. 'You are a man and we... we are girls. What's there to be afraid of?' She almost dragged him upstairs.

The staircase was on the left, very narrow. On reaching the top, Indu saw two rooms adjacent to each other, a bed lying in each room and both the rooms lit with tin lamps. Entering her room, Putul quickly smoothed out the bedsheet spread on the cot and said, looking at Indu, 'There's nothing to fear. Please make yourself comfortable. Baba should be here any moment. It may mean some waiting, no more.'

Indu felt like fleeing but his feet seemed chained to the spot. He sat down on Putul's cot. His heart was pounding hard. Putul removed the tin lamp from the stool and pushing it forward, sat down on it. Silence reigned for a minute or two.

Then Putul broke the ice. 'Indu Babu, you are a bad man,' she smiled. Indu's heart beat faster still. He made no reply and sat there withdrawn into himself. Another spell of silence.

'Are you married, Indu Babu?'

Indu could not understand the idea of this abrupt question. But it was easy to answer it. 'No,' he said.

Putul clucked, smiling, 'tch...tch...tch!'

Indu said to himself, 'What a funny girl! She thinks I am an inert clod of earth.'

He felt a strong urge to fling this girl onto the bed—she who had made herself so cosy by his side and was smiling so coyly just to tease him. He felt like biting her hard anywhere on her body drawing blood. But he restrained himself with great difficulty. By now he had been able to get the hang of the situation and his heart was filled with loathing.

About ten minutes passed in this state. Then Indu heard a male voice from the adjoining room. 'I think Beni Madhav Babu has come,' he said.

Putul laughed a different laugh this time. 'No, Indu Babu, it's Madhavi's friend, Nalin.'

Indu got up from the cot like a shot. Putul also got up with him. She looked agitated.

'Are you going? So soon? You had given Baba ten rupees, hadn't you? No, no, no...' she sang as if expressing her gratitude to him, and pressed her burning lips to his.

All this happened with the swiftness of lightning so that Indu was completely bewildered. But he felt as if someone had placed a burning charcoal on his lips. His eyes turned red with anger and his nostrils flared. With a violent jerk he pushed her away and shaking her hard by the shoulders said in a raised voice, 'Yes, I gave him money. Yes, I did. And you want to pay me back. Pay me back, pay me back...' Tense with anger, he pushed her and she fell on the edge of the cot. Indu flung the tin lamp to the ground and stormed out of the room, banging shut the door behind him.

The sound of the door banging brought Madhavi out of her room. She saw Indu walking away swiftly, while Putul was clinging to the cot and sobbing. She seemed to have injuries on her body but the greater and real injury was to her mind and this injury was not only the insult Indu had heaped on her.

Madhavi gripped Putul's hand, trying to raise her. 'Don't be mad, Putul,' she said. 'He's gone. The brute! Yokel!'

Madhavi's words of sympathy fell like venom on Putul's ears. Raising her head she stared unblinkingly at her sister and then said to her in a commanding voice, 'Go away!'

Madhavi looked into Putul's weeping but stern eyes. 'What kind of madness is this?' She said and then uttered a vile word of abuse for Indu.

Putul's eyes flashed like a dagger being honed. Like a she-serpent she hissed, 'Sister, leave my room at once!'

'Just look at this childish behaviour', muttered Madhavi leaving the room where Putul continued to sits there crying.

Many more days passed. Putul's ever sad and listless face worried Madhavi. The fact was that more than Madhavi, it was Putul who was the bedrock of the family; she was its main support. And now she had become indifferent to those who came to visit her. Madhavi could not understand her behaviour and once or twice tried to talk to Putul. But Putul seemed to have started hating the sight of Madhavi. Every time she tried to speak to Putul it just led to a war of words. One day Madhavi said to her in a biting way, 'I have seen many like your Indu Babu, impotent creatures with their airs of learning. Hypocrite!'

In reply, Putul glared at Madhavi so fiercely that she felt afraid. 'Hold your tongue!' she gnashed her teeth.

Her voice sounded like the hissing of a serpent to Madhavi. She was aching to retaliate and get even by some unanswerably stinging remark. 'So you want to be Savitri to him and he Satyavan to you?' she said with venomous softness. 'Of course, what's wrong about it?' And she burst into hearty laughter.

The laughter stabbed Putul, driving her to tears. Madhavi had hit her most vulnerable spot. She went away crying to her room and closing the door, fell on her cot, face down. She lay there a long time, drenching her dirty bedsheet with tears. The word 'he' that Madhavi had so contemptuously used for Indu Babu fluttered like a thousand glow-worms in her mind. It glowed and faded and it felt good but it shed no light, not even as much as the tin lamp which Indu had sent crashing from the alcove and which in the morning Madhavi had replaced with another. When the glow-worms shone in the darkness of her mind, they looked beautiful like white flowers. But then the darkness became denser, heavier. Putul got up, extinguished the tin lamp too and returned to her bed. The more she thought of him the more her life seemed to be a morass.

Her parents had died in the Great Bengal Famine of 1943 and this distant maternal uncle of hers had taken charge of her. The morass had started forming then and in these two and a half years it had become deeper and deeper, and now? Now nothing could be done. A deep sigh of escaped her lips.

'How can I fight this? Where do I have the strength to fight? I have none now. This is a haunted house, sucking the blood like a vampire. Nothing can be done for me. There's nothing left of me. Nobody can rescue me from this hell hole...' Her wrath turned against Indu. He had robbed her of her peace of mind by sowing there seeds of discontent and poison. Before he came, her life, whatever it was, had been drifting on an even keel. But now she could neither find any means of escape for herself nor could she shake it all off her, as Madhavi did, as if it were so much water off a duck's back. She had spent two days in a spirit of revolt but then the realities of home asserted themselves. She had to dig her own well in order to drink water from it. She could not get away from her daily routine—habits formed over a period of two and a half years which had seeped into her blood. She fell back into her old ways. Some links of the chain had no doubt snapped within her. But that did not have any immediate effect on her. She was obsessed with the overall feeling that she was caught in a cesspool for ever from which she could not extricate herself. Outwardly she was resisting Madhavi's overtures but in her heart of hearts she was laying down her weapons.

That night, on returning from Putul, Indu too could not sleep for a long time. Now and then he felt a pain rippling through his stomach, his chest and his head, giving him a strange sense of unease in which anger and remorse vied with each other. His rage had now subsided and he felt that he should not have behaved with that girl in such a savage manner. How can you be so self-righteous, do you know what compulsions others are prey to? If all had the wherewithals of a decent living, ate well, wore good clothes and had a roof over one's head, all could easily act righteous. But even so, to sell one's body seemed so dirty to him that he could not bring himself to forgive Madhavi, Putul or Bose for it.

In spite of trying hard, Indu could not sleep till two in the morning. An image that he had tried to carve in his mind crashed into smithereens at one stroke of harsh reality and it lay in a total wreck at his feet. A whiff of joy that had wafted across his mind had been snuffed into extinction. A bud that had not yet developed its perfume to become a full blown flower had been crushed by someone between his hands. Indu felt stifled.

From that day he stopped passing by their house. Now he went by a different route, which though a little longer was to Indu's liking because Bose's house was not on the way and there was no fear of Putul encountering him and calling out to him or of his coming face to face with Beni Madhav who would say with extreme courtesy: 'You came to my house the other day and it was my bad luck that I was not at home.'

A month passed since that night and its pain was no longer fresh in Indu's mind. As for recrimination, not a trace of it was left in his mind. He had nothing but compassion for these people but he could not bring himself to see them.

It was about eight at night. Indu was sitting in his room, reading, when there was a timid knock on the door. When he opened the door he saw Putul standing before him. Putul! He fell back, dodging her gaze like a man trying to save his wound from being rubbed.

Putul smiled. 'Namaskar, Indu Babu.'

He felt a strange poignancy in her smile as he returned her greeting. 'Indu Babu, I've come to ask your forgiveness,' she said.

'Forgiveness? From me? But for what?'

Putul said in a tremulous voice. 'Indu Babu, don't say that. I have seriously thought over the matter. You did the right thing.'

'Forget about it,' Indu said. 'I myself...'

'How can I forget it, Indu Babu?' Putul said interrupting him.

No one spoke for a while. 'May I beg something of you?' Putul said at last breaking the silence.

Unable to comprehend her, Indu sat still, his gaze averted. He was also uneasy lest some member of his family see him with her. Then he heard Putul say, 'Indu Babu, please save my Hashi...Save my Hashi, Indu Babu. She is still a child, sinless yet. Save her from this hell, Indu Babu.'

She was speaking very rapidly as if she feared that someone would strangle her before she had finished saying what was in her mind. Tears streamed from her eyes as soon as she stopped.

Indu felt like throwing his arms around Putul, stroking her *bokul*-scented hair and saying to her, 'Don't cry, silly. Don't cry. What would people say if they see? Here take water from my hands and wash your face. Don't be afraid. All will be well. Hashi is as much my sister as yours.'

All these words formed themselves in the inner core of his heart and he even took a step closer to her. But he stopped. Bushes, rocks, inherited ways of being... Indu could not speak...

At that moment every fibre of Putul was crying for support. But that support did not come, did not come, did not come. In those fateful moments innumerable centuries seemed to have passed. Putul moved towards the door still crying. Like a dying flame suddenly flaring up before extinction she exclaimed, 'Let be, Indu Babu. Forget that I ever came.'

Indu stood before her with lowered head, and Putul slowly merged into the darkness from which she had come.

Amarkant

The Midday Meal

The cooking done, Siddeshawari put out the fire and resting her head between her knees she abstractedly gazed at her toes and at the ants crawling on the floor. Suddenly she realized that she had been feeling thirty for a long time. Getting up groggily, she poured out water from the pitcher and gulped it down in one draught. The water hit her empty stomach. 'Hai Ram!' she groaned and lay down on the bare floor.

She lay there for almost half an hour before she began to feel normal. Feeling a little revived, she sat up, rubbing her eyes and her gaze settled on her six year old son, Pramod who was sleeping naked on a broken string cot in the portico. He was so thin that his collar bones and ribs could be seen clearly. His limbs were withered and limp like stale cucumbers and his belly bloated like a pot. Flies swarmed around his open mouth.

She got up, covered the boy's face with a soiled old blouse of hers, and then went to the door and gazed into the lane listlessly. It was past noon. The sun blazed. But for a few passers-by now and then, rushing along firmly holding umbrellas, or wet towels loosely tied round their heads, the street was quite deserted.

She kept standing there for a long time till signs of impatience began to creep over her face. She looked anxiously at the burning sky and then craning her neck forward glanced up and down the lane. There he was at last! Her eldest son, Ramchandra. He came shuffling along towards the house.

Galvanized into action, she fetched a pitcher of watch and put it by the side of the wooden platform in the portico. Hurrying back into the kitchen she placed a low stool in the eating place which she had freshened up with a coat of earth. She had just turned round when Ramchandra stepped in.

He slumped down upon the platforms and then, stretching himself on it, lay inert like a dead thing. His face was flushed, his hair dishevelled. His worn-put shoes were thickly coated with dust.

Siddheshwari did not dare go near him and watched him from a distance like a stricken deer. When he did not stir for ten minutes she got alarmed.

'Son! ...Son!' No reply. Fear-stricken she held her palm near his nose. He was breathing evenly. She touched his brow. Thank God, he had no fever. At the touch of her hand, Ramchandra opened his eyes and looked dully at his mother. Sitting up, he took off his shoes and went to wash his hands and feet. He came back walking like an automaton and sat down on the wooden seat.

'The meal is ready,' Siddheshwari mumbled uncertainly. 'Shall I serve it here?'

Ramchandra got up. 'Has Father eaten?'

'He should be here any moment,' Siddheshwari said, rushing into the kitchen.

Ramchandra sat down on the wooden seat. He was about twenty-one years old, tall, thin, of fair complexion, with big eyes and crinkled lips. He had passed his Intermediate Examination last year and was now apprenticed as a proof reader in a local daily.

Placing the plate before him, Siddheshwari sat down beside him and started fanning him. Ramchandra eyed his food without appetite—two chapatis, gruel-like thin daal, fried gram.

Swallowing the first morsel, Ramchandra said, 'Where's Mohan? Oh, what terrible heat!'

Mohan was Siddheshwari's second son. He was eighteen, and was preparing privately to sit for his High School Certificate. He had been away from home a long time today and his mother did not have the foggiest idea where he was.

Siddheshwari did not feel like coming out with the truth. 'He has gone to a friend's house to study,' she lied. 'A bright lad, he is always at his studies and talks of nothing but books.'

Ramchandra did not say anything. He took another morsel, washed it down with a long draught of water and resumed eating. He broke his chapati into small bits and chewed them ruminatingly.

Siddheshwari gazed at him with anxiety and then said in a fumbling voice, 'Any news?'

Ramchandra turned his expressionless eyes towards his mother and then lowered his head. 'No, nothing,' he replied dryly. 'When the time comes, all will be well.'

Siddheshwari did not pursue that subject. The heat had increased. In the sky over the narrow courtyard two lonely clouds hung like the sails of a boat. In the street an ekka grated past, creaking. Inside, the sleeping child breathed wheezily.

'Has Pramod eaten?' Ramchandra asked.

Siddheshwari gave Pramod a sad look. 'Yes, he has eaten,' she said.

'Did he cry?'

'No, he didn't cry today,' Siddheshwari lied again. 'A clever child. Today he wanted to go to your office. A boy like him...'

Her voice trailed off as if something had clogged her throat. Yesterday Pramod had demanded sweets and had kept on crying till he fell asleep, for more than an hour and a half.

Ramchandra gave his mother a surprised look and began eating a little faster.

Only a small bit of chapati was left in the plate. Siddheshwari made a pretence of getting up. 'I'll get you another chapati,' she said.

'No, no,' Ramchandra brushed away the suggestion with a gesture of his hand. 'I'm full,' he said. 'Even this is more than I can cope with, really.'

'Have half a chapati,' Siddheshwari persisted.

'Do you want me to get sick?' Ramchandra said, peeved. 'Must you always have your way. I would surely have taken another chapati if I were hungry.'

Leaving one morsel in his plate, he looked at the pitcher. 'Get me some water please,' he said.

His mother got up to fetch water. Ramchandra drummed the bowl with his fingers and then rested his hand in the plate. Picking up the last piece of chapati from the plate he eyed it for a second and put it into his mouth very gently as if it were a betel leaf.

The younger son, Mohan, suddenly appeared on the scene. He straightaway proceeded to wash his hands and feet and went directly to the wooden seat. Swarthy, narrow-eyed, he had a pock-marked face. He too was thin like his brother but was not as tall. He looked grave and solemn beyond his years.

'Where have you been, son?' his mother asked him, placing the plate of food before him. 'Your brother was enquiring about you.'

'I didn't go anywhere. I was here all the time,' Mohan answered gruffly, struggling with a big mouthful of food which he was finding hard to swallow.

Sitting some distance from him, Siddheshwari fanned him. 'Your brother is full of praise for you,' she said as if talking in a dream. 'He says you are very intelligent and never get tired of books and devote all your time to studies.' She looked at Mohan as if she had been caught in the act of stealing.

Mohan looked at his mother, gave a hollow laugh and kept eating. By now he had finished one chapati, three-fourths of the lentils and most of the fried gram.

Siddheshwari did not know what to do. She always felt uncomfortable in the presence of her grown-up sons. Suddenly her eyes filled with tears. She turned away her face.

Mohan had almost finished his meal.

'Son, another chapati?' she asked as if coming to herself.

Mohan looked towards the kitchen as if it were a place full of mystery. 'No, I think I've done with it,' he said in a feeble voice.

'No, son, just have one more chapati', Siddheshwari almost pleaded. 'Be a good boy. Your brother took an extra helping.'

Mohan looked at his mother closely. 'I've finished,' he said. Then he launched forth on an elaborate explanation, deliberating over each word in the manner of a teacher explaining a complex problem to a pupil. 'In the first place I'm not hungry,' he said. Secondly, your *chapatis* are too coarse. I find them difficult to swallow. They taste like I don't know what. But if you insist I'll have a little more of the lentils. It tastes good.'

At a loss for words, Siddheshwari filled Mohan's bowl with lentils.

Putting the bowl to his lips, Mohan was slurping its contents when Munshi Chandrika Prashad came in, his shoes dragging on the broken floor. With God's name on his lips, he sat down on the wooden platform and crossed his legs. Siddheshwari pulled her sari over her forehead. Mohan gulped down his lentils and picking up the pitcher made a hurried exit.

Two chapatis, a bowlful of lentils and fried gram. Like an old cow chewing the cud, Munshi Chandrika Prashad lingered deliberately over each morsel. He was about forty-five but looked much older. His flesh hung flabbily over his body and his bald head shone like a mirror. His tattered vest was only a shade better than his dirty dhoti.

The Midday Meal

Raising the bowl to his lips he sucked noisily at the lentils 'I don't see the older one around,' he said.

Siddheshwari was feeling out of sorts but didn't know why. Something seemed to be gnawing at her heart. 'He has just gone out after finishing his meal,' she said waving the fan more briskly. He said it would not be long before he started earning. your name is constantly on his lips. You are like a god to him, he says.'

Munshiji's face lit up.' Did he?—that a fool of a boy!' Looking embarrassed, he gave a thin smile.

His words acted like magic on Siddheshwari. 'Ramchandra is no fool, she began to mutter like a victim of hysteria: 'He is a clever boy. In his past life he must have been a Mahatma. Mohan holds him in high regard. Today he was telling me that his brother is highly respected in the city, especially among the learned. And as for himself, he dotes on his younger brothers. He can put up with any indignity in the world for the sake of his brothers, He cannot bear to see Pramod suffer in any manner.'

Munshiji was licking the lentils from his fingers. His gaze travelled to the alcove in the wall and he smiled. 'Yes, Ramchandra has a sharp mind,' he said, 'tough as a child he was given to too much playing still in spite of that whatever lesson I set him, he did full justice to it. For that matter, all the boys are intelligent. Pramod, for instance...' He broke into loud laugh.

After having finished one and a half chapatis, Munshiji was now trying to send down his throat a very dry morsel and finally succeeded in swallowing it with a generous quantity of water. After a brief bout of coughing he resumed eating.

They fell silent. They could hear the intermittent hooting of a flour-mill drifting down from a distance, and from the acacia tree, the persisting cooing of a dove.

Munshiji seemed to have retired into his shell. It appeared as if he had taken a long vow of silence. Siddheshwari did not know how to deal with this situation. She wished to talk to him about many things, to ply him with questions and to take command of things as in the past with assertive boldness. But now her mind was filled with vague fears.

'The rains are late this year,' she said at last to get over the oppressive silence. It may not rain at all.'

'The flies seem to have increased,' Munshiji remarked in a toneless voice, glancing around him.

'Any further news about Uncle?' Siddheshwari asked in an anxious voice. 'He was not too well.'

Munshiji sat gazing intently at the grains of fried gram as if he intended to talk to each one of them individually, and then he said, 'The marriage of Gangasaran's daughter has been arranged. The boy is an M.A.'

Again they fell silent. Munshiji was now at the end of his meal and was picking the last of the grains of gram, one by one, like a monkey.

'Have another chapati,' Siddheshwari coaxed him. 'I implore you in the name of our first-born. There are plenty of chapatis left.'

Munshiji looked at his wife like a criminal in the dock and then furtively in the direction of the kitchen. 'Chapati?' he said like an adept at an old game. 'Oh, no, I've already had my fill. Besides, its chapatis and salted things all the time. I'm fed up with them. But since you insist I won't refuse you. I'll take a chapati. Is there any *gur*?'

Siddheshwari told him that there was still some *gur* left in the pot.

'Then prepare some cool syrup for me,' Munshiji said enthusiastically.' It will take away the taste of the meal. And it's good for the digestion too. The same food morning and evening...' he laughed mirthlessly.

After Munshiji had finished eating, Siddheshwari took his used plate and sat down on the kitchen floor. She poured lentils from the pot into her bowl, but the bowl did not fill up. A small quantity of fried gram was left in the frying pan. She drew the pan near her plate. There was only one chapati left—thick, coarse, half-burnt. She was going to take it when she suddenly remembered Pramod asleep outside. Her eyes rested for a while on the child and then she proceeded to divide the chapati into two equal parts, one of which she put aside. Filling her pitcher with water she started eating but she had hardly taken the first morsel when suddenly tears began to roll down her cheeks.

Flies buzzed in the room. A dirty patched-up sari hung on the clothes line in the courtyard. The two older boys were nowhere to be seen. In the outer room, Munshiji was lying on his stomach and snoring peacefully, as if he had not lost his clerk's job in the Rent Controller's office one and a half months ago and was not faced with the ordeal of going in search of a job that afternoon!

Bhisham Sahni

Wang Chu

Just then I saw Wang Chu coming along. He was still a long way off.

Along the river bank, down the Lalmandi Road, he came with slow, swaying steps. He was wearing a yellow robe and from a distance his head looked shaven like that of a Buddhist monk. A clear blue sky, the back-drop of the Shankaracharya Hill and the road flanked by all eucalyptus trees—for a moment I felt that Wang Chu had stepped out of the pages of history. In ancient times monks from all countries must have come into India like this, crossing mountains and valleys. I saw Wang Chu walking slowly through those mysterious mists of the past. Ever since he had come to Srinagar Wang Chu had been wandering among the ruins of Buddhist temples or visiting Museums. At the moment he had just emerged from the museum at Lalmandi where many relics of Buddhist times were preserved. From his state of mind it appeared that he was divorced from the present and was wandering in some fragment of time gone by.

'So you met the Bodhisatvas?' I asked in jest as he drew near.

He smiled—a faint, crooked smile which my cousin sister called the one-and-a-half-toothed smile, for while smiling Wang Chu's upper lip rose a little only on one side.

'There are a lot of images lying outside the Museum,' he said in a soft voice. 'I kept looking at them.' And he suddenly became impassioned. 'One image has just the feet left—just the feet and nothing else.'

I thought he would say more. But he was so overcome that he could barely speak.

Together we walked towards my house.

'In the beginning they used to only show the feet of the Great One', he said in a trembling voice and put his hand on my elbow. The slight trembling of his hand felt like the beating of a heart.

'In the beginning it was forbidden to make images of the Great One. They only showed his feet under the stupa. The images began to be made much later.'

All too obviously the feet of the Bodhisatva had reminded him of the feet of the Great One and had stirred his emotions. One never knew what event at what time would move Wang Chu and transport him with joy.

'You have been a long time coming,' I said. 'I went to look for you below the pines. Everybody is waiting for you.'

'I was in the Museum all the time.'

'That's fine. But we have to be at Habba Kadal by two. If we are late it will be no use going.'

Wang Chu nodded his head thrice with short jerks and fell in step with me.

Wang Chu had wandered all over India like one intoxicated. Already he had made a pilgrimage on bare foot to Lumbini, the birth place of the Great One, with his hands folded all the way. In whatever direction the lotus-feet of the Great One had trod Wang Chu had trailed them like one mesmerized. At Sarnath where the Great One had preached his first sermon and two deerslayers had emerged from the bushes and gazed at him in dumb worship, Wang Chu had sat under a peepul tree for many hours, and he said later that he felt as if the words of the First Sermon were ringing in his ears. It was such a mystic experience that he seemed to have felt a sense of release and settled down at Sarnath. He saw the currents of the Ganga as sacred water flowing through the mists of centuries. Since his arrival in Srinagar he often looked at the snow-capped mountain peaks and would ask me, 'That path leads to Lhasa, doesn't it? The Buddhist scriptures must have been sent to Tibet by that path.' He considered the mountain range also sacred ground, for the Buddhist monks had gone across those mountain paths to Tibet.

Wang Chu had come to India a few years ago with the elderly Professor Tan Shan. For some time he stayed with him studying the English and Hindi languages. Afterwards Prof. Shan returned to China. Wang Chu stayed back, managed to get a stipend from a Buddhist institution and settled in Sarnath. Emotional, with a poetic turn of mind, he remained lost in the enchanted realms of antiquity. He had not come here in search of facts. He had come for the bliss of seeing the images of the Bodhisatvas. For months he had been doing the rounds of museums but he had never said which teaching of Buddhism inspired him the most. Neither did any fact excite him nor did any doubt assail him. He was more a devotee, less a seeker.

I don't ever remember him talking to us freely or expressing his own views on any issue. In those days I was given to holding endless discussions with my friends on politics, the state of the country religion and so forth. But Wang Chu never took part in these discussions. Sitting in a corner of the room he would just keep smiling at us. Nationalist feelings ran high in those days. The freedom struggle was at its peak and was our constant theme of discussion—what direction the struggle would take, what policy the Congress would adopt. On the practical level we did nothing but our emotional involvement with the freedom struggle was intense. Amidst all this Wang Chu's non-committal temper sometimes offended us, sometimes surprised us. He showed no particular interest either in the affairs of our country or even in those of his own country.

Questions about his country would just set him smiling and nodding.

For some time we had been discerning a change in the atmosphere of Srinagar. Some months ago a firing had taken place here. The people of Kashmir had revolted against the Maharaja. And now there was a new ferment in the city. Pandit Nehru was due to pay a visit to the city and it had been decked like a bride to welcome him. He was to be led into the city this afternoon, along the river at the head of a boat procession. I sought out Wang Chu because I wanted him to accompany us to watch the procession.

We were proceeding towards my house when Wang Chu suddenly stopped. 'Is it necessary for me to come with you?' he asked. 'Anyway I'll do as you wish.'

I felt a bit of a jolt. At a time when lakhs of people were gathering to welcome Nehruji Wang Chu's asking whether it was necessary for him to come along, offended me. However, he did not press his request and we walked homewards. After some time we were standing among the lakhs congregated at Habba Kadal Bridge—I, Wang Chu and two or three friends of mine. As far as the eye could see were people, milling crowds of people, on roof-tops, on the bridge, on the sloping banks of the river. I looked at Wang Chu from the corner of my eye just to see what effect the torrents in our hearts were having on him. Even otherwise, it had become second nature with me whenever foreigners were with us, to try to gauge their reactions to our customs and ways of life. Wang Chu stood there taking in the scene through half-closed eyes. When the boat carrying Nehru came abreast of us, the very roof-tops seemed to shake. Nehru was standing in a white, swan-shaped boat along with the local leaders, waving to the people in greeting. The air seemed to be thick with flowers. I turned round and observed Wang Chu's face. He was looking at the scene in the same passive manner.

'What do you think of Nehru?' one of my friends asked him.

Wang Chu turned his slit eyes towards my friend and then gave his characteristic one-and-a-half toothed smile. 'Good, very good!' he said. Wang Chu's knowledge of English and Hindi was barely adequate. If you spoke fast he could not follow you.

Nehruji's boat had receded into the distance but the cavalcade of boats had not yet ended, when Wang Chu said, 'I would like to go to the Museum for a little while. There's a road from here. I know it. I can go on my own.'

Without saying anything more he smiled through half-closed eyes, gave a slight wave of the hand and was off.

Eyebrows went up uninterested. He must really have been off alone in the procession, to have so soon set for the museum. 'Which jungle did you pick up this specimen from?' a friend asked me.

'He's a foreigner, you know,' I said in his defence. 'You can't expect a foreigner to be interested in our affairs.'

'So much is happening in the country and he is not interested!'

Wang Chu receded into the distance and was soon lost between the rows of trees.

'But who is he?' another friend asked. 'He never talks, never laughs. You can't even make out whether he is laughing or crying. All he does is sit in a corner and gape at us.'

'No, no, he's a very sensible man. He has been here for the past five years, he's very learned. Knows a lot about Buddhism.' I defended him again. In my eyes it stood for a lot that he read the Buddhist texts and that he had come all the way to this country to read them.

'To hell with such learning. Leaves off watching the procession, to go to the museum!'

'It's simple, pal,' I said. 'It is not India's present that has drawn him here, but India's past. Hieun Tsang too came to India to read the Buddhist texts. He too is a scholar. He's interested only in Buddhism.'

On our way home Wang Chu was still our subject of discussion. It was Ajay's opinion that now that he had been in India for five years he would stay here for the rest of his life.'

'He'll never go back. Anyone who comes to our country comes for good.'

'India is a marsh,' Dalip laughed. 'Once a foreigner sets his foot here he sinks deeper and deeper. Even if he tries he can't free himself. God knows what rare lotus he hopes to pluck from this swamp.'

'We Indians may not like our country but it has a strange fascination for foreigners,' I said.

'And there is good reason for it too. Living is cheap here and there's sunshine the year round. Besides, foreigners are left alone and not harassed. To top it all, there are half-wits like to you sing their praises and offer them hospitality,' my friend said. 'Take it from me, your Wang Chu too will die here.'

In those days my younger cousin, Neelam, had come on a visit to Srinagar and was staying with us. A vivacious girl, she was the one who had described Wang Chu's smile as the one-and-a-half-toothed smile. Once or twice I had caught Wang Chu stealing looks at her but I had not paid much attention to this as. He was always looking at people through the corners of his eyes anyway. But that evening Neelam came to me and said, 'Your friend has given me a gift—a gift of love.'

I perked up my ears. 'What gift?'

'A pair of ear-rings.' She opened her palms. On them shone two silver ear-rings of Kashmiri design. She held them against he rears. 'How do they look?'

I stood gaping at her.

'How brownish his own ears are!' Neelam said, laughing.

'Whose ear lobes?'

'Why, those of this admirer of mine!'

'Do you like his brown ear lobes?'

'Very much. When he blushes they turn deep brown.' She broke out laughing.

How cruel girls can be, how they can make fun of love they don't reciprocate. Or was Neelam just fibbing to mislead me?

But I was not unduly perturbed. Neelam was studying at Lahore and Wang Chu was living at Sarnath. In a week's time he would be gone from Srinagar, and this seedling of love would wither away of its own accord.

'Neelam, you have been thoughtless in accepting these earrings,' I said. 'It may put silly ideas into his head. Such a friendship will only end in unhappiness for him.'

'How old-fashioned you are, brother! I too have given him a present in return. A leather writing pad which was lying with me for a long time. He can use it to write his love letters when he gets back.'

'What did he say?'

'Say! His hand shook all the time and his face kept changing colour from red to yellow. He said, "Write to me! Reply to my letters." What else could he say, the poor brown-lobed creature!'

I looked intently at Neelam. But in her eyes I saw nothing except laughter. Girls are adept at hiding their feelings. I thought she was leading him on. It was a game for her but Wang Chu was bound to see it differently.

After this I felt that Wang Chu was losing his equanimity. That night I was at my window gazing at the row of fir trees when in the moonlight I saw Wang Chu strolling under the trees. He often took these strolls late into the night under the fir trees but that night he was not alone. Neelam was with him, walking along with mincing steps. This made me angry. How heartless girls are! Knowing very well that Wang Chu was going to get hurt in this game she was still leading him on.

The next evening at dinner she had another dig at Wang Chu. She brought a large aluminium box from the kitchen and held it before him. Her face was flushed like copper.

'I've brought some potatoes and chapatis for you. I've cooked them for you. And there is a sliver of mango pickle too. You know what a sliver is?'

He looked at Neelam with helpless eyes. 'Fliver,' he said. We burst out laughing.

'Not fliver. Sliver.'

'Fliver.' Another burst of laughter.

Neelam opened the box and taking out the sliver of pickle showed it to him and said, 'This is what they call a sliver of pickle.' She held it under his nostrils. 'Smell it. It will make your mouth water. Say sliver.'

'Stop it, Neelam!' I cried. 'There is a limit to everything.'

Neelam sat back in her chair but her antics continued. In an earnest, animated voice she said, 'Don't forget us when you go to Banaras. Do write to us. And if you require anything feel free to ask.'

Wang Chu understood her words but not the sarcasm behind them. He looked increasingly troubled.

'You may require the hide of a sheep, for instance. Or a rug or walnuts.'

'Neelam!'

'Why, Bhaiyya, he will squat on the sheepskin and study his scriptures.'

Wang Chu's ear lobes had started turning red. Perhaps he had realized for the first time that Neelam was laughing at him.

'Neelamji,' he said. 'All of you have been most hospitable to me. I'm very grateful.'

We all fell silent. Neelam too showed signs of embarrassment. Wang-chu must have understood her jokes and must have felt hurt. But then I thought it was just as well that he should change his feelings about Neelam. Perhaps Wang-chu, despite understanding his position, had been carried away by a very natural attraction. An emotional person has no control over himself. He realises his mistake only after falling headlong.

In the last few days of his stay with us he had begun bringing a present almost every day. One day he brought a robe for me and like a child insisted that we go out together for a walk in our robes. Even now he spent a lot of time at the Museum. A couple of times he took Neelam along with him too and on her return. Neelam spent the whole evening making fun of the Bodhisatvas. In my heart of hearts I was pleased with her behaviour for I did not want any of Wang Chu's feelings to take root in our home. Another week and Wang Chu was back at Sarnath.

After Wang Chu left, my contact with him was just the kind one has with an acquaintance. Off and on there was a letter from him and sometimes bits of information about him from someone who had met him. He was one of those who remain on the frontiers of formal acquaintanceship for years, neither stepping over the threshold nor stepping back to fade out of memory. All that I learnt was that there had been no change in his well-regulated, equable life. For some time I was curious whether things had gone any further between Neelam and him. But it looked as though even that passion had failed to take possession of Wang-chu's life.

Years passed. A lot was happening in our country in those days. Satyagraha every other day, famine in Bengal, the Quit India movement was launched, there was firing in the streets, the naval rebellion in Bombay, blood flowed and finally the country was partitioned. All this time Wang Chu had stayed put in Sarnath, self-sustained and self-contained. Sometimes he would write to say that he had taken up the study of Tantric philosophy or that he was planning to write a book.

The next time I met Wang Chu was in Delhi. I am talking of the days when Chou-en-Lai, Prime Minister of China, was about to visit India. It was by accident that I ran into Wang Chu on the road and brought him home. I liked the fact that he had come to Delhi from Sarnath on the occasion of the Chinese

Prime Minister's visit. But then I was amazed at his attitude when he told me that he had come to Delhi to sort out some problems relating to his stipend and that he had come to know about Chou-en-Lai's visit only on his arrival here. He was the same. Nor had his one-and-a-half-toothed smile changed. The same passivity and composure. He had not written any book or article in the meanwhile. And he did not show any interest on my asking about it. Tantric philosophy also did not make him particularly animated. He talked about a couple of books from which he had taken notes and then vaguely mentioned an article on which he was working. He told me that he had kept up his correspondence with Neelam even though she had been married a long time and was now the mother of two children. With the passage of time our basic ways of thinking may not change but their intensity certainly keeps changing. When he spoke of his studies, his enthusiasm and eagerness seemed tempered by stability. He was not as emotional as before. He did not go around pouring out his heart at the feet of every Bodhisatva's image. As before he ate little, read a little, walked a little and slept little. Like a tortoise he kept cheerfully and slowly walking along the path he had chosen in some distant boyhood dawn of emotional excitement.

After dinner a debate struck up between us. How could one understand Buddhism without understanding social forces? The whole field of knowledge is interlinked, and connected with life. Nothing is cut off from life. How can you understand a religion by isolating yourself from life?

He just kept smiling or nodding or philosophically watching the expression on my face. I could see my arguments were making no impression on him. It was like water gliding down the surface of a smooth pitcher.

'Well, just forget our country but take an interest in yours at least,' I said. 'Try to keep your eyes and ears open to the happenings there.'

In reply he again smiled and nodded. I knew that except for a brother he had no one in China. In 1929 there had been a political upheaval in which his village had been razed by fire and all the members of his family had either perished or run away. The one brother left alive was living in a village near Peking. Wang Chu had lost contact with this brother years ago. He had gone to the primary school in his village and later to Peking for further studies in a university. It was from there that he had come to India with Prof Shan.

'Wang Chu, the closed doors between India and China are opening,' I told him. 'This means that soon intercourse between the two countries will revive and it should be of special significance to you. The studies that you have been conducting on your own so far you can henceforth pursue as a respected representative of your country. Your country will be happy to arrange a grant for you and you will not have to plough a lonely furrow as you have been doing till now. You have lived in India for more than fifteen years. You know English and Hindi and have been studying Buddhist texts. Surely, you can form a valuable cultural link between the two countries.'

A light came into his eyes. Of course, he could get some conveniences now for the asking. The new found cordiality between the two countries could make it possible. Why shouldn't he take advantage of the situation? He told me that a month ago when he went to Banaras to get his monthly stipend, people on the road had stopped and hugged him. I told him that he would do well to go back to his country for a short time to take stock of the momentous changes taking place there. He should realise that the secluded life that he was leading at Sarnath would not do him any good—so on and so forth.

He kept listening, punctuating his silence with nods and smiles. But was not sure whether or not my talk had cut any ice with him.

After a few months I had a letter from him, saying that he was leaving for China. I felt pleased at the news. Back home, he wouldn't be the proverbial washerman's dog, belonging neither here nor there. Life would come to have a new zest for him. He wrote that he was leaving behind a trunk at Sarnath which contained some of his books and research papers. He said that after years of living in India he had regarded himself as a resident of India and that he would return soon to resume his studies. I laughed to myself. Once home, he would be gone for good.

He stayed in China for about two years. He sent me a picture post card showing the old Royal Palace at Peking, and also a letter or two. But the letters revealed nothing about the state of his mind.

In those days China was also undergoing tremendous changes. There was much zeal enveloping almost everyone. Life was entering a new phase. People went to work in groups, singing and holding the red banner aloft. Standing on the roadside Wang Chu watched them. His shy and retiring nature inhibited him from joining them but he would just stand there watching them, as if he had strayed into some new world.

He did not find his brother but he ran into a distant aunt, an old teacher and a couple of acquaintances. He went to his village. It was transformed. As he was walking down from the railway station to his house, a fellow-traveller told him that all the documents and papers of the village landlord had been set on fire under that tree, while the landlord stood there with folded hands, watching.

In his childhood Wang Chu had seen the spacious house of the landlord and he could vividly recall its coloured windows. He had even seen the landlord's horse-drawn carriage on the village road. Now his house had been converted into an office of the local administration. Many other changes had also taken place. But here too his own attitude was the same as in India.

His heart did not leap with joy. The popular upsurge slid off his mind. He was a spectator and a by-stander here too. In the first few days he was even made welcome, and at the instance of the village school teacher, accorded a formal reception at the school and recognised as an important cultural link between India and China. There was a barrage of questions about India, its people, customs, festivals and pilgrimages, but he could answer satisfactorily only those questions about which he knew something on the basis of his own experience. There was much of which he was totally ignorant in spite of his years of living in India.

Sometime later the fever of the Great Leap Forward took hold of China. In his own village people were engaged in collecting scrap iron and one morning he was roped in to join a team of workers. He stayed with the team the whole day. A fresh wave of enthusiasm had swept the entire country. At night each piece of the scrap collected was exhibited with pride and thrown into the leaping flames for melting while people sat around singing revolutionary songs. Only Wang Chu sat a little apart from them, his face drawn.

Gradually his days in China became tension-ridden and twilit. One day a man in a blue coat and trousers came to him and took him to the village administration centre. The man did not speak a word all the way to the Centre. At the Centre he was confronted with a party of five people seated at a table, waiting for him.

After Wang Chu sat down facing them, they turn by turn, started asking him questions about his stay in India. 'How long were you in India?' 'What were you doing there?' 'What places did you visit?' Learning about his interest in Buddhism one of the men asked, 'What is the material basis of Buddhism?' Wang Chu did not understand the question. He kept blinking. At last he mumbled something to the effect that Buddhism had played a significant role in the spiritual development of humanity, in giving them happiness and peace. The teachings of the Great One... Wang Chu launched on an explanation of the Eight-fold Path of Buddhism. He had barely finished when a squint-eyed man who occupied the Chairman's seat cut him short and asked him what he thought of the foreign policy of India.

Wang Chu smiled his one-and-a-half-toothed smile and said, 'You high-ups know far more about this than I. I'm only an ordinary Buddhist seeker. But India is a very ancient country. Its culture is the culture of peace and human goodwill.'

'What do you think of Nehru?'

'I have seen Nehru three times. Once I even talked to him. His mind is saturated with Western influence but he is a great admirer of India's ancient culture.'

At his answer his questioners dubiously shook their heads and frowned. Many other questions were asked. Wang Chu's knowledge of facts and of present day India was fragmentary, even laughable.

'As far as politics go you are a cipher. And Buddhism you can't examine from the perspective of social sciences. We wonder what you have been doing in India all this time. Anyway we shall help you.'

The interrogation continued for hours. Then the party bosses assigned him the task of teaching Hindi and also permitted him to work in the Museum at Peking twice a week.

When Wang Chu returned from the Party office he was tired and his head was reeling. He had not warmed to his country at all. Today he felt more uprooted than ever. When he lay down under the thatch roof memories of India suddenly wrenched at his heart. He remembered his small room in Sarnath where he used to sit and read the whole day long. He remembered the thick acacia tree under which he used to rest. The train of memories lengthened. The cook of the Sarnath canteen came to his mind. He was always so kind to him. He greeted him with folded hands and addressed him as Bhagwan. Once when he fell ill the cook came to his room on his own to enquire about his health. 'I just wondered why the Chinese Babu has not come for his cup of tea?' he said. 'Its two days now since we were blessed by the sight of you. If you had told me, Bhagwan, I would have immediately sent for the doctor.' Then came to his mind the vision of the Ganga waterfront where he used to roam for hours. The scene changed and the lake at Kashmir floated into his eyes with the snow-covered mountains behind. Neelam came to his mind, eyes gleaming, pearl-like teeth... Wang Chu's heart grew restless.

As the days went by he missed India more and more and he felt like a fish out of water. In the monastery at Sarnath there were no questions and answers. Each man was left to himself. He had a room to himself and food was the responsibility of the monastery. He had neither the patience nor the desire to study religious texts here from the perspective of new political theories. Treading the same path for years he fought shy of change. After his session at the Party office he became more withdrawn than ever. At times he also heard stray anti-Indian government sentences. Suddenly he felt extremely lonely and realized that to stay alive he would have to return to his boyhood vision when he used to imagine himself wandering through India as a Buddhist monk. He made a determined bid to go back to India. It was not easy. There was no trouble getting a visa from the Indian Embassy but the Chinese government came up with many objections. There was the question of Wang Chu's citizenship and many others. Relations between the two countries had not yet become too strained so in the end Wang Chu succeeded in getting permission to return to India. He made up his mind that he would spend the remaining years of his life in India as a Buddhist monk.

The very day Wang Chu arrived in Calcutta a clash had taken place on the Sino-Indian border in which ten Indian soldiers had been killed. He found people glaring at him. He had hardly stepped out of the railway station when two policemen marched him to the police station, where for the space of an hour a police officer kept scrutinizing his passport and other papers.

'You went to China two years ago. What took you there?'

'I had lived here many years. I just wanted to visit my native land.'

The police officer surveyed him from head to foot. Wang Chu was composed and was smiling the same crooked one-and-a-half-toothed smile.

'What were you doing in China?'

'I worked on a farm in a Chinese commune along with others.'

'But you say that you are a student of Buddhist texts.'

'Yes, in Peking I taught Hindi in an institution and was also permitted to work in the Peking Museum.'

'If you were permitted to work what made you flee your country?' the policy officer asked angrily.

What could Wang Chu reply? What could he say?

'I had gone there only for a short time,' he stammered at last. 'And now I'm back...'

The police officer again surveyed him from head to foot. There was suspicion in his eyes. Wang Chu felt uneasy. It was the first time that he was facing the police in India. Asked for references he put down Prof. Shan's name and then Rabindranath Tagore's. Both were dead. He mentioned the name of the Secretary of the Sarnath Organisation and of a couple of old associates at Santiniketan whose names he could recall. The officer noted down all the names and addresses. He was searched three or four times over. His diary in which he had jotted down quotations and comments, was confiscated. The officer noted against his name that he should be kept under observation.

When he got into the railway compartment the passengers were discussing the exchange of fire at the border. On seeing him they suddenly fell silent and kept staring at him.

When the passengers learnt that he could speak a little Hindustani and Bengali, a Bengali gentleman sprang to his feet and gesticulating wildly said: 'Either admit that your countrymen have played false with us or get out of our country. Get out! Get out!'

The one-and-a-half-toothed smile vanished. Alarm took its place. Frightened and silent, Wang Chu sat still. What could he say? The firing had come to him too as a shock. He had clear knowledge of how and why it had started and he did not wish to know any more.

When he reached Sarnath he was really overwhelmed. When he reached the Ashram with his bag in the rickshaw the canteen cook came running out. 'So you have returned, Bhagwan! My Cheenee Babu has come back! After how long I am blessed with the sight of you! Is everything all right, with you Cheenee Babu? I wondered when you would return. When you were here I could exchange a few words with you, be blessed with the sight of a good man—where is great merit in that.' Stretching out his hand he took the bag from Wang Chu. 'I shall pay, Cheenee Babu!'

Wang Chu felt that he had returned home.

'Your trunk, Cheenee Babu is lying with me. I took charge of it from the Secretary. Another gentleman came to stay in your room so I said that I would take care of your trunk. And Cheenee Babu, you had forgotten your pitcher outside your room. I told the Secretary it was Cheenee Babu's pitcher. I knew it for certain. I told him that I would keep it for you.'

Wang-Chu's heart was touched. He felt as if his unsteady life had gained stability. The lurching boat of his life found its balance again. The Secretary too met him with affection, like an old acquaintance. He allotted him a new room and told him that fresh efforts, would have to be made to get his stipend. Wang Chu spread a mat in the middle of the room and as he looked out through the window the same familiar scene sprang to view. A lost soul had again found its abode.

This was the time when I got a letter from him informing me about his return to India and about his having resumed his studies of Buddhist texts with still greater fervour. He also said that he was a little worried about his stipend and said that if I could put in a word to a certain person in Banaras it would go a long way in straightening out the matter.

The letter made me apprehensive. What mirage had drawn him back to India? If he had stayed on in China a little longer he would have gained the goodwill of the people. But there is no cure for a man's idiosyncracies. Now that he had come back what was to be done about him? I wrote a letter to the person concerned at Banaras and a small stipend was arranged for him.

But some ten days after his return, early one morning, Wang Chu was sitting on his mat happily reading when a shadow fell across his book. He looked up and saw a police inspector standing before him, holding a sheet of paper. He was asked to report at the police Headquarters at Banaras. His heart sank.

On the appointed day Wang Chu was sitting on a bench in the corridor of the police headquarters along with an elderly Chinese shoemaker. After much waiting his name was called. Raising the curtain he went in and stood before the police chief.

'When did you return from China?'

Wang Chu told him.

'In your statement in Calcutta you had said that you were going to Santineketan. What made you change your mind? The police had a hard time tracing you to this place.'

'I had mentioned both places. I intended to visit Santineketan only for a day or two.'

'Why have you returned from China?'

'I want to live in India,' he repeated his earlier statement.

'Then why did you go to China?'

He had been asked this question many times before and he had no satisfactory answer to it except to cite the Buddhist scriptures as authority.

The interview was not very long. He was ordered to report at the police headquarters at Banaras on the first Monday of every month.

Wang Chu came out but with a feeling of dismay. The journey was not a big problem but it would disturb the tenor of his life.

Wang-Chu was in such distress that on his return from Banaras he did not go to his room but first went and sat at that silent holy place where centuries ago the Great One had given his first sermon. He sat there a long time, meditating. After a long time his mind was set at rest and waves of emotion again arose in his heart.

But Wang Chu was not destined to live in peace. Barely a few days later war broke out between China and India. A veritable storm swept through the country. The same evening a police jeep came to Sarnath. The policemen took Wang Chu into custody and the jeep drove off to Banaras. What else could the government have done? Where do the rulers have the time in a crisis to screen every citizen of the enemy country with sympathy and goodwill?

For two days both the Chinese were kept in a cell in the police station. The two were poles apart. The Chinese shoemaker smoked incessantly and resting his elbows on his knees kept grumbling all the time while Wang Chu sat listless in a corner, limply resting his back against the wall and staring into space.

At the same time as Wang Chu was trying to gauge his situation a few rooms away a police officer was examining his small bag. In his absence, the police had brought his trunk from his room. Its contents lay scattered before the police officer—

bundles of papers containing passages in Pali and Sanskrit. But a large portion was in Chinese. For some time the police officer kept holding the papers against the light to see if there was a secret message in invisible ink. Finally he ordered that the whole lot be sent to Delhi, for no one in Banaras knew Chinese.

On the fifth day the war ended but it was a month before Wang Chu was allowed to return to Sarnath. At the time of his release, when he opened his trunk, he found to his horror that his papers which symbolised years of labour and which were in a sense all-in-all to him, were not there. He shook from head to foot when the police official told him that the papers had been sent to Delhi.

'Please return my papers. There is a lot I have written in them and they are essential to me.'

The officer said in a gruff voice, 'They are just scraps of paper to us and no more. You will get them back in good time.'

And then he dismissed Wang Chu.

Wang Chu returned to his room in the monastery at Sarnath. Without the papers he was half-dead. He could not bring himself either to read or to make fresh notes. Besides, he was still under observation. A little away from the window he could see a man with a staff sitting under an acacia tree. Looking utterly bored the man kept shifting on his haunches. Sometimes he paced up and down and sometimes sat on the parapet of the well. Often he would be found squatting on the canteen bench or standing at the gate. Wang Chu was now to report at police headquarters once a week instead of once a month.

This was when I got from Wang Chu a letter describing his condition. After setting down all the details, he said that a new man had taken over as Secretary at Sarnath. Being a China-hater this man might try to stop the stipend. Further, he requested me to retrieve his papers by whatever means I could. He added that it would make things easier for him if he was asked to report at the police headquarters once a month and not once a week as he was required to do now. The transport expenses alone came to ten rupees every month. But what was worse, afterwards, he could not apply his mind to his studies. He felt as if a sword was dangling over his head.

Little did Wang Chu know that I was not equipped for the job he had assigned me. In our country nothing gets done without pulling strings or recommendation. The most important person I knew was the principal of my college. Still I went to a few MPs. One sent me to the next, the next to the next. I came back each day after my round. Assurances were certainly given but they all asked one question: 'Why did he come back from China?' Or, 'Has he been doing nothing but studying for twenty years?' When I mentioned his manuscripts, they said without exception, 'That ought not to be difficult!' And they would jot down my request on a piece of paper. But the government's ways are a labyrinth and at every turn someone stands guard, reminding you back to your true status.

I gave Wang Chu a full account of my efforts and assured him that I would contact people again. But at the same time I suggested to him that as soon as the situation improved a bit, he should return to his country. That, I told him, was the best course for him.

What effect my letter had on Wang Chu I do not know. But in those tension-ridden days China had roused my ire and it was not very surprising if I had turned lukewarm towards Wang Chu and his problems.

Again, a letter from Wang Chu. There was nothing in it about his intention to return to China. It was exclusively about his stipend. The amount was still forty rupees but he had been notified that at the end of the year they would reconsider whether to continue or to terminate it.

After nearly a year Wang Chu one day got an official communication that his papers were being returned and that he could call at the police headquarters to take them back. He was ill at that time but somehow or other he made his way to Banaras.

But he was handed back only a third of his papers. The packet was still half-open. at first he could not believe it and then his face turned ashen and his legs shook.

'We know nothing,' the police officer said harshly. 'Pick these up and take them away from here or else write here that you refuse to receive them.' Wang Chu put the pack under his arm and came out. All that was left was one essay and some notes.

From that day Wang Chu felt dust rising and blocking his view.

I received the news of Wang Chu's death a month later from the Secretary of the institution at Sarnath. He wrote that in his last moments Wang Chu had desired that his trunk and some select books should be sent on to me.

At my age one is inured to hearing bad news and it does not affect one deeply.

I could not go to Sarnath immediately nor did I see much point in it. Wang Chu had no relatives there to receive my condolences? There was only a tin trunk there.

Anyway, I got there one day and the Secretary spoke the usual words of sympathy for the dead—a good hearted man, a Buddhist monk in the real sense of the word, and so on.

After giving me a paper to sign he made over Wang Chu's trunk to me. It contained his clothes, a tattered old robe (the same he had purchased in Srinagar), the leather writing pad which Neelam had given him as a present, four books in Pali and Sanskrit, a wad of letters, among them some of mine and possibly some of Neelam's and some from others.

Picking up the trunk I was coming out when I heard footsteps behind me. I turned back and saw the canteen cook running towards me. In his letters Wang Chu had often mentioned the cook. 'Cheenee Babu used to talk about you a lot. He was such a good man...'

His eyes filled with tears. Perhaps his was the only creature in the whole world who had shed tears at Wang Chu's death.

He was innocence itself and the police harassed him a lot. At first they kept him under twenty-four hours observation. 'Brother, why do you harass this poor, guileless man?' I used to ask that corporal. 'I'm only doing my duty,' he would say.

I brought home the trunk and the packet of papers. What shall I do with the papers? Sometimes I would think I should have them published. But who will publish an incomplete manuscript? My wife complains that I have filled the house with trash. She has even threatened to throw the manuscript out. But I keep it out of her sight. Sometimes I put it on a shelf, sometimes push it under the bed. But I know that one day it will be thrown into the lane outside.

Kamleshwar

Lost Directions

Chander stood leaning against the railing at the street turning. In front and on all sides, people milled past. It was evening and the lights of Connaught Place had begun to twinkle. He was so tired that his feet were giving way. He had not walked much today yet he was utterly exhausted. Weariness descending from his brain and his heart seemed to seep into his entire body. He lad wasted the day. He stood there brooding over it. He was in no mood to return home he could not even whip up an interest in the passing women. The sight added to his weariness.

Hunger...He could not decide whether he was hungry or not. He taxed his mind. He had left home at eight in the morning after having just a cup of coffee—and nothing to go with it. At this thought he felt vaguely hungry, his brain and stomach acting in consonance with each other. Generally he felt hungry only when he thought about it.

He looked up and his gaze remained glued to the sky. There were kites wheeling in the sky and the formation of the clouds made the sky look like a huge pair of stocking. He could see the dome and the minarets of the Jama Masjid under the grey sky. The minarets tapering into sharp points stood silhouetted against the sky, looking somewhat odd.

The shop behind him displayed an advertisement for blouses. Leaves slowly fluttered down from the acacia trees growing near the Regal bus stop. The buses came roaring up, stopped for a moment and sped away after disgorging passengers at one end and devouring them at the other. The traffic lights at the crossing blinked red, and yellow. Hundreds of people passed by but not one among them gave him a look of recognition. Every passer by, man or woman, ignored others us if they were non-existent or strutted along with a false arrogance.

And then Chander recalled his hometown which he had left three years ago. There even if he came across a stranger on the lonely banks of the Ganga he would nod to him politely.

And this Capital city! Here everything belongs to us, to our country, and yet nothing is ours—no, nothing is our country.

He can walk along any of these but they lead nowhere. There are houses, whole colonies, situated on both sides of these roads but he can't enter any of them. The gates outside these houses have small notice boards warning all and sundry to 'beware of dogs.' and not to pluck flowers. One must ring the calling bell and wait patiently for a response.

Back home, Nirmala would be waiting for him to return. When he entered the house, he would awkwardly settle down in a chair like an outsider because all the stuff in the room would be kept on the bed and she herself would be come busy cooking on the electric heater. He couldn't enter the house like a gust of wind and throw his arms around her because Guptaji would not have returned from the mill and Mrs Gupta, having nothing better to do, would be gossiping with Nirmala or learning a knitting pattern. He would have to behave with proper decorum, exchange a few polite nothings with Mrs Gupta. Then Nirmala would discreetly bring up the question of dinner which Mrs Gupta would take as a signal to leave.

After that he would draw the curtain of the big window and on some pretext close the window that opened on to Khurana's house. He would turn to the dining table, and on the pretext of asking for a glass of water, call his wife to him. Then he would take her in his arms, and finally be able to say: 'I am very tired.'

But that point would never be reached. Before completing this long process he would find so exasperating, he would straightaway be forced to say 'Is the food ready? What's the delay?' Gone would be that feeling of oneness with her. His voice would sound so stand-offish. In the nearby bakery shop the radio would be doling out mournful songs and then the heavy tread of Gulati's tired feet on the stairs.

A scooter would stop in the lane and an unknown man would disappear into a house. The Sikh owner of the motor repair shop would linger on till midnight, the bunch of keys in his hand, because he does not trust his mechanic even after fifteen years of service.

Then he would hear the faint scrape of Bishan Kapur's footsteps. For the past two years the just nameplate—Bishan Kapur...Journalist. All that he knows about him is that when the electric light filters through the front window and when the cigarette smoke curling against the window bars gets lost in the dense darkness then a man by the name of Bishan Kapur is in the house. And in the morning, when he finds egg shells, a bread wrapped, cigarette stubs and burnt matchsticks strewn under his window then a man by the name of Bishan Kapur has left the house.

Coming out of his thoughts Chander becomes conscious of the fact that the stench of socks has become insufferable, making it difficult for him to stand by the railing any more. He takes out his pocket diary and goes over his next day's engagements.

First thing in the morning a phone call to the English daily and an appointment for a meeting. He has also to drop in at the Radio Station. His previous cheque has to be cashed at the Reserve Bank and a money order sent home. That would account for the whole day. The Editor not being quite familiar with him, might keep him waiting endlessly before asking him in; there were always endless delays, at the Radio Station too, and or the Reserve Bank he knew no one to expedite matters; this was not Allahabad where the counter clerk would help Amarnath encash his cheque at once. As for the post office, there would be a glut of businessmen's peons at the money order counter. They tendered as many as ten money orders each. Being engrossed in calculating the commission on each money order and totalling it up, the clerk would have no time for him.

There only interaction with any one might take place when he was asked for the loan of a pen. The borrower would return the pen with his left hand without glancing at him, and mumbling thank you would continue reading what he had written on the sheet of paper while moving on to the stamp counter.

Chander was feeling so ruffled. The diary still in his hand, his gaze travelled to some high-rise buildings looming in the distance, crowned with shimmering neon signs. He was not familiar with any of those names. At least in Allahabad he knew that the leading cloth merchant was a very poor man and hawked cloth, carrying bales of it on his shoulders. And now he was so wealthy that his son had gone abroad for higher studies. He himself was a pious who adorned his forehead with sandal paste while he raked in the profits and prepared to fight the municipal election. But in this big city one didn't get to know anything about anyone.

There was one good thing about Connaught Place. It had such wide, open lawns, studded with trees under which the Corporation had placed public benches. Tired people sat on these benches while children sported on the lawns. Chander felt the children's faces and their antics were familiar to him but the golgappa-eating mummies, seemed unfamiliar because their eyes lacked the innocence and pride of motherly affection. Their bodies too lacked the beauty and dignity of motherhood. They exuded a meaningless, state challenge which one could neither refuse nor accept—a challenge that sounds in the ears of all passersby who pass on as if they are deaf.

Chander felt like sitting in the lawn for a while. But then he abandoned the idea, for he felt he had no place there. Yesterday water had crept up on him silently like a thief through the grass and had soaked his clothes.

Trees stood around in splendid isolation and there was a strange vacuity in the darkness which had gathered under the trees. At least this loneliness gave him a feeling of intimacy. But even this loneliness was disturbed because every ten minutes or so a policeman passed by on his nightly round. Discarded ice cream wrappers and empty packets of parched gram were entangled in the bushes and shrubs. Or a homeless man would depart after emptying his liquor bottle and dumping it among the shrubs.

His glance again went back to his diary. He felt so lonely in the din created by the deluge of on-rushing traffic. He felt that in these three years nothing of any consequence had happened, nothing had become part of his being, nothing had touched him, or left a feeling of joy or pain. This loneliness was like an arid, sandy waste; it was the silence of an unknown sea coast where the noise of the crashing waves only deepened the silence.

The vaulting sky shaped like a stocking, kites wheeling round the minarets of the Jama Masjid; women chased by flower sellers, orphaned children running around hawking the evening papers—the evening was still full of life.

It suddenly occurred to Chander that an age had gone by in which he had not even encountered himself. He hadn't had time even to ask, 'How are you getting along?' not to talk of having a tete-a-tete with himself. A faint smile appeared on his face. Taking his diary he jotted down against each successive Friday: 'To meet myself from 7 p.m. to 9 p.m.' Today was Friday and he resolved that he must make a start today. He looked at his watch. it was seven. But his mind played truant. Why not first have a cup of tea at the Tea House? It seemed he was not keen to meet himself and he wondered why one tried to run away from himself?

Just at that moment he saw Anand coming in his direction—the last person he would have cared to meet. Anand was a jerk, and he wanted to keep away from that infection. And was always on the look-out for a friend, not a close friend but one he could sit and talk to for a while. His talk was marked by a strange artificiality of a bookish kind. That artificiality, Chander felt, had also become ingrained in him. Like Anand, he had also imbibed it from books during his college days.

Now he felt that he had wantonly thrown that time to the dogs. He had spent it in the ruins whose descriptions trip off the half-baked tourist guide's tongues and are repeated by rote to successive batches of tourists... 'This is Diwan-e-Khas. Just look at the etchings on the walls. Here there stood a gem-encrusted throne...This is the ladies' bath... and this is the place where the King used to give a royal audience to his subjects. This is the Winter Palace and this the Monsoon Palace and this one the Summer Retreat. Now please step this way. Be careful. Just watch your steps. This is the place where the gallows were fixed.'

Chander felt as if he had wasted twenty-five years of his life with tourist guides in the midst of ruins whose life-stories he had never got to know. He was shown only the Diwan-e-Khas and its carvings. After taking him round the ladies both the guide had left him in the dark and stinking cellar where the gallows were fixed, where bats hung upside down from the ceiling. There was also a discoloured rope dating back to historic times, which entangled one's neck, till one swung to death and than only corpses remained flung into a dark well.

Was there any difference between him and those rotting bodies?

And Anand too was no different from them.

Chander wanted to give him the slip because he knew Anand would say in his studied way, 'Well, Pal how good your hair looks. Do you use Brylcream? The girls must be gone on you.'

Anand had really stopped in front of Chander. 'Hello, you here? What are you doing standing here? Driving those girls raving mad for you?' It made Chander laugh.

'Where are you coming from?' Chander asked, putting his diary in his pocket.

'Today I had a hell of a time. Not of my doing though. Come, let's have a cup of coffee.' Anand paused for an instant and then added, 'Or you want something else?'

Chander knew what he meant and dismissed the idea with a brusque 'no'. But Anand would not give up so easily. 'What else is there in life?' he said. 'Does it add up to anything? All right, let it be coffee then,' he said resignedly, giving a forced laugh. Then he pressed Chander's hand and said, 'Please, if you don't mind, do you have some money to spare?' His voice was completely uninhibited and unembarrassed. Evidently, he was short of money.

'Well, partner, I think I can manage it elsewhere,' Anand said as an after-thought. 'Wait for me. Don't go away.' And off he goes but does not return.

Chander knew this game.

After some time Chander went in to the Tea House. Walking past some tables, he went to the counter where he bought a packet of cigarettes and then settled down at a table.

'Hello!' it was a vaguely familiar face. 'I'm seeing you after ages.' The man sat down in a chair next to Chander. They were silent for a while at a loss how to start a conversion.

The Tea House was very noisy, full of hollow laughter. There was a clock on the wall which was always fast. There were three passages, marked, 'Entrance' and 'Exit'. The fourth led to the toilet, choked with napthelene balls. A mirror hung in the gallery. Everyone who went to the toilet looked at himself without fail in the mirror.

At Gaylord preparations were on for the Diner-dance. Three rows of chairs had been shifted outside to make room for the dance floor. The Volga was mostly patronised by a foreign crowd.

Just then a couple entered. The woman was nicely decked up, a flower tucked in her coiffure. The man's face was marked by a strong superciliousness. They sat down opposite each other in the part of the hall set aside for families. Before they sat down there had seemed to be no acquaintance between them, except that when the woman stepped up to a chair, the man gently placed his hand on her back as a matter of courtesy, helping her to sit down. They sat rather withdrawn from each other as if there was no common topic of interest between them.

The woman looked around, her hand going to her coiffure, while the man stared at the glass of water lying in front of him at the table. They looked around not from any interest in what was going on. They looked merely because they had eyes. They both must look around only because they must. Had they concentrated their gaze at one point perhaps their eyes would have started smarting.

The bearer served them, and they started eating without a word. After finishing, the man started picking his teeth while the woman took out her handkerchief and dabbed her lips, fixing her lipstick which had got smudged while eating.

The bearer came back with the change. The man left some coins in the tray as a tip, the woman assessing it intently. Then they both pushed back their chairs and moved out disinterestedly, the man allowing her to precede him. Then he caught up with her and walked abreast of her for the first time giving an indication of some sort of relationship between them.

Chander's heart became heavier, making him feel all the more lonely. He gazed at that vaguely familiar face which had given him a nod of recognition, no small consolation in a sea of unknown faces. Finding that he was being singled out for attention, the man was on the point of speaking but hesitated as if memory were playing tricks with him. Then he said, 'Er...you...you are perhaps working in the Ministry of Commerce. I have a feeling... he abruptly trailed into silence.

Chander's body tingled. Draining the remaining tea in the cup he said in a steady voice, 'No, I was never in the Ministry of Commerce.'

The man made no effort to make amends. As if sealing that chance contact, he said, 'All right, partner, we shall meet again sometime later.' And he got up, lighting a cigarette.

Coming out, Chander proceeding to the bus stop. There were four or five people at the bus stop behind the Madras Hotel. A policeman was sitting under the bus shelter, smoking a cigarette.

Chander went up and stood next to him. Everyone wanted to know when the bus would come but no one cared to ask. Chander silently moved away and stood under the darkness of a nearby tree. The dry leaves crackled under his feet when he shifted his weight from one leg to the other. Their sound took him back to many years. There was a deep sense of belonging in that sound. He felt reassured.

Yes, they were similar leaves, dry and yellow. He was walking along that path with Indra many years ago. He had no definite goal before him. He was just squandering his life among ruins. Then Indra had said, 'Chander, you are cut out for big things in life.' That familiar voice again rang in his ears,' you are cut out for big things in life.' And her eyes shone with irrepressible faith in him.

Looking into those love-lorn eyes, Chander had said, 'Which have I got?' Indra, I myself don't know where life will take me. I don't want you to ruin your life because of me. I don't know what will become of me. I my die of starvation. I may even go mad.'

Indra's eyes had glowed with love. 'Chander, why do you say such things?' She had said. 'Whatever you are, wherever you are, I'll be happy with you.'

Chander had looked at her intently. Her eyes had become moist. Even her eyebrows seemed to express an innocent faith. He had felt like touching her lock of hair on her brow. But he had hesitated. The ear-rings in her ears had sparkled like fishes swimming in water. He had said, 'Come, let us sit under that tree.'

There was a cement bench under that rosewood tree. Walking over the dry, yellow leaves that lay underfoot, they had gone and sat down on that bench. It was the same sound which he had heard a short while ago—the same familiar sound.

Both had sat down on the bench. Chander had held her hand and gently drew lines on her wrist with his fingers. They sat there silent although they had much to say to each other that they could not say. Then Indra had stolen a glance at him and blushed. 'Chander, why do you keep thinking in this vein?' she had repeated. 'Don't you have faith in me?'

Looking deep into her eyes, Chander had said, 'I have great faith Indra but I am afraid I will keep wandering all my life like a nomad. I can't drag you into it. The very thought of it horrifies me. You are made to lead a happy and comfortable life. I have a shroud over my head. Who knows where I may end.'

'Whatever you may end up as, good or bad, you will remain dear to me. How I keep waiting for you but you just don't have time for me.' After a brief pause she added, 'Have you written anything lately?'

'Yes,' he had said in a low voice.

'Show me.'

With perspiring hands, Chander had handed her his diary. She had hidden it among her books and had told him she would return it the following day. 'At least that will give you a reason to call on me.'

'No, no, I can't leave my diary. I must take it with me. Give it back, please.'

Indra had given him a mischievous smile and the love in her eyes had deepened.

The next day Chandra had gone to get his diary back. 'I've also written something in it,' Indra had said. 'Tear it up after reading it.'

'No, I won't tear it.'

'Then I'll stop speaking to you,' Indra had said with childlike simplicity. How lovely the childish words sounded from her lips.

And one day...

One day Indra had come to his house. After spending some time with others she came to Chander's room. It was the first time he had felt so close to her. He put a vermillion bindi on her forehead and watched her in fascination. Then he bent down and put his lips on her forehead. Indra's eyelids had fluttered and a pleasant smell had arisen from every pore of her body, her fingers trembling on Chander's arms while he soaked up the sweat on her forehead with his lips. In the heat of the moment they had together taken a vow—a vow which was wordless and soundless, which did not rise to their lips.

Since then he had always remembered these words—'You are cut out for big things.'

Just then a no. 2 bus came and sped away after halting for a brief moment. Chander suddenly realised that he was standing at the bus stop. A shock of recognition—One who was once so close to him was not living far from here. Indra too was here, living in Delhi.

He had met her only two months ago. The intimacy of four years ago was still in her eyes.

'I know Chander very well,' she had told her husband, 'His fads, indiosyncracies and all.'

'Then he deserves to be entertained lavishly,' her husband had said with great bonhomie.

And smiling as she used to four years ago, Indra had said in a teasing voice, 'Chander is allergic to milk. He swallows coffee as he inhales smoke. And if you add a second spoon of sugar to his tea it does havoc to his throat.' She had chuckled, and his memories of the past were revived—Chander really could not take two spoons of sugar in his tea.

The bus was nowhere in sight.

Standing there Chander realized that in this vast city of unknown and half-known people there was a person by the name of Indra who really knew him and still recognized him after the lapse of so many years. He felt exhilarated at the thought. He pined to meet her and to demolish this wall of separation between them.

An auto came charging in his direction. 'Gurudwara Road, ... Karolbagh. Gurudwara Road!' Chander advanced one step. Giving him one sweeping glance the Sikh auto driver proceeded towards him with great alacrity as if he had recognised Chander the moment his eyes had landed on him. 'Karolbagh! Gurudwara Road!' Seeing the note of recognition in the driver's eyes, Chander felt pleased. At least there was someone who had at last been able to place him. Chander knew the Sardar by face. He had so many times travelled to Connaught Place in his auto.

Chander got into the auto and three more passengers got in with him. Within minutes the auto had deposited Chander at the Gurudwara Road crossing. Chander took out a four-anna coin and placed it on the driver's palm. Giving him a friendly nod, Chander was about to depart when the Sikh driver stopped him. 'Saheb, how much money are you giving me?' Chander turned to look and saw the Sardar coming after him. 'Saheb, make it two annas more.'

'But I always pay four annas, Sardarji,' Chander said, giving him a knowing look. But the Sardar was adamant. There was not a trace of amiableness in his eyes. Chander reminded the man that he had travelled by his auto rickshaw scores of times and had always paid him four annas per trip.

'Sir, it must have been some other auto rickshaw. I always charge six annas...' This time the Sardar had spoken in Punjabi and had stretched out his hand before Chander in a demanding manner.

It was not merely a question of two annas. There was more to it. Chander felt hurt. Without further ado he paid the man another two annas and proceeded towards Indra's house.

She received him warmly. 'Must have strayed this side by mistake,' she joked, a note of intimacy floating in her eyes. She was waiting for her husband. 'It's going on to be nine,' she said. 'Generally he is back home by eight—the factory's closing time. I don't know what has held him up today. You will have tea, of course.'

'I can't refuse tea,' Chandra said enthusiastically, comfortably stretching out his legs. His tiredness had vanished and he was feeling buoyed up.

The maid-servant brought in tea. Indra poured out tea and he watched her arms and face. She was just the same—known and familiar. 'How much sugar?' she asked.

With a jolt, all his thoughts were dispersed. He felt his throat constricted and his weariness returning again. He began to sweat. Trying to revive old links he said, 'Two spoons!' hoping that Indra would remember everything and would ask whether two spoons of sugar wouldn't affect his throat?

But Indra put two spoonfuls of sugar in his cup and held it out him. He forced the tea down like so much poison, to the accompaniment of inconsequential talk. But there was a tinge of formality in Indra's talk and Chander felt like bolting away from her and striking his head against a wall.

He finished his tea and left, wiping his perspiration. He had not the slightest idea what Indra had been talking of.

Coming on to the road, he sighed and stood there for a while. His throat was parched and there was a bitter taste in his mouth.

At the taxi-stand at the crossing, a few drivers deep in their cups were abusing one another lustily. He saw a dog running away in the distance. Fish was being fried at a wayside stall and its smell leapt up to his nostrils. A few young men were standing at the betelnut shop, bottles of Coca-Cola held to their mouths. People were speeding away in scooters and the late stragglers, who had to go to the suburbs were anxiously looking into the distance for the arrival of their buses.

Cars, taxis, buses—the traffic had again picked up and the traffic lights at the crossing still blazed red and yellow.

Tired out, Chander was his way back home. His shoes had started hurting his toes and the foul smell rising from his socks had become unbearable.

At last, he reached home, tired and weary, and sat down on a chair like an intruder. There was nothing new in this. Nirmala greeted him with a smile. 'Tired?' she asked, placing her hand on his arm.

'Yes,' Chander gave her a loving look. His heart singed within him. Even that rented house made him feel at home and gave him a sense of belonging.

'Have a wash,' Nirmala said, arranging the food on the table.

'I don't feel like eating just now,' Chander replied.

'Why, what's the matter?' she asked lovingly. 'In the morning you ate nothing. Did you eat in the afternoon?'

'Yes, I did,' he said, his eyes still fixed on Nirmala. She hesitated and then sat down beside him.

His eyes roved over the room with an abstracted gaze and in between he turned an intense look on Nirmala.

In the light falling from behind her, her hair had a silken sheen and her eye lashes looked like soft needles. The shadows falling under her eyes were so intimately familiar. She had pushed her bangle half-way up her arm.

Chander's eyes were probing her body for that old familiar touch of intimacy. Her nails, fingers, the lobes of her ears covered with a feathery down.

He got up, drew the curtain and lay on the bed. He felt he was no longer lonely nor a stranger. The flower vase lying in front was his and so were the clothes lying over there in a heap. He was familiar with their smell.

Their familiarity was ingrained in him. Even in the dense darkness of the night his groping fingers could recognise them. He could walk through any of the doors without bumping into them.

Just then he heard the thud of Gulati's tired feet on the stairs. It made him uncomfortable. Silently, he called Nirmala to himself, made her lie down next to him and, placed his hand on her bosom.

For some time he kept listening to her breathing and feeling her rising and falling bosom. He wished every part of her body and every heart beat to serve as a witness to his deep sense of oneness with her.

In the dark his fingers groped for her nails and touched her eyelids. He put his mouth on her neck, wanting to lose himself. The familiar smell of her washed hair seeped into every fibre of his body and his hand slid over her, searching for recognition. Nirmala's breathing grew heavier.

He felt her fleshy arms and rounded shoulders. Every part of Nirmala's body was drawn to him with a unique attraction. Every pore of hers recognised him, every joint grew tense, the hot blood rose in her, and every breath was constricted. A deep recognition in every part...

Just then light came up in Bishan Kapur's window and they saw cigarette smoke curling around the window bars and disappearing into darkness.

Chander's lonely heart leaping out of the layers of loneliness was drowned in that familiar breathing, that familiar odour, that touch. He did not want anything else. One needs familiarities and in that darkness there was in him a longing to be recognised, he was looking for an old revelation in that breath, that odour, every part of that body.

Stillness reigned.

He felt secure in that silence. He clasped her in his arms, feeling tide rise. Bodily heat increase and a sea of oneness surged through every pore.

Gradually Nirmala's quick breathing slowed down. The magnetic pull weakened and the passion ebbed away.

But Chander did not loosen his grip on her arms. The ebbing tide left him alone again, like a shell on an unknown shore.

Extracting her arm from under his body, Nirmala heaved a deep sigh and lay relaxed. Gradually everything drifted into sleep and the pall of night enveloped them. No sound, no voice anywhere. Nirmala turned on her side as she descended into profound sleep. Chander watched her languidly. He had again started feeling lonely. He placed his hand on Nirmala's shoulder to make her turn towards him but his fingers seemed to have become inert and lifeless. Defeated, he lay back and did not know when he fell asleep.

After a long time the police station clock struck two, bringing Chander out of his sleep. He felt as if he had been startled out of his drowsiness. The room's stillness frightened him. In the darkness his hand groped for Nirmala, fell on her hair which lay sprawled on the pillow. He felt the silken softness of her hair and bent down to smell it. His hand slid over her body and over the curves of her shoulder. He tried to recognize its intimacy and hear the sound of her soft breathing which was so familiar to him.

Lying on her side, Nirmala moaned in her sleep. Chander's heart missed a beat lest she should come awake and give a start like a stranger, breaking that spell of intimacy.

Nirmala's breath caught, as if she were afraid, were having a nightmare. Chander felt paralysed—did she not recognise his touch?

Then he shook her up. 'Nirmala! Nirmala!' he cried frantically.

As he had feared, Nirmala woke up with a start and rubbed her eyes, trying to get the hang of things.

Turning on the light, he shook Nirmala by both shoulders. 'Do you recognize me?' he asked in a terrified voice. 'Do you recognize me, Nirmala?'

Nirmala gazed wide-eyed at him and then asked in a low, surprised voice: 'What is the matter?'

He kept staring at her. His eyes were searching for something in her face.

Rajendra Yadav

Where Lakshmi is Imprisoned

Wait a minute, this story is not about Vishnu's wife Lakshmi. It is about a girl of that name who wanted to get out of her prison. This mixing up of names is bound to create some confusion as happened initially with Govind.

When Govind woke up in tenor, he found himself drenched in perspiration. His heart was pounding so hard that he feared it might cease beating any moment. In the darkness he kept blinking, unable to make out where he was; he had lost all sense of direction and place. The clock in the adjoining hall chimed, striking one, and he wondered where the clock was—or for that matter where he himself was. Slowly things fell in place. He rubbed his neck hard to wipe off the perspiration. But the banging he had heard still resounded in his head.

Whether in a dream in reality he had felt as if someone had banged on his door several times and had said in a plaintive voice, 'Get me out of here.' The voice sounded so mysterious as it grazed against his consciousness that he woke up utterly bewildered. Was it really a human voice or merely a hallucination?

Then he gradually realized that he had been dreaming. He had dozed off thinking of Lakshmi and though he went into a deep slumber yet Lakshmi had invaded his dreams.

It was a strange voice and yet so distinct. He had often heard people saying that they knew of instances when someone called a man or woman in his or her dream, pleading: 'Take me out, take me out.' Then he would gradually worm his way into the dreamer's confidence, and tell him about a secret place on digging up which the dreamer came upon pots of gold and silver and became rich overnight. Sometimes it also happened that when the discoverer of the treasure trove was an undeserving person, the gold and silver were reduced coal or cowries. Or he became a leper or there was a death in his family. Was this Lakshmi the goddess of wealth calling him from the nether world. He kept brooding over the matter for a long time till the whole incident connected with Lakshmi came back to him. He kept lying there inert in enchanted, stunned state.

Far off, some other clock again struck one.

Now Govind could not hold himself back any longer. Tucking his quilt securely around him he put his arm out of it up to the elbow. Still lying in bed, he stretched out his hand and took out from a drawer of his almirah a half-burnt candle which had been lying alongside a heap of books. Then he rummaged through the drawer for a matchbox, taking care not to stretch his arm too far out in this wintry cold. He struck a match and succeeded in lighting it after three or four attempts. Lighting the candle he fixed it on the ink-pot lid. In the dim, wavering candle light he made sure that the door was securely bolted from inside. As he looked up, he found to his satisfaction, that the light in the upper floor which used to filter in through the skylight had long since gone out. Everything was quiet and still. Although his bed-switch was right over his wooden bed yet the fear of Lala Rupram coupled with the rigour of the winter night kept him from leaving the cosy warmth of his quilt. The first thing, in the morning Lala Rupram would remark, 'Govind Babu, these days you are studying far into the night,' the implication being that he was wasting too much electricity.

Then, very quietly, as if someone was spying on him, he fished out a magazine from under his pillow. He held the magazine in his hand which he had unwillingly taken out the folds of the quilt. He kept staring at the 47th page, which he had stared at twenty times. When the one o'clock Pathankot Express hurtled past he came out of his reverie. On the 47th and 48th pages that lay open before him, some lines had been underscored in blue. And also, the edges of the pages had been turned down. By now Govind had scanned those underscored lines more than twenty times. But he looked around warily and read those lines yet again.

At each reading he had felt elated in a strange way. His heartbeat would increase and drop again. His head would spin as it had the first time. Since then he had passed through many mental crises yet he kept staring a long time or the dark letters of the story printed in black ink. He felt as if that line of words was a barred window from behind which an innocent girl, her hair scattered over her shoulders was looking out at him. And then, a story he had heard in his childhood started taking shape in his mind. It was the story of a prince who, while out hunting was separated from his companions and strayed into a desolate spot near the sea and found himself standing under a huge fortress. He saw a very beautiful princess gazing down at him from her window. A demon had imprisoned her in the fortress. Her image, in all its details became vivid in Govind's mind, creating the strange illusion that the princess was peering at him from behind those lines in the magazine. The streaks of tears on her cheeks had dried, her lips and face wore a withered look. Her silky hair was tousled like a spider's web. The words, 'Get me out, get me out of here' seemed to rise like a cry from every part of her. Govind felt an overwhelming urge to rescue the beleaguered princess. For a moment he had a strong desire to pace up and down in the two-foot wide space between his bed and the wall, so as to relieve himself of the urge to do something.

Was it Lakshmi who had written those lines for him? But he had never set eyes on Lakshmi. If he conjured a young girl's face what would she look like? There were other reasons too which inhibited him from casting Lakshmi in the image of a beautiful girl. He was not at all familiar with Lakshmi's face and her bodily contours and age.

Govind knew only too well that all this had been written form him—the lines had been underscored to draw his attention, incredible though it seemed. He did not feel himself worthy of such gestures from a girl. He had of course heard a lot about the ways of city life. But it had not even remotely occurred to him that within a week of coming to the city after doing his Intermediate in a village he would have this lucky break....

Every time he read these lines his head would start spinning as if he were looking down from the tenth floor of a high rise building. In fact the first time he had read these lines he had jumped a if a live charcoal had fallen on his hand.

It had happened something like this. Seated on a brick platform in the mill house, he was tallying the day's accounts in a dog-eared ledger placed on top of a wooden box, when Lala Rupram's ten-year old son, Ram Sarup came and stood in front in him. He was wearing an old worn out chester, evidently his elder brother's which had been re-tailored to suit his size. Shoving his hands into his chester pockets, Ram Sarup kept steadily gazing at him.

The boy had acted in the same manner on the first day of Govind's arrival at the mill house. Lala Rupram was also present on that occasion. To show that he evinced interest in his son, Govind had asked the boy his name, age, the school he was studying in and so on. Name, Ram Sarup; age, nine years; Chungi Primary School; 4th class. From that time onwards, Govind had started sensing the boy's presence from the shadow of his chester. This obviated the necessity of confirming his presence by looking at his face. Under his chester the boy wore knickers which exposed his bare spindly legs. His feet were shod in a pair of old canvas shoes, with protruding tongues that reminded Govind of a tailless dog.

After watching Govind at work for a while the boy took out a magazine from under his chester. 'Munshiji, Lakshmi-sister wants something else to read,' he said, placing the magazine on the wooden box.

'All right, come tomorrow,' Govind had said with an edge to his voice.

Munshiji, the appellation of clerkdom that had been bestowed upon Govind on coming here, burnt his soul to cinders. A quill tucked behind the ear, a round soiled cap, an old musty coat, an outlandish seedy person—these were the hallmarks of a Munshi. The twenty-two year old Govind recoiled at the idea of his being a Munshi.

He and Lala Rupram hailed from the same village. The Lala and Govind's father were known to each other, perhaps had even studied together for two or three years in the same school. On coming to the city, Govind had approached Rupram to help him get some private tuitions or a small part-time job. Remembering Govind's late father, Lala Rupram said in most solicitous tone, 'Child, you are like a son to me. To start with, write my mill's accounts for an hour or so every day. You can live comfortably in the small room adjacent to the mill house. You can also pursue your studies there. As for flour, as you can see, there is no dearth of it here.' Overwhelmed with gratitude, Govind forthwith shifted into that dingy room. The first night, Rupram explained to him how the accounts were to be kept. Looking at Govind through his cataract-thick glasses, which spreadeagled Rupram's myopic eyes like the wings of a peacock, he smiled indulgently at him through his thick lips and in order to enhance his status, gave Govind the honorific of *munshiji*. Govind gave him a startled look and immediately decided that after making a place for himself here, he would politely tell Rupram that did not like the designation of *munshiji*.

And now hearing the word *munshiji* falling from the small

boy's lips, Govind's eyebrows shot up and that also accounted for his talking to the boy in such brusque tone.

'I must have it tomorrow,' Ram Sarup insisted.

'Yes, brother, haven't I told you I'll give it to you tomorrow?' Govind felt like saying, gritting his teeth. But he kept quiet. He had heard Lakshmi's name being bandied about in one context or the other. Although Govind's hovel-like room, overlooking the lane, was isolated from the main block of Rupram's house yet it had a wire covered skylight at the back which opened on to the yard of Rupram's house. The family lived on the first floor. The grinding mill which was on the ground floor, behind it was a store room. The word 'Lakshmi' was heard every minutes or so 'Lakshmi Bibi has said so.' 'Lakshmi Bibi has the money,' 'Give the keys to Lakshmi Bibi.' Lakshmi's reaction to these remarks would come in a thin, piping, authoritative voice and Govind had come to recognise this voice as Lakshmi's. But what did she look like? Govind's curiosity was greatly aroused. If only he could have a fleeting glimpse of her! But in the first few days of his stay in the house, he thought it was incumbent upon him to establish his bonafides and he was therefore careful not to allow his glance to rove around. Of one thing he was certain—she must indeed be an important personage in the house. What made things more difficult nothing inside the house was visible to him. Where the mill house with its four doors ended, a ten-foot long corridor began and terminated in a small square in the house. The first floor of the building was quite high and strongly built. The square which was inside the premises was covered by an iron grill which changed when people upstairs passed over it, diverting Govind's attention. Sometimes children would jump on it for fun. Unless one traversed the entire length of the corridor it was not possible to have an inside view of the house. All the taps and the improvised bathrooms were located in this corridor, making it damp and slushy. In the morning while passing by the square, Govind though walking with downcast eyes, like a decent well-behaved chap, would try to gauge what was happening upstairs. He dared not raise his eyes to look at the higher reaches of the buildings. Closing the only door of his hovel-like room he would climb onto the wooden bed and try to peer through the dusty, wire-meshed skylight with its trailing cobwebs, into the first floor. But unfortunately for him, the wire mesh had been strung in such a way that only the balcony and the iron-grilled roof partially came into focus. Many a time he would just see the soles of two small feet passing by. If he made a strenuous effort he was rewarded by a glimpse of the ankles also. Yes, they were undoubtedly a woman's feet, for once he had also had a fleeting glimpse of the border of a sari. He had sighed deeply while getting down from the bed and pushing out his chest he had thumped it in a theatrical manner, exclaiming, 'O, cruel, Lakshmi, deign to give me a fleeting glimpse of your face!'

'Munshiji, what are you looking at? Why don't you write?' Ram Sarup said as he saw Govind nibbling at the end of his holder, his eyes glued to the page of the Accounts Register. How did the boy know think that what Govind was ruminating over had nothing to do with the figures in the Accounts Register?

Realizing that he had been caught on the wrong foot, Govind gave the boy a sheepish smile. Then something flashed in his mind. Surely, Lakshmi was Ram Sarup's sister, wasn't she? Her face must closely resemble Ram Sarup's He looked intently at the boy's face to determine whether or not he could be regarded as handsome. Then he smiled at his own foolishness and yawned. Tightly wrapping the blanket round his body he said in an affable tone, 'Well kid, I'll surely give it to you tomorrow morning.' He thought of asking the boy about Lakshmi but the watchman and the mason were working within earshot....

In fact today he was feeling a bit fagged out. He quickly turned his attention to his Accounts Register.

After a lot of running about and string-pulling in high places his name had appeared on the list of candidates who had been admitted to the local college. After reading his name on the notice board, on his way back from college, he stopped to buy some books and note books. His mind was brimming with plans to carve for his future. Suddenly his mind turned to Lakshmi. Who was she? What was she like? From whom could he get all these details about her? He did not know of anybody of his own age in whom he could confide. What if he asked somebody at random? But if Rupram came to know about it? Well, he had been here for three days and something may yet turn up. Going over the titles of the magazines and story books in his possession he tried to decide which book to give her when her brother came to ask for one. He thought perhaps in the course of the next few days, while offering her a book to read, he would slip a letter between its pages, apparently addressed to a friend, but which conveyed a lot when read between the lines. It would however be so cleverly worded that it would not give him away even if it misfired. He could blandly say, 'Oh, it was an oversight!' He could vehemently assert that he had had no idea that the letter was there. In any case, he could dismiss their charge by making a score of excuses. He smiled at his inane cleverness.

The magazine lying before him had been returned by the person of whom he had been thinking so ardently. She must have held it in her soft hands, put it under her pillow after reading it or even let it rest on her bosom while chasing some line of thought emerging from her reading. His body tingled with pleasure. Would he also be figuring in Lakshmi's thoughts? While his eyes chased the figures in the Accounts Register, his hand inadvertently ran over the pages of the magazine and suddenly stopped at a page whose edge had been folded at the top. Who had folded this page? In a moment a thousand thoughts flashed through his mind. Picking up the magazine he placed it on top of the Register, opening it at the folded page. He was startled to see some lines on the page underlined in blue. Who had underscored these lines? He was sure these marks were not there before.

'I love you more than life,' he read an underscored line.

What was this rigmarole? He felt completely dazed. He warily looked at Saleem mason and Dilawar Singh the watchman. They were absorbed in own work.

Then his eyes went to the second line, 'Take me away from here.'

What!

Another line, 'Otherwise I'll hang myself.'

Govind was so scared that he immediately closed the magazine and looked around apprehensively. Did someone suspect him? Beads of perspiration appeared on his forehead and his heart started beating hard like the motor of the flour-mill. He hid the magazine between his knees lest someone should ask for it, attracted by its colourful cover. He felt a strong urge to read the underscored lines again but he suppressed the desire. Had Lakshmi really made those marks? Or was it that someone was pulling his leg for fun? But he had no friendship—who would want to joke with a person who was so new to the place?

He could not resist the temptation to look through the magazine again. Only that particular page had the tell-tale marks. He read those lines in quick succession and felt as if an aeroplane was making a droning sound in his head. His head reeled and he forgot about the work in hand. Scratching the back of his ear with his pen holder he tried to read the credit and debit sides on the page of his ledger but nothing seemed to registered on his mind. The figures kept racing on the surface of the page. He felt his heart would burst open and his brain would explode like fireworks. Whom to ask about the marks? Where the marks Lakshmi's doing?

He thought it was just too sweet a dream to be true. He had not been able to see Lakshmi but she might have seen him all right. Oh, these girls were very clever indeed. He wished he had a mirror with him so that he could see himself in it as if through Lakshmi's eyes. How did he really look he was anxious to know.

But who was this Lakshmi? A widow? A married woman? An unmarried girl? How old was she? How he wished he could climb up those stairs at breakneck speed and barge into her room, taking her by surprise! 'Lakshmi, Lakshmi did you write all this?' he would ask her, seizing her shoulders and shaking her. 'Lakshmi, you don't know how unfortunate I am. I'm not worthy of you!' He was so moved by his own chain of thoughts that tears came to his eyes.

Gazing up at the electric bulb hanging from its cord he rambled into the fathomless world of the past and the future. Then he wiped away the tears throbbing on his eyelids with the gentleness of a devotee applying sandal paste to his duty's forehead. His limp hand was still holding the magazine at that page.

He read the lines yet again. What if Lakshmi eloped with him? Where would he take her? Where would they live? And what about his studies? And the worst of it, what if they were caught in flight?

But who was this Lakshmi?

Questions came crowding into his mind as if hounds had been let lose from their kennels or as if someone were hammering mercilessly on his brain. It was such a bizarre mix-up as if the whole world was swimming before his eyes in one momentous point of time while he was being hurled down from a high-rise building.

Seated on the brick platform in front of the wooden box, Govind was poring over the accounts. The accounts did not tally and the slips of paper on which he had been toting up the figures lay strewn around him. At last, resting his elbows on the Register he closed his eyes. The veins under his temples were throbbing. He had never heard of such a thing before—

not in films, not in novels either. What did these marks denote? Did Lakshmi really make them? For that matter even a child could have scrawled those lines. Taken aback at this possibility Govind again opened the magazine at that page. No, a child would not have singled out those words for attention. And the lines were too clear and straight to have been drawn by a child. Maybe Lakshmi was just a mischievous girl playing a prank on him.

Although Govind sat there with closed eyes reflecting, yet he could not get over the fear that the mason and the watchman could have guessed into his secret. In fact he feared Lala Rupram most.

Wearing a soiled, full-sleeved jacket padded with cotton, which looked aeons old, the Lala might descend the stairs any moment, panting heavily.

And lo and behold, there he was! His cane made a staccato sound on the floor as he walked. Think of the devil and he appears! Had he seen him sitting idle? He pushed the magazine further down between his knees and fixed his eyes on the pieces of paper lying scattered around him. The mason's and the watchman's whispering suddenly stopped. Walking across the narrow corridor Lala Rupram suddenly appeared before Govind like a visitation emerging from nowhere.

Behind his thick glasses his eyes looked magnified, terrifying. A big cap padded with cotton rested on his head, its flaps resembling upturned miniature mudguards, covering his ears. In their totality, they created the impression of the horns of mythical demons mentioned in the *Puranas*. His face was covered with crow's feet and the frame of his glasses had cracked over the bridge of his nose. He had tied it up with a thick piece of thread. He wore dentures which hung loosely between his jaws and he kept working his jaws to push them back in their place, in the process giving the impression that he was chewing gum. Govind felt queasy at the strange sounds emerging from his mouth and while talking to him, Govind would keep his face averted from him. Lala Rupram's neck would keep swaying ceaselessly like a toy with a spring loose. He wore a none-too-clean dhoti which came down his knees, matching in antiquity his thick shoes which he must have picked up at a junk shop. His military stockings were also apparently bought at a second-hand shop. The stockings were covered with thick putties as a safeguard against recurring rheumatic pains. The tongues of his boots kept yapping at you. Looking at him, Govind would feel that this man was on the verge of kicking the bucket.

As Lala Rupram drew near him, Govind put on an ingratiating smile, as a mark of welcome to the old man. The brick platform was studded with about two hundred ink stains. Smoothing out the ring spread over the platform, Govind made room for the Lala to sit down. Still breathing laboriously, the Lala indicated with a gesture of his hand that did not wish to sit there. Instead, he sat down on a tin chair, facing Govind. He had difficulty breathing and kept panting all the time like a thirsty dog.

A shiver ran down Govind's spine as the Lala sat down. Had the old fogey been able to guess the secret? Although it was Lala Rupram's routine to come in after lunch, yet Govind feared that he might start questioning him. His heart again started beating hard. The Lala sat silent trying to regain his breath while Govind fixed his eyes on his Register to avoid his tormentor's gaze.

At last, trying to take control of the situation, Govind said, 'Lalaji, I got admitted into college today.'

'Really!' Lalaji's voice was drowned in a bout of coughing. One hand was planted on his cane while the other was in the sacred pouch in which he was limply telling the beads of his rosary. That hand appeared to be crippled.

The atmosphere was already getting oppressive when something happened.

Gathering his breath, the Lala had just opened his mouth to

speak when the iron mesh over the courtyard clanged loudly as if something heavy had been thrown on it. Then crashing on the roof came a pair of tongs, an iron ladle, a bucket, a cauldron and an iron pan. There was a great tumult as if the house had suddenly caught fire.

Govind sat up tense. Had a fire really broken out somewhere in the vicinity? He gave Lalaji a questioning look and was taken aback to see the old man quite cool, betraying no sign of panic. The old man did look upset but showed no sign of running to take stock of the situation. The mason and the watchman exchanged amused looks and then looked ironically at Lalaji. None of them looked agitated. The tumult inside was mounting and the iron mesh jingled again and again as more things landed on it. What was going on here? Govind felt as if his ribs would crack with excitement. He was about to ask Lalaji what was going on when the Lala heaved himself up from the chair, throwing his weight on his cane and stopping a moment to close the door, disappeared into the corridor from where he had emerged a short while ago. The mason and the watchman relaxed and smiled at one another. They cleared their throats and smiled again, this time more indulgently. Govind's eyes had been following the receding Lalaji and as he disappeared from view, Govind turned towards the mason and the watchman. He rose to his feet and, throwing his blanket over his arm, in the manner of a cock flapping its wings, he came down from the platform, his magazine tucked under his arm. He stood undecided for some time and then moved into the narrow corridor, hoping that he would be able to guess matters from there. He had just moved into the corridor when he heard a medley of sounds emerging from some crevices in the door. He could distinctly hear Lakshmi's voice rising over other voices. At least he liked to believe that it was Lakshmi's voice. Oh, God, what was happening here? Had someone met with an accident? Had a fire broken out in the house? Had a snake or a scorpion bitten someone? But judging from the manner in which these people had responded to the hullabaloo it seemed that nothing untoward had happened. But why had that old fogy closed the door behind him after going out? The iron mesh was still jingling as loudly as if someone were performing the dance of destruction on it. But that feminine voice rising above the din was so sharp and shrill that he failed to catch the words.

'Babuji, why are you looking so agitated?' It was the watchman asking Govind. 'Today the goddess Chandi is in full fury.' The watchman's remark drew a laugh from the mason.

Govind was furious. Something serious was happening inside the house and these people were taking the whole thing so lightly! In fact the wretches seemed to be enjoying every moment of it.

In the big mill house a thin film of flour lay over everything. In one corner, a small stone bathed in flour stood silent, resembling a black elephant carved out of stone, the bag which received the flour discharged from the mill looking like its trunk. In a straight line from it stood a motor, a wide strap leading from the motor was responsible for working the mill. At the other end, right near the wall was installed a motor, joined at one end to a wide strap which revolved round the motor when it was switched on to put the mill in operation. As a measure of safety this part of the mill house was enclosed by a railing. On the wall right above the motor hung a wooden board with a human skull above two crossed bones painted on it and the word 'Danger' inscribed under the illustration in red. By the side of the platform hung a weighing scale from an iron chain fixed under the roof, one pan of the scale rising from the ground in the stance of a Kathakali dancer. The other pan held an assortment of weights ranging from a *chhatak* to a *maund*. Although the watchman had strict instructions to remove the pans from the beam after the day's work was over and Lala Rupram time and again reprimanded him for ignoring his instructions yet sometimes when the mill worked till late at night and customers such as shopkeepers and office-goers starting to come in with their grain as early as five in the morning when the pans of the scale were cold as ice, the watchman hated touching them. Being an ex-serviceman, he said he had handled enough cold steel on the battle front during the war and was in no mood to handle it again in peace time. Had it fallen to his lost to handle cold steel all his life, he would ask. The weighing scale was fixed right in front of the door, and if he was not careful, while passing through the door his body would hit the pans, then he would hurl military abuses in the silent darkness.

His feet shod in mailed army boots, and an old overcoat, the vestige of his army days, wrapped around his body, the watchman was sitting on the edge of a strong bed, blithely smoking and chatting with the mason, Saleem.

A brazier rested between him and Saleem. When the fire in the brazier started sinking, one of them would lazily throw some pieces of charcoal or wood scantlings on it, and they would stretch out their legs or aims to warm them over the fire.

In his spare time Saleem also repaired cycles and was presently engaged in mending a puncture in a cycle tube. He had dipped it in a tub filled with water to locate the puncture. He had laid by the necessary tools and accessories such as scissors, pliers, screw drivers, wrenches and a tube of rubber solution. He had also collected some discarded tyres and an assortment of cycle wheels to decorate his shop. More than half the space in his so-called wayside workshop was festooned with these objects.

Govind watched Saleem at work. After wetting his copying pencil with his spit he had made a circle with it round the incriminating spot.

'Yes, Jamadar Saheb has told me all about it,' he said arching his eyebrows. 'Yes, that's what he told me,' he asserted fixing Govind with his gaze. 'If Lala is prepared to shell out some cash I can fix it in a jiffy. The girl is under the spell of a jinn.

Where Lakshmi is Imprisoned

Our Maulvi Badruddin can exorcise the jinn in no time.'

Govind looked at Saleem in alarm. He wondered if any of the Lala's daughters was visited by a goddess. This reminded him of a widow named Tara in his village. When under the spell of the goddess she also used to throw all the utensils out of the house. Her entire body would become stiff and she would start frothing at the mouth. Her eyes and tongue would bulge out and her neck would loll.

But which daughter of Lala's? Could it be Lakshmi? Oh, God, spare her, please! Govind's heart began to sink. Then the tumult above subsided. He only heard the faint sound of weeping in the distance. Perhaps someone in the house had had a fit—not serious enough for anyone to take notice of it.

In reply to Saleem's remarks, the watchman came out with a sharp retort which was equally meant for Govind's ears. 'Don't bring money into it, pal!' he said. 'Or else you will give the old man a heart attack. Son, I doubt if your Maulvi has any treatment for this kind of ailment. It requires a special kind of nostrum. Come, Babuji, sit down.'

The watchman pointed at the stool. Though he addressed Govind respectfully as Babuji, he did not think much of him. That Govind hailed from a village went against him, specially in the eyes of the watchman who had spent long years in the city. The watchman had also served in the army and had travelled as far as Cairo. Age, experience, manners—he considered himself superior to Govind on all these counts. But at this moment Govind was indifferent to all this. Sitting down on the stool he asked in an anxious voice, 'What was this rumpus about? What's going on here?'

Raising his head, the mason looked at Govind and then his eyes met the watchman's smiling eyes. Passing his hand over his salt-and-pepper moustache, the watchman said, 'It's nothing Babuji. A child must have thrown something down.'

The mason said,' Jamadar Saheb, stop telling lies. Why don't you tell him the truth? What's there to hide?'

'Then you had better tell him,' the watchman said, taking a bundle of *biris* from his pocket. Twisting the wrapper he loosened the bundle like a rolled lump of flour and extracting a *biri* from it threw it in the direction of the mason. Extracting another *biri* from the bundle he blew into it from both ends and then lighted it by holding one end over the fire in the brazier. 'Don't you really know?' he asked, picking up the threads of his talk.

Govind was irritated at this game of beating about the bush. He was sure there was something fishy that they were deliberately trying to hide from him. His tongue hanging out from his mouth, the mason was sand-papering the spot where the puncture had occurred. Whenever he concentrated on some important job, his tongue would come out of his mouth and roll over his upper lip. There was a bald patch in the middle of his pate. Govind remembered that baldness was said to be a sign of wealth. But paradoxically enough the man was far from rich for he was attending to the measly job of mending a puncture at late hours of the night.

Bending his head over his tube, Saleem said, 'Am I to mend this puncture or to tell Babuji her story? Oh, what a rotten tube! But the fellow will not think of changing it. I feel like throwing it into the brazier.'

'What are so many tubes doing here?' Govind asked making a friendly overture. 'Almost all of them appear to have outlived their lives and are beyond repairing.'

'Don't you know?' Leaving his work, the mason gave Govind an intense look. 'These are the discards of the two dozen rickshaws owned by the Lala. He owns so many rickshaws but he wouldn't care to engage a separate mechanic to undertake their repairs. He thrusts the task of repairing the tyres and tubes on me while mechanic Ali Ahmed attends to the other repair jobs. Are you new to this city, Babuji?'

'Yes, I came here only three days ago. I've come here to pursue my studies,' Govind said. He was eager to get at the heart of the matter and was looking for a new opening to revert to the subject.

'That's why,' Saleem said, 'you're asking this question. You attend to these accounts at night, don't you? Just wait. In a couple of days Lala'll put his dear, worthy son too under your tuition.' He had uttered the words 'dear' and 'worthy' with a twist to his tongue, imparting them a sarcastic ring. Pleased at his own gimmickry he lighted the *biri* which the watchman had given him.

'But why are you telling him all this?' the watchman said. 'Don't you know he comes from the same village as the Lala. He must be knowing all about it.'

'No, I'm completely in the dark' Govind said, in a reassuring voice. 'Lala's father had migrated to the city and we had lost touch with them. Please tell me what's it all about.' Govind had modulated his voice to suit his request.

Impressed by his earnestness the mason said, 'Oh, there's nothing much to tell. Lala's elder daughter is suffering from epilepsy. Some say it is hysteria. But we reckon it's nothing of the sort. Only she is under someone's spell. But under whose spell? Well, how can she know when she loses consciousness?'

'Is she a widow?' Govind asked, his heart pounding hard. How he prayed it was not Lakshmi.

This time he did not fail to notice the smiles on the watchman's and the mason's faces as they exchanged glances.

The watchman took a long pull at his *biri* and then swallowing the smoke he put on a grave expression. 'She was never married,' he said. 'Lala wouldn't marry her off.'

'What's her name?' Govind couldn't help asking.

'Lakshmi.'

'Lakshmi?' Govind exclaimed a minute too soon. All energy seemed to ebb away from his body, leaving it limp.

The watchman gave a quizzical laugh as if he wanted to say, 'So you too know the name!'

A question inevitably rose in Govind's mind. What would

be Lakshmi's age.'

'Babuji, so you know nothing about their family?' the watchman said.

'No, I don't. Haven't I already told you? I know nothing about them,' Govind said resignedly.

'But Lakshmi's story is known all over town,' the watchman said. 'You are new to the place—that's why,' he added, exchanging a glance with the mason. 'So *Mistri Saheb*, may I tell him the whole story?'

'Why ask me? What's there to hide? If he stays here he'll come to know about it anyway—sooner or later.'

'Then listen, off I go!' the watchman said blithely. 'As you know, this Lala of ours is one of the richest men of the city and an ace miser.'

'That is as it should be,' the mason said. 'A miser is bound to become a rich man.'

'*Mistri Saheb*, don't interrupt me once I've started' the watchman said testily, annoyed at the mason's inopportune observation.

'All right, proceed,' the mason smiled sagely like an old man.

'Of course, you know about the Lala's flour mill. It grinds thousands and thousands of maunds of grain every year—not less than two to three hundred maunds per day. During the War he managed to get some military contracts by bribing the big officers and their underlings. You know how profitable these military contracts are. A man gets rich in a day. You should have seen Lala's 'Lakshmi flour mill' in those days. The bags were stacked ceiling-high like sand bags on the battle front. Lala made a hell of a lot of money by selling wheat to these military people at exorbitant prices. He bought condemned grain at throw-away rates and sold it at fancy prices to complete his quotas.

To cap it all, he adulterated the condemned grain with fuller's earth. Apart from the grinding charges, he did all he could—black marketing underhand deals, theft. He set up two factories besides—a soap factory and a shoe factory. They are by his sons. He owns about two dozen rickshaws and five trucks and more than a dozen houses from which he gets handsome rents. That's not all. He lends out money on interest. If I am not mistaken he has also bought considerable land in his old village. The wretch has so many fingers in so many pies. We have only a cursory knowledge of all his deals. As for what his really worth, only he knows that. He's always busy with one scheme or another. The surprising part of it is that he has amassed all this wealth in just twenty-five years or so.

The watchman Dilawar Singh was very garrulous. He had so often narrated stories about the war, about his officers' acts of bravery and tales of his own valour with great gusto and in most exaggerated terms, that by now he had become a perfect raconteur. His voice and tone moved in rhythm with the ups and downs of his story.

While listening to the watchman it suddenly occurred to Govind that maybe she had underscored those lines in the magazine while the fit was on and as such they had no significance. This dampened his enthusiasm. But even so he feigned surprise. 'In only twenty-five years?' he said.

The watchman nodded vigorously and proceeded to light a *biri*.

Govind wondered how old Lakshmi could be.

'You yourself seen what a great miser he is,' the watchman proceeded with his story. 'He has grown old, he is suffering from some breathing trouble, his whole body shakes but if he sees the prospects of earning even one paisa he won't mind walking ten miles for it, perspiring and panting. He would refuse to hire any other mode of transport. Walk he must. In summer he keeps his body bare—he wears only a dhoti, half of it round his waist, the other half covering his torso. Even in winter he keeps to this dress, I've observed him for ten years. He won't have any of his houses repaired, or even white-washed. He keeps an eye on which tenant uses how much electricity. Why is the tap on? Why is that fan running unnecessarily? He has admitted his youngest son in a free municipal school and his daughter stays put at home. He haggles for hours with rickshawallas and truckwallas to account for every last paisa. His employees at the flour-mill are fed up with him. He teaches them all the tricks of weighing short, pinching on every paisa and what not. You must believe me when I say that his monthly income is not less than fifteen thousand rupees. But look at his appearance, like a rubbish heap. He doesn't even have an extra chair to offer a visitor. As for offering the visitor a betel or arecanut, the question does not rise. Can any one believe that he is so fabulously rich? He is getting on in years and yet how he chases money! No interest in anything else-strike or holiday, he must continue his pursuit. He leaves me alone because he trusts me. Besides, he needs me. But as for the others, he plays hell with them and they mock at him for an eccentric. People laugh at him behind his back.'

'How many children has he?' Govind asked, finding that the watchman was getting bogged down in irrelevancies.

'That's what I am coming to,' the watchman said with an air of complacency. 'I'm telling you the truth, Babuji. What amazes me is he has spent his life amassing but what will he do with it? People earn so that they can sit back in comfort and enjoy life. But this demon never takes a rest. It is money, money, money, all the time. And the poor fellow has forgotten what money is for.'

Dilawar Singh gazed at the dying embers in the brazier in a dramatic manner as if something still more sensational was in the offing. 'Babuji, I wonder when will he ever enjoy his money. It's already too late for that. Babuji, I really pity him for it. Now, suppose he dies tomorrow what good will this money do him? How helpless he is before himself—like a living dead ma   he goes on piling up money. He cannot enjoy it and he wouldn't let others enjoy it either. He is like a serpent sitting guard over a treasure. He earns money and sits tight over it—that's all he does.' The watchman sighed as if overcome with pity for Lala Rupram. Then he gritted his teeth and said, 'Sometimes I feel like going after him with a knife, sitting astride his chest, ripping it apart with the knife and churning it like mango jam. I would make him disgorge every paisa of the money that he has stuffed in his belly.'

'How many children has he?' Govind repeated his question. Wading through a mass of irrelevancies that the watchman had been spewing out, he wanted to get at the heart of the matter. He wanted to know as much as he could about Lakshmi.

Savouring the pleasure of indulging in redundancies, that had become second nature with him, the watchman smiled and said, 'Four children. His wife is dead. He won't allow any relative to come near him. And as for servants, he doesn't have any. There's an old, half-dead woman living with the family, who they say is his elder brother's widow. She looks after the house. I haven't seen anyone else in the house—himself, three sons and a daughter.'

'The two elder boys are not living with him,' the mason volunteered the information.

'Yes, they are living separately from him. They call on him once a day. Once of them looks after the shoe factory and the other the soap factory. But he doesn't trust them. He keeps all the important documents with him and personally supervises the accounts when he goes to these factories every evening and rakes in the day's intake. But the boys are much too clever for him, and unlike him, they are fond of the good things of life. I tell you, sir, the day the old man departs his niggardliness will also depart with him. These sons of his will make up for it.' Then the watchman taxed his mind. 'Well, what else did you want to know?' he asked and then added, 'No, they are not living with him as I've told you. It was all right when they were unmarried. But now they have families of their own—wives and children. You know that goddess Chandi, who is living in

Lala's house. The other can't get along with her.'

A shiver ran through Govind from head to foot. 'Who, Lakshmi?' he asked. 'Are you talking of her?'

'Yes, I'm talking of her. She is the central-figure in the house—the one who holds the key to the lock that opens the treasure. Had it not been for her where would all this bounty have come from? It is she who has brought good fortune to the family, turned the tide in its favour. Otherwise, he was just a pauper and a pauper he would have remained.' The watchman threw a halo of mystery around what he was narrating.

'But how? Will you please explain?' Govind asked. He was feeling bewildered. Once it crossed his mind that the old man was using her body to mint more money. The devil, the scoundrel!

The watchman smiled at Govind's impatience.

'The Lala's father was a man of very modest means,' the watchman began. 'And he died at a very young age, leaving minors behind. At the most one thousand each must have fallen to the lot of his two sons. Both of them were already married. This Lala wanted to start his own business. He came to the city to try his hand at the share market in the hope of doubling his money but he came a cropper. The elder brother, Rochuram started a water mill. In the beginning, he had a hard time of it but after the birth of his daughter his financial condition took a turn for the better and he never looked back from then on. The Lala was working at his brother's mill and both husband and wife lived on the elder brother's crumbs. Rochuram's daughter proved very auspicious for the family and he became fabulously rich. Their elders used to say that down the generations, a daughter was always a harbinger of good fortune to their family. The younger brother also—that is, our Lala—pined for a daughter. He went to soothsayers and spell-binders asking for the boon of a daughter through their divine dispensation. And as he so fondly wished, a girl did arrive in his family and you won't believe it, with her arrival the family's fortune took a turn for the better. It is not known whether the Lala chanced upon some buried treasure or the money rained from heaven like manna but Lala Rupram's stars shone. He was convinced that his daughter was a goddess in disguise. He named her Lakshmi and one must confess that she proved a veritable Lakshmi—the goddess of Wealth. It was not long before he set up the Lakshmi Flour Mills. Things came to such a pass that even if he touched clay it turned into gold and if he picked up a pebble it was transformed into a diamond. Then came the War and her rolled in wealth. He got military contracts, he bought one house after another. He bought trucks and minted more money by transporting goods at recklessly high rates. His elder brother Rochuram was also doing equally well and both of them used to say with pride, 'Daughters come to our houses in the garb of goddess Lakshmi. And then something untoward happened which changed the complexion of the whole thing.' Dilwara Singh paused. He knew his story was gradually working itself to a climax. He took a long pull at his *biri* and finding that his listener's curiosity had reached its crescendo he threw away the *biri* and continued: 'Gauri was now of marriageable age. Rumours were afloat that she was having affairs with young men, particularly with a neighbour's son. Neighbours started pointing fingers at the family. Before she could come to any harm, Rochuram promptly married her off. No sooner had she stepped out of her parents' home than a calamity befell the family. Lala Rochuram lost a big court case and as ill luck would have it, just at that calamitous moment his flour mill caught fire. Some people said that the Lala's enemies were behind it. Well, the upshot was that once he fell like a lumbering elephant it became difficult for him to rise to his feet. People harried him by not paying back his loans, and he became a bankrupt. He was ruined, and everything he had sold. One day Lalaji's swollen dead body was found floating in a tank. His brother, Rupram was terribly alarmed. He withdrew his daughter, Lakshmi from school and kept her under strict vigilance. From then on she never came down stairs. She has remained confined to the house. Her father does not allow any one to enter or leave the house. In the beginning a tutor was engaged to teach her at home. But when Lala Rupram learnt that it was not uncommon for tutors to seduce and elope with their girl pupils, he abandoned the idea of imparting her any education. Lakshmi raised a hue and cry but her callous father paid no heed to her remonstrations. And as for her looks—well, she's...'

'I've seen her myself,' the mason interrupted the watchman. 'Lightning flashes wherever she passes by. She's one among thousands. Dazzlingly beautiful!'

The watchman was condescending enough to accept the mason's verdict. He said, 'She was also a very good student in school. But the old fogy has ruined her. He is convinced that his daughter is the goddess Lakshmi and when she leaves the family it will spell his ruin. For fear of that, the Lala does not allow anybody to meet the girl, nor does he marry her off. He keeps a vigilant eye on her like a policeman. True, he fulfils all her wishes, indulges all her whims, he holds her in high regard, but he won't let her step out of the house. Lakshmi attained the age of sixteen, seventeen, eighteen, nineteen...what I mean is that the years passed by and nothing of note happened. Then she started quarrelling with everybody. She became very moody and irritable. She would abuse everybody, even fly at their throats. Then it came to a stage when she would lie sprawled on the floor and keep crying until late into the night. And then she started having fits.'

'What's her age now?' Govind asked, halting the watchman's flow of words.

'Nobody knows her exact age. But I reckon she must be about twenty-five or twenty-six.' The watchman gave a contemptuous twist to his lips. 'She has to have fits, a fully grown girl that she is,' he said. In fact, for the last six years or so when she has a fit she turns completely insane for an hour or to. She jumps, she utters the vilest of abuses, she cries and laughs unreasonably, she throws things around and breaks whatever she can lay her hands on. She even tears her clothes and stands there stark naked, beating her breasts and her thighs. 'You have kept me for yourself,' she wails. 'Eat me up, chew me up. Enjoy me!' The Lala stands her beatings, tolerates her abuses, but he won't relax his vigilance the least bit. Resting his head on his hand he keeps listening to her wordlessly. What a sordid life she leads! He is her father so he cannot sleep with her nor can be let her go. Oh, that is out of the question. I am past the age, otherwise I would have run away with her. And be damned to the consequences! As if I would have cared.' The watchman gave a bitter laugh and kept staring into the fire for a long time. Then he bit his lips and said, 'The old man should be branded alive with a red-hot steel rod. Then he should be tied hand and foot and shot dead.'

Govind was greatly distressed. He saw in the old watchman's eyes, the faint glimmerings of the brazier's dying fire.

Later, at midnight lying in his dingy room Govind kept thinking of Lakshmi, and in the dim candle light her image nebulously flitted past his eyes. Then in the pervading darkness he read in the dim candle light which seemed to be shedding waxen tears, the lines:

I love you more than life.
Take me away from here.
Otherwise, I will hang myself.

A question rose in Govind's mind. Was he the one and only man who had got so agitated on hearing this call? Or, there were others before him who had heard the same call and turned a deaf ear to it? But could one really ignore the call of a young girl in distress?

Ram Kumar

The Cherry Tree

The first thing that drew our attention, as we entered the gate, were the fruit hanging in thick clusters from the trees. They looked like plums. Instead of entering the house we ran towards the trees—many many trees laden with fruit. We jumped and jumped, but could not grasp any of these. They were just too high for us. Even I, the tallest of all the children, could not reach the fruit. Attracted by the noise, our elder sister came out.

'Please pluck them for us,' we all cried. 'What fruits are these? Apricots, peaches, plums?'

Sister leisurely walked towards us. Oh, how slowly she walked! On an occasion such as this she should have come running. But we were afraid that if we asked her to move faster she might walk back into the house instead of coming to us.

'What fruit are these?' she looked up at one of the trees.

'They look like apricots. Please pluck them for us quickly.'

'Some kind of wild berries perhaps,' she muttered.

'No, no, they are not berries,' we cried. 'Pluck one of them and we shall find out.'

Without taking further notice of us she just kept looking at the bunches of fruit hanging from the trees. Then she plucked one and, rolling it on her palm, examined it minutely. 'I don't know what it is,' she said. 'I have not seen such a fruit in the hills before.'

We gathered round her and tried to snatch away the fruit from her.

'No, no, you mustn't eat it. You never know. It could be poisonous. Let's first ask the gardener.' Then she turned to me. 'Do you hear me? None of you is going to pluck the fruit.' She slowly walked back into the house.

We lacked the guts to defy her and could do nothing except seethe with impatience. That evening we went round the garden counting the trees. There were other trees too but we had no eye for them. It was the first time in the hills that we had seen so many fruit trees in our own garden. All that we had come across on past occasions was a solitary apple or apricot or plum tree. To make up for it we would poach on the trees in the neighbouring orchards. But now we had so many trees in our own garden. It was veritable heaven. We felt elated.

Going into the house, Sister showed the fruit to Father. 'What fruit is this?' she asked. 'It's growing in our garden.'

'It's a cherry,' Father had promptly replied. 'But it isn't ripe yet.'

That it was a cherry made us all the happier. We had never seen a cherry tree before and now we had fifteen or sixteen of them right in our own garden! Nobody would object to our plucking fruit from them. We had certainly a right over these trees.

So carried away were we over the prospect that we even forgot to squabble over the allotment of rooms to us. Every year the question, who shall get which room—led to a crisis of sorts. Sometimes it even ended in blows. Harassed, Father would take a hand in beating one of us to take the fight out of us. But this time we accepted Sister's decision without raising an eyebrow. She placed our things where she wanted them to be and that was the end of it.

At night Sister came to my room. I was turning over the pages of a picture book.

'You haven't gone to sleep yet?'

'I'm not feeling sleepy,' I said. My younger brothers and sisters were by now fast asleep.

'I too can't sleep the first night in a new house.' She went up and stood at the window. The window was closed but one of its glass pane was broken, through which she looked out. Ever since her engagement two months ago she had withdrawn into herself. She would be married in the coming winter. The thought of her marriage thrilled us. But that she would not be living with us after her marriage also made us sad.

'Look!' she said turning round.

'What is it?'

'Come here,' she said, her face pressed against the window.

I went up and stood at her side. I peeped through the other glass pane but could see nothing in the dark except the mountain range in front. She slowly undid the window latch and put her head out through the window.

'What's it?' I asked again impatiently.

'Just look at the stars. The sky is full of them.'

I was disappointed. I thought she had seen some wild animal.

'One can see stars anywhere,' I said a bit peeved. 'What's so unusual about that?'

'They look so near as if I could pluck them just by raising my hand.'

I looked at the sky again. Like her I also felt as if the stars had descended close to me. 'The stars look near because we have come to a higher altitude.'

'No, that's not it. Last year when we were in Mussoorie they did not look so near. In Nainital...'

I lost interest in the subject.

'I have read somewhere that in this place the stars look very near,' she said.

A cold breeze was blowing into the room through the window. I returned to my bed and pulled the quilt over my body. Sister kept leaning out of the window for some time and then went away to her room. I again started looking at my picture book.

The next morning, immediately on waking up, we made for the cherry trees. 'Look, this cherry tree has started ripening,' one of us said looking up at a tree. Its fruits had turned yellow. Which tree bore big cherries and which small ones did not take us long to discover. A branch of one of the trees was bowed down with fruit. But though I jumped as high as I could the branch eluded my grasp. Then my younger brother went down on all fours and, climbing on to his back, I managed to pluck four cherries which I distributed among my brothers and sister. We fell short by one cherry and my younger sister started crying. I promised to give her half of my cherry but she refused to be placated. She threatened to complain to Sister and ran away in a huff.

After a while Sister appeared on the scene. 'Why did you pluck raw cherries?' she asked. 'Don't you know they can make you ill?'

She went away after admonishing us and we dared not repeat our pranks. If we ate cherries on the sly we knew what the consequence would be. Sister never beat us. She did not even scold us. She would just stop talking to us and this was punishment enough to keep us in check.

When we sat down to our meals the topic of cherries invariably came up for discussion.

'Now the cherries have started turning pink.'

'The ones on the upper branches are already red.'

'They should be ready in another two weeks,' Father would join in the discussion. 'Then you can eat them to your fill.'

'If they could have their way they would devour them raw,' Sister would say. 'They do not even go out these days. Always harping on the cherries!'

Mother was worried about Sister's marriage. Finishing her chores she would talk to Father about it who in turn would studiously jot down in his note book all the items required for the marriage—including the jewellery, the saris and other odds and ends. Sister's face would wear a sombre look.

With my pen knife I had carved the names of all of us on the trunks of the cherry trees, the idea being that the person whose name was carved on a particular tree would be exclusively entitled to the cherries from that tree. We would all stand under our allotted trees, praise our own tree and run down others'. Each one of us claimed that his cherries were ripening faster than the others.

One day a man came to our orchard and went round examining the cherry trees. He would stand under each tree and pulling the branches apart inspect the fruits right up to its top branch. He would pluck a cherry now from one tree now from another and nibble at it thoughtfully. He was moving in the orchard with complete abandon as if the house belonged to him. Standing together we watched him. The sight of him infuriated us. But we could not muster the courage to speak to him. After he had finished his job, he suddenly took notice of us and smiled. His two upper teeth were big and yellow.

'Do you children live in this bungalow?' he asked.

'Yes, this house is ours,' I said boldly.

He expressed a desire to meet Father and we took him to Father's room. We hated the look of his face and yet we were curious to know who he was.

When he was gone we asked Father about him.

'He is a contractor who has taken these cherry trees on contract,' Father explained to us. 'He has taken the orchard from the landlord for the season. From tomorrow his man will keep watch over the trees.'

We were not clear what a contract meant. We half understood and half misunderstood the meaning.

'We thought these trees belonged to us,' I told Father. 'How can an outsider lay claim to them when they are growing in our garden?'

Father laughed. 'We have taken the bungalow on rent,' he said. 'But the trees belong to the landlord and we have no claim on them.'

'Can't we pluck the cherries in that case?'

'No, they belong to the contractor. How can you pluck something which does not belong to you?'

That night the cherries did not figure in our talk at all. Even if one of us uttered the word absent-mindedly the glum faces of the others immediately silenced him. I could not sleep till late into the night. I peered at the garden through the window. The small cherry trees seemed to be drooping as if they had gone to sleep. Until yesterday they belonged to us but not any more. I wanted to ask Sister many things about these trees but she did not come to my room that night.

The next day the contractor came, accompanied by an old man. They had brought with them bundles of rope, old broken canisters and bamboo mats. With the mats they improvised a make-shift hut at the other end of the orchard. They spread a rug in the hut and the old man placed a hookah in a corner. We watched them at work from a distance. We were surprised at the speed with which they had raised the hut by joining two mats together. Every now and then they would look at us and smile but we made no response. My younger brother said that they were nothing short of enemies for they had usurped our land and pitched a tent on it.

The canisters were filled with small stones and hung on the trees of the ends of ropes. The other ends of the ropes were tied to wooden pegs outside the tent. When the old man shook the rope the stones inside the canisters rattled, filling the garden with a raucous sound. All this added to our curiosity.

The contractor went away after making all arrangements, leaving the old man behind who sat on a stone near the tent smoking a hookah. He seemed to have a friendlier look than the contractor whom we had found rather forbidding. Soon we approached him and he made us sit down near him. On our asking him, he explained that the canisters had been hung from the trees to scare away the birds. The birds, he told us, specially the nightingales pecked at the cherries and they turned rotten. If these birds were not kept away they would damage the entire crop o fruit.

'But why haven't you tied the canisters to all the trees?' I asked.

'That is not necessary,' he said. 'One canister can do the 'job' for three or four trees.'

'Will you sleep here at night?'

'Yes. Otherwise some miscreants may poach at the cherries.'

His hookah had aroused our small sister's curiosity. 'What's this?' she asked.

We laughed. 'It's his cigarette,' my younger brother said.

Gradually we became accustomed to the old man's presence. And also the 'Ha! Ha!' which resounded in the air at regular intervals to the accompaniment of the rattling of the canisters. The branches of the trees had begun to bend under the weight of the fruit and some of them had bent so low that I had only to jump and three or four cherries would come within my reach. But the old man was very vigilant and his eyes would keep roving over all the tree. So I could never gather enough courage to pluck the cherries.

Every second or third day Mother would send the old man a glass of tea and he would reciprocate by offering us a couple of ripe cherries. But to climb one of the trees and pluck cherries from it with our own hands of which we had dreamt in the beginning remained only a dream. It gladdened our hearts when we found a bird eating a fallen cherry without the old man's being aware of it. If we could have our way, we would have allowed the birds to eat all the cherries in the orchard. But the birds were in the habit of making a noise while eating the fruit. After eating a cherry or two they would hop across to another bough, twittering happily and the old man would immediately hear them. He would pull the rope and a canister would start rattling.

All day long Sister sat on a chair under a tree, knitting a pullover for one of us. This time in her summer vacation she had not opened any of her college books. In other years she used to keep poring over one book or the other. Only a few days ago the results of her Intermediate Examination had been declared and she had passed in the First Division. She wanted to continue her studies but Mother was in a hurry to marry her off.

There was a mountain stream flowing at some distance from our bungalow where we used to go every second or third day to bathe. Sometimes we went to the bazaar or to the cinema or on a picnic. As time passed we would think up many other diversions. But this year Sister did not join us in our activities. During our sojourn in the hills usually became very chummy with us. At night when we slipped into our cosy beds she would entertain us with stories. In the evenings she would take us out on long walks. As for picnics, we would lose count of them—for she was very generous in arranging them for us. This summer, however, she remained cooped up in her room most of the time. And if she went anywhere she went alone. She ignored all Mother's remonstrations.

One morning, as we woke up we heard many voices coming from the orchard. I lay in my bed for some time wondering what all the noise was about. I was about to get out of bed to look out of the window when Sister walked in.

'What's this racket going on?' I asked her.

'Those people have come.'

'Which people?'

'The contractor's men. They have come to gather the cherries,' she said.

I ran out of the house. The contractor's men had climbed up the cherry trees, carrying buckets with them. They were plucking cherries with both hands and dropping them into the buckets. They would lean over to reach out for a distant branch or make a creaking sound when they bent too low. People were scampering noisily around the whole orchard.

We slowly went round the orchard, stopping under each tree to look up at the men at work. It appeared as if today was the day of our ultimate defeat.

There were heaps of cherries littered under each tree. My younger sister bent down and picked up a bunch. Quickly my younger brother snatched it away from her and threw it on the ground under the tree. 'Have you forgotten what Sister said?'

'Yes, I remember, she said that no one would eat even a single cherry from here.'

Sitting near the tent the contractor was sorting out cherries with the help of other men and putting them in crates. Many empty wooden crates lay nearby. All the men were attending to their work with great speed. Noticing us standing near by watching the operations, the contractor offered us a handful of cherries each but we shook our heads.

We kept strolling in the orchard, in no mood to go anywhere else. Slowly the trees were being denuded of their fruit. The canisters, it was apparent, had done their job; there was no need to rattle them any more. The nightingales and the other birds kept wheeling over the trees without making any effort to descend on them.

'What's that lying over there?' My younger sister pointed at some object lying under a tree. From a distance we could not make out what the object was. But as we drew nearer and examined the object closely we found it was a dead nightingale. Blood had congealed on its neck. We kept gazing at it for sometime. Then I took it by its leg and shook it. It showed no sign of life.

'How did it die?'

'It seems someone has hit it with a stone.'

'These people must have done it.'

'That's why no nightingale is sitting on the trees.'

We heartily cursed the contractor and his men. We were already angry with these men and the killing of the bird had kindled our desire for revenge. We quickly thought of many ways of wreaking vengeance but each one seemed to have one flaw or the other and ultimately we abandoned this idea of revenge. Fearing that some dog or cat might carry away the nightingale we dug a hole and buried her in it.

That day Sister did not come into the garden. She did not see the dead bird nor the cherries being gathered and packed into crates. She said she could not bear the sight of cherries being plucked from the trees.

'Flowers, plants and fruits have life in them. Plucking them is as sinful as killing animals,' she used to tell us.

The men kept at their job till late into the night. Then a truck came in which they loaded all the crates and went away as soon as the truck drove off.

Suddenly a hush fell over the orchard. All that was left were the bare trees denuded of cherries. A sharp wind had risen and the branches swayed in the wind as if they were gasping for breath. Leaves lay thickly strewn under the trees. Some branches lay forlorn under the trees. They had snapped while the plucking operations were on. The evening seemed eerily silent and the trees seemed to hold a terror for us.

At dinner we kept talking about the day's happenings. We also narrated the story of the dead nightingale to Sister. But she did not take much interest in our talk. Not a word did she say. It seemed as if she was not listening to us. She ate very little.

That night I could not sleep for a long time. I could not apply my mind to reading either. My younger brother and sister, tired after the day's exertions, had fallen asleep the moment their heads touched the pillow. I was also tired and my body ached, but unlike them, although I tried hard, I could not sleep.

Then I went and stood by the window. Suddenly I saw a host of stars in the sky. They appeared to be quite near me. Our house was at a height of a mere six thousand feet while the stars were millions of miles away. Then how was it that they appeared to be so near to us? I was musing over the matter when suddenly I saw a shadowy figure under a tree. And then I discovered that it was Sister. It seemed she had also been lying awake like me.

I tip-toed out of the room. She was strolling under the cherry tree, the end of her sari trailing at her feet.

'You haven't gone to sleep?' she asked me without looking at me.

I was startled by her voice. Did she think I had materialized out of nowhere?

'I couldn't sleep,' I said in a faint voice.

The leaves rustled under her feet as she walked, breaking the silence of the night. The wind had risen.

'It's very dark tonight,' I said.

'Yes, we are having dark nights these days.'

Sometimes she raised her eyes to look at the trees through whose branches could see the stars. They were shining so brightly.

'Tonight the stars look so near,' I said.

She did not reply.

Markandaya

The Swan Flies Alone

Up to that point they had all been together. But now they had separated and no two were together. All the ten were in different fields, scratching their calves and gasping for breath.

'I've spent my life trying to knock some sense into him but he has remained a blockhead. Just let me lay my hands on him today I'll give him the thrashing of his life.' Baba wiped the blood from his bruised knee and burst out laughing.

Bhagnu Singh, his sides splitting with laughter, came over from the nearby field.

'Has he been caught, the idiot? O lord... brother. There's no sight of them.' They ran a few steps with alacrity but seeing Baba motionless, they stopped in their tracks. Both the men just looked around.

A dark rainy night and a steady drizzle.

'What can we do? We have lost our way. Don't know where we are.'

'Climb up some mound and look around. My knee hurts.'

'Did you see? The way the old man threw his hookah and ran?'

'O brother, don't talk of it.' Magnu laughed uproariously.

Then they heard loud singing:

The soul flies alone. This body will not last
Rub, wash, bathe, eat.

Do all you will,
This body....

Enveloped in darkness and fear the entire group gathered again in that small ten-*bigha* field. Their faces were not visible in the darkness but their stomachs were bloated with laughter. Just then making a sound as though swallowing spittle, he came up and started laughing.

'I made a mistake, brothers. How should I have known it was a woman? I thought it was one of you.'

Magnu said, 'You are becoming bull-headed. Can't you tell a man from a woman now?'

'No, no, she stumbled and was about to fall and I clutched blindly at the figure in the dark. And when I realised I just froze. Just then the old man gave me a powerful lathi blow. I ran for my life.' He bent and felt his leg. Thorns of prickly had got embedded in the entire length of his leg.

'Make him walk between us,' Bawa said.

Magnu said, 'Anyway, you touched a woman at least. Lucky man. It's not in your destiny to have a wife.'

People call him Hansa. Black as pitch, extremely strong, his potato-nose and pea like eyes hem in the expansiveness of his personality. The hair on his chest makes one think of dense rank grass growing on unclaimed marshy land. A knee-length dhoti and a two-yard long upper cloth made of coarse cloth and worn round the waist form his attire. Actually, he has also a thick *kurta* but that he has reserved for special occasions. When he comes out wearing this *kurta* the street urchins mark him out for special attention and chase him as if he were a bear man.

'Hansa Dada has become a bridegroom, a bridegroom!' the children cling to his legs like tiny rats. One tugs at his tuft, another pokes his whole finger up his ear and still another tickles his nose with a thin sliver of wood. A more enterprising child among them goes for his flabby protruding breast-like chest and cries 'Hansa mother! Hansa mother!' In the meanwhile a thick stick appears from somewhere which is held across Hansa's shoulder. He runs his fingers along the stick and sings in the style of a maestro. 'Is that enough?' he asks ending his performance.

'No, Dada, the other one!' the children cry clinging to his legs or swinging on his arms. Then he starts singing devotedly, 'Hansa (the swan or soul) flies alone. The body doesn't last for ever...'

That day returning to the village at midnight Hansa went straight to Baba's courtyard. He lit the lamp and began plucking out the wild berry thorns from his calves. The marks made by the thorns looked like chilblains.

Baba said, 'Where will you go to knead flour and beat *rotis* into shape at this late hour? Eat here with me.' Looking at the thorn marks on his legs Baba felt that he was having a glimpse of Hansa' real life for the first time. He had land of his own and a nice house to live in but for want of a life he kept wandering around like a wild cat. Baba got up and began plucking the remaining thorns from Hansa's calves.

He is afflicted with night blindness hence he does not stir out of the village at night. It was the attraction of the wrestling bouts at Majgaon that had dragged him there this evening. Baba was the king-pin of the wrestlers so naturally he had to go. They sat out after sunset and darkness and gathered. It was a five-mile long journey and Hansa was with a party of ten. His legs collided with others. His companies abused him and pushed him back to the rear. Hansa does not mind abuses. He is accustomed to them and even relishes them when they come from the village elders, regarding them as blessings. Sometimes he provokes just for the pleasure of being abused.

He was walking behind the others. They passed a village and Hansa lost his way in the twists and turns of its lanes and was left behind. An old man was sitting outside his hut warming his hookah. His young wife came out on some errand. Seeing ten people going in single file she moved aside. Just before Hansa came along she moved to get past him and Hansa's feet collided against hers in the dark. She stumbled and almost fell into Hansa's arms. She screamed. Throwing away his hookah, the old man ran brandishing his lathi. But Hansa slipped away. The old man's second blow fell on his wife's back. Hansa ran and so did his companions till all of them were lost in the darkness of the night, their eyes bringing them back to the right path. But Hansa who suffered from night blindness ran through the ravines stumbling and falling.

Baba was pulling the thorns from Hansa's legs. Hansa again focussed his pea-like eyes on the bear-like hair on his legs. What his eyes failed to see his hands were able to detect. Repeatedly, the incident flashed before his eyes. What would she be thinking, the poor woman? He started gazing at the Baba.

'A terrible mistake I made, brother. Lucky we got away somehow. Otherwise what would people have said? I was dying with shame that you were also there and saw it all.'

'Oh, what are you saying, Hansa?'

'Just that they would have lampooned you for the company you keep. It's a small village, the size of a boat. Word would have gone round quickly and people would have laughed.'

Hansa was not given to thinking too much but today these ideas kept nagging at his mind. If brother wanted he could surely...

The old lady came out with *puries* on a plate. Hansa got up flustered. He was seeing her after a long time. If it hadn't been night she wouldn't have come out. He greeted her. He was just going to take the plate from her hands when she said in jest, 'Out on a dacoity, son, and got your legs riddled with thorns?'

'Don't ask me anything, sister-in-law,' Hansa began but before he could say more Baba chipped in, 'Hansa almost got it in the neck today. Lucky he escaped. Otherwise he was in for a severe beating. He seized a woman...'

'Now stop sowing wild oats and get married. Life is worth living as long as the body is strong. Without that you'd go begging for food. Why don't you ask your brother? He finds matches even for the deaf and dumb, even for cats and dogs. But he doesn't seem to have a thought for you in his mind. You have everything—land, house, everything.'

Baba said nothing. His wife was about to disappear into the house when he asked her to bring some mustard oil.

Hansa sat at the head of Baba's bed with the bowl of oil.

'Massage your feet, Hansa. It'll give you relief.'

'Wonderful, brother! Ever seen me oil my body, Baba?' Hansa leant over Baba's fat thigh.

'These thighs of yours have drunk maunds and maunds of oil,' Hansa laughed. 'Some people become wrestlers just by rubbing oil on their thighs.'

Baba lay silent. The wick of the lanterns hanging from a peg on the wall, burnt low and had started smoking. Its chimney had turned black.

Sister-in-law's words were still ringing in Hansa's ears—as long as the body is strong... Turning on his side he felt the place where the old man's lathi had struck. 'I didn't do it on purpose,' he muttered. 'It just happened, I don't even look at a woman. It's this accursed night blindness of mine.'

Rolling his eyes he peered into the darkness but saw nothing. Everything was grey and foggy.

Frost or hail, after work, Hansa must visit Baba. They talk sometimes about politics, sometimes about the Ramayana and the Mahabharata. But most of all he enjoys talking about 'Gandhi Mahatma'. Someone had put it into his head that the Mahatma was a divine incarnation.

There was nobody in the courtyard that day. It was evening and a brazier was burning near the Baba's bed. The cattle stood listlessly, their heads buried in their managers. Rain pattered down. Kalua, the dog had dug up the soaked earth with his paws and lay curled in it. When the ticks harassed him beyond endurance, he moaned and scratched his neck with his paws. Just then a man, clothes drenched in the rain, came in, pushing his bicycle through the slush. When he came in and stood his cycle against the wall, Hansa greeted him: 'Jai Hind, Ganesh Babu!'

'Jai Hind, brother Hansa, Jai Hind!'

He pulled out a bundle of handbills from his bag and placed it in front of Baba while Hansa sat down next to Baba! Baba read a handbill and looked up. 'It can't be done. Not in the rainy season.'

Hansa did not understand a thing. Overcome by curiosity he said, 'What's it all about, brother?'

'One Sushila Behen wants to give a public talk on Gandhiji. It's a notice from the District Committee.'

'What does the notice say?' Hansa gaped at Baba. 'Just read it out to me, brother. Will there be singing too?'

'Yes, the same song—'Wake up, you, who wear the Gandhi cap!'

Hansa took down his hand drum from the peg on the wall and hung it round his neck. Then he strung a tattered tri-colour on his stick. He beat twice on the drum—'Wake up, brother, the man with the Gandhi cap has come,' he sang. Then he banged on the drum... dharam—dharam—dham-dham—dharam—dharam—dham—dham!

Within minutes fifty children assembled there with more coming. Hansa's procession started. 'So sing Susheela's party, it's valiant Jwahar's story.'

'You boys, big and small, shout, the whole lot of you...
'Gandhi Baba ki Jai!'

And then again—'Wake up, brother...!'

Hansa's drum beat ceaselessly. In a moment he seemed to have woken up the entire village. People poured in from all directions. The children knew nothing of Gandhi Baba. Hansa was their leader. One boy walked ahead, waving the flag. 'Speak up, speak up! Victory to brother Hansa!'

Some said 'Jai!' others 'chai!' and peals of laughter rose on all sides.

Some old men flaring their nostrils and inhaling snuff twirled their spindles and chuckled, 'The lout has finally found something to keep him busy. Let him become a follower of Gandhi Baba. At least it may get him a low-caste Congress wench. Gandhi has no scruples. He doesn't mind eating from the hands of tanners and cobblers.'

Hansa had no time for them. Babu Saheb's wooden cot and Baburam's shiny bedsheet must be procured.

Baba sits silent. Gradually the whole village converges and, packs the courtyard to overflowing. Darkness spreads thickly like a sheet. The rain patters down. Four lanterns have been lighted.

'Well, you've dragged all those people here in this rain and slush. And created a fine tumult. But where will Susheela stay? And what about her food?'

'Don't worry—we'll arrange it when she comes. My house is practically empty. And don't worry about food either—I'll manage,' Hansa said as he came out.

He walked with extreme caution, step by step. Everything looked so foggy to him, as if greyness had seeped into his eyes and he could do nothing about it. Led by a child he managed to come up to Babu Saheb's courtyard. He hauled the heavy cot on to his head. Staggering under its weight he crawled back to Baba's courtyard.

Baba was angry. 'The wretch is bent upon killing himself,' he said.

Hansa was very pleased to hear that Susheelaji had arrived. Sitting down next to Baba he drank in all that she said.

She was sitting right in front of Hansa. Although the lantern was burning he could not see how she looked.

'The voice is firm. And this fresh sugarcane-like smell—where is this coming from?'

Hansa was lost. The song she had sung a year ago: 'Wake up, my beloved, the Gandhi cap ones have come!' throbbed on his lips. Dark complexioned, she was tall as slim, with rough, ungroomed hair and bright eyes. How beautifully she sang. Hansa thought.

The *kirtan* started. After that Susheelaji and others spoke and then congregation broke up singing, 'India is uneducated, day by day it grovels in humiliation.' Hansa sat on, lost. The clanging of the cymbals and the twang of the tambourine echoed in his ears. Susheela's sharp voice kept piercing his heart and he kept reliving the evening's happenings. Those eyes of hers—what couldn't they make you do! His veins tingled with blood rushing through them. Suddenly the words, 'Victory to Gandhi Mahatma' fell on his ears. 'Victory, Victory' he repeated in a resounding voice.

The night has advanced. In Hansa's house preparations are on to make *puries*. The flour is being kneaded. Vegetables are being chopped. The fire is burning. But who is to bring the clarified butter from the store room at the back of the house? Hansa wanders around the house, his eyes chasing Susheela's voice. Susheelaji avoids Hansa's gaze but soon her eyes get entangled in the dense jungle of Hansa's hairy chest. How manly he is, she thinks.

But for Hansa she is no more than a shadow endowed with everything except form—she has a sweet languorous voice and the smell of fresh fruit on trees. He is very happy. What a difference the presence of a woman in the house makes! How good one feels! His mind is occupied with these thoughts when the ghee is asked for. He gets up, but bumps into the cot and

The Swan Flies Alone   179

falls down. Susheelaji rushes up and helps him to his feet. He feels very embarrassed.

Damn these eyes! He hastily gets to his feet.

Susheelaji keeps hold of his hand. 'Not hurt, are you?' she asks.

Rubbing his eyes he smiles, the down on his arms tingling and his heart pounding.

'Hansa Dada has night blindness,' someone says.

'Night blindness? Then tell me where the ghee is. I'll go with you,' Susheelaji says.

Vishwamitra's hand on Maneka's shoulder, the dark monsoon and a night gentle drizzle. A cold breeze blows.

The two cross the courtyard, getting wet in the rain. 'Want a lantern?' a voice asks.

'But you have only one. We can manage without it.'

The dark storehouse. Both grope in the dark. Hansa says something. Susheela hears something else. Eyes see something. Hands go in quest of something. Neither knows what is where.

In the dark the seeing eye is the same as the unseeing eye. Both want support. Sometimes he stumbles, sometimes she. And both become seeing—endowed with divine vision.

In the morning to the barking of dogs the caravan advanced. The bullocks' bells jingled. Cicadas trilled. Baba picked up his ancient fifty-six spokes bamboo umbrella and proceeded towards the village pond.

On the way he met Magnu Singh. 'Well well, Hansa's boat has struck port,' Magnu laughed.

'Why, what happened?'

'Asking me, brother? You should know. The news had spread through the village last night. That wretch is not fit to cross anyone's threshold. They all say,' Foist some widow or tart on him to help him keep straight.' They held a panchayat at Babu Saheb's house last night. They decided that no more meetings will be held in this village and no female will be allowed to come here and speechify. Our daughters and daughters-in-law may be led astray. The fact is that the Raja Saheb is fighting against the Congress behind the scenes. Babu Saheb supports him. He has not been able to express opposition openly out of fear of you. Now he has got a chance.'

'What chance?' Baba asked testily.

Magnu moved closer to Baba. 'Last night Hansa turned the tables on us,' he said.

'What do you mean?'

'The truth. No food was served. When it got very late Banga went in with a lantern and then rushed out and spread the news all round the village. Now he has gone to the riverbank with her luggage on his head to put her in the boat.'

Baba walked on silently. He could not stand gossip but for some reason he wanted to laugh. Then he heard Hansa in the distance signing in his heavy voice:

My sister-in-law has wrought her magic,
She has cast her spell of Brahma, she has won over Vishnu,
She makes Shivji dance to her tune...

Baba stopped. Hansa approached slowly. The darkness was thinning. Hansa was scared. How am I to face brother, how...?

They stood silent for a while, Baba saw Hansa had some *khaddar* clothes in his hands, but his eyes were glued to the ground.

'Hansa!' Baba said in a harsh voice. 'You have reached the point of no return. There is no coming back, you must know.'

'Brother you can cut me to pieces but how can this happen?'

Hansa was about to go when Baba said, 'Go home and come straight back with your things. Today we'll catch fish and we shall cook it by the abutment of this field.'

'All right, brother,' Hansa went away wiping his button eyes.

The village was in the grip of election fever. Babu Saheb was pitted against the Congress tooth and nail. His men tore up the opposite party's posters hung on his trees. Pro-Congress farmers were called and threatened. Their lands, they were warned, would go and their animals be carried away. They alluded to Hansa's and Susheela's story as an example of moral corruption. The Congressmen have no code, no creed. Gandhi is an oil crusher, they said.

Hansa has become a full-fledged Congress volunteer. Khadi kurta-dhoti and the tri-colour fluttering on a long lathi held aloft. A bugle hanging at his side he goes about distributing handbills with the message of Bapu.

'Do everything as Babu Saheb says. Stuff yourself with sweets in Raja Saheb's tent. Take money and food from him, Ride in his car. But remember the Congress of election symbol. When you reach there forget about what you have eaten. The Congress fights for your freedom. No more ejection from your lands. No more untouchability. People's rule. No shout at the top of your voice, 'Victory to Gandhi Mahatma!' Victory! Victory!

Every house, every throat rang with Susheela's sweet songs. The village children hovered around Hansa Dada, carrying coloured flags made from newspapers.

Ramlila was round the corner. The roles of Ram and Lakshman were assigned to men belonging to Babu Saheb's party. But they could find no one to play Ravana. The belief was that the man playing Ravana invariably died an untimely death. Nobody was prepared to take the role.

Baba was supervising the Dussehra arrangements. How could Hansa see anything going wrong when Baba was at the helm of affairs? And especially when Susheela was to round off the function with a speech! Hansa kept wondering how to got about this business. Suddenly the children started clapping and surrounded Hansa Dada. They put Ravana's black robes round his face. Hansa got into the spirit of it. Flourishing his sword he thundered, 'I'm Ravana. Where's that scoundrel Rama?'

A child wrenched off the tri-colour from his stick and draped it round Ravana's head. People laughed uproariously. Someone from among the crowd shouted, 'Victory to Gandhi Mahatma!'

Facing the crowd, Ravana began to orate, 'Brothers, Rama was a king. Now look, no low caste man is ever allowed to be Rama. They are only fit to play the role of Rakshasas. Birahim, Kalu, Bhulai, Feddar—all are members of our Party. This is the people's war. Go all out! Attack!' And flinging his arms about and waving his hands in the air, Hansa plunged forward, his army of demons following him. The peasant lads wearing monkey masks and brandishing maces, joined the people's army. Rama was left sitting there alone. The recitation of the Ramayana stopped. Tiwari cried himself hoarse to maintain order but who listened?

'Victory to Gandhi Mahatma! Victory to Hansa Dada!'

Baba's sides were splitting with laughter. He couldn't speak. Seeing the black-painted faces of the demons and the tri-colours in their hands, people threw the garlands meant for Rama's head on Hansa.

At this juncture Susheelaji plunged into the crowd with the swiftness of an arrow. 'Who's doing Ravana?' she cried. 'Is this what the tri-colour is for?' She ripped the mask off Hansa's face and stood aghast on seeing him.

'So is this how a volunteer behaves?' she cried. 'You are dishonouring our flag. Stop this nonsense and perform the Ramlila properly.'

The people returned to their places. Baba watched silently. Holding her bag, Susheelaji came up and stood next to him.

The Rama-Ravana battle continued. The drums boomed. Coloured arrows flew ceaselessly. But Ravana refused to die. He just wouldn't oblige them. The couplet announcing his death was sung repeatedly while Vyas prompted again and again, 'Lie down and go to sleep!' But who listened? Why should Hansa's army be routed?

Just then Lakshman stumbled and fell and his crown slipped from his head. Running hither and thither, Rama felt dizzy and started vomiting. A cry went up, 'The people's army has won!' Then another cry went up, 'Hansa Dada's party will also bag the votes in just this way!'

Day and night now Susheelaji went about playing her tambourine and in the night stayed at Hansa's house.

The people of the opposite party had letters sent out. Susheelaji must be called. She is creating a bad impression on the people.

Two days before polling she was sent a notice that she was violating the Mahatma's ideals and hence was forbidden to do party work.

She greeted the notice with a laugh. God had separated her from her husband and now these false followers of the Mahatma were trying to separate her from the people.

The tambourine jangled louder and her singing became sharper.

There were just two days left for the election. Susheelaji fell ill. She was staying at Hansa's house. Her body was burning with fever but she would not allow anyone to come near her. When Hansa returned at night she would ask him to sing. Hansa would immediately start singing his favourite song:

The soul flies,
This body will not last...

The song over, he would recount the day's developments and then she would rest her head on his bushy chest.

Election day arrived but Susheelaji was too ill to leave her bed. Peasants passed by in bunches shouting slogans of victory. She would toss restlessly in bed. Hansa would try to stop her but she would get out of her bed to meet the peasants. Baba reasoned with her but she wouldn't listen to him.

She was carried to the polling booth in a palanquin. While she was sitting under a tree there her head reeled and she fainted.

The voting went on. The peasants ate in the Raja Saheb's camp, drove to their booths in his vehicles and cast their votes for the Congress. They will win self-rule, they will win freedom, they all thought thus.

There was a heavy downpour in the afternoon. Sushilaji got drenched while making for shelter. Baba put her in the palanquin and sent her back home. The voting continued.

Hansa was working with the fury of a demon. When the thought of Sushila oppressed him, he would try to suppress it and work all the harder. Very few votes went to the Raja Saheb. Evening fell. The Raja's camp was filled with defeated workers. The very sight of them made Hansa angry. Sushila was in his thoughts all the time.

'Brother, something more must be done,' Hansa said to Baba.

'First let me go away from here,' Baba said, catching Hansa's hint.

Armed with scythes, about thirty people planted themselves outside Raja's tent. Nobody knew why they were standing there. Hansa blew his bugle and the big tent came crashing to the ground in the twinkling of an eye. A roar went up. The peasants returned home shouting slogans.

Susheelaji developed pneumonia. Her breathing became laboured. Baba sat at her side day and night while Hansa moved heaven and earth but to no avail. Again and again she uttered Mahatma's name, asked Hansa to sing his song and then closed her eyes.

The election result was announced and the leaders flocked to her, seeking forgiveness, but she turned away her face, as if saying, I know your dirty tricks.

Hansa got up and went out of the room.

In the end, one day, Susheela stopped breathing. Cries of grief broke out all around. Even children wept. Hansa stuck the tri-colour on the staff meant for breaking green leaves for goats. Holding the pole aloft, he blew his bugle. And then he started laughing. His laughter struck terror into people's hearts but he kept laughing.

To this day, Hansa knows only three words—'Ganni Mahatma,' 'Jawaharlal' and 'People's army.' Children mob him the same as ever. But now he cannot lift the huge wooden bed. Yes, he watches those who can and laughs and laughs for hours.

His fields are overgrown with grass. His house has crumbled. But the pole with the tattered tri-colour and the bugle Susheela gave him still hang from a wall. Sometimes he goes around cleaning up all the lanes in the village.

When freedom came he got money. He was a political sufferer. He laughed holding the wad of notes in his hands. One by one he hung up the notes on the walls of the village.

Twice, people took him to Agra and put him in the mental hospital. But after a few days the village lanes echoed again with: 'The soul flies alone...'

Even now he sometimes swears he will procure freedom. The veins in his flushed face stand out. Blowing his bugle, he wanders through the fields of paddy, sugarcane and maize and sings:

The soul flies alone...

Shekhar Joshi

The Miller of Kosi

Time hung heavy on Gosai Singh. Even the *chillum* failed to divert him. Getting up from under the shade of the *mehal* tree, he once again went into the mill-house. The funnel was still one-fourth full of unground wheat. Bending over, he shoved his hand into it and lazily turned over the grain. Then he scraped the flour from the millstone and collected it in a small heap.

Before coming out he again looked into the funnel. The upper millstone was revolving with a slow grating sound but the level of the grain had not decreased. The door of the mill-house was low and he had to stoop to go through it. A white film of flour had settled over his head and arms.

Leaning against the pillar he swore under his breath. Not even a maund since morning—and the sun had gone so far in the sky.

The situation was indeed exasperating. It was the month of June and not a cloud in the sky. In other years the transplanting of paddy used to be over by this time. But this year the brooks were dry. There was no water to irrigate the fields and even the seed beds were withering. The water-mills near the small streams had stopped working long ago. Gosai was more fortunate. His mill was on the Kosi river. Even so, its pace was lazier than that of a sluggish pack-pony.

In the nether part of the mill the churner emitted a feeble

murmur as it cut through the water. Even the cowherds churning curds could make a louder sound. Pulling up his army trousers over his knees, Gosai lowered himself into the stream, keeping a watchful eye for holes to plug. Every drop of water was precious in these days of drought. By putting up a small embankment upstream he had been able to divert the channel towards his mill. His job done, he waded back through the water to the mill.

In the distance he saw a man, a bundle of grain poised on his head, coming towards the mill.

'Hey, listen,' Gosai shouted. 'You won't get your turn here not for the next two days, anyway. My hands are full. Better try Umaid Singh's mill.'

The man looked at Gosai hopefully and pitching his voice higher, shouted back, 'I'm badly in need of flour. Can't you serve me out of turn?'

Gosai smiled. The fellow shouted as if the mill was making a deafening noise. 'Everyone is in a desperate hurry,' he said, keeping his voice low. 'Try your luck elsewhere.'

Sitting down in the shade of the tree, Gosai raked up the embers of a dying fire, got his hookah going and began to puff at it.

The grinding stone went round and round with a monotonous drone. The grain trickled down the chute, making a pecking sound. The churner coughed wheezily.

There were no other sounds. The water of the Kosi flowed sleepily. Could ankle-deep water make any noise? The rocks lay naked, exposed to the sky. The birds were silent in the afternoon heat.

Gosai thought that he should not have turned away the man so soon. When he saw so many bags piled up. The man would have gone away himself. And it would have given Gosai an opportunity to talk to someone.

At times, his loneliness got on his nerves. Not the loneliness of the Kosi, but the other loneliness which had seeped into his very being. He had nobody to call his own. Not even a pet animal. Had life any meaning for a man who had no home, no wife, no children?

He rolled down the ends of his army trousers. They had got wet in the water and their wetness pleasantly tickled his skin, making his lips curl in a faint smile. These trousers brought back memories... in fact they had bequeathed him a legacy of loneliness. What was the use of recalling these things? But he could not forget the Havildar's trousers.

Havildar Dharam Singh had come to his village wearing military trousers. Smart, laundered, with razor-sharp creases. The ambition to wear such trousers had lured Gosai into the army. When he left the army, after long years of service, he had brought his loneliness with him along with the trousers.

Other memories too were linked with them. For instance that time when he had come home on leave...

It was his first annual leave. He was smartly rigged out in his regimental uniform and a pointed cap with a crest of crossed spears rested on his head at a jaunty angle. The news of his arrival in the village had spread like fire in a pine forest. Young and old, all had come to greet him. His uncle's room was packed with visitors and a red and blue striped rug had to be spread in the courtyard to accommodate the callers. But the girl Gosai's eyes were searching for was not there.

Lachma did turn up the following day, from the village across the brook, on the pretext of looking for her buffalo calf.

At first Gosai feared he would never be able to meet her. The boys of the village would not leave him alone. He had become the cynosure of their eyes. The village headman, Narsingh, had remarked that even Sohnia's son had started wearing his tattered cap at an angle. Day and night, these urchins followed him around like so many lost kittens, hoping for a cigarette or a chat.

One day with great difficulty he managed to get away from his fans. He had seen Lachma going towards the forest and telling the boys that he was in search of wild game, he managed to get rid of them and followed her there. Far from the village, her head resting on Gosai's knees, Lachma ate ripe juicy *kafal* fruit. Gosai playfully squeezed her hands and the blood red juice of the fruit squirted on to his trousers.

'Never mind!' Lachma had said. 'Leave your trousers with me and I'll have a shirt made for myself out of them.' Then she had burst into laughter.

How long ago it seemed Gosai could not remember what he had said 'I'll get a velvet blouse made for you, my pet', or something to that effect.

Then Gosai had sounded her father through an intermediary for Lachma's hand. But her father had rejected him, saying, 'How can I give my daughter to a man who lives in distant lands and whose life hangs by a thread before the barrel of a gun?'

Did anyone buy a velvet blouse for Lachma? Did Ramy, who had come to marry her from a village across the hill?

This he had learnt from Kishan Singh, a sepoy of his own unit. Standing in front of the Quarter Master's store, one sad winter evening, Kishan Singh was explaining why he had had to have his leave extended. 'Ram Singh of our village insisted on my joining his marriage party. Friend, he has got a fine wife. She's beautiful too. Real fireworks! And very cheerful by nature. Lachma or some such name. You must have seen her. She hails from near your village.'

It was Rum Day. Normally Gosai Singh did not go beyond half a peg of rum. But that evening he took two pegs and made a spectacle of himself. Next day the Havildar Major had pulled him up. 'That bloody Adjutant!' Gosai swore as he recalled that evening of long ago.

Vividly he remembered the day before he was due to leave his village to join his unit. He has sought out Lachma. 'I swear by Ganganathji,' Lachma had said. 'I'll do as you order me.' there were tears in her eyes.

He thought grimly that if he ever chanced to meet Lachma he would ask her to atone for her sin before Ganganathji. False oaths before the gods always brought misfortune. But he did not know if he would ever meet Lachma again.

Even while serving in the army he did not once visit his village. Not did he ask anyone about Lachma. Naik Gosai Singh's name was always on the list of those who asked for voluntary transfers from one military station to another. Fifteen years he had stayed away.

Then a few months ago he had returned to his village for good. After fifteen years' service his name had been put on the reserve list. When he had joined the army his hair had been black; now it was pepper and salt. He had not married. Had there been anyone here in this solitude today. Gosai would have told him his life's story. How many words he had read in that book, how much he had seen, heard, experienced.... But this shade of the tree by the burning sands of the river, this sound of the mill and Gosai pulling at his pipe! No one in sight all around! Everything altogether empty, motionless, desolate...

As his gaze wandered he saw a woman approaching along the footpath, a bundle of grain on her head. Gosai thought he ought to call out to her to go back. Why force her to walk all this way along the slippery moss-covered stones of the Kosi and then send her back! But he was fed up of arguing with people from a distance at the top of his voice. So he didn't shout to her. She had now left the field-path and reached the road by the river.

Noting a change in the sound of the mill, Gosai went in. The grain in the funnel was almost gone. He emptied a small bag into it and shut off the cock. The sound stopped and he started filling the bags with flour.

'Can you grind my wheat?' Gosai heard a soft voice behind him. 'I've no flour left for the evening meal.'

It was a woman. Her voice sounded familiar. Startled, he

turned round. One end of the cloth that loosely held the bundle on her head had fallen over a part of her face and Gosai could not make out her features. He wanted to come out to confirm his suspicion but instead he started beating against the grinding stone and Gosai's heart beat in tune with it.

Wheat flour lay scattered on the floor of the small mill-room and Gosai's body was covered with a white film which made him look very old. The woman could not recognize him.

She again repeated her request. The bundle resting on her head, she stood in the sun, waiting.

Unable to avoid a reply any longer, Gosai said, in a low voice, 'You see this big mountain of grain? It may take a long time.'

Without a word the woman turned to go. Bending low, Gosai came out of the mill-room. As he saw the woman turn, his suspicion turned to conviction. He kept watching her go, then, dusting the flour off his clothes, he took a step or two forward. Some inner force seemed to compel him to call her back. He opened his mouth but no sound emerged. Some hesitation, some incapacity, stopped his mouth. The woman had by now reached the river. Gosai felt his whole inner being was in a state of fierce agitation. He could not stop himself and called in a wavering voice. 'Lachma!'

His agitation had prevented him from calling loud enough. The woman did not hear him. Gosai gathered himself together and called again, 'Lachma!'

Lachma stopped and looked back. Everyone in her parental village called her by this name. She was used to it. 'Did you call me?' she asked raising her voice.

'Yes, bring your grain. I'll grind it.' Not wishing to suddenly reveal his identity, Gosai stood in the shadow of the tree. Depositing her bundle of wheat in the mill-room, Lachma came out wiping the perspiration from her face and looked around for a shady place to rest. There was no such place except the tree, so she moved towards it.

'May your children live long,' she said with gratitude as she approached Gosai. 'You are kind to me. I would never have had my turn at the other mills.'

Suppressing his amusement at the blessing bestowed on his unborn progeny, Gosai, without giving her time to look at him, reciprocated her good wishes. 'May your children live long. When did you return to your parent's home, Lachma?' Gosai spoke in a controlled voice, as if he were an ordinary acquaintance.

Lachma, who was clearing the leaves away to make a place to sit, looked at him with a start. She could not have been more surprised had the slow-moving waters of the Kosi suddenly flooded the banks. She gazed at him wide-eyed, as if unable to believe this was indeed Gosai, the man she had known long ago.

'You...?' she wanted to say more, but the words stuck in her throat.

'Yes, I retired from the army last year,' Gosai said. 'I've put up this mill just to keep me busy.' He attempted a smile. 'Are your children well?' he asked after a pause.

Without raising her eyes, she nodded. Then she picked up a flower that had fallen from the tree and began plucking its petals, one by one while Gosai raked the fire.

To keep up the conversation, he asked her how long she intended stay with her parents.

Now Lachma could not hold herself back. She bent her head and tears fell, one by one. Gosai looked on, watching her sob, her shoulders heaving. He did not know in what words to express his sympathy. Then he noticed that her throat was bare of the ornament which betokens a married life. It meant she was a widow and he was angry with himself for being so unobservant.

They had met so unexpectedly that he could not remember the things he had always wanted to speak to her about. Now he wanted only to be a listener. Responding to his silent sympathy, Lachma began to talk about herself. 'Whom God forsakes, everyone else also forgets,' she said, wiping her tears. 'Living with my brother-in-law and his wife became unbearable. I came back to live with my mother. Now she too is dead. I've only a small son with whom I share my misfortune. But for him, I would have tied a stone round my waist and drowned myself.'

'Do you live with your uncle now?' Gosai asked.

'In hard times no one comes to one's help. That is the way of the world. Uncle has his eye on my father's property. He is afraid I'll claim a right to it. I have told him I don't covet his property for I know how to fend for myself. I can work in the fields, if it comes to that. I don't want to be a thorn in anyone's side.' Gosai said nothing, only looked at her with sympathy.

Lachma sat leaning against the trunk of the tree, her legs folded under her. Fifteen years had gone by and they had left their mark on Lachma's face too. Yet in her care-worn features Gosai could still glimpse the girl of fifteen years ago.

'The heat is unbearable this year,' Lachma said, changing the subject.

Gosai watched the sunshine filtering through the leaves of the tree lighting up her body, turning a lock of her hair to gold. 'The sun is too hot here,' he said, getting up. 'It's better under the other tree.'

'I'm all right here,' Lachma said. He looked away.

The grain in the funnel was almost finished. Gosai lifted Lachma's bundle and poured the grain into the funnel. Then he went to an adjoining room and returned with some brass and aluminium utensils. He went to the river, drank water, and returned.

Collecting some wood, he revived the fire and poured water in a charred kettle. 'It will soon be time for tea,' he said as he passed by Lachma. 'When the water starts boiling put tea leaves in it. The packet is lying there.'

Lachma did not reply. She watched him as he walked along

the footpath that led to the river. It took him some time to get milk from a wayside shop. On his return, he saw a six-year-old boy sitting beside Lachma.

'This boy will not leave me alone even for a minute,' Lachma said, to introduce the child. 'Now he has trailed me here to harass me.'

Gosai saw that, avoiding his eyes, the boy was every now and then pressing his mother for something. 'Be quiet!' his mother at last rebuked him. 'We shall soon be back home. A little patience is not going to kill you.'

After adding milk to the tea, Gosai again went into the mill-room. He came out carrying some flour, squatted on the edge of the river and kneaded the flour into dough.

Lachma got the tea ready and Gosai poured it into a tumbler, a mug and a mess-tin. Then he got down to baking *chapatis* in a stove improvised from stones.

Putting aside her tumbler of tea, Lachma volunteered to make them. She looked so determined that Gosai could not say no to her. Crisp, brown, swollen *chapatis*. Gosai had not seen such for ages so different from the ones he was accustomed to eating in the regimental mess or those made by himself. Lachma's hands moved swiftly as she rolled the dough, her silver bangles jingling softly.

Gosai looked at the child as he sat there, holding the mug of tea, his eyes fastened on him.

'The *chapatis* will get cold,' Lachma reminded Gosai. 'Eat them with your tea while they are hot.'

'They are for the child,' Gosai said. 'It's too early for me to eat.'

'He has had his food,' Lachma said with great embarrassment. 'I gave him something to eat before coming here.'

The child had been following their conversation attentively. His restraint had reached the snapping point. 'Mother does not mean what she says,' the child said tearfully. 'There are no *chapatis* in the house.'

'Shut up!' Lachma glared at him, blushing deeply.

'Don't be hard on the boy,' Gosai said. 'Children do get hungry.'

He held out two *chapatis* to the boy, who looked greedily at them and then at his mother.

'Now take them,' she said curtly. 'Wherever he goes, he displays his worst traits.'

The child was about to cry. Gosai placed a lump of jaggery on the *chapatis* and offered them to him. He started eating looking with tear-filled eyes at this strange friend. His little jaws worked busily as Gosai looked on, amused. He sensed that this brief interlude had made the atmosphere tense, so he dipped a piece of *chapati* in his tea, smiled and said, 'It's true, food made by women has a different taste.' He forced a laugh. Lachma looked sadly at him. 'If I had some vegetables the child could have eaten one more *chapati*.' He looked helplessly at the boy.

'Had he been so lucky he would not have been born in our house,' Lachma said. 'We have gone without food for two days. Today I earned some money. I'll buy a few things.'

Gosai felt in his pocket. 'Lachma!' he took out a note. 'Keep this to go on with,' he said, offering it to her. 'I've enough for myself. I received my pension day before yesterday.'

Lachma shook her head. 'No, no. I can manage. That's not what I meant. I just happened to mention it.'

Gosai was ruffled at her refusal. 'What good is a man if he does not stand by others in their need?' he said dryly. 'I earned a lot in my life and threw it away without a thought. What use was it to me? Money is worthless if you don't help others. Utterly worthless. I'm not doing you a favour, money is mere mud if not used. Nothing but mud and dust.'

But in spite of Gosai's ingenious logic Lachma was adamant. She gently stroked her child's head and said with philosophic calm, 'If god Ganganath is on your side, evil days pass off somehow. As for the stomach, it is like the funnel of a mill. The more you put into it the more it demands. If people speak to you kindly it is enough to lighten your burden.'

Gosai looked at Lachma. Gone were the storms and tides that had a risen years ago; that sea was held within bounds and was calm now. He could not force the money on her. With a deep sense of frustration, he slowly walked away towards the mill. Suddenly he took a few quick strides, stood in the door and looked back furtively. Lachma was standing under the tree, her back towards the mill. He disappeared into the mill-room. Quickly he added a few seers of wheat flour to Lachma's heap from his own lot and came out, carefully wiping his hands.

He spied someone near the embarkment. 'Who's there?' he shouted. Perhaps someone was trying to make a breach in the embankment and divert the water towards his field.

He quickly walked up to Lachma and told her that her flour was ready. He stood uncertainly before her. 'Lachma!'

She looked up at him with puzzled eyes. She felt embarrassed by his gaze. Who knows what he wanted to say but all he said, hesitantly, was: 'When you have put by some money don't forget to make a sacrificial offering to god Ganganath and beg his forgiveness for mistakes made. Those who have sons should avoid the wrath of the gods.'

Without waiting for a reply he hurried towards the embankment. When he returned after dealing with the trespasser, he saw that Lachma, the bundle of flour on her head, was slowly walking along the path, the child at her side. He kept looking at her till she disappeared round the bend.

The wooden cock was still pecking at the grinding wheel, making a sharp, staccato sound. The mill stone went round and round with a monotonous drone. The churner bit into the water coughing wheezily. No other sound anywhere, all was silent... motionless...!

Krishan Baldev Vaid

My Enemy

At the moment he is lying unconscious in the next room. Today I doped his whisky for the neat stuff which he drinks like fruit juice has no effect on him. His eyes get streaked with red, the furrows of his forehead gleam with sweat, the venom of his lips increases—and that's all. Mentally he remains alert.

It beats me why I did not think of this strategy before. Maybe I did. And then for some reason suppressed the thought. I always for some reason or the other suppress my thoughts. Even today I feared that he would recognize the difference in taste at the very first sip and catch me red handed. But as the level of liquor in the glass sank his eyelids began to droop too and that gave me courage. I felt tempted to wring his neck. But when I thought of the consequences I abandoned the idea. I think every coward has a strong imagination which saves him from taking risks. Still, taking my courage in my hands, I did look him straight in the face. No mean feat this for, normally, I keep looking sideways in his presence and my eyes flutter. Normally, I tend to behave abnormally in his presence.

Anyway, now his eyes were closed and his head was lolling. Before falling to his sides, his arms like two laden and swinging branches had raised themselves towards me. Seeing him so helpless, I imagined for a moment that he was in the throes of death.

But I knew that the wretch might spring to his feet any

moment. He would not utter a word on coming to himself. His strength lay in his silence. Even in those days he talked very little. But now he seemed stricken dumb.

Even the thought of his dumb disapproval sends ripples of unease through me. I have told you, haven't that I am a coward.

I don't know what put the idea in my head that all these years of staying away from him had freed me from my fear of him. Perhaps it was this happy thought that had made me bring him to my house that day. Maybe somewhere in my mind I was hoping against hope to cut him to size. I had hoped that showing him my lively beautiful wife, my healthy, up-and-about children and my spacious and magnificent house would make him run from the battlefield and rid me of him for ever. Perhaps I wanted to prove that having rid myself of him I had taken control of my life to a very fortunate extent.

But these are lame excuses. The reality perhaps is that it was not I who brought him home; he came in spite of me. He who wanted me to eat humble pie and not the other way around. This subtle design of his had obviously escaped my attention at that time. I never grasp the right point at the right moment. That is the trouble with me. I have many other troubles. But to dwell on them at this stage would be pointless.

Anyway, that day I tried to give some such lame explanation to my wife, Mala but it left her unimpressed. The very sight of him made her wild. It took me only a moment to understand the gravity of the situation and to realize my folly. I should have got rid of him on some pretext, right there on the road, far away from home. If, breaking through my enforced silence, I had pleaded with him, explaining to him my compulsions and had given him a clear picture of Mala the situation could have been saved. 'Look, *guru*, have pity on me and stop pestering me,' I should have told him, and we might have come to some compromise there and then. In any case he might have given me some breathing space. I would have been saved the ordeal of fighting two battles at the same time. In any case, it is now clear to me that I should not have brought him home with me. But this belated wisdom was of no use now. Mala and he were glaring at one another as if they were old sworn enemies. For a moment I felt reassured, hopefully confident that Mala would be able to handle the situation. But the very next moment I was on guard for I feared that Mala might turn nasty. So I said to her in a soft, ingratiating tone reserved for such critical occasions, 'Darling, please let us in. We are returning from a long ramble and are dead tired. Let us just have a breather and after that you are free to punish us in any way you like.'

She stood aside to let us in but her severe look had not softened. Nor did she let me sit down. My friend looked at me as though saying, 'So that's what you are—a slave to this woman!' As for me, I looked from one to the other as if wanting to conspire with each one against the other.

Mala took me aside at the first opportunity and started reprimanding me. 'Who is this vagabond-like protege of yours. Must be an old crony! Isn't he? You have been married so many years and yet you haven't changed. What will my children say? What will our neighbours think? Say something now! Don't stand there tongue-tied.'

I didn't know what to say. Generally, I weigh every word before speaking to Mala which makes her all the more irritated. Of course her anger is never without reason. Our successful marriage is founded on this fact—she is always right and I readily and silently acknowledge all my mistakes. She may keep railing at me but she fully trusts my loyalty. It is just to keeping my morale that she sometimes complains: 'I can't understand why you enjoy opposing me over every small thing?' she says. 'I grant that you are more intelligent than me. But why can't you be indulgent to me once in a while and let me have my way?'

I love her baseless recriminations though they don't please me overmuch. But she thinks these are necessary to keep me happily deluded. And I know its she who rules the roost. And that is as it should be.

There was Mala gritting her teeth and saying 'Will you answer me? When my children return from the park and find this tramp sitting in the drawing room what will they say? What kind of impression will it make? Oh, what a dirty man! The whole house stinks! Tell me, what will I say to my children?'

Now obviously, I couldn't answer her. I stood before her with a hang-dog look while she let lose a barrage of words on me.

I think I must straightaway make clear one point: Mala did not bring those children with her. They are as much mine as hers. But on occasions like these she always calls them 'my children', separating them from me as if she is taking gems out of muddy soil. I feel pained by it sometimes. But when I think it over coolly I feel that whatever the physical reality, in spirit the children are really Mala's. I have played a very small role in their development. And this is as it should be. Had they been like me it would have taken a long time to straighten them out, as it is taking me. I am happy that there is a bright future ahead of them and my contribution to this brightness is only that I am their legal and perhaps biological father, and that I earn for them, serve their mother day and night with great dedication.

Anyway, after standing there for a while with downcast eyes I at last raised my head and said in a very affectionate voice, 'Listen, dear, believe me, I recognize this nuisance only vaguely. there is no question of friendship with him. If I run into somebody on the road...'

I don't know how my sentence would have ended... or whether it would have ended at all. She stamped her foot and said, 'Lies... downright lies!'

She went away in a huff and I stood for some time with downcast eyes. The I returned to the other room where he was smoking a *bidi*. He was smiling as if he knew the ordeal I had passed through.

What had happened that evening was that I had taken permission to out for a short aimless ramble. Normally she does not give me permission so easily nor do I dare request it for she hates aimless wandering. Whenever I have to go somewhere, meet someone, do or not do anything, she decides the purpose in advance. She is right. I appreciate her good sense. Whatever the purpose, however, I rarely manage to go far from home all by myself. I have got so habituated to Mala's company that I feel lost without her. When she is with me my mind never goes wool-gathering. Everything looks so solid and meaningful. My thinking also becomes orderly and rational like a room arranged by Mala, in which everything is in its place, is neat and tidy. And when Mala is not with me, what happens is what happened that evening or something like it, for exactly that had never happened before.

As I have said, that evening I had strayed away from home. Ordinarily, even when I am away from home I keep thinking of home. Not because of any problem at home. The vehicle of my life moves smoothly and well—what else can it do. When its steering is in the hands of a woman like Mala? I don't have a worry in the world. I earn a handsome salary, have a good wife, good children, good influential friends with good buxom wives, a good government house with a nice pleasant lawn, a good neighbourhood, a well-laid table in spite of soaring prices, a good cosy bed and a good bed-life. What else can a good human being ask for? But still, when alone I derive great satisfaction by counting my blessings of home and hearth—the satisfaction that a healthy man gets looking at himself in the mirror. What I mean is that it keeps off boredom. This too was entirely a fall-out of Mala's good influence. I remember another time of my life when I was always a prey to boredom.

Perhaps that evening my mind had for a while strayed back to precisely that past era. I had drifted far from home. And then I suddenly found him standing before me.

At first I thought this dangerous looking stranger lying in

wait had seen me alone and tried to waylay me. I stopped in my tracks. Slipping from his dagger-like eyes my gaze was focussed on his smile. I saw fleeting glimpses of bygone days spent with him, dim like a mirror covered with dust. I felt as if after absconding for years I had been caught and hauled up before someone. The sheer enormity of being brought to trial weighed my head down.

For a short while—or perhaps for a long stretch of time, we stood face to face in that naked darkness. If a third person had been observing us he would have thought we were praying over a dead body, or were silently reciting an incantation before pouncing upon each other.

Of course, it's true that the moment I recognized him Mala had come to my mind. Maybe I was unknowingly invoking her help, as I do in times of crisis. At the time my first impulse was to scamper off. At the same time I was seized by a vague desire to surrender myself to him and instead of going home just drift along with him, with Mala none the wiser. The thought had shocked me at that time and I still marvel at it for, after all it was only to shake him off that I had taken refuge in Mala's lap. If a few years ago I had not revolted against him... But to call that escape a revolt is to delude myself, I thought, and my face burned with shame. My face often burns in this fire.

That bastard must have guessed my discomfiture. None of my weaknesses is hidden from him, and that was a major reason for having sought asylum in Mala's lap. I could hear the rustling of dry leaves in his laughter and that sound brought alive a myriad memories of the life I had spent in his shadow. I raised my eyes with great difficulty and looked at him. He had stretched out his hand towards me. Terrified, I fell back two steps and his laughter grew louder. Gritting my teeth I faced his eyes. I put my hand in his rough hand and, with the stench of his breath on my face, I felt that after all these years of freedom I had again given myself up to him. Funny, the feeling did not bother me as much as it should have. Perhaps every runaway convict has a secret desire to be apprehended.

No words passed between us on the way home. Wrapped each in our own silence we walked slowly along. As if like pall bearers we were carrying a corpse on our shoulders.

So, after facing the brunt of Mala's wrath when I returned to the drawing room, with my hang-dog look, I found the rascal at ease, smoking a *bidi*. For an instant I felt it was his room, not mine. Then regaining my composure, I flung open all the windows of the room and turned the fan on at full speed. I kicked his dirty shoes under the sofa and was about to turn the radio on, when I heard his cracked laughter. Feeling a bit jittery, I jumped back and sat down in a chair at the far end of the room.

I felt like going up to him in abject surrender and laying bare the whole situation with folded hands. 'Look, friend, take pity on me. Go away quietly before Mala enters the room. Or else the consequences will be disastrous.

But I didn't say anything. Even if I had he would have dismissed my request with a venomous laugh. He is heartless. He goes to the root of every matter in a moment and abhors sentimentality.

I stealthily watched him as his eyes roved over the room. Seated on the sofa with folded legs he looked like an animal. His condition looked eroded but his face still bore some resemblance to me.

This angered me and at the same time made me strangely happy. There was a time when he was my sole ideal and when we roamed together for hours on end. We resigned together from several jobs, not to mention the jobs from which we were sacked together. We considered ourselves superior to all those who tread the beaten path and waste their whole lives in building squalid and run-of-the-mill homes and who remain confined within the four walls of their homes. Their feelings were swayed only by the pranks of their children and they danced to the tunes of their stupid wives, and their only concern was to preserve their white collar status.

For some time I stayed lost in the memory of those by-gone days. I felt as if he had brought a message from that same world, and was once again trying to ensnare me in that romantic wasteland from which I had escaped and made for myself a bed of roses, a bed on which every night Mala demanded a proof of my conjugal fidelity and where I am very happy.

He was smiling as if he could see into my mind. Seeing him re-establish his away over me with such ease, I asked him, changing the subject, 'How long are you going to stay here?'

His laughter shook the decorous atmosphere of our house and I feared that Mala would soon come charging into the room and scratch his face. But this fear only shows that even after all these years of servitude I haven't really understood Mala. In a little while she did come into the room in a beautiful sari, smiling. Folding her hands in a charming manner she said, 'You look very tired. There is hot water in the bathroom. Do have a wash and something to drink later, to refresh you. We have dinner rather late.'

I was greatly pleased. Mala had taken the matter in her own hands and I had been fretting for nothing. I felt like kissing her. I looked at the bastard from the corner of my eye. He certainly was looking subdued. I thought if he did not bolt now I would consider all Mala's tactics and feminine wiles futile.

What fun it would be, if instead of running away, the skunk fell under Mala's spell. Then I would ask him, 'Now tell me, do you understand how things are?' I close my eyes, saw him dancing attendance upon Mala, then getting into bed with her. It gave me a strange kind of satisfaction.

When I opened my eyes, he had already disappeared into the bathroom and Mala was bending over the sofa, tidying it up. I looked into her eyes and tried to smile. But her face had again become taut and I lowered my eyes. It was evident that she had not yet forgiven me.

He emerged from the bathroom wearing my clothes. In the meanwhile, Mala had taken out bottles of beer and was filling his glass. 'How do you like your food?' she asked. 'Hot or less spiced?' I had trouble restraining my laughter. The wretch probably hardly ever got a square meal.

Over the beer, Mala kept up some small talk with him. How did he like this town? Was the beer cold enough? Where was his luggage? He kept glancing around nervously. Our children trooped in and greeted their 'uncle', sat on his knee, turn by turn, told him their names, sang songs and then with a 'Good night' went away to their room.

Mala's behaviour made it seem as if he was a friend of our own circle, with us on a few days visit and that his limousine was parked at our front door.

I was very happy and when Mala went to lay the table for dinner I looked him straight in the eye for the first time. He had tossed off three glasses of beer and his face looked less pale. But after Mala's departure, his smile was as venomous and challenging as ever. He seemed to be telling me, 'I like your wife all right, But son, warn her. I'm not as malleable as she thinks.'

For a second I felt deflated again. The problem was not to be solved so easily, I felt. I recalled that even in those days he liked beautiful and well-dressed women. But their spell did not last long. Still, I thought, things had gone out of my hands and I could do nothing but wait.

The dinner that night was delicious and afterwards Mala herself went to show him his room. But that night Mala did not talk to me. I cracked a joke or two. 'After his bath he looked quite nice, didn't he?' I teased her, made many overtures, but Mala would not let me near her. I couldn't sleep that night. But I was sure that Mala would succeed in driving him away the next morning.

But I was wrong. Granted that Mala is very clever, very

sensible and very charming too. But she is no match for that bastard's thick-skinned obduracy. For three days Mala danced attendance on him. In my clothes he looked very much like me. It looked as if Mala had two husbands. I drove away to my office early in the morning and I don't know what they talked about in my absence. But whenever she got the chance she would take me to her room and lash out at me, 'Won't this bastard ever leave? As long as he is around we can neither invite anyone over nor visit anyone. My children tell me the fellow doesn't even know how to talk properly. What does he want, anyway?'

What could I tell her what he wanted? I would say, 'Be patient. He must surely be thinking of leaving now.' Or I would say that I was myself embarrassed. Sometimes I would blame it all on her. Who asked to lavish such care on him at first? If she had been cold in the beginning and a little curt...

Mala's behaviour did not change. But on the fourth day she went away to her brother's house along with the children. I tried to stop her but she did not listen. That day that rascal guffawed, loudly, again and again.

It's five days since Mala left me. I have stopped going to my office. He has come out in his true colours. Taking off my clothes he has again put on his soiled kurta-pajama. He says nothing but I know what he wants: This is the chance of a lifetime. She is gone, and you would do well to vanish from here before she returns. Oh, no, there's no need to worry about her. She is quite capable to looking after herself.

And today, at long last, I have succeeded in making him unconscious for a while. Now I have two alternatives. One, to do away with him before he regains consciousness. Two, to collect a few essentials and as soon as he revives both of us take the same path from which I had run away a few years ago to seek refuge in Mala's arms. If Mala were here, she would have found a third way out. But she is not here and I don't know what to do.

Shailesh Matiyani

Exorcism

Kewal Pande had swum half way across the river. It was the waxing quarter of the year and although there was only knee-deep water in the upper reaches of the ghat still the current was swift. Suddenly it occurred to Pande to make his obeisance to the evening sun. But just as he faced the sun with water in his cupped hands some comet-like object flashed between the sun and his eyes. On looking carefully he saw smoke spiralling up from the north end of the burning ghat of Bondsi where the shudras cremated their dead. In the strong wind the smoke bending bow-shaped had gathered in wispy curlicues and hung suspended like a comet before the sun.

Om Vishnu Vishnu Vishnu...

Kewal Pande's knees knocked together under the water and the water slipping through his loosened fingers fell back into the river. A fear rose in his subconscious mind. Had poor Kisanram breathed his last?

The thought of Kisanram again set his legs atremble under the swift current of the water. Pandit Kewalanand Pande, a professional priest, felt that it was not a comet that had come between him and the sun but it was plough-hand Kisanram's soul hanging there like a ghost. For some time he remained submerged in his own thoughts rather than in the swirling waters of the Suyal river. He didn't know how, but the feeling that Kisanram's had died wove itself round him. The sacred thread round his neck, the mark of sandal paste on his forehead, and the ideas of caste in his blood. Again and again he was appalled at the thought that the water of the Suyal river, polluted by the dead body of an untouchable floating down from the burning ghat, bones and all, was swirling past his legs. They might even have thrown the half-burnt body into the river. He had seen many dead bodies floating down the river like logs of wood, especially in the river at Banaras when he was studying Sanskrit there. The village forest was immediately on the bank of the river. The high pine trees cast their shadows eastwards. Far off, on the river slopes herds of cows and goats were grazing. For some time Kewal Pande stood looking into the distance, and then, instead of crossing over, turned swiftly to the bank from where he had entered the river. He felt as if he had lost the strength to wade through the water to the other bank. Even before he had seen the smoke spiral, when he was halfway across the river he had suddenly thought of Kisanram. He had felt his legs were cutting through the river water as powerfully as the blade of Kisanram's plough cut through the earth. And then why did this comet of suspicion hang with such persistence in the firmament of his imagination, this suspicion that Kisanram wad dead and that it was his corpse that was being burnt? After all, it could well be that some other pyre was burning or that some fishermen had lit a fire on the bank of the river.

Kewal Pande felt a strong urge to scoop the water on the bank into his palms and examine it closely. He recalled that whenever while ploughing his field, Kisanram would stop his bullocks and walk across to him, rubbing tobacco powder between his palms, a strong smell would emanate from the plug of tobacco while it was being unplugged, a smell as strong as the smell of his soiled clothes. Would the same smell rise from the river water? He wanted to laugh at his imagination running riot in this manner but he could not. Kewal Pande had a soft corner in his heart for Kisanram and the thought of his death kept nagging at his mind. Abandoning the idea of crossing the river for he was no longer in a mood for it, he started walking along the river bank in towards the north, towards Binsar hill. The cremation ground was at a distance of about a furlong from there.

Gliding along the vast stretch of sandy earth like a pregnant snake, the Suyal created the illusion of flowing upstream. As the rays of the moon fell on the surface of the water along the bank, the river gave the impression of flowing backward and if you kept walking along the bank for some distance, the river like the moon also seemed to be walking with you. If Kisanram's half-burnt body had been thrown into the river would it too float upwards towards the north?

A little further off was a deep pond. What if his dead body had floated down into this pond and fishes were feasting on it? Pande stopped for an instant to look into the pond. He resumed his walk, accelerating his pace.

Those who have seen the Suyal river know that at the beginning of the mouth of *Kartik*, when the floods are over, the river water is transparent. But since the second quarter of the year had just ended one could not keep one's foothold in the river. Like silver rupees strung at regular intervals on the necklaces of hill women the ponds are studded along the river bank till the point where the Suyal merges with the Kosi.

Kewal Pande's clientele also extends along the length of the Suyal in a similar pattern. Looking down from the stone embankment the asela and paparua fishes frolicking on the river surface and the minnows leaping up a few inches and then falling plop into the water like pebbles made a fascinating sight for Kewal Pande. He recalled that before they had built a dam over the river he used to come with Kisanram and low caste boys of their age to catch fish in the pond. Like those boys he also used to jump into the pond without any inhibition. No one ate fish in his family. But the joy of catching frolicking fish...it was irresistible. Pounded Ramban leaves have been cast in the water. On the dammed water foam churns like soap lather ... and fishes stunned into semi-consciousness circle around the surface. They can be caught just by stretching out a hand.

There was not much difference in age between Kewal Pande and Kisanram. Perhaps Kisanram was two or three years older but he had started looking old much sooner than Kewal Pande. Pande was over sixty-five years of age but he did not have a single crow-mark on his florid face to match the sandal paste marks. In contrast, Kisanram had developed a stoop. He knew Kisanram since childhood and both had grown together like two trees in a forest. Kisanram's father had three wives and a large family and there was barely enough food to go round. Most of the time they had to live just above starvation level. The father had to sell his labour and work day and night to eke out an existence. Pande did not remember a single day when he saw the exuberance of youth reflected in Kisanram's face or saw him indulging in childish pranks. Whenever he saw him he always found him submerged in work either behind the plough or holding hammer and sickle.

Passing his childhood in his village from where he passed his middle level examination, Pande went away to Nainital to live with his maternal uncle. After doing his high school there he went away to Banaras for his graduation and returned to his village after rounding off his studies. His younger brothers were still studying and his father had grown old. His clientele was very large and both on economic and moral grounds it was necessary for Pande to take care of it.

Returning home for good after his studies, Pande learnt from Kisanram himself that in the meanwhile his mother had passed away and he was now living with his maternal uncle. His uncle was a blacksmith but Kisan only knew farming although he could also handle odd jobs. One day while hammering red-hot iron, the fingers of his right hand got crushed, rendering the hand useless. His hand out of service, his uncle turned him away and he returned with his wife, Bhawani, to her parents' home. His in-laws gave asylum to their daughter and showed him the door. 'Gosaiji, those low-caste creatures have taken my wife away' he had said to Pande, not using the words 'their daughter'.

The three crushed fingers of the hand damaged at his uncle's smithy, slowly festered and fell off. With the remaining two he held his stick to drive the bullocks and used the other hand to hold the handle of the plough. Among the first sounds that Pande had heard on the outskirts of the village on returning home after a long absence, was Kisanram's high-pitched voice prodding his bullocks forward. On coming nearer when Pande stopped to say 'May God bless you, Kisanram, are you all right?' Kisanram began to talk at a breathless pace as if he had been conserving all sorrows to narrate them just to Pande. His eyes gradually filled with tears as he explained his plight. Repressed sorrow rose like mist lifting from a deep valley; moisture came to his eyes like water level raised when a river is dammed up.

This was the first time Pande had seen Kisanram crying. Mostly he had seen only a pitiful smile lurking in his dry eyes. When his body was drenched in perspiration from hard labour one wondered did Kisanram shed tears from the pores of his skin?

And even at such times, Pande would have the odd fancy that Kisanram was perhaps an accursed Indra in whose body a myriad eyes had appeared. He used to wipe his perspiration as carefully as if he were wiping tears from his cheeks. When one watched him at such moments, one felt a bitterness rise through one's whole being.

When Kisanram was hard at work one wondered if he shed tears through the pores of his skin in the form of perspiration....Pandeji was overcome by bizarre thoughts whether Kisanram was under the curse of god Inder to have grown eyes all over his body. He would mop up perspiration from his body in such a manner as if he was wiping tears from his wet cheeks. As Pande watched him steadily without blinking his eyes the taste in his mouth became bitter.

At that time his body did not smell of tobacco being unplugged. After returning from Banaras, Pande had noticed that despite being older than himself, Kisanram, in contrast to Pande's fair, sturdy and developed frame, looked as if nature had hammered the iron of his body with the hammer blows of adversity to adjust it to herself. He could plough the field, fell a tree or break stones without any apparent strain as if he were perfectly attuned to nature.

Pande vividly remembered that uncommon sight when as a boy of fourteen Kisanram was taking his newly-wed bride back to her parents for a day's visit. He had met them when he was on the way back from his Middle School. A squat little wheat complexioned girl, she was wearing a flamboyant skirt, and a rose-coloured veil and was walking behind him in complete abandon, smoking a *bidi*. 'Maharaj,' Kisanram had made obeisance by bending down and touching the ground with his forehead. His bride had hastily extinguished her *bidi* in her palm and had burst out crying.

It had made Pande laugh. Kisanram had also joined him in laughter. 'Gosaiji, in our community girls learn all the tricks of life at a very early age,' he had said. And then he had asked, a little abashed, till what age, according to the Shastras, it was forbidden for a young pair to take freely to each other family concerns?

Pande recalled that while uttering the word 'Shastras' Kisanram's voice shook a little. Pande had a sharp mind of which he had given evidence from his childhood. He had understood at once that something was disturbing Kisanram's mind. Some village elders' quaint ideas must have taken root in his mind. He had taken a great liking for the naive Kisanram and now he had also had a glimpse of his wife with the curiosity of one of the same age-group. 'Friend Kisanram, to tell you the truth, I have yet to study the Shastras,' he had said. 'My father is thinking of sending me to Kashi to study Sanskrit. When I become a full-fledged Shastri after ten or twelve years I shall initiate you into these mysteries.' And they had both laughed like flowers in the forest.

Kisanram's wife was carrying a basket on her head. It contained *puries, ganderies, spinach* and potato curry, all properly covered with the end of her bridal head gear.

After many years, when Pande came home on vacation, he had asked Kisanram, 'Have you had a child!' and from Kisan's answer he had felt as if he were still waiting for the day when Pande would reveal to him the secrets contained in the Shastras.

On returning after completion of the Shastri degree at Kashi, Pande had again wanted to ask Kisanram the same question but his tale of woe filled him with grief. He felt that this time, instead of putting out her *bidi* in her palm, his wife had rubbed it against Kisanram's heart. He felt as if she was somewhere nearby, laughing in her sleeve at his display of sympathy for her husband.

Kisanram's marriage had taken place at the dawn of boyhood and it had broken at the dawn of maturity. Now Kisanram was living alone. Although many had warned Pande's father against it yet he had engaged Kisanram as his ploughman.

One day Pande's mother said to Kisanram, 'Kisanram, the bird that sat on your branch flew away. Why are you renouncing life for her? If you marry again, at least our land would be better taken care of. As you know even bullocks work in pairs. You are a ploughman, if you can't take another woman for your wife, you could at least bring the first one back.' Earlier, Pande had also given Kisanram similar advice.

Kisanram was conscious of his limitations. A tiller of the land cannot put in his best without a wife. And what was worse, his right hand was disabled. But Bhavani? There was no chance of her coming back to stay with him. It was like conjuring up false visions. One day he had confessed to Pande's father that he was unfit for work and bringing his stepbrother to work in his place, had said weeping. 'My master, if I am unable to restore the flesh that has dropped from my hand how can I bring back one that has gone out of my heart?'

In those days the whole village had talked of the tenderness of a mature woman's heart, which is like a mother's. Kusmavati had herself wiped Kisanram's tears. That a Brahmin woman and that too belonging to the priestly class should with her own hands wipe the tears of a low caste man—well, it was something unheard of. Eyebrows had gone up. But Bhiron Pande had thought differently. He said that to do so was to become pure, not impure.' When Kewal Pande asked Kusmavati about it, tears came to her eyes. 'Kewal, whether rich or poor, all suffer alike,' she had remarked. 'When I wiped Kisanram's tears he picked up the dust from my feet and putting it to his forehead, said that if the philosopher's stone could convert an iron trough into gold why couldn't my touch wash away the sins of his previous births. He is a low-caste by birth but he is full of compassion and of detachment.'—this Kisan. Bhavani has tarnished her name by deserting this poor simple man.'

It was not lost upon Pande that Kisanram was deeply in love with Bhavani and that was why he felt this estrangement so intensely. That is why he seemed to have lost all interest in life.

In those days he had taken to washing his clothes once a week and he cooked his meals at regular hours. If he happened to be working in the fields the food would be sent to him from Pande's house. Expressing his gratitude to Pande's wife he would say, 'Please send my *rotis* on time, Brahmin lady of the house.'

One day after finishing his work in the fields, Kisanram was washing his clothes by the Suyal. Clad in a bare loincloth he was standing in the water like a stork lost in thought, legs submerged in water and torso bathed in sunshine. The end of his loincloth fluttered in the strong breeze as if seeking flight from the hip cord. He had spread out the remaining clothes to dry when Pande, who was returning from a visit to his clients, passed by. Kisanram stood aside to let him wade through to the other bank. He was careful to keep at a distance from Pande so that the water touched by his feet should not pollute Pande. Giving Kisanram a portion of the sweets which he had received from his patrons, Pande remarked, 'Bhavani has not done a good thing, Kisan. You could have been spared the drudgery of washing clothes and cooking food. And, you and I used to go fishing together—why are you trying to fall back from the bank? I am not that kind of touch-me-not Brahmin.'

Kisanram joined his hands together, a faint smile on his lips. 'Maharaj, the day I received the benediction of the older lady's golden fingers—the ache in my eyes and my heart went away. It's more than enough for me. Otherwise I the impure and you the pure...'

Years passed. Kewal's father, Bhairon Pande, and then his wife, Kusmavati, passed away. Kisanram's back became more stopped but he did not give up the plough. Until he gave up the plough himself, they would not engage another ploughman, so Kewal Pande had decided. Whenever necessary he would engage an extra farmhand on a daily wage. Everybody would ignore Kisanram's lapses. Kewal's wife, Chandravati too, like her mother-in-law, Kusmavati, had a soft corner for Kisanram. Sometimes Kisanram, overcome by her kindness would remark, that though the body of the older lady had gone her soul had housed itself in the younger lady's body. Often this was the springboard for Kisanram to launch out on all kinds of questions about the soul and god. 'Maharaj, I'm told the Shastras are replete with wisdom relating to the soul and the world soul. I am your slave. Your feet are the right place for me. I am told the answer to these questions is given in the form of incantations. If the sound of a couple of incantations falls in my polluted ears it would wash away the stains of my soul. What am I to do, Gosaiji. I'm no better than an animal. Not a grass-eating animal but a grain-eating one. Gosaiji, I'm your slave through the cycles of births. Blow a few incantation in the direction of this fat-head who has taken refuge in you.'

What remained unsaid after this could be read only in Kisanram's eyes. Changing the subject he would ask, 'Maharaj where does the soul go after death? Does it go to the other world or keep wandering in this world?'

Kisanram learnt that in the human cycle of 84 lakh births and deaths one birth could also be that of a phantom. This had greatly aroused his curiosity. He wanted to know whether, if the soul was unwilling, it could still turn into a phantom at the behest of the body?

When not visiting his clients Pande would spend the time inspecting his fields. He had noted that when his wife, Chandravati, was in the fields Kisanram would work with greater zeal. But when Pandeji was there, on the pretext of chewing tobacco, he would go to him time and again and ask him all sorts of questions. Although his questions did not make much sense yet Pande could not be harsh with him and suffered him gladly. And his dazed, groping speech made it fairly clear to Pande that Kisanram was progressively turning an introvert. His eyes had sunk deep into their sockets where they seemed to shine like a fish-like substance at the bottom of a pond. Pande sometimes feared that this portended his imminent death.

Once Pande had told Kisanram that those who did not have a wife or children did not gain release from this world. Holding torches in their hands they kept wandering from place to place at night like phantoms in quest of a wife and children. Sometimes they did so in groups. Pande had also apprised him of the fact that those belonging to the higher caste were spared this ordeal despite their having no wife or children, the redeeming feature being that they could seek their salvation though a study of the Shastras. Henceforth Kisanram constantly pestered Pande with all sorts of outlandish questions seeking enlightenment on so-called 'salvation'.

Only a few days before, he had again asked, 'How to liberate oneself if one begins to haunt the person one had desired?'

Pande tried to fathom the reason of Kisanram's mental trepidation. After persistent questioning Kisanram opened up a bit. 'Maharaj, you are like a god to me,' he said. 'Why hide anything from you? My body is getting feeble. My appetite is gone. My bile has increased and sleep is fitful and I am losing the strength to bathe and wash my clothes. My stomach burns with hunger and I keep coughing. The spasms make me feel as if my body is going to pieces. When I look around I am assailed by my own smell and my own corpse-like shadow. Gosaiji, then my mind goes out of control. Now on the eve of my death, I smother with fierce and dirty abuses. Even those against whom I didn't say an unkind word in my young days. Swinging in the hangman's noose my soul keeps cursing me, 'Curse on you, Kisanram! You scavenger who are turning into a demon at death's hour. Now on your way to the cremation ground don't call your wife a whore, you butcher!' These two stumps on my hand smouldering like *bidis* go for my skull. I cry—'You slut! If you had not wrenched my heart out, in this old age of mine someone else if not you would have been around.' Gosaiji, what if I turn into a phantom?'

'Kisanram, you haven't forgotten your Bhavani. If she had shown the same faithlessness to any other man he would have spat on her face and taken another woman in her place to warm his bed. I see, with advancing years you have become more bitter towards her but your infatuation for her has not waned. Your abuses are not those of a fiend but of an aggrieved man.'

'Gosaiji, the broken branches of a tree grow again but when a tree is uprooted it never grows again. As long as my limbs were in fine condition, I ate on time to satisfy my hunger and washed my clothes on time. If I had not kept my mind occupied I would have spat out abuses at Bhavani. Maharaj, you yourself saw her flitting around me like a butterfly. If I had brought an elderly woman to live with me, I would have felt that she was not hovering round me like a butterfly but bumping against me fore and aft. Maharaj, you must be saying to yourself, this man has gone senile, what nonsense he's talking. But Gosaiji, I couldn't bear to drive that butterfly so far away that I should lose sight of her, that I should keep scanning the sky for her and she should become invisible like a star in daytime.'

Looking at Kisanram's sunken eyes which shone like a fish in a pond he felt as if it was the Kisanram of bygone days who lay drowned in his own stagnant waters. Was this the man who had gone to the fields with that young Bhavani who had stubbed out her *bidi* on her palm and was this the man who had asked: 'Maharaj, the Shastras say the relationship with a wife is eternal, in all births, is it not so?'

Only a few days ago he had said to Kewal Pande, 'Maharaj, I am in anguish these days. I come of a low caste and that is bad enough. Over and above it, I have a crooked mind at loggerheads with this world of strife. I have been denied the right to hear our holy scriptures. Nothing sacred must fall in my polluted ears. For that matter who would care to recite them to me? Sometimes I retire to the solitude of the forest and lie there with closed eyes in the hope that taking me for dead, a heron, the bird dear to Vishnu, may perch on my head and utter some sacred words in my ears. Maharaj, I'm not so much worried about my own redemption. What deeply concerns me is that in my next birth, if I become a phantom I may start haunting her. Maharaj, that my father's ghost had entered my stepmother's body and her sons had tried to drive it out by branding her body with hot iron tongs. That ninety-year old woman would writhe in agony. I live in fear lest Bhavani's sons should also brand her body with hot iron tongs... I had a right over her but as long as she was with me I didn't utter a harsh word to her. I thought: 'Leave her alone, Kisanram, a beautiful girl, agile like a butterfly! Let her flit about where she likes. Let her sit where she wants to.' How will I stand the sight of her being branded after my death?..... Tell me, Gosaiji, if a man plucks out his eyes and offers them to the heron will he remain eyeless if born as a phantom?'

Pandeji noticed that the nearer Kisanram drifted towards his end, the more Bhavani fluttered in his mind, making his thinking more clouded and his resistance more feeble, unable to withstand the vagaries of life. Pande became apprehensive lest out of some wild belief Kisanram should gouge out his eyes. Glancing into his sunken eyes Pande would feel as if Kisanram, holding a fishing net firmly, had spread it wide into the inner depths of his being in which his own unfulfilled desires had been caught wriggling. Tense with anger as he tried to gather the various strands of the net of illusion, the wrinkles round his eyes would shrink as if the fishing rod had been pulled up, the water profusely dripping from its cords.

How oppressive such eyes must feel in one's body—eyes that are unbearable to others! The glitter in the depths of ignorant and unlettered Kisanram's eyes was like a dead fish's lustre in a tank, reminding Pande of the Yaksha-Yudhishtra episode in the Mahabharata. He would feel that unless the questions in his eyes were answered, Kisanram would not leave Pande either in life or thereafter. He began telling Kisanram, 'The Shastras also say that the man who performs penance with a pure heart definitely attains Paradise after death.'

The moment Kisanram asked a question Pande would say, 'Kisanram, you are an honest man, without an enemy, serene and tranquil. Through their pious deeds people like you attain Heaven. They don't become phantoms.'

Such reassuring replies only diminished Kisanram's questions, not his anxiety or his pain. Previously, he used to express his anxiety in his endless questions. Now he gathered it into his being to ooze out drop by drop like water oozing from a rock... Pande feared that if his anxiety did not abate there would be no salvation for him. Even if his body was sent floating in the river, his soul, clinging corpse-like to the bamboo support, would rise to the surface, would become invisible... One could already see shadows of death lurking in Kisanram's eyes. How terrifying those people look whose life ebbs through their eyes!

Walking along the bank of the Suyal, his mind lost in memories, Pande felt that someone was pulling down from his back the bag containing offerings received from his clients. An old client had passed away in a distant village and Pande was returning after performing the dead man's thirteenth day rites. Among other things his bag contained barley and sesame seeds and also a set of utensils.

After Kisanram's death, his step-brothers must have taken away the few utensils he possessed and most likely the mean louts had not even offered utensils to the priest as was customary. Pande recalled that Kisanram was careful not to touch the pitcher which Pande's wife Chandra brought to the fields. He would put his cupped right hand to his lips for Chandra to pour water in it from a distance and he drank in sharp explosive gulps. Even at that time his thirst seemed endless. How clear the sound of his gulp was! His Adam's apple seemed to dance to its rhythm.

While walking Pande suddenly felt as if Kisanram was following close behind and, tilting the pitcher tied to his back, he might any moment put his lips to it. His feet grew heavy. He recalled that once on the death of a client he had promised Kisanram, just to console him, that on his death he would perform his last rites. Kisanram had felt reassured. 'Maharaj, the sesame seeds for the dead offered by your noble hands will wash away all my sins,' he had mumbled smacking with satisfaction. 'I hope it will not go against you, Gosaiji,' Kisanram added quickly. 'A pious Brahmin performing a low-castes' death rites! It would only be adding to my sins. I may be punished for it.'

Pande also knew that to perform Kisanram's death rites was strictly against religious codes but this seemed the only way of reassuring Kisanram. 'The body is made of earth, Kisanram. When the earth falls off only the soul remains and the soul, as you know, is intangible.'... But it was no occasion to enter into any controversy. But he was caught in a dilemma—if Kisanram was dead would he be able to keep his promise?

Suddenly he realized that he had been praying under his breath, 'May it not be that Kisanram is dead...May it be someone else.'

There were only two people whose deaths were considered likely by the villagers at that time—one of them being Kisanram and the other his step-mother.

For a moment Kewal Pande debated if it did not amount to a prejudice against Kisanram's mother, to prefer her death to her son's. Then he felt that a person over ninety had undoubtedly reached the time of farewell. The person must die, tomorrow, if not today.

As Pande reached the cremation ground walking on heavy feet he found that only one pyre was burning in its last stages. The mourners had gone and the cremation ground was deserted. With the murmuring of the running water the stillness also seemed to be speaking as if telling the story of a last departure.

To all outward appearances, Pande regarded low-caste people as untouchables, but he did not feel as if they were untouchable. He had inherited large-heartedness and compassion from his father and mother but he was shackled by hide-bound custom in which there was no place for sentiment.

Standing in that lonely spot a tremor ran down his spine. The desire to know about Kisanram increased but there was nobody around whom he could ask whether it was Kisanram or his step-mother that had died or someone else. But from a distance he could see no body on the pyre. Perhaps the body had got burnt. Or perhaps a half-burnt body had been sent down the river. But whom to ask? The river or the forest? On all sides only the valley stretched dressed with trees.

The strong desire to know impelled Pande forward. His mind was in a quandary and doubt pulled at his feet. If some farm-hand in the field or coming along the way saw him messing around in the burning ghat God knew what he would think. What was he searching for after an untouchable had been cremated? Suddenly something like a piece of cloth clung to his feet and he fell back startled. He saw it was a plaited two-peaked black cap like the one Kisanram wore and used to hold before his wife, Chandra to receive the *rotis*. No, there was no mistaking the cap. He was now seeing the cap without Kisanram's head but he had never seen Kisanram's head without this cap.

Kisanram! Omvishnur! Kewal Pande felt that Kisanram's spirit must be somewhere around, looking at him with beseeching eyes—'Maharaj!'

'Hey Ram!' Tears of grief and pain came to Kewal Pande's eyes. Like a snake hissing in the dark his doubts were confirmed. His feet suddenly became light and his fear, dissipated as it happens when face to face with a calamity disabusing one's mind of all illusions. Kewal Pande retraced his steps and after walking some distance proceeded towards the road leading to the village. He just had to walk along the Suyal bank a short distance but a little way out of the cremation ground he felt as if his feet were weighed down with a heavy weight. He felt that Kisanram had been left behind but he was still holding his cap before him. What could he have wanted to ask in his last moments? Just an entreaty that his soul be released? Maybe before breathing his last he had asked someone to remind Pande about his promise to perform his last rites.

He recalled the whole thing. In his last days there was a glow in Kisanram's eyes showing confidence in his liberation. It was no ordinary glow. Its reflection lay in his speech, hearing, eating, even in his gait. Now he did not look agonized or sad but tranquil and serene. His decaying body had gained an even momentum as if from an inner rhythm. Pande's assurance to him that he would perform his last rites in solitude according to the Shastras, seemed to have wrought this miracle. It had sent him into an impenetrable serenity like that of a mystic. Or was it that his soul after his death was hovering around to see if Pande lived up to his promise?

As Pande advanced further he felt Kisanram was imploring him back to return and there was only one way out of this impasse—to perform his last rites. Yes, this was the only way of liberation from all his dilemma. He could not perform the rites with the knowledge of the community. He must perform the rites in the solitude of the Suyal valley with God as the only witness for whom there was no difference between one and another, for whom a scavenger and a Brahmin were alike. But if he performed the rites near the cremation ground a passerby might see him and stare at him with questioning eyes. He might even spread the rumour that now money-minded Brahmins had surreptitiously started performing the last rites of untouchables.

A little further up a small stream joined the Suyal. Pande walked up and put down his bag on a slab of stone near the confluence of the two streams. As he opened his bag the pitcher tumbled out as if impelled by providence. Pande's heart brimmed over. For some minutes he remained lost in the memories of the childhood he had spent with Kisanram. Then he filled the pitcher with water from the river and made an altar with the earth near the river bank. He put the pitcher on it. All his life he had received money from his clients. Why not reverse the process for once and make a votive offering in the name of his devotee? Taken up in the generosity of thought he even forgot that he was performing the rites of an untouchable. He took out the plate, glass and bowl from his bag. He put some sesame and grains of barley in the plate and plucked some blades of kusha grass from a nearby field. With all the ingredients neatly arranged in place he began the recitation of '*Kisanram pret pretarth*' in readiness for the first offering of sesame seeds: While reciting he had a strong urge to get back to the ghat, fetch Kisanram's cap and make the grain offering into it...'Vishnu-Vishnu!'

After completing the rites, when he came close to his village it suddenly occurred to him that he had also to perform his father's annual memorial rites following day. Today he had performed an untouchable's rites and tomorrow he would be performing the memorial rites of his pious father learned in the Shastras. Pande looked at his hands. They had become polluted, he felt. In great anguish, he ran his fingers over his face and he felt the atmosphere permeated by the stench of unplugged tobacco.

Pande was thinking, after secretly performing the rites of an untouchable he ought not perform his father's memorial rites without consulting the members of his family. Such deceit to his departed father might prove harmful. He knew that despite his father's kindly disposition towards untouchables he was not broadminded enough to defy the orthodox tenets which greatly influenced his thinking. He had lived by the belief that whatever the Shastras enjoined was true humanity. How could Pande perform with his polluted hands the memorial rites of a person who had never in his life acted against the norms laid down by the Shastras?

Kewal Pande was drawing near his village. The long journey full of mental turmoil had proved very tiring. He was feeling apprehensive. To perform the rites with a pure heart he would have to tell the truth even if he had to face his family's wrath. He felt by now Kisanram's spirit must have been liberated. But now the same phantom of penance had possessed him on account of the sacrilege of performing rites for an untouchable. His forehead grew wet with sweat as he looked in the direction of the cremation ground and thought of Kisanram. It seemed to him as if his own spirit had wedged itself between him and the setting sun and was hanging from its lower disc. As if stunned, he sat down on a stone by the edge of the footpath.

After cremating his step-mother Kisanram was returning home by another route when he saw Pande sitting by the footpath, lost in thought. He was looking so woebegone.

'Maharaj,' Kisanram said prostrating himself before Kewal Pande.

As if coming out of a reverie, Kewal Pande looked up as if in response to some inner call. Kisanram was standing before him, bare-headed, beads of perspiration glistening on the bald patch in the middle of his head. Kewal Pande looked at him, astounded, unable to take his eyes off his face.

Kisanram joined his hands together in salutation and bowed his head before him. 'May you live long,' Kewal Pande blessed him. As he raised his hands to bless Kisanram he felt as if he were struggling to release himself from the clutches of a phantom dangling in the sky.

Shivprasad Singh

Nanho

As the postman knocked at her door, Nanho Sahuain angrily stirred the lentils in the pot with the ladle as if the pot was the culprit. Holding the ladle in her turmeric-smeared hand she emerged from the kitchen and then, covering the ground in long strides, taking one step where she would have normally taken two, she came to the door in a huff.

'Who's there?' Still holding the ladle in her hand, she removed the door chain from the door with the other hand and peeped out. She fell back a step as she saw the postman standing outside the door. Covering the turmeric mark on her sari with her hand, she pulled down her veil the length of a hand and stood behind the door like a lizard clinging to the wall.

'I don't expect a letter from anywhere, Munshiji,' she mumbled. 'Have you checked the address? There could be a mistake.' Her ear-ring was dangling from her ear, its end taut like a lizard's tail.

'The letter is for you. From Calcutta. From a man named Ramsubhag Sahu. The address is correct.'

'Ramsu...!' The word remained incomplete as if she had tried to swallow it down with water and it had hit her stomach, making her squirm. Her ear-ring seemed to impale her sari like a nail. 'Yes, it's mine, Munshiji,' she said.

Nanho

As the postman handed her the letter her ear-rings shook and the letter fluttered in her hand like a captive bird. She closed the door behind her with a bang and moving into the courtyard she stopped beside the platform used for keeping pitchers of water, and read the letter.

It was a short, three-line letter, conveying the information that Ramsubhag was coming. She went through the letter laboriously, lingering over each word and taking a long time to finish it. The water falling from the platform, drop by drop, had made the soil under it quite damp. Some barley seeds must have fallen on the damp soil and had sprouted. She stood there a long time looking at them with unblinking eyes.

Five years is indeed a long time—five long, long years. It was after five years that Ramsubhag had suddenly remembered his sister-in-law. For five years he had never tried to find out whether she was alive or dead. When her own husband was gone who would care to share her joys and sorrows? Nanho pulled up a low seat from under her string-bed and sat down on it. Her turmeric stained fingers had left their marks on the postcard, giving it the auspicious look of a wedding invitation. At the thought of a wedding her eyes sparkled like the scales of a fish. How many times she has recalled her wedding! She wanted to forget about it, to drive this sorrowful thought out of her mind for good. Why regret what was not in one's fate? But what kind of woman is she who does not think of her marriage—and especially a woman in whose life marriage came as a document, an event which made her life desolate, an arid waste.

Nanho was also married off like all the other girls of her village; her wedding was no different from other weddings—turmeric, vermilion, feasting, music, merry-making, laughter and tears everything was as usual.

But there was one difference. Her marriage was not performed at her parents' home; instead it was performed at her in-laws' home. There was nothing exceptional even about a marriage of this kind. Those parents who, despite their ardent desire, can not afford the cost of the celebrations, do not welcome the bridegroom's procession to their home, but rather send off the bride to his house for the wedding. Nanho's marriage also took place in the same manner. There was nothing unusual about this either. Nanho's husband, Mishrilal, was congenitally lame in one leg. Even when he was a young man, one leg was thin and soft as a child's arm. He walked, or rather hopped, by leaning on a stick. He was not bad to look at, but being dark-complexioned and having high cheekbones gave him a bleak appearance. He ran a grocer's shop in the village where, besides the daily necessities of life, he also stocked such items as tobacco, *bidis*, matchboxes and vegetables. There being few buyers of vegetables, they did not sell fast and often went stale by being kept overnight. Their prices being at par with food grains, even well-to-do people went in for vegetables only when they had guests to entertain at home.

Nanho's father had felt very happy when her marriage was arranged with Mishrilal, because the boy her family had been shown as Mishrilal was quite good looking and smart. He had his hair combed back and though not fair, had a glowing complexion which looked beautiful. Therefore, when the bridegroom's people said that they would not come with a marriage procession but would conduct the wedding at their own house, Nanho's father consented after putting up some token resistance. This arrangement, he knew, would work to his advantage, as he would be able to avoid many expenses.

The bridal palanquin was brought outside Nanho's parent's house, many rites were performed all day and that night, with music and ceremony Mishrilal and Nanho became husband and wife. The music had blared forth happily and the paper buntings gaily fluttered in the breeze, the professional women singers sang songs of the auspicious marriage of Rama and Sita but all the time, Nanho was trying to dry her tears under her veil, though nobody saw her doing so. With a heavy and ugly millstone hung around her neck she was lowered into a fathomless sea of pain and sorrow where she could not even hear the sound of her own sobs.

'So, sister-in-law, it was I whom your father had inspected but it was Mishrilal who married you!' said Ramsubhag to Nanho the day after her marriage when she was sitting huddled up in a corner. He smiled and added, 'To each his own fate, I am not lucky enough to get a wife like you, lovely as the moon.'

It is customary for younger brother's-in-law to jest with their older sisters-in-law. But what answer can one make to such a joke? The tears she had been holding back for the last twenty-four hours flooded her eyes now.

Ramsubhag got scared. He had said it to hurt her, but the injured bird does not always fall at the hunter's feet. Sometimes, only drops of blood fall on the ground and the bird flies away with the arrow lodged in its breast.

'You are right, Lala, to each his own fate,' Nanho replied tears still throbbing on her eyelids.

Ramsubhag was Mishrilal's cousin—his maternal uncle's son. Most of the time he stayed with Mishrilal, mainly because he did not like to live with his own family, his father drove him too hard and taking the cue from him, Ramsubhag's elder brothers also would come down him at the slightest show of resistance. Besides, Mishrilal wanted to have Ramsubhag with him for he was a great help and made most of the purchases to replenish the stocks at his shop. Ramsubhag felt quite at home with Mishrilal and treated his house as his own. He was greatly pleased when he learnt that Mishrilal intended to marry. A woman in the house would enliven the atmosphere and also Ramsubhag would be spared the drudgery of cooking which he often had to undertake.

But on seeing Nanho, Ramsubhag felt as if something unwarranted had happened of which he had never dreamt. Nanho was not the kind of woman whom he could unhesitatingly think of as Misri's wife. He had come without any inhibitions to have a chat with Nanho and to impress upon her that he was indeed a somebody and a pivotal point in the scheme of things whom her husband could ignore only at his cost. She must know that she could not find a better brother-in-law than Ramsubhag. And for that matter, while negotiating her marriage, her father had actually selected him to be her spouse. But there was something in Nanho's downcast eyes which made him forget the speech he had planned. She was sitting bundled up on the coloured mat, her arms thrown round her knees, her eyelashes like the legs of a butterfly which had got wet in the rain. She was staring into space, perhaps at the picture of a field in her mind, a great field ready for harvest, into which someone had suddenly thrown a burning torch.

Ramsubhag sat silent for a long time, his eyes roving over the courtyard. He wanted Nanho to break they silence and give an indication of what was rankling in her mind. Perhaps it was yet not too late to mend matters. But Nanho remained silent.

The ceremonies connected with the second day of the wedding were under way. The women of the village had gone round, worshipping at the altars of the Satis, the devoted wives, and asking for blessings for the couple, on behalf of Mishrilal's dead mother. The professional women singers, wearied of night-long singing, still continued to sing of Ram and Sita in their thick, raucous voices. Some laggards were still busy eating, soiled leaf-plates lying strewn around them.

The silence was getting too much for Ramsubhag. 'All right, sister-in-law,' he said getting up.

'Well, young man, do you like your sister-in-law?' a jovial professional singer asked Ramsubhag in her thick voice as he was leaving of courtyard.

'Yes, yes, very much!' Ramsubhag replied. He had not missed the sting in her voice. He even tried to force a smile on his face but failed, and sat down with bowed head on the string-bed by Mishrilal's side. Mishrilal was chatting with some relatives. His dhoti, dyed yellow for the occasion, showed to good effect on his swarthy body. There was no change in his expression: his face still looked bleak. His forced cheerfulness was akin to the piece of camphor kept in a discoloured rusty tin. The metal bangle on his right wrist dangled loosely like a dead spider. Ramsubhag could not explain it, but today Mishrilal looked to him uglier than on other days. He wondered how a man could look so ugly in his wedding clothes.

After attending to his visitors, Mishrilal turned to Ramsubhag. 'Subhag, what do you think of your sister-in-law?' he asked him. 'Do you like her? Tell me the truth. You went to meet her, didn't you? What did she say?'

'No, nothing much. She seems quite cheerful,' Ramsubhag said. 'Normally girls seem sad when they leave their parents' home.'

Mishrilal gave a hollow laugh. '*Arre*, Sumbhu, you turn out to be very smart at assessing brides! You're right—why should she looked sad? Had she gone to a house with a large family she would have had a hell of a time coping with her older sisters-in-law; they would have kept pestering her day and night. But here we are only the two of us. She will rule the roost. Don't you think so?'

'Hm!' Sitting with bowed head, Ramsubhag had not been listening to his cousin. He had corroborated his statement absent-mindedly.

Near the charpoy, Nanho was sitting huddled up on the coloured bridal mat, with her legs drawn up, her long eyelashes like the twisted legs of a wet butterfly. She had a distant abstracted gaze. Or maybe she was looking inwards at a swaying field laden with ripe grain over which one had just now thrown a burning stick.

Ramsubhag was sitting on the charpoy with bowed head and downcast eyes. 'Hm!' he said absentmindedly as if he had heard only half of what was being conveyed to him.

'Mishri Sah!' a woman called standing at the door. 'Babaji wants you. You must come and sit on the chowki to perform the rites. The auspicious hour is passing.'

Mishrilal slowly rose to his feet and jerkily sat down on the chowki. Wrapped in red *chunni*, Nanho who was carried in her arms by a woman like a doll and deposited by the side of Mishrilal.

A week had passed since Mishrilal's marriage during which period Ramsubhag had found time to chat with Nanho on numerous occasions. Every time he would feel as if he had erred somewhere and his heart would fill with remorse. He would decide that he would not go to her again. What had to happen had happened and could not be reversed. But his resolution would weaken and he would again find himself sitting near her. Nanho was formal with him and talked only in monosyllables. She never looked straight out him but there was something even in those drooping eyelashes which drew Ramsubhag towards her. Those eyes never looked at him; they were always looking elsewhere and yet they stirred up a tornado in him. Time and again he thought that perhaps if he had not stood before Nanho's father posing as a bridegroom, Nanho would not have come to this house. The agony he saw in those drooping eyes was of his making. He was the culprit, the criminal. Perhaps he pined to go to Nanho to atone for his sin but strangely enough her presence gave him no solace. His mother had sent him two rupees as a gift to the new bride. But he lacked the courage to offer her the money. He had bought a silk handkerchief from the market to wrap the money in before formally offering it to her. But the handkerchief kept burning a hole in his pocket and never changed hands.

'*Lala*, why are you always looking so morose?' one day Nanho asked Ramsubhag. 'Don't you find this place congenial? Do you miss your cousins and nieces?'

'Oh, no, I don't look sat, do I? Not when you are here.' Ramsubhag smiled.

'Oh, yes, I do spend some time with you. But I can only share my sorrows with others. How can I share happiness to them when there is no joy in my heart? I was born in the lap of woes and I grew with them. My mother passed away at my birth and as I grew up I became a burden to my father. How can I dispel other's sorrows?'

'Look, sister-in-law,' Ramsubhag said in a tone of deep intimacy, 'what had to happen has happened. What's the use of taking it to heart? It will only eat into your vitals. Try to be happy. Laugh sometimes.'

Nanho began to smile. 'Well, *Lala*, since you say so I will try. I'll laugh. But don't take me amiss. It takes time to cultivate a habit which does not come naturally.'

Ramsubhag went away looking very happy. A load was off his mind, as if a thorn had been removed from his flesh. How fascinating Nanho's smile was! For that matter whether she looked sad or smiled he found her equally fascinating. while roaming around in the village or when gossiping with friends or sitting at the shop her face would haunt him and the thought of her would grip his mind, coming in wave upon wave like concentric circles in a tank when a stone is cast in its water.

After the harvest the breeze grew warmer. Laden with the smell of acacia flowers, it had gained a new momentum, driving dry leaves, withered branches and ripe ears of corn before it which landed in Nanho's courtyard in profusion. After having his midday meal, Mishrilal would move into the courtyard for his siesta while Ramsubhag would avail of the time to go to the bazaar to make purchases for the shop. Nanho would sit alone in the house, watching the dry leaves fluttering in the courtyard.

Not far from the courtyard there was an acacia tree rising above the rubble of some ancient ruins. In the season when the acacia was laden with green fruit, Nanho would pluck the fruit in huge quantities, bring it home, extract juice from it and playfully apply it to her face or make patterns with it on her milk-white cheeks. When she looked in the mirror she would look like a doll made of turmeric and rice, reminding her of the boys who played the roles of Rama and Sita at the Ramlila.

A strong blast of wind flung the door open with a bang. Ramsubhag was standing before her, smiling.

'Sister-in-law' he sat down next to her on the string-bed. 'may I have a glass of water. I'm feeling thirsty.'

'Where did you go in this heat?' Nanho said pouring water for him into a glass from the pitcher on the platform.

Under the impulse of the moment, Ramsubhag's two hands grazed past the glass of water Nanho was holding before him and encircled her wrist. Her arm shook and, stiffening like a serpent, it wriggled out of Ramsubhag's grasp. The glass of water fell to the ground.

'Don't you feel ashamed of yourself?' Nanho hissed like a snake. 'If you were a man you should have taken my hand in everybody's presence. But then you acted like a trickster, standing proxy for someone else. Now don't you feel ashamed of taking the hand of another man's wife.'

'Sister-in-law, I...I... came to give you this.' Ramsubhag took out a handkerchief from his pocket, with two rupees tied in it.

'What's it?' Nanho asked angrily.

'The customary offering for the first glimpse of your face. I had thought of giving it to you before but could not bring myself to so.'

He placed the handkerchief on the bed and walked out of the house, staggering. The entire courtyard swayed before his eyes like a swing. The village lanes, the very doors of the houses seemed to be jeering at him. That day he returned to this village.

Two months passed. There was no news from Ramsubhag. Sometimes Mishrilal talked about him but finding that Nanho did not pick up the thread he would lapse into silence. Ramsubhag used to make the bulk fo the purchases to replenish the stocks at the shop. With him gone, it became quite a job for

Mishrilal to fill the breach. He would hire a pony man or a cart-man but he found it difficult even to accompany them to the market. He would return home in the afternoon under the blazing sun, leaning on his walking stick, the hot wind searing his face. One such afternoon when he was returning home he had a heat stroke and took to bed. Nanho gave him a concoction made of mango leaves and applied mango paste to his hands and the soles of his feet, but the fever did not come down. He kept writhing with pain. Nanho did not go out of the house alone and it was difficult to seek help. She sent word to Ramsubhag's village, asking him to come post haste. It was long past midnight when Ramsubhag arrived at Mishrilal's house and found a crowd gathered outside the door. He heard women wailing inside. Mishrilal's dead body was lying outside his room. Nanho had become a widow.

Ramsubhag was so busy with Mishrilal's last rites that he had no time to speak to Nanho. Even if she happened to pass by, he did not have the courage to stop her and say a few words of solace to her. Glass bangles too play the strange game of destiny. When Nanho did not want to wear them she was forced to wear them and now that she didn't want to take them off other people forcibly took them off her wrists.

Later on when she had some respite she would sit on her coloured wedding mat and gaze out into the courtyard. Ramsubhag would get agitated at the sight. Her sad eyes would pierce his heart. As far as possible, he avoided staying in the house and spent most of the time looking after the shop or sitting at others' doorsteps.

Many months passed. The rains came and ceased and the rain clouds drifted away. The showers filled the gaping wounds of the crumbling walls. Repaired with fresh earth, they put on a happy exterior as if the rains had never tried to pulverize them.

On the full-moon night of Kartik they were having a religious congregation at Chamtoli where they sang hymns in praise of God. They had placed the image of their patron saint, laden with flowers garlands on a wooden platform in the middle of the gathering. The incense fumes went spiralling up, purifying the village's polluted atmosphere. The kirtan party sang on while men, women and children listened with rapt attention:

> You have bound us with the bonds of love
> You are the cloud and we the peacock,
> You the moon and we the wild goose.
> Madhav, even if you break this bond we cannot break it.
> If we break off with you,
> to whom shall we join ourselves?
> Yours may be infatuation but I hold you fast with bond of love
> Try hard as you may but I'll not let you go.
> You are *Girvar* and I a peacock in trance
> You are the moon and I the *chakora* in thrall.
> Madhav, you may desert me but I'll still cling to you
> By breaking away from you to whom else shall I go?

The singing continued late into the night. When Nanho returned home the lines from Saint Raidas's hymn were still echoing in her ears: 'Even if you break this bond, we cannot break it...'

Ramsubhag had closed the door of the courtyard. He opened it on hearing the rattling of the door chain.

'Sister-in-law, it's not right for you to roam around so late at night,' he said, slipping aside to allow her to enter. Where had he got the courage go question her like this?

'Hm!' Nanho grunted.

'I'm talking to you...'

Nanho turned on her heel and fixed her eyes on his face. 'If you are so concerned you should have married me. You're getting wild with me as if I'm your wife. What right have you over me? I'm telling you, in future don't you dare glare at me like that!'

Ramsubhag sat down holding his head between his hands, his body burning with anger and shame. Pulling up his bed-sheet he covered his face with it and kept seething with anger.

That was five years ago. This was the first letter from him in those long years. He had informed her that he was coming to the village from Calcutta. Nanho had had a hard time of it for he had disappeared that very night five years ago. Nanho's eyes had got swollen with crying. She had nobody whom she could call her own. Perhaps she was born to lead a lonely life. How forlorn she looked. Had she done wrong by attending the religious congregation that night? Everybody from the village had gone there. Why make an exception in her case? Was it because she was a widow for whom all festivities are taboo?

'Where's that young man gone?' the next day a woman had asked Nanho. 'Look, take my advice and marry him. Such marriages are not forbidden in your community. How long can you live like this?'

'Don't talk rot!' Nanho had reproved the woman. But the next moment she had felt ashamed of herself. How was it that people were able to pry into your innermost thoughts? The more you tried to hide those thoughts the sooner people brought them to the surface.

'I'll keep my mouth shut, if that's what you want,' the woman had said. 'But you'll regret it. You won't be able to get a better husband than him. He won't remain unmarried all his life for your sake. Such opportunities rarely come a women's way. Your father had seen him, hadn't he? It was through trickery that Mishrilal had married you.'

'I say keep your mouth shut!' Tears came to Nanho's eyes. 'My life has been one long fraud—fraud heaped upon fraud. No one can erase what's written in my fate.'

Nanho Auntie! Nanho Auntie!' a small boy shouted from the shop.

'Why, what's the matter?' she asked entering the shop. 'Why are you creating this hullabaloo?'

'Look, Kishna has decamped with a big lot of wild berries!' Jannu said with a child's lisp. He was looking greedily at the luscious red berries heaped in a basket.

'Lease Kishna alone!' Nanho said good-humouredly. 'Here, have these berries and run away.'

The boy filled his pocket with berries and went away smiling. Nanho closed the door after him and went into the kitchen.

The train from Calcutta arrived at about seven in the evening. Nanho was lying on a bed strung with jute string. Its rough edges hurt her bare feet. The wind had lost some of its chill. Instead, now there was a touch of warmth in it as it came wafting wave after wave. Nanho's dark hair dangled in thick curls from the edge of the bed and kissing the ground. She lay there staring at the stars in the blue sky. The moon would soon rise from behind the eastern wall of the courtyard, for a mass of light had started scintillating as it ricocheted against the parapet of the roof of her house.

The door chain rattled.

'Sister-in-law.'

Ramsubhag had returned after five years.

Nanho opened the door and found Subhag standing before her. She peered at him through the darkness.

'Please come in.' Her voice, sharp like the cracking of a shoulder bone pierced the stillness and was lost again. Both sat in studied silence, Ramsubhag on a bed in the courtyard, an eerie stillness surrounding him.

After finishing his meal, Ramsubhag again returned to his bed to sleep. Nanho pulled up a stringed low tuffet and sat down next to his bed.

'Babu, you have remembered me after such a long time,' Nanho said breaking the silence at last. 'You look so thin. Were you ill?'

'No, I'm all right, sister-in-law,' Ramsubhag replied. 'For five years I've been trying to forget you. Many a time I thought of visiting you and seeking your forgiveness. But my courage failed me. This time I decided I'd once for all spill out what's on my mind. I had erred unknowingly, sister-in-law. I didn't have a ghost of an idea that that small lapse of mine would recoil so heavily against me. What I did, I did for Mishri Bhaiyya's happiness. But a wrong is a wrong, irrespective of one's intention.' Ramsubhag was looking at the ground with downcast eyes. 'Who else will forgive me, if not you?'

'What wrong are you talking of, *Lalla*? What you call a misdemeanour is a consequence of my fate. You may be under the impression that my father knew nothing about it. He came to know about it the moment your people broached the suggestion of the bridal send-off. People do have a foreboding when something is likely to go wrong. Those who have the means can prevent things from going awry. But those who are weak take umbrage by calling it deceit. As I have said my father had seen through your game but he could not back out because he did not have the money which another boy's family would have demanded. You became a handy excuse. But you were not to blame for it.' Nanho wiped her tears with the end of her sari. Ramsubhag kept gazing stupidly at Nanho through the darkness.

'Babu, you must be tired after your long journey,' Nanho said. 'I'll talk to you in the morning.' She got up and went to her room.

Ramsubhag stayed there for three days. He did nothing but talk to Nanho, night and day,—about Calcutta, about his parents, about his brothers and cousins—in fact, about everything under the sun. Nanho looked so changed to him. Her eyes had lost their old sparkle. Now they looked so mellow and full of maternal affection. Seeing Nanho in this new guise, Ramsubhag's mind was filled with hope. Could it be possible? Could the reckoning of fate be tallied up afresh? But he had always found it difficult to open his heart to Nanho. He had not been able to live down those two past events and they had kept rankling in his mind. But Nanho too was not like this before.

Today Nanho was also thinking in the same vein about those old days and Saint Raidas's lines kept echoing in her mind: 'Even if you break the bond, we can't break it. If we break off with your, to whom shall we join ourselves?'

She seemed to be in a happy mood but Ramsubhag had no peace of mind. He kept turning over the idea in his head that if he brought up the question of his going away, things might come to a head and Nanho might become more explicit about her intentions.

In this hope, the next morning he said to her, 'Sister-in-law, I intend leaving for my village by the night train.'

'But why so soon? Are you unhappy here?'

'I like it here all right, but...'

'All right, it's entirely up to you.'

Ramsubhag failed to catch the meaning of her reply. He kept sitting in his room, hoping against hope. Maybe at the time of departure she might try to persuade him to come back.

In the evening, when Ramsubhag came out after packing his things, Nanho emerged from her room.

'So you are ready to leave, *Lalla*?' she said.

'Yes.'

Extending her hand to him, Nanho said: 'Here is, your handkerchief, *Lalla*'.

'What handkerchief?' Ramsubhag asked. He seemed to have turned into dead wood. 'But sister-in-law, I had given it to you as an offering for the first glimpse of your face,' he said.

'On seeing your face, my father had bestowed upon me the blessings of an unforeseen married life in perpetuity. You mother had also given you those two rupees to perpetuate that memory. What my elders gave me I accepted with good grace as if in honour bound. Babu, I was weak and lost the battle against my fate. But today I am standing on my own feet. Today you must save me from being vanquished. Your handkerchief had shackled my feet and I am therefore returning it to you. You must not take offence.'

Ramsubhag silently took the handkerchief from Nanho. She could not bear the sight of his going. Her eyes were swimming with tears, through which the flame of the lamp seemed to be divided into many parts like the petals of a full blown flower: Nanho closed the door but could not put up the door chain to bolt it.

Krishna Sobti

The Encircling Clouds

Lying in the small cottage at Bhowali Sanatorium, I look at the hills stretching away in front of me. I look at the encircling clouds, swollen with rain, and at the barren ones, wisp-like and shrivelled. I look at the mist groping in vain, and at my own body, bare as a tree that has shed its leaves. In front, the path to Ramgarh is etched into the dry vegetation of the sloping mountain, like the thick veins standing out on my arm. The breeze, wayward like my own breath, now caresses and now pummels at the window. My body tucked inside the blanket gradually disintegrates like a thin layer of lime slowly dissolving in water, and I live in constant dread that my life, woven with the warp and woof of years will suddenly stop pulsating.

The curtains at the door and the windows hang listlessly, silent like me, day and night, morning and evening. Nobody lifts them with firm hands and stands at the threshold to greet me with a smile. Night, morning, evening gather turn by turn around my bed. I lie in the iron bed and look with dimmed eyes not at darkness and light but at myself, at my wasting body from which life is ebbing away. I am helpless. Nothing else remains.

I look at my thin arms sticking out of my shoulders and am reminded of those plump arms, that perfumed hair, and those soft lips which gave my life. I had everything. Living together, sleeping together, walking together. Early in the morning someone would bend over my bed and say, 'Won't you get up? It's morning.'

With closed eyes, I would put my arms around that alluring body, draw it to me to smell those moments of the night and mumble, 'Where's the hurry?'

A laugh and the arms would relax, eyes open and domesticity dawn.

Breakfast in the garden. The mistress of the house, chic and debonair, confident of her authority, would turn the dream of the night into tangible reality. I would look at her fingers while she poured milk into the cup, those fingers which had caressed my hair in the night, and the end of her sari jealously hiding her gently heaving breasts. For a fleeting moment I would wonder if what I felt deep down in my being was merely the outer trappings and the reality lay somewhere still deeper in those transient moments where two beings become one... But the night here at the sanatorium is tubercular and dark. Lying under the blanket, I look at the phials of medicine, read their labels over and over again and realize that when the sap of life dries up, bones and flesh become wood, not earth, because from the earth life sprouts once. I am yet to turn to earth.

In the vacuity of this dreary existence I try to resurrect that memorable night when on receiving a message I hurried to her room. Under the blue light of the lamp two tired eyelids fluttered and after gazing at an infant, sleeping in the crook of an arm, two eyes came to rest on my face. They seemed to say: 'I have given form to your embrace and made it live.' I got up, touched her cold brow with my lips and marvelled how love that is born in the body grows of the body can also take a form, and come into the world.

But there is another form of love which never comes to fruition, like the mountain clouds which promise rain but never break into a shower.

It was years ago. I had gone to the hills one summer. One bright morning we had just got up from breakfast table when my aunt introduced me to her. I still remember those beautiful eyes. 'Ravi, meet Minni. She's here just for two days.' My aunt's introduction lacked warmth—A sigh escaped her lips. There was something hollow about the way my aunt said that she was here for two days. I didn't like it.

She acknowledged my greeting with a nod and I perceived a faint smile on her face. Thin but lively, her face wore a far-off expression. I could not take my eyes off her face with its tightly swept back hair. I was left feeling as if I must atone for someone else's reproach.

When we came out, aunt's children became playful. They tugged at Manno's sari and clung to her arms and cried, 'Mannojiji! Mannojiji!' My aunt about to go in, turned round on hearing the shrill laughter of the children. I still remember her face as she tried to hide her stern expression. With a firm hand she pulled away the children. Looking coldly at Manno, she said in a limp voice,' Manno, better go out for a stroll. These children will not let you alone.' Seeing the reproach in their mother's eyes the children ran off.

My aunt's arms fell to her sides. Manno looked at her steadily.

But before my aunt could get over her discomfiture, Manno was out of the gate.

'Tell me, aunt,' I asked my aunt, 'What's this mystery?'

My question had apparently irritated her. 'She is ill, Ravi,' she said shortly, and then added, 'For two years she has been staying at the sanatorium. Now her father has bought her a cottage there; and an old family servant looks after her. When she gets fed up with the place she comes to the city for a brief spell.'

I was too shocked to believe her words.

'Ravi, when I see her on her rare visits I lose my appetite.'

'But you shouldn't have sent the children away so abruptly,' I said trying to probe her further. 'Didn't you see she felt hurt?'

My aunt looked hard at me, as if she thought it futile to explain things to me, and went inside. The children were busy playing. I stood there puffing at a cigarette, trying to blow away my vague apprehension with the curling smoke. I walked out of the gate and climbing down the ridge took the road running along the bank of the lake. In the sunlight, little waves shimmered and broke against the bank. I stopped in front of the Naini Temple, and leaned on the railing to watch the boats. In one boat two young men, rowing strongly, sped past towards Tallital, leaving behind an old man dozing in another boat. Then followed a few European women in the club's boat.

Suddenly I see that pale face in the water, those big eyes, those thin arms. I repeat the name, Manno, Manno, Manno... I stand on the high bank and Manno flows towards me on the water. Pulled back curly hair, unblinking lashes... But Aunt says Manno is ill, Manno is ill.

Turning away from the railing I looked in the direction of my aunt's house. The Cheena Peak stood firm in its exalted glory, looking down at me... I stood on the road bewildered. Everything was the same as on other days, but for two eyes, their image imprinted deep in the caverns of my mind, and that illness behind those eyes, inaccessible and beyond release.

My aunt had gone out with the children. I went into the drawing room, and having nothing better to do, looked at the decor and admired my aunt's taste. On the cabinet stood the family photograph, in a heavy frame. What was there so attractive about my aunt's husband that she spends days and nights, months and years bound to him? But no, it was unbecoming of me to harbour such thoughts in aunt's own house.

I climbed the stairs to my room. Lighting a cigarette, I gazed out of the window. Bright-red tin roofs dotted the hills and grey hill tracks meandered over them. Aunt would be back soon...and Manno. I kept turning the pages of an old magazine.

'May I lay the table Saheb?'

'When will aunt be back?'
'She said she won't have lunch.'
'And the guest?'
'She will lunch alone. Upstairs.'

I crushed the cigarette under foot, relieved that I should not be tortured by her presence—or was it at my helplessness that I could not keep company with her? What else passed through my mind I do not remember. All that I remember is that I toyed with my food absent-mindedly and kept looking out.

I was at the end of my last course when I heard hoof-beats.

'Will you be able to get there in two hours?' The voice was low but firm.

'Yes, hazoor.'

I heard her going upstairs. Lunch was over, but I did not go up. Even after helping myself to another cup of coffee, I kept sitting at the table. It struck me that to be disturbed by such a brief encounter was a sign of terrible weakness. Why should a casual introduction make me so restless?

After an hour I found myself climbing the stairs. A curtain hung across the open door. I knocked.

'Please come in.' Manno was standing by her suitcase, holding a Cashmere shawl. She did not lose her composure on seeing me. 'Please sit down,' she said, removing clothes from the sofa.

This was the brightest room in aunt's house. New furniture, costly curtains, and Manno wearing light yellow clothes. it cheered me.

'You've had your lunch, of course?' I asked just for the sake of saying something.

'Yes.' She gazed at me.

'Is aunt out?'

Manno nodded. She folded the shawl and put it in the suitcase saying, 'I'll be gone before the evening. Please tell aunt I came for a day only.'

'But she'll be back soon.'

She aid nothing, nor did she indicate anything by her expression.

'Won't you stay for another day?' I asked.

Silently, she bent over her suitcase, putting things into it. After a pause she said, laughing, 'What's the use? This small city holds no attraction for me after a big village like Bhowali.' After so many years, her laughter still rings in my ears and the pallor of her face is still vivid in my mind.

We came down together, I carrying her coat on her arm. The servant and the gardener bowed and were given tips.. The syce patted the horse.

'Will you ride?'

With a fleeting glance she looked at the coat. 'No, I would rather walk. Lead the horse.'

I wanted her to ride, but could not force the words out of my mouth.

At the gate she turned her head as if she was taking a last look at the house. She quickly collected herself and started off briskly down the slope. We walked in silence.

Her things were put in the taxi. The driver sensed the tense situation.

'Shall we start?' he asked.

With a blank look she stretched out her hand for the coat. As she sat down in the car, the attendant took a rug and with professional dexterity spread it over her knees.

She looked tired. I could see the fish-faced golden bangles on her wrists. But what was in her eyes? I could not make out for the life of me. She gazed steadily at her hands lying inert on her knees.

The car started and I looked back. No arms were raised. No lips moved in farewell. Till the car disappeared round the bend I kept looking at the ribbon tied in a simple knot round her hair falling at her nape and hearing that painful thank you—'No, no, that's all, thanks.'

Even today when I conjure up those moments something happens to me. After the road had swallowed up the speeding car, I turned back and trudged along the bank of the lake. In vain I tried to blot out her face; it kept bobbing up before my eyes, again and again. It was a slow ascent to the house, halting and weary. The thought of it tires me even today. The coolies were shifting the furniture on the verandah. Something clutched at my heart. So it was all a game, a make-believe! Manno's room had been furnished with hired furniture. I saw aunt in a new light; the favourable impression I had formed of her was suddenly reversed. My aunt was standing at the door. 'Ravi, go and wash,' she said in a strained voice. 'Tea will be ready in a minute. Don't be late.'

We sat down to tea. The children were not about. Only my aunt. She poured tea and pushed the cup towards me.

'Aunty!'

She pretended she had not heard me.

'Aunty.' I said again, 'Why did our visitor leave so abruptly?—She had come for two days, right?'

Aunt kept stirring her tea. Her silence made me more cruel.

'She asked me to tell you that a day's stay was enough for her.' Why do I think of all this now? Why these futile thoughts?

Aunt seemed unable to hear any more. Sighing deeply she looked at me and said,' Say no more, Ravi,' and left the room, leaving her tea untouched.

That night uncle was to return from his tour but the servant told me a telegram had arrived to say he would be two days late. I wanted to go to my aunt's room but felt shy. Finally I found myself on the stairs in front of Manno's room. I went in and put on the light—all empty, no curtains, no furniture, no Manno—I looked at the wood piled in the fireplace and thought, had she been here tonight she'd have sat up late into the night and perhaps I would have come here like this to her and... why am I thinking all this! Why...

Gripped by a vague nervousness, I hurried down. I switched off the light and tumbled into my bed. Lying awake I thought of that small cottage in Bhowali where Manno would have reached by now.

'Ravi!' It was my aunt.

She came and sat down near me and fondled my hair. For a moment her hand became still and then passed over my brow.

'I'm not fondling you but that unfortunate girl,' she said in a trembling voice. 'This hand will never touch her again.'

My hand trembled in her grasp. I felt I was holding Manno's hand.

'Ravi, stop thinking of her. She will not be in our midst for long.'

I trembled at my aunt's touch. 'Aunty, I may not live long either.'

Today, years later, lying in a cottage in Bhowali, I think countless times what made me utter those prophetic words, whose horrid truth I feel in my pulse-beat, day after day and night after night. I don't know how aunt reacted to those words. But I remember her suddenly switching on the light and looking full in my face with reproachful eyes. 'Have you gone crazy?' she said. 'Do you want to compare yourself to a girl who gropes in a blind alley and for whom there is no point of return?'

She sat down in the chair. 'Ravi, you have seen her only for one day. But I've known her for years and my heart has been squeezed dry of all feeling. All the care I have lavished on her has been in vain. There was a time when I eagerly looked forward to her homecoming and now I wait anxiously for her departure and keep my children out of her way.'

She looked at me uncertainly, got up to go but stopped suddenly. 'Ravi, this will lead you nowhere.' Her voice was stern with warning. 'There's no use pining for a derelict for whom all doors are closed.'

That day I did not understand my aunt. I wouldn't even if I wanted to.

The next day I roamed about like a lost soul. I raced the horse to Lariakanta, and back to the Band Stand. When I turned homewards I found that I was bound for elsewhere. I stood at the ridge thinking. In the afternoon when I descended the slope to Tallital, I was clear in my mind about my destination. I had to go to Bhowali.

I got out of the bus. At the Ramgarh bus-stand I saw heaps of luscious red apples and I knew I was not far from Bhowali. While in the bus I had imagined it would be a small congested place. But here the tall pines swayed in the breeze and the place was drenched in sunshine. Bhowali looked beautiful. Passing through the square I came to the post office, and obtained her address. The way to 'The Pines' lay through a small bazaar. A narrow path at the turning of the main road took me off towards a small hill. I looked down from the railing. Between the hills lay a small valley, criss-crossed with small fields like a piece of patchwork. Far off, towards the south, a lake shone like a sheet of silver.

After this, my first visit, I came to Bhowali times without number. But not like this. This visit was different, utterly different. I walked on unthinkingly; unaware that I was going to Manno. I just walked on, that's all I was aware of. 'The Pines' was boldly etched into the trunk of a tree. I pushed open the wicket-gate. Walking between the two rows of flower-pots, I came to the verandah and treading softly on the carpet I knocked gently. A bent man with a shrewd face answered the door.

'Anybody in?'
'Son, are you looking for the child?'
I nodded in reply.
'The child has gone to the lake. She should be back soon.'

I sat down in the open and waited. After a while I turned my back towards the gate. When you decide a person won't come soon, he turns up soon.

The sound of horse-hoofs. I forced myself not to look back.

'Baba,' someone called. I felt two eyes on my back. I got up. Of course, I knew it could be none else than Manno. There was no surprise, no eagerness in her eyes. Nor were they sad. They were just two eyes, very much like Manno's, looking at me steadfastly.

'Baba!'

The old servant came towards the horse in swift strides and said in a caressing voice, 'Child, get down. It's already late.' He held out his hand to help her dismount. Manno said, 'Please call Amma. I'm not feeling well.'

'I hope there's nothing wrong, child.'

She gave a little laugh on seeing his anxious look. 'Please tell Amma to prepare my bed.'

The servant pulled up a chair for her. 'Want to lie down?' he anxiously asked her.

'Yes, Baba.'

She avoided the servant's gaze as if she was guilty of some indiscretion.

Then she bent towards me, 'Have I kept you waiting long?'

'Oh, no,' I shook my head. 'Are you unwell?'

In reply Manno closed her eyes.

The old maidservant came running with a shawl and wrapped it round her shoulders. 'Manno, that old man is put out by trifles. You'll come round in a moment. May I bring tea for the gentleman?'

Manno did not know what to say. 'Amma, ask him yourself. He may not like the idea.'

Her meaning was lost on me: I said, 'No, no, I'm not thirsty.'

Manno didn't seem to have heard. Nor did she look at me.

'How is aunty?' she asked after a pause. 'Is uncle still away?'

The maidservant now knew who I was. 'You should have informed us you were coming. I would have asked you to bring a few things for Manno.'

'Amma, please make the bed. I'm tired. I can't sit any longer.'

I sat on looking a fool. How thoughtless of me. I should have at least brought some fruit for her.

Manno seemed to have read my mind. 'It wasn't necessary,' she said as if musing to herself. 'It's not proper to bring anything or take anything from here.'

I cursed myself for my senselessness. I followed her into the cottage. Amma put her to bed, loosening her hair. She pushed a chair towards me and left the room.

'Manno!'

Without speaking, she stretched her thin arm towards me and then suddenly withdrew it. Today when I am myself reduced to Manno's state, I would make a thousand sacrifices to win back that hour. While sitting there why didn't I touch that arm, stroke that hand? As if some mysterious force held back the flood, I sat glued to the chair, motionless.

Why this hesitation? It must have been the same fear which now keeps away my near and dear ones from me. That night when I got up to leave her room, love and fear waged a grim struggle within me. When I reached the dak bungalow I felt a great sense of release from a bond whose every oppressive moment had held me in its shackles. I wish Manno were alive today to see the fruits of that liberation.

I couldn't sleep properly all night. Each time I woke I felt I was still in Bhowali in that room at 'The Pines', with its large windows. I was lying in Manno's bed and sitting by the bedside Manno was gazing at me. I stretched out my hand. Manno laughed and shook her head. 'Tuck it under the rug. Who would care to touch it?'

'Manno!'

Manno says nothing, only laughs.

After this phantasmagoric night when I woke again, I saw my aunt. 'Ravi, it will lead you nowhere.'

That morning I rushed to the bus-stop. The thought came to me, 'The Pines' ...no...no...nothing...go back.'

When I got home my aunt looked sharply at me and asked, 'Where were you yesterday?'

'Went to Ranikhet, aunt.'

'Why didn't you tell me?'

'What was there to tell, Aunty?'

In the afternoon I met Uncle. He had returned the previous day and as always he wore a grave expression. I caught his expression when he raised his eyes from the plate. I had no doubt that uncle and Manno's father must have been brothers. His eyes had the same tranquility and steadiness as Manno's.

Getting up from the dining table, Uncle said, 'Ravi, your aunt wants to go to Lucknow. Do you mind going with her?'

'Uncle, I'll accompany her.'

My aunt, children and I were coming down from Nainital. As the bus took a turn down the broad hill road, I saw Bhowali shrouded in a haze. The same Bhowali I had visited yesterday. And then on to Kathgodam and Lucknow.

After a day's stay at Aunt's place when I went to take leave of her, she insisted on my staying with her for a few days more. She was not prepared to take a no from me, it seemed. But I was adamant. 'But where will you go?' she asked at last.

'I don't know,' I said.

Something seemed to be weighing on my aunt's mind. 'But your uncle wants you to go back to Naini.'

'No, Aunty, I'll go south, to father.'

'Ravi, you didn't enjoy yourself at Naini this time.'

'No, no, Aunt.'

Parting I touched aunt's feet. Aunt is not much older than myself. But I felt I was in need of her blessing.

She was taken by surprise. 'Ravi, you have touched my feet,' she said smiling. 'I'll bless you for it. May you get a beautiful wife.'

She had said this half in jest, and when I stood glum she felt embarrassed.

After buying my ticket I left the luggage with the coolie and began to stroll on the platform. There was no train in the yard. The straight railway line stretching into the distance, seemed to have uncoiled the skein of my tangled thoughts. I kept thinking not about Bhowali, 'The Pines' and Manno but of the blessings of my aunt. A cosy home, a beautiful wife and I...

My aunt's prophecy came true. I did set up a house, and marry a beautiful girl. That is a different story though. But the train did not take me to the destination I was bound for.

The train steamed in and the coolie found a seat for me and put in my luggage while I stood watching the rushing crowd—passengers, coolies, women, children, old men.

'Saheb, the train will leave in a minute.'

I looked at my watch and nodded my head. Adjusting his turban the coolie said, 'Saheb, don't you see? The green light is on.' I looked at the green signal. And then everything swam out of focus... the same bright thin figure, the same pallor on the face.

'Coolie, take down my luggage!'

'Saheb!'

'Hurry up, quick'....

The coolie was again following me with my luggage. I returned the ticket and purchased a new one. I bought baskets of fruit, gulped some tea, and took the train to Bareilly. I would go where I liked. Who was there to stop me—and why?

In the afternoon I sat basking on the front lawn under the winter sun. Mother came from inside and sat down by my side. 'Now that you have come on leave why are you in a hurry to go? Why be so stubborn?'

I smiled like the wise prodigal son. Contrary to her expectation, I said, 'Mother, any girl who is acceptable to you is acceptable to me.'

'Son, would you like to see the girl then?'

'Yes, mother.'

I felt mother was smiling to herself.

After dinner when I returned from a stroll the room was quiet.

I no longer had that youthful eagerness, curiosity, desire to see someone. Having lived so long alone, I perhaps had no hope of companionship.

I started dozing while reading in bed. I dreamed I was working my way up a hill. I saw a thick cluster of pines. The sky was empty, a voice resounded in the silkiness of the night and then a trembling hand groped towards my neck. The same feeble wrist, the same thin trembling fingers... I woke up with a start. My brow was damp with fear. I parted the window curtain. The lawn lay covered with light, filtering from father's room.

I came to myself, sighed, touched my hair, my cold brow. A terrifying desolation, and in the dark that hand...that hand.

Why was I reminded of this hand that night, a hand that I had almost forgotten and had seen for the last time, many years ago, while coming down from 'The Pines'?

I won't say I touched it because to move your head forward numberless times with the intention of touching is not to touch.

Staying in Naini for a month and returning time and again from Bhowali, there came one final day when I returned from Manno and wished to turn that return into a point of no return. Three times I descended, and three times turned to ascend again.

Manno, a shawl thrown over her shoulders was reclining in an easy chair. I was standing by her side. 'Tomorrow I will be gone from Naini,' I said breaking the ice.

Manno slowly gathered the shawl which had slipped from her shoulders. The far off expression which I had seen on her face a month ago, had again returned.

I wanted to say something. But what should I say? Should I tell her that I would soon return?

Every passing moment confirmed my resolve to return. But the way she looked at me suggested that I was going away for ever.

'Manno...' I said.

'Ravi.'

For a fleeting moment her face became taut and then it was suffused with a faint smile. She joined her hands in farewell, 'Namaskar.'

I stood rooted to the ground speechless, looking at those folded hands, wanting to step forward and bid farewell, but unable to move.

'You are getting late, Ravi.'

I lowered my eyes and without a word of parting hurried on. Would I return again, or was it the final parting?

I looked back and stopped for a moment. Manno was sitting in the same posture, like a statue.

Perhaps she had a hunch that I would turn back. 'Please sit down, Ravi.' she pointed towards a chair. There was no anguish in her voice nor any sign of surprise. She looked at me questioningly as if she knew I had something on my mind.

'I don't feel like going, Manno,' I said with the simplicity of a child.

I looked at her, tense with expectancy. Oh, how excruciating her silence was.

She wanted to say something, as I could see. But the words seemed to stick in her throat. 'But you'll have to leave sooner or later,' she said at last.

I was overwhelmed. I could have touched, could have kissed the very timbre of her voice. 'Manno.'

I stepped towards her. As if to arrest the outpouring of my heart she raised her feeble hand. 'Manno.' I want my plea to reach her. 'No.' And nothing more.

Then she raised her thin hand in a gesture of farewell. Feeling empty and helpless, I took my way down 'The Pines'. My eyes had become misty. I looked back, bewildered. I was again standing on the bank of the lake and Manno was drifting by in a boat. She had not seen me. Her bowed head was hidden by her uplifted hand. Perhaps her eyes were closed. Or may be she was weeping. The thought of that stern wounded pride made me throb.

I heard her sobbing inside. In my heart I cried out, 'Manno, Manno.' A voice seemed to reply, 'Don't wait. Don't stop.'

Then I ran towards the road, increasing the distance between me and the cottage, the inmate of the cottage and those two eyes. But I could not blot out the memory of Manno. Even today the thought of her is fresh in my mind. I vividly recall that afternoon when Manno and I went for a walk along the big lake. The afternoon was drenched in mild sunshine, golden and glorious. I was carried away by the pallor of her face. Her shoulders, covered with a shawl, in spite of her tired gait, were proudly erect. I gazed at her curly hair, her shoulders, her feet.

When we came to the end of our promenade, we sighted two small temples under a giant tree. Their tin doors were closed. Manno stood thinking for a moment, and then taking off her shoes, she stepped over the rocks and plucked a lotus from the temple pool. She covered her head with her shawl and placing the lotus in front of the closed door she bowed her head in worship.

When she got up, she looked strangely different, as if she was not Manno but an incarnation of her own helplessness which had bowed its head before the closed door of its destiny.

Anguish rose in me for this melancholy loneliness. 'I'll look around for the priest and have the temple door opened,' I said.

'No, Ravi, no need,' she said shaking her head. 'I've no blessings to ask for. All doors are now closed to me. May those doors remain open for those from whom I have been separated.'

Casting to the wind the fear of catching infection from her disease which stood in my way, I bent over her head. 'Manno...'

She gently pushed my hand from her shoulders.' Ravi, don't stretch out your hand for that which you can't endure.'

There was no reproach in her voice, no irony, no bitterness. She simply said what had to be said. That day I could not answer her. Not even though I went to her again and again, not even in those moments of farewell when I left Manno weeping. The weakness that made me a coward has me in its grip today. Today I curse that cowardice, on my own behalf, on Manno's behalf.

The house was full of gaiety. Mother had got a bride after her own heart and I a life companion. When I looked at Meera's innocent face, I completely lost my head. A throng of relatives and friends—it gladdened my heart to see the house of marriage ringing with laughter. We went on a month's honeymoon to the seaside and then to my place of posting where we set up a new home together. My life had found its equilibrium.

In our newly discovered world, endless and fathomless like the sea, we would roam for hours together, doting on each other. Morning, evening, day and night we would lose ourselves only to find ourselves again. Lost in ourselves we saw everything and yet saw nothing.

And thus ten years passed. Oblivious of the impending doom, absorbed in each other. Torn away from Meera and the children, when lying in the cottage, I recall those halcyon days I feel as if I still hear somebody breathing by my side. I wish I could peep into someone's eyes and tell her how happy we were then. But now there is no one at hand to listen to me. Because of the children, Meera has become cold towards me.

Last month, while going to Ranikhet, Meera had dropped in for an hour with the children. Lying in bed I saw the three of them coming up. For a brief moment she had paused at the wicket-gate. Then she had gathered the children and led them up.

'Rani, Munna, bow to your father, children!' They raised their hands awkwardly at their mother's bidding and then looked at me with curiosity. Their own father was a stranger to them.

Meera cried all the time. She was too shaken to talk coherently. For fear of infecting them, I dared not fondle my own children. I kept gazing at Meera who had come to see me. I tried to search the wife in this woman, who I had once called my own.

I was hurt by the heartlessness of Meera looking at her wristwatch with tear-filled eyes.

Abstractedly, I stared at the wicket-gate through which my own family would presently pass, leaving me alone to my fate. I was overpowered by a strong urge to hold Meera's hand and say, 'I won't let you go. No, I won't let you go.' But the apathetic look in my children's eyes tore through my desire to its very end.

I looked up startled. Meera had come up. Bending over me, Meera lightly brushed my forehead with her lips and then stepped back. Wiping my tearful eyes which had become wet with Meera's tears, I looked around through misty eyes. The dam had burst. The torrent of emotions had carried away everything. There was no Meera by my side, nor the children.

Propped against the pillow I looked out. They were now at the third turning of the descending path. With her back towards me, Meera stooped slightly as she walked. Holding hands, the children walked on, now looking at their mother now at the path.

With bated breath I watched them, hoping that they would look back at me. But no heads turned. Only my daughter's ribbon, tied round her head, kept bobbing in the air, as if proclaiming, 'Daddy, we are going, we are going for ever.'

Yes, they were gone—all of them. They left because I was also preparing to depart. In the same way, I too had sped down the path when I sensed that Manno's end was near. Like me Manno too had wept. Now I know what it means to cover your face and shed tears in sequestered loneliness with no one around to console you.

That time when I parted from Manno I did not think of her for years together. But whenever I saw her in sleep, I saw the same thin body, the same big eyes and the arms resting over the blanket. I would wake up, greatly agitated, and shifting closer to Meera cuddle myself against her.

I had come to Lucknow on tour and visited my aunt. We sat chatting when my aunt's tone suddenly changed. 'Ravi, do you know, Manno is no more in this world.'

I was stunned. But hiding my feelings I put on a grave expression befitting the role of a newly-made father.

'Yes, she passed away in sleep,' my aunt looked at me as though I was still the Ravi of those bygone years. 'The maid-servant was on leave. When Khayali, the old servant came in the morning there was no life in her.'

'Aunt...' I said in a chocked voice, on the verge of asking something.

'Ravi, you should have written to her once, at least,' Aunt said in a strained voice, wiping her tears.

I put my handkerchief to my eyes to wipe my tears.

'And she had left a packet for you,' Aunt added. 'It contained a woollen jersey.'

'I again called on aunt the next day. Touching her feet in a hurry I said, 'Well, Aunt...'

'Ravi...' Aunt said in the same strain in which she had been speaking to me yesterday.

Shaking my head I said in a defeated voice,' No, Aunt, no.'

Aunt realized that I didn't have the heart to dwell on the subject. Her heart brimmed over for Manno. 'I wonder why Providence had doled her out a love which could not be requited,' she said.

When I returned from Lucknow her memory kept haunting me for many days. I saw her sitting in 'The Pines', knitting a jersey for me. The same hands, the same visage.

After lying in bed at home for a year at last I found myself at Bhowali with its mild sunshine and its cold wind rushing through the pines. Yes, I was here again. But this time I did not have to call at the post office to find someone's address. The first time I moved into the accursed cottage facing 'The Pines', I wept bitterly. The whole night I kept repeating the same name, 'Manno! Manno!' If she had been alive today...

Meera, whom I had known for years, now looks remote and alien. The woman whom I had loved ardently, kissed passionately. But when my heart brims over and I pine for someone, it is of Manno I think and not Meera.

Tired of my dreary existence, when I gaze out of the window, I still see her curly hair and her face dimly outlined in the encircling clouds.

The frequently changing colours of the medicine bottles remind me that my soul will not grope for long in this transient body. One day while looking out of the window I will merge in these clouds... in these encircling clouds.

Nirmal Verma

Birds

Passing through the dark corridor Latika stopped short. Supporting herself against the wall she raised the wick of her lamp. On the steps her shadow began forming a shapeless, ragged shape. From room No 7 strident laughter and the chatter of the girls could still be heard. Latika knocked at the door. The noise ceased at once.

'Who's there?'

Latika stood still. For some time muffled sounds of whispering went on in the room. Then came the sound of the latch clicking. Latika went in. In the flickering flame of the lamp the girls' faces emerged like close-ups frozen on a movie screen.

'Why is the room dark?' There was an edge to Latika's voice.

'The lamp ran out of oil, Ma'am'.

It was Sudha's room, so Sudha herself had had to answer. She was perhaps the most popular girl in the hostel. For, on all holidays, and everyday after dinner, the girls from the other rooms crowded into hers. The chatter and the leg pulling would go on till late into the right.

'Why didn't you ask Karimuddin for oil?'

'Ma'am, I've told him so many times. He just doesn't remember'.

A ripple of laughter ran from one corner of the room to the other. The oppressive air of discipline that swirled in with Latika's entry, suddenly drained out. Karimuddin was a servant in the hostel. Stories of his laziness and shirking had been circulating among generations of students.

Latika suddenly remembered something. Holding up her lamp she ran her eyes over the room. The girls sat in a circle, huddled against each other. Familiar faces all, but in the lamp's pale light it was as if something had changed, as if she was seeing them for the first time.

'Julie, what're you doing in this block so late?'

Julie was sitting at the head of a bed, near the window. She lowered her eyes. The lamp light shrank and fell on her face.

'Have you signed the night register?'

'Yes, Ma'am'.

'Then...?' Latika's voice hardened. Abashed, Julie started looking out of the window.

Ever since coming to this school, Latika has felt that despite scoldings and harsh words, this particular rule of the hostel is never obeyed.

'Ma'am, our vacation starts from tomorrow, and we decided that tonight...'

Without completing her sentence, Sudha looked at Hemanti and started smiling.

'Hemanti is going to sing for us tonight. Won't you also join us for a while?'

Latika felt a sense of unease. Was she really a kill-joy? For years she had been living in this hill station yet each year she failed time to mark the moment when time gliding past the beleaguered days and summer, of autumn, curled up into the lap of the winter vacation.

Feeling like a thief she stepped silently out of the room. Her face lost its tautness. She smiled to herself.

'Is none of you going to stay back to see the snowfall with me?'

'Ma'am, aren't you going home for the holidays?' The girls' eyes were fixed on her face.

'Nothing's decided yet. I love the snow.'

Latika recalled that she had said the same thing last year and perhaps the year before too. She felt that the girls were watching her with suspicious eyes, as if they didn't believe her. Her head reeled, as if, from some unknown corner, a cluster of inky clouds were about to rise and enfold her. She laughed a little and then tossed her head.

'Julie, I want to have a word with you. See me before returning to your block. Well, good night.' Latika closed the door behind her.'

'Good night, Ma'am. Good night, good night.'

Instead of descending the steps from the corridor Latika stood leaning against the railing. She turned down the wick of the lamp and put it in a corner. Outside, the blue layers of fog had thickened. The rustling of the pine trees on the lawn outside flowed in, now gently, now sharply, blending with the rise and fall of the wind. As she felt the bite in the air, the thought of the holidays beginning from tomorrow strayed again into Latika's mind. She closed her eyes. She felt that her legs were tied to her body like bamboo stilts, the joints slowly coming undone. The dizziness in her head had not yet left, but now it seemed no more confined to her head, but to have become a part of the fog outside.

The sound of voices on the stairs served to wake Latika from her reverie. She wrapped the shawl round her shoulders and picked up the lamp. Dr Mukherji was coming up with Mr Hubert, humming an English tune. The stairs were dark, and Mr Hubert had to grope his way up the stairs with his walking stick. Descending a few steps Latika lowered the lamp. 'Good evening, Doctor. Good evening, Mr Hubert!' 'Thank you, Miss Latika!' Mr Hubert's voice rang with gratitude. Walking up was a strain for him, and, as he leant against the wall, he was panting. In the light of the lamp the pallor of his face had acquired a copper-like hue.

'What are you dong here all alone, Miss Latika?' The doctor whistled softly under his breath.

'Just checked up on the girls. What brings you up the stairs at this time of night, Mr Hubert?'

Hubert smiled and tapped Mukherji's shoulder with his stick. 'Ask him. He's the man who has dragged me here.'

'Miss Latika, we were coming up to invite you. Tonight we are having a small concert in my room, at which Mr Hubert will play Chopin and Tchaikovsky, and then we shall drink coffee with cream. And then, if time permits, we shall confess all the sins we have committed this year.' A smile rose and played on Dr Mukherji's face.

'Doctor, please excuse me, I'm not feeling too well.'

'Good. In that case you would have had to come to me anyway'. The doctor held Latika by her shoulder and turned her towards his room.

Dr Mukherji's room was at the other end of the block, almost jutting into the roof. He was half Burmese, which was evident from his flat nose and small, vivacious eyes. After the Japanese attack on Burma he had sought asylum in this small hill station. Apart from his private practise he also taught Hygiene and Physiology at the Convent School, for which he had been given a room in the hostel. Some people said that his wife had died on the trek back from Burma, but nothing could be said of this with certainty for the doctor never talked about his wife.

In the midst of a conversation, he sometimes said, 'Before I die, I shall definitely visit Burma once,' and for an instant his eyes would film over. Even though she wanted to, Latika could never ask him any question. She felt that the doctor did not want anybody raking up his past or showing sympathy for him. The very next moment, dispelling his sombreness, he would break into a laugh, a dry, wan laugh.

Homesickness is the only ailment for which no doctor has a cure.

They set out a table and some chairs on the roof. Inside the room Dr Mukherji put some water in the percolator for coffee.

'I hear that in the next two or three years we shall have

electricity in this place,' Dr Mukherji said, lighting the spirit lamp.

'I have been hearing that for years! The British too had made some elaborate plans, don't know what became of them.' Reclined in his easy chair Hubert was looking at the lawn outside.

Latika brought two candles from her room. Fixing them at the two ends of the table, she lit them. The darkness on the roof shrank before the pale light of the candles. A dense soundlessness spread all around. The sighing of the pine trees in the wind threw trails of whistling echoes down and up, in the gorges and over the cliffs.

'This year the snow will be early perhaps, there's already a dry chill in the air,' Dr Mukherji's cigar glowed like a red dot in the darkness.

'I don't know why Miss Wood has to insist on this theatrical Special Service,' Hubert said. 'Is it necessary for the girls to listen to Father Elmond's sermon before going home on vacation?'

'I've been listening to him for the last five years. Not a word changes in Father Elmond's sermon.' The doctor couldn't stand Father Elmond.

Leaning forward in her chair Latika poured coffee into the cups. Every year before the school closed for vacation, these were the two fixtures in the programme—a special service in the chapel, and then a picnic in the afternoon. Latika recalled her first year at school when she had gone to the club with the Doctor after the picnic. The Doctor had gone into the bar. The ballroom was filled with the officers of the Kumaon Regiment. After watching a game of billiards, they glanced into the library on the right, when Dr Mukherji came up from behind. 'Miss Latika, this is Mr Girish Negi'. He paused amidst the din of guffaws and loud laughter from the billiard, room. A finger on the page of a book, Girish Negi was looking out of the library window. 'Hello, Doctor,' he turned back. At that moment...

Just at that moment, one did not know why, Latika's hand shook slightly, and a few hot drops of coffee spilled on her sari. In the dark nobody noticed that a sleepy emptiness had over spread her face.

In the gusts of wind the candle flames flickered. Looming above the roof level, on the Kathgodam Road, the last bus of the U P Roadways went, carrying mail. In its headlights the bushes around cast shadows on the house walls and, gliding along, disappeared.

'Miss Latika, will you be staying here during vacation?' the doctor asked her.

The doctor's question remained suspended in the air. That very moment Chopin's Nocturne, gliding from under Hubert's fingers, slowly began to dissolve in the darkness on the terrace like soft whirlpools glinting on the surface of water and rippling far, far away towards some distant shore. Latika felt that from far off peaks of snow, flocks of birds were descending and flying away to unknown lands. These days she often did see them through her window—like bright tops tied to a string they flew in long zig-zag lines, away from the solitude of the mountain ranges towards the strange cities where she would never perhaps go.

Latika started dozing in her chair. Dr Mukherji's cigar was silently glowing in the dark. The doctor wondered what was passing through Latika's mind, and Latika wondered, was she getting old? The face of Miss Wood, the principal, swam before her eyes, a toothless, hollow cheeked woman with bags of flesh swinging under her eyes, roused to irritated anger at the slightest provocation, and screaming raucously. Everybody called her Old Maid. In a few years Latika too would become exactly like her—a tremor ran down her body, as if she had touched something dirty. She recalled that a few months ago she had received a love letter from Hubert—sentimental, full of pleading and a lot of god knew what, she had not understood a word. She had felt amused at this childish antic of Hubert's, but she had also felt pleased at heart—she was not yet past the age at which she could attract people. Hubert's letter did not make her angry, it only made her compassionate. If she wanted to, she could have cleared the misconceptions he was labouring under, but some force stopped her from doing so, some force that helped keep her confidence in herself, as if her illusion of happiness was linked to Hubert's misconceptions.

Why Hubert alone? Could she love anyone with the fervour which she no longer had, which hung over her like a shadow, neither fading away nor giving her release? She felt as if the cluster of clouds were again descending over her, her legs again becoming cold and lifeless.

She got up with a jerk from her chair. 'Excuse me, Doctor, I'm feeling very tired...' Without completing her sentence she went away.

For a while the terrace was steeped in silence. The candles were on the point of going out. Dr Mukherji took a fresh pull at his cigar. 'All girls are the same—foolish and sentimental'.

Hubert's fingers lost their tautness on the piano's keyboard. A hesitant echo of the last bar stayed fluttering in the air for sometime.

'Doctor, have you noticed that for some time past Miss Latika has been behaving in a stranger way?' In Hubert's tone was a studied note of indifference. He didn't want the doctor to have even an inkling of his feelings for Latika. The doctor would turn to ridicule with one bellow of laughter the tender sentiments that he had been harbouring so long.

'Do you believe in destiny, Hubert?' the doctor asked. Hubert waited with bated breath. He knew that before saying anything the Doctor philosophised. The doctor leant close against the railing of the terrace. In the pale moonlight the shadows of the pine trees fell on the lawn. Sometimes a glow worm disappeared in the air after spraying green light into the darkness.

'I sometimes wonder why human beings live, don't they have anything better to do? Thousands of miles away from home, I am washed up here. Who knows me here...I may even die here. Hubert, have you ever thought that to go as an alien to a foreign land is quite dangerous...?'

Hubert looked at the doctor with some surprise. This was the first time that he saw Dr Mukherji in this light. He had always been reserved about his personal affairs.

'There's no one dependent on me, this gives me a strange carefree feeling. But some people's death remains an enigma till the very end. Perhaps they expected too much life. We can't even call their lives tragic for till the last breath they are not conscious of the phenomenon of death.'

'Doctor, whom are you talking about?' Hubert asked, upset.

The doctor kept smoking his cigar, then fixed his eyes on the dying candle flames.

'You know there was a time when Latika used to go to the club regularly. She got acquainted with Girish Negi there. He told me everything the night before he left for Kashmir. I have never told Latika about that meeting. But that day who knew that he would never come back? And now... now what difference does it make? Let the dead die.' The Doctor's dry, wan laughter was filled with a hollow vacuity.

'Girish Negi? Who was he?'

'He was a captain in the Kumaon Regiment'.

'Doctor...Latika...' Hubert could say no more. He suddenly remembered the letter he had written to Latika. How meaningless and bizarre, as if each word of it was wrenching at his heart. Slowly, he rested his head on the piano. Why hadn't Latika told him about it? Wasn't he worthy even to be told?

'Latika...she's a child, and silly. Does one die with the dead?'

After a short silence the Doctor again repeated his question,

'But Hubert, do you believe in destiny?'

In the gust of wind the candle flames flared sharply and then died. On the terrace, Hubert and the doctor could not see each other's faces, but still they were looking in the direction of one another. The sound of a mountain stream flowing along the ground some distance from the school, was heard clearly. When, after a long time the bugle of the Kumaon Regiment sounded, Hubert got up hurriedly. 'I must be going, Doctor. Good night.'

'Good night, Hubert. Excuse me. I'll go to bed only after I finish cigar.'

In the morning the sky was overcast. No sooner had Latika opened her window than a balloon of fog entered her room as if it had been shuddering all night in the cold, waiting just for this moment when it could trespass into her room. Above the school the road leading to the chapel was hidden in clouds; only the cross was visible, silhouetted against the screen of fog as if in pencilled lines.

Latika averted her gaze from the window, and found Karimuddin standing in the room with the tea tray. Karimuddin had served in the army as an orderly, so after putting the tray on the table, he stood to attention. Latika sprang to attention herself. Ever since she had woken up she had been dozing fitfully, out of sheer lethargy. To get over her embarrassment, she said, 'Chilly, isn't it? Don't feel like leaving bed.'

'Ah, Mem Saheb, this is no cold, let Christmas come and your teeth will keep chattering with the cold. That's the real winter.' Putting his hands under his arms Karimuddin shrank into himself as if the mere thought of those days had given him the shivers. He had dyed his hair round the edges of his bald pate, making it look tobacco brown. Whatever the talk he had the knack of bringing it to a level at which he could express himself freely.

'One year there was such heavy snowfall that the entire stretch of road from Bhowali to the dak bungalow was totally blocked. So thick was the snow, Mem Saheb, that even the branches of trees wrapped themselves against the trunks of the trees—like this'. He demonstrated by bending low and assuming a hen's posture.

'What year are you talking of?'

'That I can tell you only after calculations, Mem Saheb. But I very well remember that the British were still here. There was no national flag on the cantonment buildings. Very smart these British were—within two hours they had had the snow cleared. Those days just one blast of the whistle drew out fifty horsemen from nowhere. Now, all the sheds are lying deserted. Those people knew how to make others wait upon them. Now everything is different'. With a sad expression Karimuddin looked out of the window.

This was not the first time that Latika had heard about the good old days of British Rule from Karimuddin—the Angrez Bahadur who had made the place a heaven.

'Mem Saheb, are you spending your vacation here this year too?'

'So it seems, Karimuddin. I'm afraid ill be pestering you.'

'What are you saying, Mem Saheb? Your being here keeps my spirits up. Otherwise in vacation time the dogs have a free run of the place.'

'Tell the mason, please, to repair the roof. Last year water or snow kept leaking out of the crevices.' Latika recalled that last winter whenever snow fell she had had to retreat to a corner of the room to sleep.

Picking up the tray, Karimuddin said, 'Hubert saheb may leave tomorrow. Last night he again took ill. He came and woke up at midnight. Complained of pain in the chest. Winter doesn't seem to suit him. He said that he would try to leave tomorrow by the girls' bus.'

Karimuddin closed the door and went out of the room. Latika thought of going to Hubert's room and enquiring about his health. But then she didn't know why the slippers kept dangling from her feet and she kept looking out of the window at the rushing clouds. When Hubert's face looks at her and becomes pleading and different, she feels that he is reproaching her in his dumb, helpless supplication—she can neither dispel his misconception nor say anything about herself in self-justification. She feels that whichever strand she catches hold of in order to extricate herself from the web, turns into a knot.

It had started drizzling—the tin roof became noisy with the pitter-patter of rain. Latika got out of bed. She re-made it neatly. Then dragging her feet in her slippers to the big mirror, she sat on the stool before it and undid her hair. But for some time the comb remained sunk in the hair and she looked at herself in the mirror with a unseeing eyes. She had clean forgotten to tell Karimuddin to keep putting by fuel-wood. These days the wood was cheap and dry. Last year her room had got filled with smoke and she had had to keep the window open even in the bitter cold.

Latika looked at her face in the mirror—she was smiling. Last year, to escape the chill and dampness of her room she often went to sleep in Miss Wood's room on the sly. Miss Wood's room stayed warm even without a fire. She fell asleep as soon as she lay down on the downy, springy sofa. The room remained empty during vacations, but Miss Wood did not have the common humaneness to give it to her for use for the two months. Every year she stuck a lock on the door. Last year she had forgotten to lock the bathroom door from within, so Latika had used it to steal in.

The first year she had been frightened here alone. During the vacation the whole school and hostel rooms boomed with a ghostly silence. When her fear became too much and she could not sleep she would keep Karimuddin engaged in small talk, and when she started dozing, he would extinguish the lamp and slip out. Sometimes she would call the doctor on the pretext of illness and force him to sleep there, having an extra bed made up for him in the adjoining room.

She extracted a bunch of hair from her comb and walked to the window to throw it out. Outside, the rain water was falling in thick streams from the sloping roof, onto the lawn below.

On the overcast sky, the mountain peaks disappeared and appeared again behind the scudding clouds as if they were being seen from a moving train. Latika put her head out of the window and blinked as a cold blast of wind hit her face. As she remembered each task she had to attend to, her lethargy mounted. Money had to be given to the school peon to reserve bus tickets for the girls. The luggage they were leaving behind had to be stored in the godown. Sometimes she had even to help the smaller girls pack their things.

She does not really hate these tasks. Everything gets done in time. A lapse here, an oversight there, all get set right later—every chore leaves behind some anxiety and strain—but sooner or later it does get done.

But when the last bus load of girls leave, she suddenly feels out of sorts—aimlessly she wanders through the empty corridors, now entering one room, now another. She doesn't know what to do with herself—the mind doesn't get involved with anything but wanders, always.

And then everyone asks her facilely, 'Miss Latika, aren't you going home during the vacations?' What can she say?

Ding! Ding! Ding! The special service bell rang in the school chapel. Latika withdrew her head from the window. Slipping out of her sari, she threw a towel over her shoulder and entered the bathroom in her petticoat.

Left—right—left—left—

A formation of the sepoys of the Kumaon Regiment was marching in fours on the road leading to the cantonment. The heavy and rough thud of their army boots bounced off the chapel walls and went reverberating through the prayer hall inside.

'Blessed are the meek...' Father Elmond was reading the Sermon on the Mount, in a rasping voice, chewing each word. Under the statue of Jesus Christ the light of the candles on both ends of the candelabrum fell on the girls sitting in the front rows. The rows in the back were enveloped in darkness. There sat girls, heads bowed in prayer, whispering among themselves. Miss Wood had already delivered her valedictory address, congratulating the students and staff on the conclusion of a successful school session—and now, sitting behind the Father, was muttering something to herself as if prompting him.

'Amen!' Father Elmond put down the Bible on the pulpit and picked up the Prayer Book. For a moment the silence of the hall broke. Standing up, the girls pushed back the benches purposely, making a grating sound. The sound of laughter rose from a corner of the hall. Miss Wood's face became taut and her brows knitted. Again a hush fell over the hall—through the bleak shadows of the hall Father Elmond's sharp, splintery voice was heard, 'Jesus said, I am the light of the world. He that followeth me shall not walk in darkness but shall have the light of life...'

Dr Mukherji yawned with boredom and fretfulness. 'When will this business end?' He asked Latika in such a loud voice that she looked the other way in embarrassment. All through the special service, a special, ironic smile lingered on Dr Mukherji's face, and he kept softly tugging at his moustache.

Father Elmond's costume sent a ripple of amusement through Latika. When she was a small girl she often wondered whether these padres wore anything under their robes. What if the robe accidentally lifted?

Left...right...left! The sound of the marching army boots receded from the chapel—only the echo hung in the air.

'Hymn No 117,' Father Elmond said, opening his Prayer Book. Each girl in the hall opened the Hymn Book kept on her desk. The sound of rustling pages slithered from one corner to the other.

Getting up from a bench in the front row, Hubert sat down on a stool at the piano. Being the Music Teacher he had to accompany the school choir on the piano every year. Hubert blew into his handkerchief. He always did this to hide his nervousness. Casting a glance over the hall with stealthy eyes, he opened the Hymn book with trembling hands.

Lead kindly light...

Muffled and shy, the notes of the piano met together. Hubert's long, yellow fingers, covered with thick down, opened and closed. The voices of the girls forming the choir, locking with each other, fused into soft-sweet waves.

Latika felt that her bun of hair had come loose, as if hanging, at the nape of her neck. Avoiding Miss Wood's eye, she carefully re-secured her hair with hair clips.

'What an obstinate man... In the morning I stopped him from attending chapel, yet he's turned up.'

Latika remembered what karimuddin had told her... the whole night he had coughed...and was talking about leaving tomorrow...

Crooking her head to one side, Latika tried in vain to have a glimpse of Hubert's face. From so far behind, nothing could be seen clearly. Only Hubert's head could be seen bent over the piano.

'Lead kindly light...' The notes of the music seemed to have climbed a high mountain, and, scattering wisps of breath into the vast emptiness of the sky, were climbing down. The soft, rain-drenched light is glistening on the oblong glass panel of the chapel window. And one single ray of light falls aslant on Jesus Christ's image. The smoke from the candles traces a blue line in the light, now floating in the air. In the momentary pause of the piano, Latika hears the murmuring of leaves, from somewhere far away. For a moment she had the illusion that the chapel's dim darkness, winding back from the four corners of the prayer hall, had encircled her thickly—as if someone had brought her to this place blindfolded, and had suddenly whisked away the bandage from her eyes. She felt there was nothing solid or real in the smoky illumination of the candle—the ceiling of the chapel, the walls, the doctor's strong and supple hand on the desk—and that the notes of the piano piercing the fog of the past had themselves become part of the fog.

A crazy memory, a bizarre feeling—beyond the glass of the chapel, in the dry mountain wind, the trembling branches of the weeping willows bending in the wind and, under foot, the soft, familiar rustling of pine leaves... Just there Girish is standing, holding a khaki military hat in his hand. Broad, upraised shoulders, if you put your head on them he would withdraw into himself. Charles Boyer—that was the name she had given him. It made him laugh with embarrassment.

'Who selected you for the army? You are a major in rank but you are worse than the girls. Your face turns red at the slightest touch.' All this she had never said, just thought it—thought she'd say it some time, but that 'some time' never came.

> The red flower (rhododendrons?)
> Brought it
> You have, haven't you?
> Liar!

His khaki tunic carried war decorations on its pocket. From out of it came a wilted red flower.

> It has withered
> Hadn't even bloomed
> (How clumsy!)

Girish's hand is entangled in her hair. The flower doesn't stay, then he secures it under the clip.

> 'There!'

She turned round. But before she could speak, plonk came

Girish's military hat over her had. She stood there spell-bound. Girish's hat is on her head—a small red mark on her forehead. On it is a stray, flying hair. Girish has touched the red mark with his lips, he has enfolded her now unhatted head in both his hands.

'Latika!'

'Man-eater of Kumaon!' Girish teased her. She had started laughing.

'Latika, listen!' His voice sounded, like what?

'No, I don't hear anything.'

'Latika, I'll be back in a few months.'

'No... I don't hear a thing.'

But she does hear—not what Girish is saying, but what he is not saying, what never got said afterwards.

'Lead kindly light.'

The girls' voices rose and fell to the sound of the piano.

For a fleeting moment Hubert turned his head and looked at Latika. Eyes closed, she was standing like a statue in meditation. Was this stance and emotion for him? Has Latika made him her companion in these moments? Hubert took a deep breath, and from the breath swirled a mass of weariness.

'Look, Miss Wood is dozing in her chair!' The Doctor whispered under his breath. It was the Doctor's favourite joke that Miss Wood slept under the pretence of praying.

Father Elmond gathered the ends of his robe from his chair and, closing his Prayer Book said something in Miss Wood's ear. The sound of the piano was fading, and Hubert's fingers lost their tension. At the conclusion of the service Miss Wood read out an Order. The unexpected rain had called for an alteration in the programme. It would not be possible to go to Jhula Devi temple for the picnic. Instead, after breakfast, the girls would assemble at Meadows, just at some distance from the school. They would have to take their lunch packets from the hostel kitchen. Only the evening tea would be prepared at Meadows.

Rains in the hills are unpredictable. A short while ago smoky clouds were thundering, the whole town was shivering and wet—now the sun-washed blue sky was emerging from behind the fog and spreading. Latika came out of the chapel, and saw glistening rain-drops falling from the branches of the weeping willows.

After coming out of the chapel the girls have collected in the corridors in small and big groups. Breakfast was still three quarters of an hour away and no girl was in the mood to go back to the hostel. The vacation had not yet started but precisely for this reason perhaps, they wanted the foretaste of freedom in these last moments of stockaded discipline.

Miss Wood frowned at the girls' noisy behaviour but she could not give them a talking-to in Father Elmond's presence. Suppressing her anger, she smiled and said: 'Tomorrow all these girls will be gone and the school will be deserted.'

Father Elmond's long, impressive face had taken on a deeper red here in the chapel's oppressive heat. Hanging his walking stick on the corridor railing he said, 'Who's staying behind in the hostel during the vacation?'

'Miss Latika, I reckon. For the last three years she has been spending her vacation in the hostel.'

'And Dr Mukherji?' The Father's upper lip stretched slightly.

'The Doctor stays here all the year round—summer and winter.' Miss Wood gave Father Elmond a surprised look. She could not understand why Father Elmond had brought the doctor into the conversation.

'Doesn't Dr Mukherji go anywhere during the vacation?'

'It would be hard to visit Burma in a two month vacation, Father,' Miss Wood laughed.

'Miss Wood, I don't know what you think. But I cannot understand why Miss Latika should stay in the hostel all by herself.'

'But, Father, it is a rule in our school that any teacher can stay in the hostel at vacation time, at her own expense.'

'I am not talking of school regulations at the moment. Miss Latika will be left alone with the Doctor and, to tell you the truth, Miss Wood, I don't have a very high opinion of Dr Mukherji.'

'Father, what are you talking about? Miss Latika is not a child.' Miss Wood had not expected Father Elmond to harbour such dark thoughts about anyone.

Father Elmond was a little take a back at her vehemence. 'Miss Wood, I don't mean that,' he said evasively. 'You know there was quite a scandal over Miss Latika and that military officer. How long does it take for a school to earn a bad name?'

'Poor fellow, he is no more. I knew him, Father. May God rest his soul in peace,' Miss Wood made a sign of the cross.

Father Elmond was so put off by Miss Wood's stupidity that he didn't say anything further. He had never got along with Dr Mukherji, therefore he wanted to run down the Doctor in Miss Wood's eyes. But here was Miss Wood shedding tears for Latika. To continue was useless. He took his walking stick from the railing and, looking up at the clear bright sky, said: 'You changed your programme unnecessarily, Miss Wood. No sign of rain there.'

When Hubert came out of the chapel his eyes were momentarily blinded by the glare. He felt that someone had suddenly sprayed a handful of bright, boiling light into his eyes. The notes of the piano still fluttered in his head, like strands of wispy cotton-wool. Playing the piano always put a heavy strain on the lungs and his heartbeat increased. He felt that in the effort of transmitting one note of music to the other, he was crossing a dark chasm. What I experienced in the chapel today, how extraordinary it was, he thought. I felt that each note of the piano, emerging from the dark caves of eternal silence, cutting through and chiselling the blue, spreading fog, extracted some half forgotten meaning out of it. Every descending pause was a small death, as if a trail had got lost in the trembling shadows of a dense cluster of trees, a small death which bequeathed the remnants of its cadences to the coming notes... which dies but is not destroyed, not destroyed, therefore alive even in death, immersing in the other notes.

'Doctor, does death come like this?' If I ask the doctor he would laugh it off. I feel, that for the last few days he has been hiding something from me—I do not like the echo of sympathy in his laughter. Today he tried to stop me from coming to the special service. When I asked why, he slurred it over. What is this something that the Doctor fights shy of telling me? Perhaps I am just becoming suspicious by nature, that's all.

Hubert saw the rows of girls descending on to the road leading from the school to the hostel. In the bright sun, their vari-coloured ribbon, blue frocks and white belts shone. Some girls of the Senior Cambridge class had plucked roses from the chapel garden and tucked them into their hair. The sepoys from the cantonment are making obscene remarks at the girls; sometimes heads bent lightly, whistling.

'Hello, Mr Hubert!'

Startled, Mr Hubert turned his head. Latika was standing there, a fat register under her arm.

'Are you still here?' Hubert's gaze remained riveted on Latika's face. She was wearing a full sleeved, cream coloured woollen jacket. Her neck was round like the Kumaoni girls. Under the hot sun her wheat-coloured complexion had turned slightly rosy as if even after constant washing some scattered rose spots had stayed.

'Had to take down the names of the girls who are leaving tomorrow... I had to stay back. You too are leaving tomorrow, Mr Hubert?'

'That's my intention as of now. What would I do here? Are you walking towards the school?'

'Come along!'

The crowds of girls had increased on the macadam road. So they took the footpath circling the polo grounds.

The wind had risen. With every gust of wind pine leaves fell from the trees and rose on the footpath in sudden big heaps. Hubert made a way through the heaps with his walking stick. Latika watched him, standing behind each time. Baby clouds coming from the Almora valley veiled the sun, like silk handkerchiefs, and then drifted away with the breeze. In this game the light became dim sometimes, sometimes spreading out its bright mantle, gathering the entire city into itself.

Latika suddenly walked ahead of Hubert. Hubert's breathing grew heavy, and he followed her panting. When they left the polo ground pavilion, and turned to the right of the cemetery, Latika stopped for Hubert to catch up with her. She recalled that during the vacations when time hung heavy on her, sitting in her room, she often walked up to the cemetery. Climbing the hill which bordered the cemetery, she would watch the pines from whose snow-laden branches snow fell like fluffs of cotton. In the bazaar down below the children sleighed. Standing on the hill she would visualise the road—now buried under snow—that passed by Father Elmond's house, led to the military hospital and the post office, and then got lost somewhere outside the church steps. The thrill one gets from solving jig-saw puzzles, Latika got by tracing roads buried under snow.

'Miss Latika, you walk very fast,' Hubert's face had wilted with tiredness. Beads of perspiration shone on his forehead.

'Were you ill last night?'

'How do you know? Do I look ill?' There was an edge to Hubert's voice. Why did every one talk about his health, he wondered.

'No, I wouldn't have known but for Karimuddin. He told me about it in passing,' Latika was slightly abashed.

'No, it's nothing serious. The same pain began again. I'm perfectly all right now.' In confirmation Hubert threw out his chest and slightly accelerated his pace.

'Did you speak to Dr Mukherji?'

'He came in the morning. I just don't understand him. He always contradicts himself. He said that I must take leave for six months and have complete rest. But if I'm all right where is the question of taking rest?'

The touch of anxiety in Hubert's voice did not escape Latika's notice. 'You worry for nothing, Mr Hubert,' she said, dodging his question. 'The season is changing, even perfectly healthy people can fall ill.'

'Do you think so?' Hubert's face beamed with happiness. He gave Latika an intent look. He wanted to set all doubt at rest by making sure that she was not saying this merely to console him.

'That's just what I was thinking, Miss Latika. The Doctor's advice gave me a scare. What would I do along, with six months' leave? In the school the children divert me. To tell you the truth it is hard to get through even these two months in Delhi.'

'Mr Hubert...you are leaving for Delhi tomorrow...?'

Latika suddenly stopped in her tracks. In front spread the polo ground, at one end of which military trucks, were heading for the cantonment. Hubert felt as if Latika's eyelids had dropped and half-closed, as if a forgotten dream had slipped into them.

'Mr Hubert, so you are going to Delhi'. This time Latika did not repeat it as a question—in her voice was just a sense of immense distance.

'Many years ago I went to Delhi, Mr Hubert. I was very young then—I don't know how many years ago it was. I have lost count of the years. My aunt was married there, in Delhi. i saw many things, but now the memory has faded. I remember that we climbed the Qutab. We looked down from the topmost storey—a strange sensation it was! The people walking below looked like clockwork toys. We threw monkeynuts at them, and were very disappointed that none of them looked up at us. Perhaps my mother scolded me, and I got scared just looking down. I hear that Delhi has now changed beyond recognition...'

They resumed their walk. The wind subsided. The fleeting clouds now seemed to relax, their shadows falling on the hills of Nandadevi and Panchchuli. As they neared the school the pine trees receded into the distance, here and there around the apricot trees the red-brown flower shone in the sun. In getting to the school they had covered the entire length of the polo ground.

'Miss Latika, why don't you go somewhere in the winter vacation? In winter this place must be desolate.'

'I like it here now,' Latika said. 'The first year the solitude oppressed me somewhat. But now I have got used to it. On Christmas eve there is a dance at the club, they run a lottery. And there is singing and dancing till late in the night. On New Year's day the Kumaon Regiment puts up a carnival on the parade ground, there is skating, and the military band plays under a lot of coloured balloons, the army officers take part in a Fancy Dress show—all this happens every year, Mr Hubert. Then a few days later the English tourists start arriving for winter sports. I am introduced to them and they promise to return the following year but I know they won't, and they know it too. But that does not make any difference to our friendship. Then after some time the snow starts melting on the mountains, the vacation draws to a close and you people start coming back—and, Mr Hubert, I don't even realise when the vacation started, when it ended.'

Latika saw that Hubert was looking at her with consternation. She fell into an embarrassed silence, as though all this while she had been prattling in a mad, delirious way.

'Forgive me, Mr Hubert, sometimes I get childish and get carried away.'

'Miss Latika...' Hubert said in a low voice. He stopped walking. Latika was startled at the heaviness of his voice. 'What is it, Mr Hubert?'

'That letter...I'm ashamed of it. Please return it to me. Consider it never written.'

Latika understood nothing—lost and transfixed, she stared at Hubert's yellow, troubled face.

Hubert gently placed his hand on Latika's shoulder.

'Yesterday the Doctor told me everything. If I had know I...I...' Hubert's voice faltered.

'Mr Hubert...' But Latika too, could not speak further. Her face had turned white.

For some time they stood in silence at the school gate.

Meadows—a small island surrounded on all sides by goat tracks, leaves and shadows, like a nest esconced between two valleys. Immediately on entering it, stones charred by picnickers, semi-charred branches of trees, old newspaper sheets spread out to sit on, now scattering in all directions, meet the eye. It is a favourite spot for tourists and picnickers. A crooked mountain stream cuts through the meadow, looking from a distance like a white ribbon under the bright sunlight.

There is a bridge over the brook, made of old logs of wood. The girls are teetering across the bridge.

'Dr Mukherji, you are going to send up the whole jungle in flames! Miss Wood said, stamping with her high-heeled sandal or a burning matchstick which Dr Mukherji had carelessly flung on a pile of pine leaves. He was sitting a little away from the brook, under the interlocking shade of two pine trees. In front of him a goat-path led towards a small village down below, where, in the lap of the hill, terraced fields of beet could be seen. In the stillness of afternoon the sound of sheep and goat came floating down with the breeze.

Remaining stretched on the grass, Dr Mukherji smoked his cigar.

'Have you seen a jungle on fire, Miss Wood? It slowly spreads like an intoxication in all directions'.

'Have you seen one, Doctor?' Miss Wood asked. 'I feel

terribly afraid.'

'Many years ago I saw cities burning,' the Doctor looked at the sky, lying on the grass. 'One after the other, houses fell like a pack of cards. Unfortunately it is only on rare occasions that one sees such splendid sights.'

'Where did you see it, Doctor?'

'In the war, I saw my own city, Rangoon, burning.'

It gave Miss Wood a jolt, but her curiosity did not wane.

'Your house—was that too burnt down?'

The Doctor was silent for a while. Then he said, 'We left it... and came away. I don't know what happened afterwards.' To speak about his personal affairs is very difficult for the doctor.

'Doctor, don't you ever think of going back to Rangoon?'

The Doctor yawned and then, turning on his side, lay face down. His eyes closed and strands of hair fell across his forehead.

'What is the good of thinking, Miss Wood? When I lived in Burma, did I ever imagine that I would spend the fag end of my life here?'

'But, Doctor, say what you will, one never feels at peace anywhere but in one's own country. You may live here for any number of years and yet you will feel like an outsider.'

The Doctor slowly blew the cigar smoke in the air. 'For that matter, even there I would be regarded as an outsider, Miss Wood. After so many years who would recognise me now. To start a new life at my age would be difficult. I won't be up to it.'

'But Doctor, how long can you vegetate in this hill town? If you have to live in this country set up practice in a big city.'

'Where will I knock around to expand my practice? Miss Wood, one can find patients wherever one lives. I came here only for a few days, and then I stayed on and on. Whenever I get bored I shall move on. If one does not put down roots anywhere, one leaves nothing behind. I have no illusions about myself, Miss Wood. I am happy.'

Miss Wood did not pay much attention to Dr Mukherji's statements. In her heart she regarded him as something of an eccentric, careless and self-willed. But she had faith in his character—she didn't know why, because she could not recall the doctor wittingly or unwittingly, ever having given evidence of it.

Miss Wood sighed deeply. She always thought that if the Doctor had not been so lazy and indifferent he would certainly have made a mark in his profession. That was why she was angry with him and at the same time felt sorry for him.

She took out a ball of wool and knitting needles from her bag and then prised out a flat coffee tin wrapped in newspaper in which egg sandwiches and hamburgers lay compressed. Pouring coffee from a thermos, she said, 'Doctor the coffee has gone quite cold.'

The Doctor muttered, still stretched out. Miss Wood bent down to see. Resting his head on his elbow he was sleeping. The upper lip had stretched a little and turned, as if he were smiling before making a joke.

His cigar, pressed between his fingers, dangled upside down.

'Mary, Mary, what do you want?' Second standard students, Mary, raised her alert, vivacious eyes as the circle of girls advanced and receded in rhythm.

'I want—I want blue!' Swinging her arms in the air Mary shouted. The circle broke like water. The girls ran helter-skelter, tumbling over one another, to touch a blue-coloured object.

Lunch was over. Small groups of girls were scattered all over Meadows. Girls of a senior class had climbed up some trees to break twigs to build a fire to boil water for tea.

At that afternoon hour Meadows seemed to be dozing languidly. A stray gust of wind, and the pine trees set up a rustle. Sometimes, to get over its lethargy, a bird flew down from a tree and settling down on the bank of a channel plunged its head in the water. Rising up it wheeled around aimlessly, and then lurk again in the bush.

But the silence of a jungle is never voiceless. Sounds and voices, like dreams in deep sleep, keep furrowing the light gossamer curtain of stillness, flutter in the air like mute waves, as if someone on tiptoe glances in, and goes, making an invisible sign—look, I'm here.

Ruffling Julie's short hair, Latika said, 'I called you last night.'

'Ma'm, I went to your room, but you weren't there.'

Latika recalled that last night she had sat a long time on the Doctor's terrace when Hubert was playing Chopin's *Nocturne* on the piano.

'Julie, I wanted to ask you something.' She felt that she was trying to shield herself from Julie's eyes.

Julie raised her face, eagerness and curiosity in her brown eyes.

'Do you know anybody in the Officers' Mess?'

Julie shook her head with an air of uncertainty. Latika riveted her with how look.

'Julie, I'm sure you will not tell a lie.'

The curiosity in Julie's eyes had now changed to fear.

Taking out a blue envelope from her jacket pocket, Latika flung it into Julie's lap. 'Whose letter is this?'

Julie stretched her hand to pick up the envelope, but for an instant her hand trembled, and remained arrested in the air.

The envelope bore her name and her hostel address.

'Thank you, Ma'm. It's a letter from my brother. He lives in Jhansi.' Nervously Julie hid the envelope in the fold of her skirt.

'Julie, show me the letter.' Latika's voice had hardened and shrilled.

Julie helplessly surrendered the letter to Latika.

'Does your brother live in Jhansi?'

This time Julie made no reply. Her bewildered eyes kept gazing at Latika.

'What's this?'

Julie's face was drained of colour. The seal of the Kumaon Regimental Centre was staring her in the face.

'Who's he?' Latika asked. Some vague rumours had already travelled down to her that Julie had been seen with an army officer in the club. But such rumours were common and she did not believe them.

'Julie, you are too young for all this.'

Julie's lips trembled. There was entreaty in her eyes.

'You may go. I will talk to you when you return from your vacation.'

Julie looked at the envelope with greedy eyes. She was on the verge of saying something, but she went away wordlessly.

Latika stayed looking at Julie for a long time, till she vanished from sight. Am I in any way better than an old spinster? Why am I venting my frustration on others?

Maybe—who knew—perhaps this was Julie's first introduction to that experience which a girl guards and keeps close to her heart. An indescribable joy which carries pain, a high-tide which drowns joy and pain, which contains both in itself—a pain which is born of joy and which hurts.

Under this very pine trees she had felt the same pain when Girish asked her, 'Why are you quiet?' Eyes closed, she was thinking about—thinking about? no, living—that moment which was pressed between fear and surprise—a bewitched, mad moment. If she turned back now, she would see Girish's nervous smile, and the past from that day to this afternoon would break like a bad dream. This was the pine tree on which she had carved Girish's name with a hairpin. The pin got blunted again and again, the bark of the tree wouldn't peel, and then Girish had etched her name under his own. When a letter came out crooked, she would laugh, and Girish's trembling hand tremble more.

Latika feels that what she remembers she wants to forget too, but when she really begins to forget, she gets afraid lest something of hers taken away from her, something be lost forever.

In her childhood, whenever she lost a toy, she would go very quiet and try to remember where exactly she had put it. When she found it after a lot of searching around, she would pretend that she was still searching and had not found it. Skipping the place where the toy was lying, she would look for it in all the other nooks and corners of the room. The lost thing was not lost anymore, so there was no fear of forgetting where it was—

Today why couldn't she play the childhood game of make believe? 'Make believe'—perhaps she does make believe, the make believe of remembering him who is getting beyond remembrance. Days and months pass, and she remains entangled, without being aware of it. Girish's face fades. She tries to remember, but it is like wiping dust from the glass of an old picture. Now the pain is not like before, she just remembers, in a matter of fact way, something that used to exist. Then she dislikes herself. She deliberately scratches the wound that is healing of itself, despite her resistance.

The faded names on the pine tree stared at Latika with a silent, helpless expression. In the heavy stillness of Meadows the voices of the girls at play on the other side of the stream, came echoing: 'What do you want?... What do you want?'

Butterflies, glow worms, crickets, cicadas—in the descending evening shadows of Meadows it was difficult to tell one voice from an other. The voices which one could recognise individually in the afternoon had got merged into an undifferentiated monotone. Wiping his feet on the grass, somebody crawls along. From the thickets of foliage and bush, somebody springs up in flight, fluttering his wings—but look up, and there's nothing. The sound of the gurgling stream of Meadows—like a train going through a dark tunnel in a rush, and the screams of whistles and wheels lingering long as echoes do...

The picnic would have gone on a little longer. But layers of clouds were climbing on each other thick and fast. The picnic things began to be gathered together. The girls who had dispersed to the corners of Meadows gathered around Miss Wood. They brought with them various odds and ends. Some had thrust birds' feathers into their hair, some had made sticks of branches of trees with pocket knives, and some girls of the higher classes had trapped in their handkerchiefs small fishes from the brook, and were secretly showing to them to each other, evading Miss Wood's eye.

Miss Wood walked ahead with the groups of girls. From Meadows to the tarred road was a four furlong or so climb. Latika started panting. Dr Mukherji was behind everybody. He stopped at Latika's side. Kneeling with both knees, and bowing to her, he said in courtly Elizabethan English, 'Madam, wherefore dost thou look so worried?'

Dr Mukherji's dramatics brought a tired, limp smile to Latika's face.

'Dying of thirst, I am, and this climb doesn't end.'

The doctor took his thermos off his shoulder, and handing it to Latika, said, 'There's still some coffee left in it. It may help you somewhat.'

'Where were you all this while, doctor? I did not see you at the picnic.'

'I slept the whole afternoon—with Miss Wood. I mean Miss Wood was sitting near me. I think Miss Wood is in love with me.' Before making a joke Dr Mukherji chews one end of his moustache.

'What does she say?' Latika swallowed the coffee from the thermos.

'She might have said something, but unfortunately I fell asleep. Many such beautiful moments of love in my life have been left incomplete because of this wretched sleep of mine.

And as they walked on, talking in this vein, the rows of pines and bamboos climbing up Meadows and the motor road, began to sink in the evening dusk, as if, they had quietly bowed their heads in prayer. Somewhere above these trees the chapel cross stood silhouetted against the clouds. Below it, along the mountain terraces, the fields looked like running squirrels suddenly arrested in motion in expectancy of someone.

'Doctor, Mr Hubert did not come to the picnic?'

Holding a flashlight Dr Mukherji was walking ahead of Latika.

'I advised him against it.'

'Why?'

In the dark and with the crunching of pine leaves it was difficult to hear clearly. Dr Mukherji coughed slightly.

'For the last few days I have been suspecting that Hubert's pain in the chest is no ordinary pain.' The Doctor laughed a little, as if he did not relish his gravity of tone. He waited, perhaps Latika would say something. But Latika kept walking silently behind him.

'It's just a suspicion. I may be wide of the mark. But he would do well to get one of his lungs X-rayed. It will at least set all doubts at rest.'

'Have you talked to Mr Hubert about this?'

'Not so far. Hubert worries even over trifles, so I have not had the courage to tell him.'

The doctor felt that the sound of Latika's footsteps following his had suddenly stopped. He turned back and saw, in the dark, Latika standing like a shadow in the middle of the road.

'Doctor...' Latika's voice sounded blurred.

'What's the matter, Miss Latika? Why have you stopped?'

'Doctor, is Mr Hubert...'

The doctor flashed his light on Latika's face. It had turned pale and she was trembling.

'Miss Latika, what's the matter? You're looking bad.'

'It's nothing, Doctor. I...I...suddenly remembered something.'

They resumed their walk. After walking some distance they raised their eyes to the sky. In the smoky sky was a flock of birds flying towards them in a triangular formation from behind the mountain range. Latika and the Doctor watched the birds. Latika remembered that every year, just before the winter vacation these birds flew towards the plains, breaking journey for some days at these hill stations, waiting for the snow, then flying downwards to strange, unknown lands...

Were they also waiting for something—she, Dr Mukherji, Mr Hubert? But waiting for what destination? Where would they go?

No reply came to her in the darkness, except for the haunting sound of the brook of Meadows, and the rustling sound of the pine leaves. Nothing else was heard.

Latika gave a start and looked round. Leaning on his walking stick the Doctor was whistling softly.

'Miss Latika, let's hurry. It is about to rain.'

By the time they reached the hostel lightning was flashing. But that night it did not rain for a long time. The showers would hardly get a start, when buffets of wind pushed the clouds away. The next day, the bus had to be caught early in the morning and, therefore, after dinner the girls went to their rooms to sleep.

When Latika entered her room the bugle of the Kumaon Regimental Centre was playing, Karimuddin was pumping gas in her lamp, humming a hill refrain. Latika lay down without changing, doubling her pillow under her head. Karimuddin gave her a fleeting glance and then resumed his work.

'How was the picnic, Mem Saheb?'

'Why didn't you come? The girls were asking for you.' Latika felt that the day-long tiredness was clinging to her tissues. Involuntarily her eyes closed under the weight of sleep.

'If I had come who would have looked after Hubert Saheb? I sat the whole day glued to his bed. And how he has disappeared.'

Karimuddin removed his soiled towel from his shoulder and started polishing the lamp's glass chimney.

Latika's half-closed eyes suddenly opened. 'Is Hubert Saheb not in his room?'

'God knows where he is wandering about in his state of health. I had gone out to heat some water and when I returned the room was empty.'

Karimuddin went out muttering. Without getting up from the bed Latika slipped her slippers off her feet under it.

Where had Hubert gone at this hour of night? But her eyes closed. The day's fatigue locked out all worries and questions, as if, after a day-long game of blind-man's buff, she had touched 'target' in her room. She was safe now. In the four walls of her room nobody could catch her. In the bright light of the day she was witness, she was defendant, everything in conflict with her, while now, in this solitude, there was no complaint, no grievance, no recrimination, all struggle ended. What was her own had now become her very own, indubitably her own, it gave no cause for pain, demanded time to stamp it with possession.

Latika turned her face towards the wall. The shadows of the trembling curtains shook in the dim night of the lamp. In the flashes of lighting, the window panes threw a blinding glare and the doors rattled as if someone was knocking at them from outside. The laughter and snatches of talk of the girls passing the corridors to their rooms—then everything stilled, but yet, in uncertain sleep, she kept hearing for a long time the hissing of the lamp. She was not aware when the hissing sound too stilled, after becoming a part of the silence.

After some time she felt subdued voices coming from the stairs, somebody crying out at intervals, and then, the cries slowing down.

'Miss Latika, please bring your lamp here'. It was Dr Mukherji calling from the bottom of the stairs.

The corridor was dark. She descended three or four steps,

and lowered the lamp. By the balustrade stood Mr Hubert, resting his head on it. One arm was dangling while the other which the doctor had clutched firmly was swaying over the doctor's shoulder.

'Miss Latika, please lower the lamp a little more... Hubert... Hubert!' Supporting him the Doctor pulled Hubert up. Hubert raised his head. A strong whiff of whisky cut through her. There were red streaks in Hubert's eyes, his collar was upside down, the knot of his tie had loosened and slipped. Latika placed the lamp on the stairs with trembling hands and stepped back against the wall. Her head reeled.

'In a back lane of the city there is a girl who loves me.' His head resting against Dr Mukherji's shoulder, Hubert was climbing up the dark stairs with teetering steps.

'Doctor, where are we?' He suddenly shouted so loud that striking against the corridor's ceiling his unsteady voice reverberated for a long time in the air.

'Hubert...!' The doctor lost his temper suddenly, then was annoyed at his own loss of control, and patted Hubert on the back. 'It's nothing, Hubert, old boy. You're just tired.'

Hubert fixed his eyes on the Doctor's face. In them was the pleading of a frightened child, seeking an answer from the doctor's face.

Reaching his room, the Doctor laid him on his bed. Hubert allowed his shoes and socks to be removed without resistance. When the Doctor began removing his tie, Hubert rose on his elbows, kept staring at the Doctor for a while. Then he held him by the hand.

'Doctor, am I going to die?' he asked.

'What kind of talk is this, Hubert?' The doctor released his hand, and laid Hubert's head on the pillow.

'Good night, Hubert!'

'Good night, Mr Hubert!' Latika said in a shaky voice.

But Hubert did not make any response. He fell asleep immediately on turning on his side.

Returning to the corridor Dr Mukherji stopped by the railing. Outside, whenever the layers of cloud thinned under strong blasts of wind the moonlight, like smoke from a dying fire, spread over the hills.

'Where did you find Mr Hubert?' Latika leaned over the other end of the railing.

'In the club bar. If I had not come along, he would have kept sitting therefor I don't know how long.' Dr Mukherji lit a cigarette. He had yet to call on two patients. He stood there, debating if he should cancel the visits. Sitting in his quarters downstairs, Karimuddin was playing on old film tune on his mouth organ.

'The sky remained overcast the whole night, but it did not rain beyond a drizzle.'

'Till Christmas, perhaps, the weather will continue this way'.

They stood silent for some time. The crickets' calling from the lawn stretching in front of the school, made the pervading silence still more dense. Sometimes the soft whimper of a dog came from the motor road above.

'Doctor, did you speak to Mr Hubert about me last night?'

'Nothing in particular... only what people already know. Something which Hubert should have known too but didn't.' The Doctor looked at Latika. She as still leaning on the railing.

'Each of us has some kink or other.' Doctor Mukherji smiled in the dark. 'Some people iron it out, others nurse it to the end.' Dr Mukherji's smile had a touch of stoicism.

'Sometimes I think, Miss Latika, that if it is wrong to be unaware of something it is as wrong not to forget it, to stick to it like a leech. When my wife died on the way from Burma I thought my life was useless. But, as you see I am still living, and hope to live for quite some time more. Life is quite interesting. If it weren't for my age I would perhaps have married again. In spite of this, who can say that I did not love my wife? I love her even today...'

'But Doctor...' Latika's voice became strained.

'Yes, Miss Latika?'

'Be that as it may, Doctor, what is it that keeps us going? Even when we stop we are carried forward by its momentum.' Latika felt that she was not able to say what she wanted to, as if something had got lost the dark, could not be round, and perhaps never would be found.

'Only Father Elmond can tell you about that, Miss Latika.' All his idiosyncrasies, bordering on irreverence, surfaced in his hollow laugh.

'All right, I must be going, Miss Latika. I'm quite late.' The Doctor struck a match and looked at his watch.

'Good night, Miss Latika.'

'Good night, Doctor...'

After the doctor was gone, Latika stood leaning close against the railing. The mist which gathered in the corridor trembled in the rising wind. The heaps of old note books, newspapers and wastepaper that the girls had put outside their rooms, while packing the evening before, had now scattered in the strong wind down the corridors.

Latika picked up her lamp and moved towards her room. Walking along the corridor she saw a thin ray of light coming through a chink in Julie's door. Latika remembered something. For some minutes she stood at Julie's door, holding her breath. After a while she knocked. No sound came from within. Latika gently pushed open the door. Julie had forgotten to put out her lamp. Latika took out the blue envelope from her pocket and gently pushed it under Julie's pillow.

Mannu Bhandari

Trishanku

The four walls of a house give one a sense of security but they also hold one within their confines. Schools and colleges while developing the brain and mind of a person also curb personality in the name of discipline, rules and regulations. The fact is, friend, that everything carries the seeds of its opposite within itself.

No, these are not precepts culled from tomes. I don't go in for such bulky, pretentious books. These are just fragments of the debates and discussions that go on night and day in our house. Our house, that is, the haunt of intellectuals. Here, amidst cigarette smoke and cups of coffee, imposing edifices of words are raised, verbal revolutions are activated. In this house there is plenty of talk but little action. I can't quote chapter and verse in support of my contention but based on the observation of what goes in my house, I have a strong feeling that action is barred for intellectuals. Every day my honourable mother does her three-hour stint at college and feels liberated. Then she does a little bit of reading and writing and spends the rest of the day stretched out on her bed or wagging her tongue. She labours under the happy delusion that the mind is sharpened when the body is at rest. In this manner, out of twenty-four hours she spends at least twelve sharpening her mind. As for my honourable father, he is two steps ahead of my mother. Left to himself, he would bathe at his desk.

We expend the largest volume of words on one subject—modernity. But wait! Please don't get me wrong. This is not the bobbed hair and fork and knife variety of modernity. There is nothing ersatz about it; it is the genuine article. What it actually is even I do not know. But there is a lot to it, especially with regard is going off the beaten track. But you have to pay the price for everything and even then, more often than not, get it in the neck.

Our discussions tear to pieces everything under the sun. But one topic is a hot, perennial favourite and that is the institution of marriage. Marriage, that is, the first step towards disaster. Starting on a light note, the discussion soon rises to an intellectual level. The institution of marriage, it is argued, has become an empty husk. The husband and wife relationship is false and extraneously imposed. And then a thousand innuendoes are cast upon the institution of marriage. In these discussions men are ranged against women in a clear distinction of male from female. Soon the atmosphere gets so surcharged that I fell sure a couple of divorces are on the way. But nothing of the sort ever happens. All of them are as firmly esconced as ever in their marital bliss. And of course, the tone and momentum of the discussion are the same even today.

Just think, if you pick holes in the institution of marriage doesn't it follow that you do the same with free love and free sex. In particular, men wax so eloquent about it that even mere discussion of the subject gives them vicarious pleasure.

Father himself is a great votary of these ideas. Or was, till one day a distant and quiet young cousin of his, in whose mouth even butter would not melt and never took part in the raging discussions in the house, sprang a surprise by giving a tangible shape to these ideas. At one stroke our modernity vanished in thin air. It transpired that ultimately Mother handled the situation with great skill and made the girl's life 'meaningful' by binding her in the meaningless bond of marriage. All this happened long ago and I only heard it whispered about.

For that matter Father and Mother too had had a love marriage. It is of course a different matter that since I came of age I have never seen them behave like a couple in love but only like a couple in hot arguments. Before taking this daring step Mummy too had to argue a lot with her maternal grandfather. This pre-marriage session of arguments extended over a long period of time and spilled over into the post-marriage years too. Even so one cannot call theirs a marriage of arguments but a marriage of love all right. Mummy speaks of it with great pride. Not pride in the marriage but in the manner in which she had trounced my maternal grandfather. She has so often narrated the wranglings between grandfather and herself that now I can reel them off by heart. Even today when she talks about it her face glows with pride at having gone off the beaten track.

Well, this is the atmosphere in which I am being brought up—so very uninhibited and independent. And suddenly one day I realized that I had grown up. This realization of being grown up came not from within me but from outside. There is an interesting story behind it. The thing is that in front of our house there is a one-room *barsati* set with an open terrace. Every year a couple of students come to stay in this flat, poring over their books and promenading the terrace. But I never took much notice of them. Perhaps I had not reached the age of taking notice. This time I saw two boys there. Just two. But by evening either friends would be storming the place. What a racket they created! The whole neighbourhood rang with it. They sang and laughed, teased each other and threw innocent-seeming comments at any girl who swept their attention was our house—to tell you the truth was me. I had only to step out on to the verandah or just flit by and remarks would come flying at me, like a shot hitting the bull's eye. A tremor would go down my spine. For the first time I felt that I existed, not only existed but was the cynosure of someone's eyes. To be honest, the first feeling was thrilling. I became new even to myself—new and grown up.

It was a peculiar situation. I would fume when they made me the butt of their jokes, although there was nothing indecent about those jokes. It was all innocent fun. But when the boys were not there or were engrossed among themselves I would miss them. A vague uneasiness would take hold of my mind. Things came to such a pass that my thoughts were centred on them ceaselessly and I found a thousand pretexts to come out onto the verandah.

But the hullabaloo that these young men made became a cause of concern for the entire neighbourhood, it almost drove away their sleep. Our neighbourhood was mostly inhabited by businessmen from Hathras and Khurja. They had their daughters to think of and these boys had become pests. The elders thought it was time they rolled up their sleeves and dealt with these young chaps with a firm hand. But strangely enough, Mummy and Papa were blissfully ignorant of the goings-on. The fact was that they had become an island onto themselves; they lived in the colony and were yet not of it.

One day I said to Mummy, 'Mummy, the boys living in the opposite flat keep passing remarks at me. I won't have any more of it. I'll pay them back in the same coin.'

'Which boys?' Mummy asked me in surprise.

Incredible! So Mummy knew nothing about it! With a mixture of dislike and elation I told her the whole story. But it created no impression on her. 'Show me the boys,' she said cooly and went back to her book. I did not like my mother's indifference. Any other mother would immediately have gone into action and whipped these boys right and proper so that its memory would have gone down to the seventh generation of their family. But here was Mummy looking so unconcerned.

In the afternoon when those boys assembled on their terrace I said to Mummy, 'Look, those are the boys who ogle me all the time and pass comments on whatever I do.'

It beats me completely why Mother reacted in the manner she did. She just stared at me and smiled. For a while she scrutinized those boys. 'They appear to be college boys,' she said. 'But they are just children.'

I wanted to ask her if she expected old fogey to tease me and not boys. But before I could open my mouth, she said, 'I will invite these boys over to tea tomorrow evening and you can get to know them.'

I was stunned.

'You mean you want to invite these blokes to tea?'

'Certainly. In our times when boys and girls could not meet they had to content themselves by throwing glances and long-distance banter. But times have changed now.

I was in the seventh heaven of delight. How daring of Mummy to make such a suggestion! She was indeed great and out of the ordinary.

So these boys would step into our house and make friends with me under our own roof. Suddenly I felt I was very lonely and in need of friendship. I did not mix with anyone in our colony. Only Papa's and Mummy's friends came to our house.

I spent the next day in great uncertainty. I wasn't sure whether Mummy would keep her word or had said it in the excitement of the moment. In the evening I said meaning it as a reminder, 'Mummy, are you going to call on those boys?' These were the words but what I really meant was, 'Mummy, go to them, please.'

And Mummy actually did go to them. She rarely went out visiting in the colony and this was one of those rare occasions. I waited with bated breath for her to return. What if Mummy brought them with her? What if they were rude to her? But no, they looked a decent lot. Mummy returned after an hour or so. She was looking cheerful.

'They were utterly taken aback when they saw me,' Mummy said. 'So far people had been threatening them from their own doorways and they thought I was walking right into their den to break their bones. But they fell over themselves to entertain me. Such sweet kids really. They have come from outside and couldn't get into the college hostel so they have taken this room. When your Papa comes in the evening we shall call them over.'

I had never realized that time could pass with such excruciating slowness. When Papa returned from office, Mummy told him the whole story with gusto. She was feeling exuberant at doing something out of the ordinary, going off the beaten track. Papa was not to be outdone. 'Call them over,' he said delightedly. 'Let the kids have a good time. When else will they let themselves go if not at their age?'

Here was an opportunity for Mummy and Papa to prove their modernity. Papa sent the servant to fetch the boys and they showed up the next minute. Mummy introduced them with great decorum. Hi's and Hello's were exchanged. 'Tanu, dear, get the tea ready for your friends,' she said.

Damn it! Tanu dear! I had to prepare tea once for Papa's visitors, Mummy's guests and now for these boys too. Tanu dear had to be on her toes.

In any case tea went off very well. There was great fun and a great deal of laughing and joking. The boys defended themselves by declaring that the neighbourhood was unnecessarily prejudiced against them and that there was nothing wrong with their behaviour. It was all just for fun and no harm done.

Papa supported them. 'Everybody does it at your age,' he said. 'If I had a chance I would do it still.'

Waves of laughter followed his observation. Two hours later, when they were leaving, Mummy said, 'Look, treat this as your own home. Drop in whenever you feel like it. You will be good company for our dear Tanu. You can help her with her studies.

And listen, if there's anything special you want to eat, let me know and I'll cook it for you.'

They went away bowled over by Papa's open-mindedness and Mummy's friendliness. But the poor girl who was supposed to make friends with them was relegated to the role of a mere spectator.

We kept talking about these boys till long after they were gone. To invite these eve-teasers to tea, especially when the target of their attack happened to be the host's own daughter sounded so thrilling. From then on Mummy talked about it to all and sundry—in fact to everyone who dropped in. Mummy was a raconteur par excellence. She could make anything, however drab, sound highly interesting. And here was a tailor-made episode which would bear telling to great effect, without requiring any frills. 'Only you could have hit it off,' Mummy's friends said. 'You have a very healthy attitude. People talk big but they keep their children on a leash all the time. If they become suspicious they even spy on their own children.'

And melting in the praise, Mummy would say, 'Don't I know? Be free and let others be free—that's what I believe in. In our childhood we reeled under so many dos and don'ts that our lives became hell. At least let our children be spared so much oppression.'

But Mummy's pet daughter was passing through another kind of crisis at that time. In the drama that was being enacted, Mummy had herself assumed the role of the heroine—a role which rightly belonged to her child.

The upshot of the tea party was that the behaviour of these boys underwent a sea change. The decency that had been foisted upon them made it obligatory for them to act in accordance with norms of good conduct.

Standing on the roof, whenever they spotted Papa or Mummy then would send across a namaskar to them wrapped with the proprieties and on seeing me they tossed a Hi wreathed in smiles. Instead of badinage we would have a regular dialogue, open and uninhibited. The distance between our verandah and their roof was not large and by raising our voices we could converse freely. Of course it was another matter that our neighbours also heard us without difficulty and with keen interest. As soon as we got going, half a dozen heads or so would suddenly appear in the neighbouring windows. Not that there were no love affairs in our colony. There were many, even elopements. But all this would happen under the cloak of secrecy. When our neighbours' probing eyes got wind of these goings-on, they got a kick out of them and discussed them with savage delight. The men would twist their moustaches and the women wave their hands in the air, and broadcasting these events from one end to the other, with many embellishments. Some of them would boast of being highly experienced and say none could throw dust in their eyes. They would snigger without words as if they had divined what was brewing. But in our case the situation was very different. There was nothing clandestine about it. Actually, we were so open that our inquisitors had to be posted behind barred windows and even so, to their chagrin, they could find nothing incriminating in our talk.

But as generally happens the whole affair snowballed. What happened next was that these meetings came to be held in my room, and not on the terrace as before. Every day, two or three boys would drop in and we would have a whale of a time, gossiping and laughing. We would sing and keep up the tea drinking. In the evening when some friends of Papa or Mummy dropped in they would find one of the boys still entrenched in my room. The very people who advocated liberation now frowned at our activities. As I could discern, their eyes would darken with a strange kind of suspicion. One of Mummy's friend, even said in a subdued voice, 'Tanu is going very fast.' Mummy herself had lost her zest for going off the beaten track. She had perforce to face the naked truth, that her daughter, a raw, inexperienced girl, was hobnobbing with three or four young boys. Mummy was in a quandary. She could neither fully accept the situation of her own making nor could she disown it.

One day she called me and said, 'Tanu, my child, these boys come every day and set up camp here. This is seriously interfering with your studies. How long can things continue like this?'

'I study at night,' I said.

'Oh, do you? Don't give me that crap. There's hardly any time left for studies, as I can see. I don't like this rumpus, I tell you. I don't mind their dropping in once in a while. But they have made it a regular practice. One or the other of them is always hanging around.' The note of irritation in Mummy's voice was mounting.

'You have become so free with them,' Mummy continued. 'I know they won't take it amiss if you tell them to look sharp about their own studies and also leave you to yours. If you think you are not up to it, can't I tell them?'

But the need for all this never arose. Partly because of their studies and partly because of the various diversions provided by a big city like Delhi their visits decreased. But Shekhar, from the opposite room, came regularly, sometimes in the afternoon and sometimes in the evening. What I had not noticed about him in the company of those boys surfaced now with force. He spoke little but the little that he spoke was loaded with meaning. Suddenly I began to understand this unspoken language of his. Not only did I begin to understand it but also to respond to it. It did not take me long to realize that something which they called love was growing between us. I would not have known the meaning of it. But those who are fed on Bombay films do not find it difficult to understand the implications of this phenomenon.

As long as there was nothing between us, our minds were free-wheeling and everything was open, but as soon as something appeared, the wish to hide from others, also appeared.

The other boys would come pounding up the stairs, talking loudly. But Shekhar came up almost on tip-toe and would talk in whispers. Actually there was nothing special about our talk—just about college and studies. But the ordinary gains special meaning when spoken in low whispers. If love gathers an aura of mystery it becomes thrilling, otherwise it is flat as flat can be. But Mummy had a sixth sense by which she could smell out the secrets of all members of the family. Even Papa suffered because of it. Even if Shekhar came secretively, Mummy would appear from nowhere or ask from her own room, 'Tanu, who's in your room?'

I saw that Mummy was greatly perturbed by this behaviour of Shekhar's and an expression of dismay swam in her eyes. But I never imagined that she would be so dismayed. A house in which love affairs had been the staple of conversation—scandals, extra-marital affairs, love triangles and so on—the infatuation between me and Shekhar should have passed unnoticed. If I was friendly with boys I could as well be in love with one or two. Mummy perhaps thought that this affair would develop along the lines of Bombay art films, of which she was a great admirer and in which nothing sensational happened from start to finish.

In any case, I shared Mummy's anxiety to some extent. She was not only mother but also a friend and companion. We discussed things with each other without reservation. I wanted her to say something about this affairs but she just did not oblige. Only when Shekhar came she shed her indifference and hovered around my room with alert eyes.

One day I was coming downstairs to go out with Mummy when we ran into a lady of the colony right at our door. After greeting Mummy she came straight to the point, 'Those boys living in the house opposite yours—are they related to you?'

'No.'

'Oh, I see! Since they come to your house almost every evening I took them for your relatives.'

'They are Tanu's friends,' Mummy said with such nonchalance that the lady turned away, her dart completely missing the target.

We got rid of her all right but I feared that there would be an aftermath, that Mummy would give me the works to unburden her mind of the anger that was lying bottled up within her.

But what she said came to me as a bit of a surprise. She said, 'Haven't these people anything better to do except poke their noses into others' affairs?'

I felt not only reassured but also took it as a signal and stepped up my pace. I did take care to devote to my studies one hour of the three that I spent with Shekhar. He taught me with all his heart and I enjoyed being taught by him. In between he would scribble sweet nothings on slips of paper and hand them to me. They would galvanize me to the very core. Even after he was gone, the words he had written would keep ringing in my ears and send a thrill down my spine. It was like wallowing in a sea of emotion.

A new world, very bright, very full, was taking shape within me. I needed no one these days. I was fulfilled and self-sufficient. Even Mummy, my constant companion, was moving out of my life. I had stopped taking any notice of her except to exchange trivialities.

Days passed. Lost in myself, I was sinking more and more into my own world and had almost become oblivious of the external world.

One day I returned from school, ate my food with gusto, and I had just returned to my room when Mummy who was resting in bed called out to me, 'Tanu, come here!'

When I went to her I found that her face was flushed with rage. My heart missed a beat. She picked up a book from the side table took out from it five or six pieces of paper from the book and flourished them before me. Heaven help me! When I was going to school Mummy had asked for a book to read and I had given her this one, forgetting that Shekhar's scribbled notes were in it.

'So this is how your friendship is sailing along!' she said sarcastically. 'So this is what you study and this is what he comes to teach you!'

I was silent. There would be no greater folly than joining issue with Mummy when she was in a temper.

'I gave you freedom but it does not mean that you should change it into license.'

I was silent.

'A slip of a girl and look at her doings! The more I give her a long rope the more she runs amuck. One resounding slap and all your romance will vanish in thin air.'

Her last sentence made me shiver with rage. With a jerk I raised my head and glanced at Mummy and then fell back in amazement. This was not Mummy at all. Neither was this foul temper hers. And yet what she said seemed very familiar. Hadn't I heard all this before? And it flashed through my mind—my maternal grandfather—my *Nana*. But my *Nana* had passed away many years ago. How had he come back to life? And that too in Mummy—Mummy who fought him tooth and nail and opposed him in everything?

Mummy's grandfather-like sermons continued for sometime. But most of it left me cold, the only thing that bothered me was how Nanaji had got into Mummy.

A strange, tense silence fell over the house—to be practise a silence between me and Mummy. No, between grandfather and me, for Mummy was really not in the house. It was grandfather speaking through her. Generally Mummy and I operated on the same wavelength. I could put my thoughts across to her and she could to me. But Grandfather? I did not understand his language, much less his tone of voice. To communicate with him was out of the question. As for Papa, he was indeed my friend but in an entirely different way. I played chess with him, played the game of bending elbows with him and wheedled him into granting me the favours I had failed to get from Mummy.

As a child, I used to have piggy-rides on his back and even today I can ride on his back without a second thought. But in spite of his being such a friend it was only with Mummy that I shared intimate secrets. And here she was, utterly silent. *Nana* had taken complete hold of her.

I showed Shekhar the red flag and he studiously stayed away from the house. The evenings hung heavy on my hands.

Many times I thought of going to Mummy and asking her openly, 'Why did you get out of temper with me?' She knew of my friendship with Shekhar. I had not hidden this fact from her. So why this sudden volte face? did she think ours was a brother-sister relationship? Then suddenly it occurred to me that it was no use talking it over with Mummy. She had no independent views of her own, having been eclipsed by grandfather.

Four days passed and I hadn't had a glimpse of Shekhar. On the slight hint from me, the poor boy had even stopped coming out on the terrace, let alone coming over. His friends were not seen on the terrace either. If any one of them had dropped in I could have asked him about Shekhar. I knew he was sentimental to a fault. He didn't know what had passed between Mummy and myself but her anger seemed to have cast its long shadow over everything. Seemingly, the thought of her anger had sent everyone into hiding.

Actually since yesterday Mummy's face had been looking a little less taut as if the three days' anger which had congealed on her face had started melting. But I had decided that it was for Mummy to take the initiative to get us out of this impasse.

After finishing my bath I was ironing my school uniform behind the door while Mummy was getting the tea ready and Papa sat engrossed in his newspaper. Probably Mummy was not aware that I had finished my bath and was there. I heard her talking with Papa. 'You know what happened last night?'

she said. 'I felt very bad after that and could not sleep.' Her voice was soft and gentle. I stopped ironing. 'It was about midnight. I got up to go to the bathroom. The terrace opposite was plunged in darkness. Suddenly something red glowed like a star. I peered into the dark. Shekhar was standing on the terrace smoking. I came back on tip-toe. After two hours I peeped out again. He was still standing there and smoking. Poor chap, I felt very sorry for him. And for Tanu too. She had also been in low spirits of late.' Then she said in a voice that sounded full of self-reproach. 'First we give them a long rope and when they start prancing we suddenly pull short. Does it make any sense, really.'

I heaved a deep sigh of relief. I felt so overwhelmed that I felt like running up to Mummy and hugging her. It appeared that after a long time my Mummy was once again her real self. I held myself back at that time, deciding to have a frank talk with her later on. For the last four days my mind had been swarming with questions. But now it was all over. Now Mummy had come out of grandfather's spell and I could talk all I wanted with her.

But when I returned from school in the afternoon I was astounded at what I saw. Shekhar was sitting in the chair holding his head between his hands and Mummy was sitting on the arm of his chair, caressing his back. Seeing me she said in a most natural way, 'Look at this idiot. He has missed college for the last four days and has not eaten a scrap of food. Ask him to sit down with you at lunch.'

And Mummy sat down and cajoled him into eating. But Shekhar did not stay after lunch. He went away weighed down by gratitude towards Mummy. As for me, such a flood of joy broke within me that all my questions were swept away in it.

It took time for things to settle down in their old grooves but settle they ultimately did. Shekhar started coming to our house but only once in two or three days. And we spent most of the time talking about our studies. Shekhar was apologetic at his behaviour and promised Mummy that he would not give her a chance to complain again. The days on which he did not visit us we would make up by talking with each other from across our houses. Since the goings-on between us had my parents' approval, the neighbours' tongues had stopped wagging. They blamed the times for it and hopefully waited for things to go wrong.

But I did notice one thing. Whenever Shekhar stayed on a little longer in the evening or turned up in the afternoon, grandfather would start tossing and turning in Mummy's mind and his presence would be reflected in her face. She did her best not to allow grandfather to speak. Yet she found it hard to put him completely out of the way.

Yes, the situation had become a subject of discussion between me and Mummy. Sometimes she said in jest, 'This Shekhar of yours is slithery and soft as jelly. At his age, boys should be footloose and carefree. They should steel themselves to take the hard knocks of life. But all he does is to hang around on the roof like Majnu and stare this way.'

I just laughed this off.

Sometimes she would get sentimental and say, 'Child, why can't you realize that I have high hopes for you? The dreams I have for your future!'

I would laugh and say, 'Mummy, you are just wonderful. You dream your own life and you dream my life too. Please leave some dreams for me.'

Sometimes she was in a mood to pontificate. 'Look, Tanu, you are too young to understand the ways of the world. Apply your mind exclusively to studies and drive out these silly ideas from your mind. Of course, when you are grown up, get involved in this rigmarole of love and go in for marriage too. I am not going to look around for boys for you. I'll leave that to you but you must be mature enough to make the right choice.'

I would catch the hint that she did not wholly approve of Shekhar as a life companion for me. I asked Mummy, when she fell for Papa, did grandfather approve of her choice?

'My choice? Don't forget I had completed my studies and was twenty-five years old when I chose him. With complete understanding. There was little possibility of my going wrong. Do you understand?' She would say, changing her bewilderment into anger. 'Studies and age—these are the things about which she was always at me. Age was the only point on which she could score over me. I was good at studies so Mummy could not nag me on that account. As for age, I felt like telling Mummy that what her generation did at twenty-five our generation could do at fifteen. Couldn't she understand such a simple thing? But I would not press the point for fear of arousing grandfather in her.

My half-yearly examination was close at hand and I studied hard for it, closing the doors on all visitors. Mummy was pleased; she felt reassured. After finishing my last paper I felt as if a load was off my mind.

'Mummy, tomorrow Shekhar and Deepak are going to the pictures. May I go with them?'

I had never gone out with them but after such strenuous studies I was in a mood to relax and I had a right to some liberty, so I believed.

For a moment Mummy scanned my face and then said, 'Come here, sit down by my side. I want to have a word with you.'

I sat down by her side wondering what there was to talk about. Mummy is given to talking. Even 'yes' or 'no' does not come easily to her. It is wrapped in a torrent of words and becomes explicit only after fifty or sixty sentences.

'Now that your exams are over I was myself planning to go to the pictures. Which picture would you like to see?'

'Why can't I go with them?' I was feeling so irritated that Mummy just kept gaping at my face.

'Tanu, my child, I've given full liberty to you to do all you like. But walk just fast enough for me to walk with you.'

'You tell me plainly whether you will let me go or not? Why this useless talk of your keeping pace with me? Who's talking of your walking with me?'

Caressing my back, Mummy said, 'Walk together we must. If you fall headlong there must be someone near to help you get up.'

I realised that she would not let me go with them. If she said 'no' so sweetly one could not even quarrel with her. And if one argued with her it meant a long sermon in return—regular class of fifty minutes. But for the world of me, I could not understand what harm there was in my going with the boys. Must she always be negative? As she had told me once, she used to resent being denied freedom in her childhood—don't do this, don't go there—and now she was denying the same freedom to me. She just talked big. I had seen through her. I got up and walked off in a huff to my room. But not before I had tossed a sentence into the room, 'Mummy, those who walk must fall, and those who fall will rise and walk again. They won't need others' help.'

I don't know whether it was a reaction to what I said, or a sense of guilty but I found that in the evening she had called over Shekhar and three or four of his friends for a get-together in my room where she regaled them with mouth-watering delicacies. We had such fun that it washed off my afternoon's resentment.

The exams were over and the weather was pleasant. Mummy also seemed to be in congenial temper. Subsequently my friends resume their suspended rounds of visits. Things went on smoothly. But I was in for another jolt.

One day when I returned from my girl friend's house I heard Mummy calling me in a hard voice, 'Tanu, come here, will you?'

The tone of her voice was a danger signal. For an instant I lost my nerve. Mummy was looking very stern.

'Do you go to Shekhar's room?' she fired at point blank range. It instantly occurred to me that someone in our colony had been wagging their tongue. I wanted to tell Mummy that whoever had passed on this information must have told her the rest too, with some frills added. But Mummy seemed to be in a nasty mood and so I discreetly held my tongue. But what could be at the back of Mummy's anger? There must be more to it than was apparent to the eye. Could my going to Shekhar's create such havoc? But Mummy doesn't act on reason only. She is often governed by moods.

My silence made Mummy more edgy.

'Don't you remember I had forbidden you at the very beginning not to go to his room? Isn't it enough for you that he pitches camp here for three to four hours at a stretch?'

Sorrow, anger and fear were battling on her face. I did not know how to explain things to her.

'The good woman living across the lane put me wise to the whole thing,' Mummy said. 'Do you know that I have not bowed my head before anyone? But I felt so humiliated that I could not look her in the eyes. I have lost face on account of you. Oh, how they deride us!'

Good heavens! This time the entire colony seemed to be speaking through Mummy. Surprising how she was speaking the language of the very people she had been so snooty about.

Mummy continued with her harangue while I withdrew into my shell and just closed my ears to her vituperations. I thought I would discuss the whole thing with her after she had cooled down. Why was she making a mountain out of a molehill. I would ask her.

The atmosphere in the house had again become tense. It appeared this time Mummy had taken Papa also into her confidence. He did not join issue with me though he had surprisingly kept himself out of the whole affair. But this time I marked the tension on his face.

Two months before when things had first come to a head I was shaken to the core. But this time I had resolved that if Mummy wanted to act like grandfather. I would have to take her up in the same manner in which she dealt with him. I was firm about it in my mind. I shall show her that I am her daughter, true to her grain. She had deviated from the beaten path and had always boasted about it. But now that I had taken the first step she had herself wavered and was trying to pull me back to the line drawn by her.

I had a lot of arguments tucked away in my mind to be brought forth when it came to a show-down with Mummy. I shall tell her plainly that if she wants to keep me in chains she should have from the beginning brought me up differently. Why this pretence of freedom when she did not mean it? This time I was so worked up that my mind was burnt to embers. I decided that I would remain cooped up in my room. If my feelings overflowed I would give vent to them through tears. I, who was the cynosure of all eyes, who chirped happily all through the day, had now retreated into myself. I kept repeating to myself the refrain,—'Mummy, you must realize that come what may, I shall do just what I want to do,'—although I didn't even have the ghost of an idea what it was that I wanted to do.

I don't know what happened during these three or four days. I remained confined to my room, planning my strategy to beat Mummy at her own game.

But that afternoon I could not believe my ears when I heard my Mummy calling at from the verandah: 'Shekhar, tomorrow all of you will be leaving on your vacation. Have dinner with us tonight. Bring your friends along too.'

I don't know what kind of crisis Mummy had to pass through to reach this stage.

Shekhar was at the dinner table that night along with Deepak and Ravi. Mummy was all attention to them. And as was his wont, Papa was indulging in his light-hearted banter. A few faces were visible plastered against the neighbouring windows. Everything had fallen into place, with not a note of discard anywhere.

Only I stood apart from the whole scene, taking a detached view of it. Then it suddenly occurred to me that grandfather was grandfather—hundred percent himself, which must have made it easier for Mummy to hold her ground against him. But how am I to fight with Mummy, who is grandfather one moment and Mummy the next?

Usha Priyamvada

Return

Gajadhar Babu ran his eyes over the luggage collected in the room—two boxes, a basket and a bucket.

'What's in the small tin, Ganesh?'

Ganeshi was tying the bed-roll. My wife says you are fond of *laddus*.' It made him proud to think that he could be of service to his master. 'We'll miss you,' he added.

Gajadhar Babu was excited at the prospect of going home. But his happiness was tinged with sadness. He was snapping ties with a world which had become familiar and dear to him and where he commanded respect.

'Please don't forget us,' Ganeshi said tying the string around the bed-roll.

'Drop me a line if you are ever in difficulty. And yes, don't delay your daughter's marriage. Fix it up by September.'

'If you don't help us, who will?' Ganeshi said wiping away tears with his napkin. 'Things would have been easier had you been here.'

Gajadhar Babu was getting restive. With all his belongings packed up, the room in the railway quarter where he had spent the major part of his life now looked denuded and ugly. In anticipation of his leaving, the neighbours had even uprooted the flower plants and shrubs which he had so carefully nurtured in the courtyard. In their place big holes gaped at him. But the pleasant anticipation of joining his near and dear ones stifled the mild wave of anger he felt rising in his heart at this act of vandalism.

Gajadhar Babu was happy, very happy. After thirty-five years' service with the railways he had retired and was proceeding home for good. During his long tenure of service, he had spent most of the time alone, far from the family. The thought that one day he would go to live in the midst of his family had sustained him in his lonely moments. Judged by worldly standards, it could be said that he had not fared badly in life. He had constructed a house of his own. His eldest son, Amar, and daughter, Kanti were married and settled. Another son and daughter were in college.

Most of the time Gajadhar Babu had been posted at small stations. When the question of his children's education came up his wife went to stay in the city with them. Gajadhar was an affectionate person who needed affection. With the family gone, his life had become a vast emptiness. It became difficult for him to stay in the house. When his family was with him, on returning from duty, he would spend his time happily at home: joke with his wife and have fun with the children. He did not have a poetic turn of mind, yet he would keep remembering his wife's loving words and gestures. She would keep the hearth going even up to two in the afternoon so that she could serve him a hot meal. In spite of his protests that he had had enough she would force upon him another helping and sweetly cajole him into doing full justice to the food. When he came home he found her standing at the kitchen door, greeting him with a shy smile...Gajadhar Babu's memory glowed with numerous small details and he felt nostalgic. And now after a long wait the time had come when he would again live in the midst of that affection and respect.

Gajadhar Babu put his cap on the string bed and hung the coat on the wall nail. Every now and then he would hear loud cachinations from within the house. It was a Sunday. In the next room, the boys and girls were collected round the table, having breakfast. Still smiling, he went in. Narendra, his hands on his hips, was mimicking a dance seen in last night film, at which Basanti, his daughter doubled up with laughter. Amar's wife, oblivious of all decorum, sat with her head uncovered, hugely enjoying the whole thing. As Gajadhar Babu appeared on the scene a hush fell on the room. Amar's wife quickly covered her head, and Narendra, dumped himself in a chair and put a cup of tea to his mouth. The effort to suppress her giggles kept Basanti's shoulders shaking.

'What's going on, Narendra?' Gajadhar Babu said, amused.

'Nothing, father,' Narendra replied looking completely put out.

Gajadhar Babu wanted to join in the fun and their sudden silence irked him.

'Basanti, may I have some tea,' he said sitting down. 'Your mother hasn't finished her worship yet?'

'She should soon be here,' Basanti said, glancing towards mother's room. She proceeded to prepare a cup of tea for her father.

'Child, the tea doesn't taste nice,' Gajadhar Babu said taking a sip. 'It's insipid.'

'I'll add some more sugar.'

'No, don't bother. I'll have another cup when your mother prepares some for herself.'

Amar's wife had already left the room. Narendra also slipped away quietly. Only Basanti remained, out of deference to her father but she kept looking towards the door. Soon her mother came in, pitcher in hand, mumbling some mantras. She poured water on the basil plant.

'Sitting alone!' she gave a start on seeing her husband sitting all by himself in the room. Basanti had also gone in the meanwhile. 'Where are the others?'

Gajadhar Babu felt a constriction in his heart. 'They must be busy somewhere,' he said. 'Children are children, you know!'

When his wife went into the kitchen she knitted her brows at the sight of unwashed utensils scattered all over the kitchen floor.

'Oh, God, am I to pollute myself washing these utensils after a bath! Nobody even cares to collect them in one place.' She called out for the servant, but there was no response. She called out again, this time a little louder, and then looked at Gajadhar Babu. 'Amar's wife must have sent the fellow to the bazaar!' she sighed and fell into a sullen silence.

Gajadhar Babu patiently waited for his breakfast. He was reminded off Ganeshi. Every morning before the passenger train arrived he used to prepare *puris* and *jalebis* and serve them with tea. Nice tea, exactly to his taste. Three spoonfuls of sugar and thick creamy milk. The train could be late, but not Ganeshi with his glass of tea.

He felt pained at the plaintive tone of his wife. 'I've to fret over things the whole day,' she said. 'Even the servant is no help. Work, work, work, all the time. It has made me prematurely old. Nobody cares to share my burden.'

'Doesn't Amar's wife help you?' Gajadhar Babu asked.

'She sleeps all the time. And as for Basanti, she has to attend college.'

Gajadhar Babu, thoroughly worked up, called out for Basanti. She came out of her sister-in-law's room and stood before him.

'Basanti, from today you must cook the evening meal. Your sister-in-law will cook the morning meal.'

'But I've got to study, father,' Basanti pulled a long face.

'You can study in the morning,' Gajadhar Babu said in a conciliatory tone. 'You know your mother is not so strong as she used to be. Between yourself and your sister-in-law you should be able to manage the house.'

Basanti maintained a sullen silence.

'Her mind is not in her studies,' her mother said when Basanti was gone. 'Most of the time she is at Sheila's house.

There are grown up boys in her house, I try to stop her but she won't listen to me. A load will be off my chest when she is married.'

Breakfast over, Gajadhar Babu went into the sitting room. The house was small and there was hardly any space which he could have entirely to himself. As in the case of a guest come for a short stay, they had improvised some space for Gajadhar by shifting the chairs against the wall and putting a string-bed in the empty space. While lying on the bed Gajadhar Babu would feel that his status in the house was no better than that of a bird of passage, and he was reminded of the trains which halted at the station briefly and were then gone. His wife, no doubt, had a room to herself but it was cluttered up with odds and ends. A corner of it was filled with jars of home-made pickles and jams, canisters of rice and tins of ghee. In another corner lay quilts and rugs, rolled into a huge bundle tied with string. Besides her own and Basanti's trunk, there was a huge tin box which contained the family's wardrobe of woollens and winter clothes. And to top it all, a clothes-line was slung across the room, on which Basanti flung her clothes in reckless disarray. Gajadhar Babu avoided going into this room.

The second room was occupied by Amar and his wife, and the third room which opened onto the front had been set apart as the sitting room. Before Gajadhar Babu came to stay in the house, the room contained a cane-chair set, which formed a part of Amar's wife's dowry. The chairs had blue cotton covers and cushions embroidered by Amar's wife.

When Gajadhar Babu's wife wanted to unburden her mind she would pull her mat into the sitting room and lie down maintaining a stubborn silence. That day when she pulled her mat into his room, Gajadhar Babu broached the subject of their domestic problems. He had observed the way the house was being run and mildly hinted at the need to economise. 'Now that our income is reduced we must cut down our expenses,' he said.

'But I can't starve the family,' she retorted. I've scraped and scrounged all my life. I never ate well nor wore decent clothes.'

Gajadhar Babu looked at his wife with melancholy eyes. She knew that they were not well off, and it was but natural that she should feel the pinch and talk about it. But what worried him more than her complaint was her unsympathetic tone. Had she suggested that they should put their heads together and devise a way out of their difficulty, he would have squeezed some solace even out of the present predicament. But her perennial nagging made him feel as if he was solely responsible for the family's misery.

'What do you lack, Amar's mother?' he said. 'You have a daughter-in-law, and sons and daughters. Money is not everything in the world.'

As soon as these words were out of his lips, he realised that this manifestation of his inner being was beyond his wife's comprehension. He felt still more isolated.

'The daughter-in-law is a great help indeed!' his wife said sarcastically. 'She is doing the cooking today. You'll see she will make a hash of everything.'

She abruptly closed her eyes and soon lapsed into slumber. Amazed, Gajadhar looked at her face. Was this the woman, the memory of whose soft touch and captivating smile still lay enshrined in his heart and had helped to lighten the burden of life? He felt that that charming woman, the companion of his life, had fallen somewhere by the wayside. This heavy woman who lay sprawled before him was utterly unfamiliar—uncouth and ungainly, her withered face coarse and lustreless. He kept looking at her for a long time. Then he lay down and stared at the ceiling.

Something crashed to the ground. His wife woke with a start. 'It's the cat!' She got up abruptly and ran in.

When she returned, her cheeks were flushed. 'Do you see your daughter-in-law's doings? She left the kitchen door ajar. The cat has upturned the pot of lentils. I don't know how I am going to feed the family. And half a jar of ghee is clean gone on *parathas* and one vegetable curry. She has no heart, no conscience. Men sweat their guts out, earning a living and she squanders everything without a thought. I told you she is no good at running the house.'

Gajadhar Babu felt that if she continued with her dirge his ears would start tingling with pain. He clenched his lips and turned his back on his wife.

In the evening, Basanti designedly cooked such rotten food that it became difficult to swallow even a single morsel. Gajadhar Babu somehow gulped the food down and got up. But Narendra pushed away the plate. 'I can't eat this rotten stuff.'

'Then don't,' Basanti said in a huff. 'No one is forcing you to eat.'

'Who asked you to cook?'

'Father, who else?'

'Father gets funny brain waves.'

His mother somehow mollified Narendra and had some food specially cooked for him. Gajadhar Babu later on said to his wife, 'Basanti is no longer a child. It's a pity she has not learnt cooking.'

'She knows how to cook. She was just feigning.'

Next evening, finding her mother in the kitchen, Basanti changed into new clothes and' was about to go out when Gajadhar Babu stopped her.

'Where are you off to?'

'Just next door—to Sheila's house.'

'You had better not. Go in and study,' Gajadhar Babu said in a peremptory tone.

For a moment Basanti stood undecided and then re-traced her steps.

When Gajadhar Babu returned from his evening stroll his wife said, 'What did you say to Basanti? She is lying with her face covered. She has not even eaten her meal.'

Gajadhar Babu was upset. From his wife's tone he felt as if he was the guilty one. He decided to marry off Basanti as soon as he could.

From then on Basanti always avoided her father. When she had to go out she went by the back door. Once or twice when Gajadhar Babu asked his wife the reason for Basanti's strange behaviour she told him that she was angry with him.

Gajadhar Babu exploded with rage. 'What impudence! So she doesn't deign to talk to her own father?'

Then his wife broke the news that Amar was thinking of living separately from the family.

'Why?' The news came to him as a hammer blow.

His wife gave evasive replies. He realised gradually, that Amar and his wife had a number of complaints against him. Since the time Gajadhar Babu had come to occupy the sitting room, they had no decent place to receive visitors. Further, Amar's wife had to drudge in the house and her mother-in-law taunted her for her inept ways.

'Did any such thing happen before my coming here?'

Gajadhar's wife shook her head. Previously, Amar was reckoned the head of the family. His wife too had her own way in everything. Amar's friends had made the sitting room their haunt where they were regaled with tea and refreshments, even at odd hours. Basanti also liked things that way. With Gajadhar's coming their liberties were curtailed.

Gajadhar said in a feeble voice, 'Well, ask Amar not to act in a hurry.'

When Gajadhar Babu returned from his walk, he found his bed was missing from the sitting room. He was about to go in to enquire when he saw it lying in his wife's room in the midst of jars of pickles and bundles of quilts. He took off his coat and ran his eyes along the wall for a place to hang it. Then he folded it and, pushing away some clothes from the clothes-line, flung the coat on it. Without having breakfast he stretched himself on the bed. Though still active, age had started telling on him; he went for a walk, morning and evening, but the exertion tired him.

Gajadhar Babu was reminded of his spacious railway quarter, his carefree life and of the flurry of activity on arrival of the passenger trains, of the familiar faces and the rattling of wheels which fell on his ears like music. The roar of the mail and express trains which hurtled past the station was the sole companion of his solitary nights. Often people from the Seth Ramjidas Sugar Mills came to gossip with him. The orbit of his friendship did not extend beyond these people. He felt those good old days would never come again; in them he had lost a valuable treasure.

Lying on the bed, he listened to the noises coming from within the house; brief exchanges of arguments between his wife and daughter-in-law, water dripping from the tap, the brittle sound of utensils being scraped, and over them all a tete-a-tete between two sparrows.

Suddenly he decided that henceforth he would not take any interest in home affairs. Well, if this was the only place in the whole house for the head of the family, he would stay put without protest. And if they shoved him off to some other corner, well, let it be so. If he could not enter the lives of his children, he would rather live like an alien.

And true enough, from that day onwards, Gajadhar Babu never poked his nose into the affairs at home. Narendra asked him for some money. He gave it to him without asking a question. Basanti would stay away from home for hours, he would not raise even his little finger in protest. But what galled him most was that his changed attitude went unnoticed even by his wife; she was utterly oblivious of the fact that he was weighed down by a terrible mental strain. Rather, she was pleased that her husband did not poke his nose into her affairs. Sometimes she even went to the extent of saying, 'This is as it should be. You should not meddle with your children's affairs.

They are now grown up. We are doing our duty by them. We are giving them proper education, and when the time comes we will perform their marriages.'

Gajadhar Babu gave his wife a hurt look. He felt he was nothing more than a money-making machine for his wife and children. An entity whose existence entitled her to put vermilion in the parting of her hair and ensured her a certain status in society. All that was required of her was to provide him with two meals a day—and with that her responsibility towards him ended. She was so absorbed with the tins of ghee and sugar that they had become the whole world to her. He could not hope to be an integral part of her world. He could not be the focus of her life. He even lost interest in his daughter's wedding.

In spite of having stopped interfering with the family affairs he could not become at one with the family. He felt as out of place in the house as the bed looked in the well-furnished sitting room. The joy of coming home was overcast by a pall of gloom.

However, despite his grim resolve not to impose himself upon the family, one day he faltered. His wife, as was her habit, was denigrating the servant—that he was a shirker, that he stole money, and ate too much. Gajadhar Babu had all along felt that the family was living beyond its means. The servant, to his mind, was a luxury which they could not afford. He paid him off on the spot.

When Amar returned from office he called for the servant.

'Father has dismissed the servant,' his wife said.

'Why?'

'He says the servant is too expensive.'

A bare statement of fact. But Gajadhar Babu did not miss the sting of sarcasm in his daughter-in-law's voice. Being slightly out of sorts that evening, he had not gone out for his evening constitutional. Unaware of his presence in the house, Narendra said, 'Mother, why don't you bring father round? Had he nothing better to think of than packing off the servant? If he thinks I'll carry the load of wheat on the cycle carrier for grinding, well, he is expecting too much of me!'

'Yes, mother,' Basanti chipped in, 'I can't attend college.and sweep the house at the same time.'

'He is getting senile,' Amar muttered. 'Why can't he leave things alone?'

'And imagine his asking our daughter-in-law to do the cooking!' Amar's mother rejoined. 'Fifteen days ration goes in five.'

Before Amar's wife could retort she swiftly disappeared into the kitchen.

After some time she went to her room and switched on the light. She was taken aback. Gajadhar Babu was lying on his bed with his eyes closed.

Gajadhar Babu came in, waving a letter and called out for his wife. She came wiping her hands on the end of her sari, and looked at him expectantly.

'I've got a job in Seth Ramjidas Sugar Mills,' Gajadhar Babu said. 'It's better that I earn something rather than idle away the time. He had made me an offer once before but I had declined it.'

He paused and then as if the dying embers had suddenly kindled, he continued in a low voice, 'I thought after years of separation I would stay with you for good...anyway, I'll be leaving the day after tomorrow. Will you come with me?'

'I?' His wife fumbled for words. 'Who will look after the house if I also go away? Such a large family... and a grown-up daughter.'

'Yes, you are right,' Gajadhar Babu said. 'I just asked you in case...' And he lapsed into a long silence.

Eagerly Narendra tied the bed-roll and then fetched a rickshaw. Gajadhar Babu's tin trunk and the small bed-roll were deposited in it. Holding a bundle of *laddus* and salted *mathris*,

Gajadhar Babu climbed into the rickshaw. He cast a glance at his family and then looked away. The rickshaw started.

They came in after seeing him off at the door.

Amar's wife said to her husband, 'What about going to the cinema?'

Basanti jumped, 'Brother, I'll also come with you!'

Gajadhar Babu's wife went straight to the kitchen. She put the remaining *mathris* in a tin and brought the tin to her room.

'Narendra, take away Babuji's bed. As it is, the place is already so cramped.'

Giriraj Kishore

The Paperweight

The sight of the shepherd, staff in hand, walking behind his herd of sheep, made Mrinal Babu laugh. The shepherd was uttering weird sounds to keep the sheep together. Sometimes he smacked his staff hard on the ground scaring the animals, setting them bumping pell-mell into each other.

The peon, came in and said, 'Hazoor, Saheb has come.' Although Mrinal Babu had expressly come to meet Shivnath Babu, the information unbalanced him for a moment. Immediately he realized that the peon was keenly watching the fast-changing expressions on his face. He swiftly proceeded towards Shivnath Babu's office. A looking glass hung outside his room. A glance at his face in the mirror told him he was unnecessarily worried that he looked nervous. Gently pushing the curtain aside, he wiped his shoes on the doormat, coughed, and entered the room.

Shivnath Babu was busy wading through files. To prevent the Chief Minister getting distracted from work Mrinal Babu locked his hands together and settled down in a chair. About two or three minutes later he realized that he was sitting rather stiffly on the chair, not at ease. To sit like this was a sign of nervousness. He leant back against the cushion, and stretched his legs. They struck the wooden foot-rest under the table. His face changed at once, and his gaze travelled to Shivnath Babu's face. But the sound of his feet hitting the footrest had not affected the C M in the least. His eyes remained glued to the file. Mrinal Babu sat on, as if observing his working skill closely, as if trying to learn something from him.

Shivnath Babu would pick up a file, untie its red string and turning it to the flagged page, start reading. Sometimes he would have to go back some pages. His lips also looked busy while reading. He would either make a noting in the file, or put a question mark and throw it on the floor. There were very few files which he signed as they were. Watching the process Mrinal Babu got bored. His glance flitted around. Closed from all sides, lamp burning and the circle of lamp-light falling over the files...it looked like the den of a philosopher. The rest of the room was barely touched by light. The continuous sitting hurt him in the posterior. He changed position. When Shivnath Babu raised his head from the file Mrinal Babu reacted with some embarrassment. Maybe he thought that before raising his head Shivnath Babu would give some indication. He had to force a smile on his lips, and his dry lips stretched like rotten rubber. Hiding his own characteristic smile under his thick moustache, Shivnath Babu said, 'Tell me, then, the work in your Department is going on well?'

This was precisely what Mrinal Babu had come to tell him about. Since Shivnath Babu's return from abroad he had made several attempts to meet him, but pressure of work had made it difficult for Shivnath Babu to give him time. Before going abroad, Shivnath Babu had inducted him as minister. He had said to him, 'I want you to show the same speed and intelligence here too. It was, after all, your exceptional vigilance that forced Shantisharan to give in his resignation...I think... you will be well able to understand all exigencies and situations'. Then, giving a faint smile, he had added, 'I am fully aware that honest and hard-working people like you are scarce.' He boarded his plane. Almost everyone kept standing and looking and until the plane took off. For many days after

Shivnath Babu's departure, Mrinal Babu felt like a child whose father disappears after admitting him into school.

Shivnath Babu's words were indelibly etched on the tablet of Mrinal Babu's mind and he did his utmost to introduce radical changes in the department before Shivnath Babu returned. He had given strict instructions to his staff that no file was to be kept pending for more than a fortnight.

Mrinal Babu had noted that on his return from abroad Shivnath Babu had had a good word for the work of all the ministers at the cabinet meeting. But he had said not a word about his ministry. A funny change was discernible more often than not, in the working of his ministry too. Whichever file he asked for, would be with the Chief Minister. Even the Secretary was often at the Chief Minister's. Mrinal Babu was convinced that the Secretary was a rascal. If the Chief Minister wanted to talk about a file he was supposed to call the minister, according to protocol. He had heard that the Secretary was currying favour with the Chief Minister.

Raising his head Shivnath Babu rang the bell and then turned to Mrinal Babu. 'You haven't told me what you wanted to see me about?' The same peon entered in response to the call bell. He took in Mrinal Babu with a swift glance. 'Put me through to his Secretary, Mr Rai,' Shivnath Babu said, pointing at Mrinal Babu. 'I wish to talk.'

Mrinal Babu did not like the idea of his Secretary being called in his presence. But he kept quiet. On Shivnath Babu's gesturing at him with his eyes and muttering 'Hunh', Mrinal Babu asked, 'Is there some departmental work with Mr Rai?' Shivnath Babu kept looking at his files as if he had not heard Mrinal Babu. For an instant Mrinal Babu's face lost colour. Then picking up courage he said again, 'For some time now I have been trying to understand all the ins and outs of my department. I've many schemes in my head'.

Shivnath Babu received this statement with a long-drawn 'Hunh'. Mrinal Babu failed to understand whether he had uttered this 'Hunh' at what he had said, or at something in the file. Tying up the file, he said, smiling, 'All right.'

Mrinal Babu was bucked at Shivnath Babu's 'All right', and said 'Mr Rai is not cooperating with me at all. No file is placed before me. When I ask he says it is with the Chief Minister. Now, what can you have to do with these files? After all, it's you who have made me minister. I enjoy your confidence. But Mr Rai... you know well...he is a smart chap.' He paused, hesitating, and then said, 'Mr Rai thinks I will never have the courage to speak out to you...that I'm a new man...'

Seeing Shivnath Babu again engrossed in his files Mrinal Babu took it as an affront. When the peon came and informed him that Mr Rai was not in his bungalow and had gone to the temple, Shivnath Babu abruptly got up from his chair without saying anything. Joining his hands together in a namaskar, he said to Mrinal Babu, 'All right then.'

Mrinal Babu felt that he had been thrown out of the office. Swiftly he came out. As soon as he came out, his eye fell on the peon. He was explaining something to his driver very theatrically. There was a kind of smile on his face, that looked as if he was mimicking someone and enjoying it thoroughly. Mrinal Babu did not like it. 'What was the peon telling you?' he asked the driver after the car had gone some distance.

The driver was not prepared for such a question. He became nervous and said, 'Nothing, sir.'

'What do you mean, nothing?' Mrinal Babu said in a hard voice, repeating the driver's word.

The driver tried to save his skin by telling him that it was something between him and the peon, but Mrinal Babu was not satisfied. 'Was he saying something about me?'

The driver turned slightly to look at him. He was sitting in the left corner of the back seat. The mirror was also fixed in the other corner. He had to say, looking in front: 'Hazoor, he was only asking is the Chief Minister angry with your Saheb? It is only a short time ago that your Saheb was made minister.'

Mrinal Babu was furious. He wanted to say, 'Why should Shivnath Babu be angry with me, it is I who am angry with him: He didn't say it. He just closed his eyes and sank back into his seat. Even with closed eyes he could not regain his equanimity. His nostrils flared and he tried to formulate in his mind the thought of sending in his resignation immediately on reaching home. The behaviour of Shivnath Babu before he had made him a minister was very different from what it was now. He suddenly realised that he had been talking to himself. He sat up straight and looked at the driver to make sure that he had not seen anything. But when his gaze went to the mirror he found that it had been set at a different angle. He felt he was his own prisoner, that all situations contrived to make him so.

The present situation had become totally different from what it was before. When Shivnath Babu came with an invitation to him for a minister's post, how soft-spoken, and amiable he was. He could recall the conversation between them word for word. 'I know you are a straightforward and incorruptible man. You had opposed me in defiance of the party whip. Shanti Sharan had to submit his resignation entirely because of you.' Shivnath Babu had given a faint smile. He had then said, with a grave expression. 'If I had wanted to, I could have divested you of the membership of the party and the Assembly both. But I knew there was no other member in the party with your grasp and understanding.'

At the swearing-in ceremony too Shivnath Babu had heaped praises on Mrinal Babu in the presence of the Governor. On the oath-taking day he had sent his own car to take him to Raj Bhavan. Mrinal Babu remembered, that that day there was a childlike simplicity and guilelessness on Shivnath Babu's face. But his face today...

The driver rammed on the brakes with such force that Mrinal Babu thought there had been an accident. A baby goat had narrowly escaped being run over. Mrinal babu was full of pity for the baby goat.

His car stopped in the portico, and many people were assembled in the verandah. His first impulse was to get down from the car and quietly slip away. They had met him the day before. He had promised them that he would give them a definite reply the following day. He had been sure that he could prevail upon the government to consider their problem with sympathy. It was a question of an industrial take over. The government wanted to acquire the dwellings of the people in the area and in return people wanted permanent jobs in the factory and dwellings in the industrial area on less rent. The government objected to the idea of giving employment. It was ready to compensate them monetarily and no more. The same problem had arisen at the time of Shanti Sharan and it was still unsolved. It was about this problem that Mrinal Babu had gone to the Chief Minister, and sought a meeting. Even after the representative of the workers had gone he had phoned the Secretary to come over with the relevant files. Mr Rai had got away by telling him that the files were with the Chief Minister. Mrinal Babu had got so enraged that he had shouted at the Secretary over the phone, saying that no file was to be sent to the Chief Minister without his knowledge and consent. The Secretary had not thought it necessary or fit to make any reply.

But Shivnath Babu's behaviour was trying in the extreme. He now found himself in a most embarrassing position with the slum dwellers. He decided finally that it would be best to send then to the Chief Minister. To act on his own without consulting the Chief Minister would land him in the same impasse in which Shanti Sharan had found himself.

When Mrinal Babu suggested to them that they should meet the Chief Minister, an Assembly member of the Opposite party and a leader of the deputation, lost his temper. 'You are talking like Shanti Sharan. Is the department under your charge or the Chief minister's? The Chief Minister says, 'You people labelled Shanti Sharan dishonest and dumb Now I have put the ministry in charge of the ablest and most honest member of the house. Even now you come running to me...' Mrinal Babu stood silent. He felt as if the hinge had come off while he was attempting to open a door. He wanted to tell them clearly that he was minister only in name. But he could not acknowledge this in the hearing of all of them. He thought it best to say, therefore, 'All right...If there's anything in my power that I can do, I shall...' Joining his hands in salutation he came back into the house.

Mrinal Babu felt as if he had been forced into a situation especially prepared for him. Once again he felt like sending in his resignation. 'But...' This 'but' had assumed the proportions of a mountain for him. He envisaged in a rush, the whole scenario that could arise from his resignation. If Shivnath Babu had some other plans for him the resignation would only come in handy. People would say, 'what thundering speeches he used to make on the floor of the house! But when it came to real action he turns tail and flees.' Or, they might even spread the story around that he had been forced to resign.

He picked up the paperweight lying on the table and rotated it fast. The sight of just a little pressure from his fingers setting the paperweight spinning swiftly made him wonder what to call this motion. The telephone extension buzzed like a bee. He felt a wave of indignation at his P.A. Why didn't he stop these calls? Where was the need to put them through? Just presses the buzzer for the asking. People think I am a minister. My recommendation can move mountains... He wanted to pick up and put down the receiver without speaking or listening. But the peon came in and told him that the Chief Minister was on the line. To pick up the receiver seemed to him like picking up a heavy object. At the other end Shivnath Babu himself was speaking. He spoke just two sentences. 'Please over come. It's something important.' The voice was comparatively mild. Mrinal Babu echoed in rage: 'It's something important!'

He came out of his room. In the PA's room the driver, the peon, and the bodyguard were chattering amidst loud and frequent guffaws. Mrinal Babu shook with rage. He marched into the PA's room and began shouting, 'Aren't you ashamed of yourself, guffawing and gossiping with these people? Have you no dignity to keep up?' Seeing the PA getting it hot, everyone slunk out of the other door and resumed their various positions of work with diligence. The driver began wiping the car, the bodyguard sat on the bench, the peon disappeared within.

Driving along, the driver kept apprehending Mrinal Babu's pouncing upon him at any moment. The bodyguard was also tense. But Mrinal Babu was exclusively occupied with and greatly oppressed by the thought of Shivnath Babu's behaviour. He was thinking that if Shivnath Babu's mood permitted he would bring this up.

Reaching the Chief Minister's residence he stopped short in the verandah. The PA came running up and showed him into the drawing room with the utmost courtesy. For a minute or two Mrinal Babu compared this welcome with the cold reception he had been accorded earlier in the morning. But right in front of him, on the divan, Shivnath Babu sat reclining, his left elbow resting against a bolster. The left knee lay flat and the right knee stood at a ninety degree angle, while an expansive smile played on his face, and he said 'Welcome', with his right hand he motioned towards the sofa. Mrinal Babu sat down without a word.

'I don't suppose you have had your lunch?' Shivnath Babu asked, still smiling, affectionate.

'No, Sir. I'll have it when I back.'

'Lunch with me today. Ever since my return from abroad I haven't had a moment's respite. This morning too I couldn't speak with you. I felt very bad about it later. Actually a file had put me off completely. Please don't take it amiss. Sometimes under mental strain I do funny things.' He emphasised the last sentence and also smiled.

The Paperweight

Mrinal Babu did not think it appropriate to have lunch with Shivnath Babu. He made an excuse, 'I've invited some people over for lunch.'

'All right, then I owe you a lunch,' Shivnath Babu said with engaging frankness. His face now wore the same look as on the occasion when he had invited him to join his ministry. 'Yes, you were telling me something about Rai in the morning. I know him well.' Shivnath Babu laughed loudly.

'Have you heard this fable—a crafty wolf sat on the bank of a river, and boasted: "I've eaten up a whole field of melons." The crocodile thought this totally improbable, and when the wolf bent down to drink water, the crocodile caught him by the throat. "Out with the field of melons!" he cried. "Ate it all up yourself?" The wolf laughed loudly and called out, "You there, melon field! Come out behind". The crocodile leapt towards the wolf's hind-side and the wolf ran away.'

This story of Shivnath Babu's made Mrinal Babu laugh. But Shivnath Babu assumed a grave expression and said, 'You are raw yet. Try to understand things little by little. You don't know the ways of these government officials.'

Mrinal Babu did not like the adjective 'raw' for himself. He said respectfully, 'Babuji, for how long am I to be labelled raw? You too think of me as a greenhorn'. After saying this Mrinal Babu felt he had overstepped the line. He smiled to make light of his remark. Shivnath Babu's face reverted to the hard expression it had worn that morning.

'Mrinal Babu, I had taken you for a politician,' Shivnath Babu said. 'But you have turned out to be an emotion-ridden child that smiles on getting sweets, and cries on getting a little hurt. A politician has to be like iron. As long as the iron is cold it is in a position to inflict injury...'

Shivnath Babu could have said more but Mr Rai's coming in just then made him stop. It took some time for Mrinal Babu to reclaim himself from the tense situation, but he began thinking, even as a minister I have too seek permission to meet the Chief

Minister, whereas, Mr Rai, a mere secretary, and in the presence of his minister, can walk in unannounced...'

Shivnath Babu said to Mr Rai in a stern, reprimanding way, 'Mr Rai, I attach great importance to the carrying out of orders. Even the secretary of the Assembly appointed by me is as pivotal as the Chief Minister. Every representative of the people is an inseparable limb of the government. I wouldn't like to hear in future the complaints I have heard just now. In matters of administration too, any kind of interference is intolerable to me...'

With the last sentence Shivnath Babu gave Mrinal Babu a meaningful glance. After a pause he continued, 'The responsibility of upholding the rights of the people falls upon the Chief Minister. It is these rights that he delegates to his minister, secretaries, in other words, to all the limbs of the government. But it is the Chief Minister who is answerable for the least lapse.'

Shivnath Babu ceased speaking. Turn by turn he looked at Mrinal Babu and then at Mr Rai. There was undoubtedly a difference in the two looks, but Mrinal Babu felt that he too had a share in the upbraiding given to Mr Rai. The only difference was that Mr Rai stood with lowered head while Mrinal Babu sat on the sofa.

Shivnath Babu asked Mr Rai in the same tone, 'Have you brought the file?'

Mr Rai produced a file from under his arm and respectfully extended it to him.

'You may go,' Shivnath Babu said, taking the file without glancing at it. 'But bear in mind what I've told you.'

Mrinal Babu noticed that walking towards the door Mr Rai smiled faintly.

After Mr Rai had gone Shivnath Babu pushed the file towards Mrinal Babu. 'Tomorrow you will have to answer in the Legislative Assembly.' There was a note of command in his voice.

Mrinal Babu started turning the pages of the file. He sensed that Shivnath Babu was intently studying his face, taking note of every change of expression. Then he heard Shivnath Babu saying, 'You can, of course, study the file at home. But you may as well glance through it in my presence. I am going out of station just now. I will come straight to the assembly tomorrow morning. You are an idealist and given to sentiment. I wouldn't like that later, when you look at the file, you should feel your ideals are being violated.'

Mrinal Babu felt that Shivnath Babu was telling him in different words, 'I place great importance on my orders being carried out...'

Shivnath Babu got up and going into the other room said, 'You have understood?' Mrinal Babu didn't get a chance even to fold his hands in farewell.

Getting into his car Mrinal Babu thought Shivnath Babu does funny things under stress...'

When he opened the file at home, he found it dealt with the question of the industrial settlement and the rehabilitation of the slum dwellers. With a slight change of wording, the same answers had been written that Shantisharan had made in the assembly.

Mrinal Babu felt that every member of the assembly was repeating the sentence that he had once used for Shantisharan: 'We do not want dogs who jump for a bone.'

And Shivnath Babu says with a smile: 'Shantisharan was dishonest and dim-witted. But now the most honest and trustworthy member of the assembly who enjoys your confidence is saying the same thing...'

Hridayesh

The Parrot

It was hard to say who woke first in the morning—Lala Asharfilal or the parrot—and whose waking brought the morning to the house, or at least the feeling of morning. Sometimes Asharfilal's was awakened by the parrot's trilling, and sometimes, it was only Asharfilal's footsteps, as he moved onto the verandah after leaving his bed, that made the parrot raise its neck from the hollow of its warm feathers. The parrot would circle around a couple of times in the cage, reciting, *tain...tain...tuun...parho paththe Sitaram... Sitaram*. And then Asharfilal would echo the parrot gently, *Paro paththe Sitaram... Sitaram*. Sometimes the two things happened together—the opening on Asharfilal's eyes and the cry of the parrot. The interval between the two events, if there was any, was so slight as to be practically unnoticeable.

Today too, Asharfilal watched, through sleepy eyes, the darkness dissolving into the luminosity of morning, while the parrot recited, *Sitaram...tain...tain...parhopaththe Sitaram... Sitaram...*

Asharfilal came onto the verandah, joined in the parrot's morning ditty for a minute, and then went away to attend to his own morning rituals. Before his bath he cleaned up the parrot's cage and sprinkled a little water from his pitcher over the bird.

The Parrot

His worship over, Asharfilal pushed a slice of melon into the cage, which the parrot fell to pecking. He himself drank his milk, which his widowed sister warmed and brought for him.

There were only two people living in the house—he and his widowed sister. And the third living being was the parrot. Earlier, there were two girls also, and his wife too. The girls married and the wife died. No. Three years ago, another woman had come. The parrot was not here then. With the coming of the second woman the eerie silence of the house vanished. The house began to feel like a home again.

He hadn't suggested it. He hadn't even given any hint. Whenever the subject came up he just shook his head. 'No. It won't be right.' But his widowed sister understood that he needed another woman. He looked like a plant wilting for lack of water. He no longer ate with relish the semolina pudding and other sweets which he loved. His betel-reddened, ever-fresh lips were now dry. He would go to his shop in a soiled kurta. He did not sleep well at night. The stars were still in the sky when he rose. When his sister brought a girl and stood her before him, he saw something so appealing about the girl that he could not say no to remarriage. Before, he had refused for fear of being swept away thus by forces beyond his control. He forgot now that he was over fifty, that half the hair of his moustache and head had turned grey, that he was grandfather to his two daughters' children, and that the world would laugh at him.

The sister had a mole on the right side of her lower lip, on which a bunch of hair grew. Sometimes the sister looked very wise. With smile on his face, he said, 'It looks as though you cannot do without a sister-in law in the house.'

Within a fortnight on the date which the priest set, the girl arrived as a bride in his house.

To prove true to his name, Asharfilal offered his bride a necklace of *asharfis*—dazzling gold coins. He also gave her several flashy saris with rich floral designs. On his return from the shop every day he brought her sweets.

He would say to her, 'Give me a son.'

The wife would burst out laughing, walk mincing and swaying. The covering on her head would slip again and again. She would twirl her wrists and set her bangles jingling. She would put a finger between her lips and suck it. She would dig her toe into the ground and scratch the floor. When he left for his shop, she would come up tinkling her jewels and bar his way. 'Give me a rupee. I'll eat *chaat* today. If you see tamarind somewhere get it. And also *kaitha* leaves. I love to eat these things with salt.'

More of a girl than a wife—Asharfilal thought. Sometimes her waywardness alarmed him too. He would try to look younger. He started dyeing his hair. And trimmed his moustache. In the morning he took a tonic with his milk as recommended by the doctor. But he saw that the gap of thirty or thirty-two years between him and his wife could not be bridged by him alone. If he reduced his age she would have to increase hers. That was the only way a bridging was possible.

But it was as if his wife had firmly caught hold of time. She preferred to remain a wayward girl. She would colour her eyes thickly with collyrium, rub her soles to make them soft and smooth, and plait her hair, standing in the middle of the courtyard.

When his widowed sister, on his return from the shop in the evening, tightened her hair-grown lips and complained—that Suman Bhabhi kept standing at the window for hours on end, that today Suman Bhabhi chatted with the postman, that today she gave a drink of water to the knife-grinder, a low caste man, that today she had the bear man give a performance on the platform of the house, that today she went to meet the school teacher's wife, saying she would be back in half an hour and stayed on for two hours—his fear grew.

He scolded his wife and told her she ought not to talk with strangers, nor should she go out of the house. 'Should I rot in the house, shut up inside?' she asked him, covering her anger with a laugh.

The season of Holi had come. The wife stood at the door like the spring incarnate. Two high-spirited boys, Tarun and Shyam, studying in the college down the lane, splashed colour on her. They chased her into the courtyard and rubbed coloured powder, all over her face.

Where he heard about this, his eyes grew dark with anger. 'I don't like this rowdyism.' She turned round and said, 'You mean I should also be an old fogey like you?' He was stunned for a minute, as if the clock in his mind had suddenly stopped, or as if his consciousness had petrified. But then, sizzling with anger he bent her double with blows and kicks. 'Turning into a slut, are you, witch? I know how to set you right.'

But in his heart of hearts he got even more scared of her.

The next day he brought her gold earrings. And then a gold brocade sari, costing four hundred rupees.

Without telling him his wife went to the films with a neighbour's wife of her own age.

In the evening he again bent her double with violent blows, but the next day, brought her a gold ring studded with a gem.

A few days later was the annual country fair. The women of the neighbourhood and the other girls were going. In spite of the widowed sister-in-law's admonitions, she went with them. She sucked ice, ate *gol gappas* and circled wide and high on the giant wheel. Merriment gave her wings. She was radiant.

In the evening he beat her again. Cowering under the deluge of kicks, slaps, and blows with shoes, she felt that her tender dreams were being bloodied.

The next day when he was in his shop a man came running up and broke the news that his wife had taken her life. On coming home he found her body swinging from the hook on the ceiling, her neck stiffened in the noose she had made with her sari.

When he gave her the best of food and clothing, why did she have to give up her life, just because of a few restrictions imposed on her? Asharfilal could not really understand it.

It was getting on to be nine, and carrying the bunch of keys, and the red cloth bag containing the cash, Asharfilal set out for his shop. If it had been winter he would have left for his shop at ten. Going by the weather, ten was the hour for the market to open. He dealt in coconut fibre, cotton goods and wicker work articles. Feeling the pulse of the market, he also off and on laid by, stocks of lentils, groundnut and such commodities and unloaded them at a profit. A seasoned speculator, he rarely incurred losses.

He was still at the job of opening his shop, when the newsboy flung down the newspaper. He bought one newspaper in Hindi. What interested him most were the latest news about taxes, income-tax raids, accidents and miracles. International news or news about the life of the common people, he skipped. The first thing he read was about trends in the various markets. On Mondays astrological forecasts for the week were published, and this too interested him. He knew of some ways to placate the bad phases of planets. The next day the paper became defunct, and was put to use as wrapping paper.

It was afternoon by the time he finished with customers. The shop servant brought his food from home in a tiffin carrier. He always ate his afternoon meal in the shop. Because it was eaten in the shop it was fully cooked. At night, the food eaten at home included raw foods.

In the third quarter of the day the rush of customers slackened. And he availed of this time to draw up the day's accounts—the intake from sales, the amount outstanding against customers, and what he owed others.

At seven he called it a day. Before leaving he pulled at the locks again and again, testing them. This had become second nature with him. A year and a half ago he had a servant boy who slept in the shop at night. The boy got a place to sleep and also kept watch over the shop.

He was a hill boy of thirteen or fourteen, and, like any other boy from the hills was short, with a flat, smooth face and tanned skin. A peon at the Panjab Bank, Lakshman Singh, had brought him to Lalaji. He had said, thickening his 'S' sounds, like all hill people, 'Lala Shaab, engage tnish boy to look after your shop. He will do all your work and give you no chansh to complain.'

He certainly was in need of a boy. The old servant he had in the shop frequently fell ill. Even otherwise, when there was a rush of work, he would think with a sense of urgency, that there should be an extra hand to cope with the work'.

Lakshman Singh had asked him to give the boy two meals a day, and twenty five rupees. After seeing his work perhaps it could be raised a little. The boy would stay around and wait on him body and soul.

He calculated. Food and stuff would come to seventy-five rupees at the most. These days a good servant couldn't be had, even for the searching, for less than one hundred and twenty five or one hundred and fifty rupees. This was cheap.

Sitting in the shop, he would buy things for the house—a winnowing basket, a sieve, a mat. He had bought the parrot the same way, sitting in the shop. But that was after he had engaged the boy.

He had decided that the boy would have his meals in the house, but stay in the shop. The shop was quite big. At the back was a toilet for out of time use. There was also a hand pump and other amenities. Overhead, was an iron grille.

The first night, locking up the boy in the shop, he had asked: 'Won't be scared, will you?'

Flashing his maize-white teeth, the boy had said in his hill accent, thickening the S's, 'Lala Shaab, I am not afraid of anything. Back home I ushed to go all alone to the jungle to chop wood. The jungle wash infeshted with bearsh'.

In the morning, unlocking the shop, the Lala said to the boy: 'Weren't scared, were you?'

This time the boy said without flashing his teeth: 'Too many rats in this shop. They kept scurrying about throughout the night. I just couldn't sleep.'

At this he laughed. 'Now that you are here the rats will run away. They will think that a mountain cat has come to live here.' The boy had bluish eyes and they did shine like cat's eyes.

Every evening he locked up the boy in the shop and freed him the next morning. On Fridays, the bazaar was closed. On that day he would bring the boy home, have him clean the rooms, tighten the cots or wash the clothes, and do sundry chore.

The boy's name was Jeevan Singh. In the hills his father owned land. His mother was dead and his father had married again. The step mother was harsh to him. She did not give him enough to eat, and had him beaten, making false charges against him to his father. After the birth of a brother, things became worse. He had come away from home for the first time in his life...

Asharfilal found the boy honest and intelligent. He did not have to tell him anything twice. The boy was active and alert. He would climb up the rack like a monkey. Without loosening the bundle of string unduly, he would snap it at the measured point with one sharp tug. Once a customer tried to slip away without paying and the boy caught him. A twenty rupee note slipped out of the Lala's pocket one day, when he was changing his shirt, and the boy held it out to him. 'Lala Shaab, your money. It fell from your pocket.'

After a mere fifteen days he started giving the boy tea-money. He told his widowed sister whom the boy called 'Maji', to give him some extra tit-bits with his regular meals.

He had given the boy an old cotton carpet to sleep on. He also told him that if he kept working diligently as he did, he would have new clothes made for him on Dussehra, Diwali, and Holi days.

Past experience had taught him that servants vanished after a few days. Now that, with luck, he had got such a good domestic he did not mean to lose him easily. His presence made things better for him. So that mean-minded fellow shopkeepers would not entice him away, Lalaji did not let him mix around freely. Shy by nature, the boy would stay in the shop even when done with work, and watch the bustle of the bazaar. His shyness made his face look more innocent. There was always a poignancy about him, especially around his flat nose and full lips. And this too looked agreeable.

Looking at him attentively, he would feel that the boy had improved in health. And he would ask: 'Jeevan Singh, are you happy here?'

'Everything ish fine,' the boy would reply with lowered eyes.

Almost two months went by. He was pleased with the boy and the boy with him.

It was the weekly holiday in the market. At seven o'clock in the morning he had unlocked the shop and brought the boy home. After washing the floors the boy asked, 'Lala Shaab, ish there a river shomewhere nearby? I want to wash my clothesh and bathe in running water.'

'You can wash your clothes in the running water of the public tap, and also bathe at it.'

'No, a river is good. In the hills I bathed in the river.'

The boy was overjoyed to see the river. With fascinated eyes he watched its blue waters. He felt that the river had eyes and was smiling at him. The river had hands and they were beckoning him. The river had feet and they were running, maybe towards his village.

He got down into the river and started swimming, sometimes on his back, sometimes on his belly, and sometimes below the surface of the water. He gave his hands to the hands of the river, his feet to its feet.

A high mound rose on the bank, and getting out of the water, he climbed the mound. Two goats were grazing on top. On seeing him they immediately bounded away and ran down the mound. In his village too, there were goats and they too leapt like this. From the mound the luminous sky seemed to him stretching far, far, into the distance.

He dried his clothes and returned after two hours.

In the evening, after feeding him, Asharfilal, as usual, locked him up in the shop.

The next week, on the holiday, the boy again insisted on going to the river. That day too the river seemed to beckon and sign to him with its arms, to run and smile at him with its eyes. That day too the boy swam like a fish in the river.

Then he climbed up the high mound. As he stood there he saw a train crawling in the distance on its rails and he watched the moving train with wonder and fascination. A bird flew down and perched on his head and flew away. He watched wide-eyed, the bird flying in the blue sky.

Returning home he told Asharfilal to settle his account, for he wanted to go back to his village. Asharfilal simply could not understand what had happened so suddenly, to make the boy want to go away. Only this morning he had given the boy sweet *puras* for breakfast.

The parrot circled round and round the cage and recited. *Tain...tain...tuun..Parho Paththe...Sitaram...Sitaram!*

Asharfilal went to the cage and lovingly called the refrain: '*Sitaaa-raam! Sitaaaram! Tain Tain...Sitaram.*'

Even if he omitted the phrase '*parho paththe*', the parrot would sing it on its own. Asharfilal would often think that perhaps he ought not to have taught it the rowdy phrase. He would often feel that the bird's cry *'parho paththe'* was directed at him.

The parrot rested its head on the bars of the cage. He understood that it was saying, caress my neck. He pushed his fingers through the gaps and did so.

Round the parrot's neck, a circle had started forming. The circle was at places deep red in colour, and at other places a soft yellow. Around it a black velvety line was also forming. This was an indication that the parrot had come of age.

When he had bought it, it was an inert thing. He doubted if it would learn anything. But the fowler had assured him that baby parrots learnt fast. It was not just wizened old birds that came out with 'Ram Ram'. It would grow into a beautiful bird.

The parrot really did learn to speak soon and became beautiful too.

He threw a piece of banana into the parrot's cage, and it started pecking at it.

The day's paper carried the news of rebellion in some country. But he was not interested in this kind of news, and skipped it after racing his eyes over the beginning lines.

Returning home in the evening he threw a piece of sweetmeat into the parrot's cage.

Before going to sleep he hung the cage from an iron hook in the verandah. In winter he also threw a thick cloth over the cage.

When selling the parrot to Lalaji the fowler had impressed upon him: 'Lalaji, buy it. When it starts speaking in its sweet way, you will think it is your kith and kin'. Bought for two rupees the parrot had indeed become a member of the family.

Tain...tain...tu...parho paththe...Sitaram...Sitaram...

It was morning. Asharfilal put a piece of peeled litchi into the cage.

Tain...tain...tu...parho paththe Sitaram...Sitaram...

Another morning had dawned. Lala Asharfilal threw an apricot into the cage.

Tain...tain...tu...parho paththe...Sitaram...Sitaram...

Another day. Asharfilal put plum in the cage.

When the parrot stood on one leg and dropped its white eyelids over the rounds of its eyes, it looked like a sage lost in meditation. On its tail, with the green feathers, were a couple of yellow, and also a couple of blue. Its tail had become long. The cage became small and Lalaji bought a bigger cage, in which was a small swinging platform.

Tain...tain...tu...parho paththe...Sitaram...Sitaram!

Another morning had arrived.

In the newspaper there was an item about a dependent country of the third world becoming free. Asharfilal ignored the news.

In the paper was another piece of news about harijans refusing to work gratis for the Thakurs of the village, and the harijan's huts being burned down. Asharfilal found no interest in this piece of news either.

Tain...tain...tu...parho paththe...Sitaram...Sitaram...

Another morning had come.

Asharfilal was cleaning the parrot's cage. Someone called him and he went out. When he returned he found that he had left the window of the cage open, and the parrot was sitting outside on the cage, its wet wing spread out on one leg to dry. He placed a slice of apple in the cage. The parrot hopped down and went in. The same thing had happened once before too. The parrot had evidently come to regard the cage as its permanent abode. Asharfilal kept gazing at the bird's coral red beak and then put his hand inside the cage and fondled its soft, feathery neck.

Tain...tain...tu...parho paththe...Sitaram...Sitaram... Another morning had dawned. *Tain...tain...tu.,..parho paththe...Sitaram...Sitaram...* Another morning.

The Parrot

The sky had started turning very blue. The sunlight was filled with a sparkling brightness. The branches of trees had grown vari-coloured moss. In the fields the gold had condensed into the corn. Fragrance had taken its abode in the air.

A parrot with a long green tail descended from the sky above, perched on the cage, and started chattering. The parrot in the cage also took a few excited turns inside, and squawked in response. The parrot outside rose in the air, took many somersaults, again settled on the crest of the cage and started trilling. The parrot inside fluttered its wings and called at the top of its voice, in considerable excitement.

The parrot outside rose again and flew off, describing the vast expanse of the sky with its wings.

When Asharfilal returned from his shop in the evening he found the parrot very restless in the cage. It was furiously trying to pluck at the bars of the cage with its beak. From its tantrums it looked like a different parrot. He threw a piece of sweetmeat into the cage but the parrot ignored it and kept twisting the bars of its cage with its beak. He tried to fondle its neck to calm it but it sprang at his finger.

It was morning. Like all mornings. No, different. The parrot was not calling. Asharfilal came into the verandah. A bar of the cage was twisted and through the gap the parrot's neck lay extended. The slightly spread wing and bent leg made it look as if the parrot was flying away with the cage.

Even today Asharfilal has not understood why the parrot snapped the delicate strand of its life by thrusting its neck through the bars of the cage.

Shaani

Hell-Bound

I padded in warily and slowly pushed open the outer gate, careful not to make any sound. The front door of the house was also closed, as always. I pushed it open, slowly, very slowly. In fact I wanted to catch Jameel by surprise—like an unpredictable heart-attack.

It was a typical Bhopal afternoon, languidly declining towards evening. A still and lazy afternoon, inducing sleep. I knew Jameel must be having his siesta and was therefore sure to be at home. Not because of the tone set by the city but because of the nature of his preoccupations. He went to college in the morning and his evenings and afternoons were always free.

Jameel was lying on the diwan, facing the wall. Hearing my footsteps he turned round and his eyes remained fixed on me in surprise. '*Arre!*' He got up from the diwan excitedly and caught me in an embrace. It was a powerful hug. His arms were long and firm and I feared his palms would sink deep into my back. For the first time I realised that even fingers could speak so eloquently.

'When did you come?' he asked me drawing his face away. His voice was thick with emotion, though his face being still so close to me I could not see the expression on it.

'This morning,' I said, 'by the Southern Express.'

Disengaging ourselves we sat down on the diwan.

'Will you belive it, I was thinking of you this morning?' Reclining against the bolster, Jameel looked at me intently. It was a full gaze which must have taken in everything in one sweep.

Pushing aside the curtain, his wife, Kaneez, emerged from the next room, smiling. She asked me how I was, sat down by my side and beamed at me happily.

'How is Baji?' I asked. 'Please give her my greetings.'

'She is saying her *namaz*,' Kaneez said looking in the direction of the other room. 'What would you like to have? Yes, you will have lunch, of course.'

'At this time?' I laughed.

I knew she would insist and I would acquiesce in the end. She went in.

'How is Baji now?' I asked Jameel. I had a glimpse of Baji in the other room as I entered the house. She was saying her *namaz*. It was an awkward question. Jameel started looking for his packet of cigarettes. Fishing it out from somewhere on the diwan, he lighted a cigarette and then looking at me, gave an imperceptible nod, implying that she was none too well. He smiled wanly. Baji, his mother, had been keeping indifferent health for many months,—even before Bhaijan had passed away, Jameel said. Bhaijan was hale and hearty when he went to sleep at night and the next morning he was gone. It was just like that!

'Who is it, Allan?' I heard Baji asking from the other room. Perhaps she had finished her *namaz*. By Allan she obviously meant Jameel. He told her my name and said that I had come from Delhi and wanted to pay her my regards. She blessed me from the other room in a tired voice. She kept muttering for a while the meaning of which I failed to comprehend. I thought of going to the door to have a look at her. But I could not bring myself to do so. I was afraid I would not be able to face her.

'And so?' Jameel said as if bringing me back to earth. 'How is your Delhi?'

'My Delhi?'

Jameel smiled.

Delhi was so better than an Inferno, I used to tell people. Four years ago I had left this city in a bitter mood. Due to the cussedness of the government, I had been exiled from this place. I felt that I had not been sent to Delhi but had been kicked into it. Of course, time had healed the wound, but Jameel knew that I could not belong to Delhi nor could Delhi be kind to me.

'If not at Delhi, you must have sampled the communal riots at Meerut,' Jameel said. 'How are things there now?'

'The history of Meerut riots is quite old. They date further back than 1947. I have nothing new to tell except repeating what you read in the newspapers. I hear there is great tension in Aligarh and Moradabad.'

'Can you rely upon newspapers?'

I refused to be drawn into this controversy.

'Those who are at the epicentre should know,' Jameel said.

'Where's the epicentre?' I asked.

'Delhi, of course,' Jameel said. 'It's the epicentre of the country. Meerut, Jamshedpur, Bhagalpur—they all take their cue from there.'

I started staring at the walls of the room on which hung paintings of various sizes, all by Kaneez. I could easily discern Hebbar's and Husain's influence in them. It was however, evident that both of us wanted to steer clear of this controversy, all the more so, because we feared we would get involved in the happenings of which the controversy formed the subject.

'Your old expression has returned,' Jameel said. 'In your last illness it had kept playing hide-and-seek with you.'

'It's a boon bequeathed by my last heart attack,' I said, giving a triumphant laugh, as if I had conquered a fortress.

'I hope you are now fully recovered.'

'I don't know whether I have recovered fully or not. But I feel quite fit. I mean as fit as a heart patient can reasonably feel.' I said this out of a sense of self-pity. 'I've stopped caring about it,' I added nonchalantly. 'If another attack has to come, come it must. Nobody can stop it from coming, not even a doctor, much less me.'

'For a long time we knew nothing about your illness,' Jameel said. 'There were only vague rumours. Tense with anxiety, we phoned up people at Delhi. But your friends said there as nothing to worry about. They told us that you were in the hospital, in the intensive care unit. But it had nothing to do with your heart, so they said. Only Pankaj, who had come from Delhi, told us how grave your condition was. But how did it happen?'

'Why, as it generally happens—like a bolt from the blue.'

'At home?'

'No, at the office.'

'But how?'

'I was talking with a visitor when I suddenly started feeling uneasy followed by a tightness in my chest. Then a pain shot through it. I was drenched in perspiration and my voice became feeble. I felt as if my heart was sinking. I wanted to get up but I had no strength to do so. I wanted to sit still but I could not do that either for I was feeling very restless. At last I lay down on the floor and started writhing in pain.'

I stopped talking for I found Jameel's face contorted in pain—precisely the kind of expression I wished to see on his face. I was happy that I had paid these people back for having taken my troubles so lightly. I had also a grouse against my Delhi friends. True, they had tried to minimise the gravity of my illness from a sense of expediency. But that expediency had dectracted from my sense of importance. Today I had returned to this city after a lapse of one year, not as somebody worthy of being specially noticed, but just like any other mortal.

'Do you remember I wrote you a letter of condolence?' I said. 'It was the 7th of April and I wrote the letter an hour before the attack came. Little did I realize that within an hour I too would be treading the path from which Huseen never returned.'

Kaneez came in, with *rotis* and a plateful of *kababs* which she placed before me on a small table. 'Eat,' she said, pulling up a stool and sitting down on it in front of me. As I took the first morsel of food I realized that it was very indiscreet of me to have mentioned Huseen's name. In fact I had no intention of bringing up his name but it had inadvertently come up. Had I not come to condole with them about his death—the very man, who until recently used to visit the city to condole others' deaths and did not feel up to the job for he did not know how to conduct himself on such occasions. He would just sit in a corner, apart from others, staring into space with expressionless eyes.

I had got the news of Huseen's death in my office in Delhi. It had come not from Bhopal, nor from Jameel but from Syed Mahmood of Birhanpur. He had written in his letter—'You will be grieved to know that our dear friend, Huseen Ahmed Siddiqui passed away in Nigeria of a heart attack. Naseera Bhabi had flown his dead body to Bhopal. I returned only yesterday after burying him. We were all greatly distressed over his death. It is difficult to describe a young woman's plight who is bereft of a husband, with none to care for her three small children. Fate could not have dealt her a more cruel blow.'

I sat for a long time holding the letter in my hand. I read the letter over three times, each time lingering over Huseen's name. I did not want to believe that what Syed Mahmood had written was true. No, I just couldn't believe it and at last when I resignedly did so, a sigh escaped my lips. The agony was so deep that it was like a sign of relief. I seemed to have bottled up all my grief within me. It was a most painful experience.

'It makes no sense to me,' I blurted out to everyone who came to meet me afterwards. 'It was not the time for him to die. And that too of a heart attack! He was two years younger than I. A God-fearing man, who led such a temperate life. He did not even smoke.'

These remarks clearly bespoke my fear and I used them as an armour to ward off fear. The fear of death had kept chasing me all the way from the office to my home. This fear seemed to be so strongly entrenched in me that I had become tongue-tied. It was momentous news but I had kept it even from my wife for far that Huseen's death would monopolise our talk and Huseen's face keep haunting me all night, driving away sleep. I managed to snatch some sleep at last but it was nothing short of nightmarish. His face kept invading me from all directions and I kept seeing his dead body in my dreams. It looked many days old. The same thing happened the next night and the night after. But I kept the whole thing to myself without giving anyone an inkling of how mentally upset I was. Even the letter of condolence to Jameel I wrote after postponing it for three days. Like Huseen, I was also innocent of how a letter of condolence should be worded.

It may sound odd, but to tell the truth, I had stopped considering Huseen my friend, specially after he left for Nigeria, or maybe even earlier, when I had drifted closer to his younger brother, Jameel.

Fifteen years ago, when I had come to Bhopal, Huseen was the one with whom I had first struck up a friendship. Both of us had come from different places and had no links with Bhopal. Huseen had a strange, manly sort of attraction about him which could draw people towards him without any reservations. Tall and slim, he had already started showing signs of balding. I had sized him up at the very first encounter: a man of fine sensibility, and aggressive and volatile by nature, he could even laugh at himself. He could spin such fine yarns, most of them plausibly grotesque, that one could not help laughing over them and admiring him all the more for his whimsicality.

In those days we lived in the Amirgunj lane of old Bhopal. Huseen was teaching Philosophy at a private college and I was an ordinary pen-pusher in an office. Amirgunj was preponderantly inhabited by aristocrats of the old vintage and Huseen and I struck a discordant note among them because we eked out a hand-to-mouth existence. I fact our friendship was the result of our being kindred spirits, both financially vulnerable, at odds with the world and given to tantrums at the slightest provocation. We became a solace and comfort to one another. Although our vocations were radically different, I was the one who was first drawn towards him, though it was not long before he too took a fancy for me. Though he taught philosophy, he was very orthodox and religious-minded and went to the extent of claiming to be a true votary of religion. As for myself, I did not teach Philosophy at any point even with a barge pole. Just because of that doubtful attribute I called myself a progressive, having an ultra-modern outlook. And taking things to their logical conclusion, judging by orthodox religious criteria, I boasted of being a sinner who would rot in hell fire. As such, I was in utter contrast to Huseen. But the fun of it was that each of us regarded the other as a sinner, dubbing any third person who did not conform to either category as a colourless 'non-entity'.

'You're a hypocrite,' Huseen said to me one day in anger. 'A first rate cad and utterly wicked!'

'Even a bigger hypocrite than you?'

'I'm nothing compared to you. Not even the dust of your feet!'

'That you are not, even otherwise.' I tried to laugh off the whole thing.

'I know you to your very core,' he said. 'You want to have the best of both worlds.' He almost plucked at my hair in anger. 'You are not even an atheist, or whatever you call yourself. You are just a fake, a show-off!'

'You mean even a bigger show-off than you? You, who claim to be such a conformist, observing fasts and so on!' I retorted.' Stop observing those religious fasts, pal. One can see through your game.'

I was not tired of driving home the point that those who sincerely and devoutly observed religious rites such as fasting were not punctilious about what they ate in the morning before going on fast or what they ate when they broke the fast in the evening. During the month of Ramzan I singled out for mockery these people who rushed out to the market in the morning, dangling fat purses from their wrists, to buy hens, partridges, fish, biryanis and the like, as a prelude to their fasting. Such jokes hurt. But that was exactly I wanted. It gave me vicarious pleasure to see them frothing at the mouth in anger.

'You are neither here nor there,' Huseen would fulminate against me. 'You are neither of the *shias,* nor of the *hias.* May Allah have mercy on you.'

Not that he did not fall out with me once in a blue moon. Persiflage had in fact become a common pattern of our daily lives. We even threatened to stop talking to each other. But we would make up the very next day or the day after, as usual. And them get into a squabble all over again.

I am talking of the times when communal riots were rampant in the country. There had been a rash of them—Jabalpur, Bhiwandi, Jalgaon, Ahmedabad, Jamshedpur and so on.

But we were living in Bhopal which had no history of communal riots. Even so we lived in fear for there was tension in the city. The government was alert and had posted homeguards and policemen at strategic points in the city. There were rumours afloat, most of them from outside, carrying news of communal carnage. The Hindus and the Muslims who had lived together in harmony for ages had now started looking at one another with suspicion and fear. They had divided themselves into small groups.

'You can see for yourself,' Huseen said to me one evening,' 'the havoc these sons of animals have done to the country after partitioning it.'

He had read some alarming news in the morning paper. His chin was unshaven and his hair dishevelled. He looked balder than on other days.

'Now this country is not worth living in,' he said. 'One day we too will be hacked to pieces and thrown on the garbage heap with no one left to mourn our loss.'

'Why, I'm with you.' I laughed. I wanted to make light of his fear—like a song sung in the dark.

'You won't be spared either.' Huseen looked daggers at me. 'Tomorrow when that herd of infidels storms your door with knives and hatchets and choppers it won't ask your views on subtle matters. These people will only go by your name and that will be the end of it.'

'But you yourself told that a name is not enough to identify a person.'

'Yes, I did say so. But that was in a different context. Don't try to mix up things. I know you sometimes try to be very clever.'

Yes, indeed I was trying to be clever. The cleverness of wanton ignorance. The cleverness of running away from hard realities. I did not want to see eye to eye with Huseen. To agree with him was to allow the ground to slip from under my feet.

Then something strange happened for which I was not prepared. Huseen suddenly became inaccessible to me. He had his college in the morning and I had my office in the afternoon. It was only in the evenings that we used to meet and spend some time together. But for the last few evenings he was not to be seen anywhere. His doors had always been open to me and I knew his brother, Jameel, quite well. He studied in the same college where Huseen taught. When I dropped in at Huseen's for a chat Jameel was often present and we would have tea together. One thing peculiar about Huseen's family was that when a visitor came all the members of the family made it a point to meet the visitor together. Sometimes I disapproved of this practice for the presence of the elders placed me under certain constraints. Nevertheless I liked Jameel's company. In fact I had taken a liking to him from the very beginning.

Now that I think of it, I feel that my meeting with Jameel through the medium of Huseen was just one of those happy coincidences. For, otherwise, I would have directly made friends with him to the exclusion of Huseen. This fact impinged on my mind all the more when I had once gone to enquire about Huseen and happened to meet Jameel when he was alone. As time passed I drifted away from Huseen.

'These days it is difficult to meet Huseen Bhai in the evening,' Jameel told me. I had missed him on the two previous evenings when I called at his house. 'He's caught up in that rigmarole,' Jameel had added, noting my puzzled expression.

'What kind of rigmarole?' I asked him.

'It's surprising that you don't know. Bot of them are trying to get away from the country.'

'Go away where?'

'Somewhere, anywhere—the Middle East, Libya, Africa. Anywhere they can manage to get a job. Syed Mahmood is driven to it out of necessity. His teaching job makes it difficult for him to make both ends meet. And he has four daughters to marry off. And the worst of it is his son is a victim of polio. As for Huseen Bhai, he wants to lead a better life.'

Syed Mahmood, who was quite friendly with us, was in those days teaching English in a college in Bhopal. He was secretive by nature, so it was not easy fathom his mind. He always seemed to be in a hurry, his restlessness did not allow him to stay in a place for more than two minutes. He never sat down when he came and if he did, it appeared he mentally started counting the minutes the moment he sat down. What Jameel said about Syed Mahmood caused me no surprise. He and Huseen, being friends, must have joined hands in pursuit of a common objective even though their reasons happened to be different.

'So you want to run away?' I sniped at Huseen.

Huseen gave me a belligerent look, which momentarily reduced his small eyes to pinpoints. 'Who is running away?' he said.

'You. Who else?'

'I'm not running away. I'm going.'

'It amounts to the same thing.'

'No, it's not the same thing,' he said emphatically. 'Those who wanted to run away have gone to Pakistan and they are gone for good—never to return.'

'As if you will return!'

'Do you mean to say I am going there to die among those African negroes?'

'Who knows?'

'I knew good friends like you would wish me such luck! Well, please yourself.'

'But you are certainly turning your back on the battle-field.'

'To go away for three or four years cannot be construed as leaving the battle-field,' Huseen said, incensed. 'Have I no right to think of my own and my children's future? You mean I should keep rotting here? See those scoundrels, loafers and rascals flourishing around me? And burn my blood? No, I can't do that any more.'

'I too have children and I too have to think of my future.'

'If you want to keep wallowing in mud who can stop you? You don't want to rise in life, nor are you capable of it.'

'You mean running after money to rising in life?'

'Yours is the philosophy of cowards and drones,' Huseen cried. 'Keep your philosophy to yourself.'

He left in a huff.

This was my last meeting with Huseen before he left for Nigeria. At least on that subject. We did meet subsequently on different occasions but in a most perfunctory manner. Our relations, it was evident, had already cooled down. And then I learnt that he had left for Nigeria. I was deeply hurt. He hadn't even come to say a formal good-bye. For that matter Syed Mahmood too was gone. But in his case it was like taking a plunge in the dark in high hopes. He had sold his wife's jewellery and some ancestral land and had gone away to Saudi Arabia whereas Huseen had got a regular teaching job in Nigeria and had been given air fare join duty there.

'Would you like to have something else?'

I gave Kaneez a startled look. She was standing before me and I seemed to have forgotten her very existence.

'What else?' I asked.

'Some *kababs*. Another *roti*?'

'Thanks, that'll do, I've already stuffed myself. I should have skipped the meal. Doctor's orders, you know.'

'And you have been obeying doctor's orders blindly,' Jameel laughed.

He knew that for the last three years or so, while in Delhi, I had constantly been knocking at doctors doors. I had just arrived in Delhi when I learnt that I was suffering from a very serious disease which could even prove fatal. I was at the end of my tether. I had become grumpy and full of hate but that was of no avail. At last I sought admission in a hospital and was promptly reduced to a file—Case No 535.

Those days were like hell...

Kaneez stood there holding the wash bowl. Then she fixed her eyes on me and said, 'I hear you had some trouble. That it was your heart or something.'

I was appalled at the manner in which she talked of it. I had passed through hell and she was not even aware of it. I had thought they would be worried about me and the house would be steeped in gloom because of my grave condition and that when I visited them they would receive me joyously as if the prodigal, of whom they had lost all hope, had returned.

'He was in very bad shape,' Jameel explained to his wife. 'It was a massive heart attack and for fifteen days he kept hovering between life and death. Luckily, he happened to be in Delhi where all medical facilities were readily available. But for the pace-maker which came to his rescue, anything could have happened.'

For an instant Kaneez's face turned white with fear. Her brother-in-law had died of the same trouble and her sister too. And then her father-in-law, the latest being Huseen.

'Listen, don't give up smoking,' she said. 'All right?'

After a while tea came, everything neatly arranged on a tray. Kaneez pulled up a stool near the teapoy and started pouring tea. Baji was in her room, but nobody seemed to be aware of her existence. When I entered the house she had been busy with her *namaz* and after finishing her *namaz* she had not come out to meet me. Nor had I ventured to go in to pay my respects. I just sat there staring at the walls where Kaneez's paintings hung. They had been there for many years and exactly in the same places. But as I sat there I felt for the first time that they were hitting me in the eye. They were interspersed between pieces of calligraphy—one calligraphic writing regarding Allah, the other Mohammed and above the door which opened into the room there was a full verse from the Holy Quran, inscribed in Calligraphic embellishments, saying Allah was with those who exercised forbearance.

'Did I ever show forbearance?' I asked myself, while taking the last sip of tea. Had I forgiven those friends who had failed to call on me while I was in hospital? And why had I mellowed towards my enemies who had unexpectedly called on me?

'Oh God' It was Baji's voice emanating from the other room.

Kaneez gathered the tea things, making more noise than was necessary, consigned them to the tray, one after another and walked out slowly.

'It must have been quite a job managing Baji,' I said after a pause.

'Oh, they all somehow fend for themselves,' Jameel replied. 'When the news of Huseen's death came from Nigeria, Baji was very ill. We feared she might die any time. I was in a predicament. When I asked the doctor, he said she may not be able to bear the shock. But it would have been folly on our part to keep her in the dark. How long could we hide it from her? For two days I kept pleading with others that it would be wise not to break the news to her. You know she loved Huseen Bhai more than any of us. We could have kept posting her fake letters supposedly coming from Nigeria. If there was any lapse she would have at the worst charged Huseen Bhai with being an undutiful son. But how long could we keep up this game? At last I had to give in. The news of her son's death was ultimately broken to her and you know the rest.'

Then I put him the inevitable question though I immediately realised its absurdity. It was a question which every one used to ask me during the course of my illness and which always put me in a temper.

'Were there any prior indications of Huseen's trouble?' I asked.

'No, one,' Jameel replied. 'He had of course complained that he had been feeling a little out of sorts two days before the attack came. That day too he had attended to his duties as usual. Before leaving the house he had told sister-in-law that he would go to the doctor in the evening. He was about to leave for the doctor's clinic when a Pakistani friend dropped in. He wanted a video cassette from Bhai. And then they sat down to watch a film. Perhaps you don't know that Bhai had collected a large number of Hindi films cassettes and LPs of Indian music.'

No, I didn't know that. When Huseen had come here seven years ago, he used to detest Hindi films and had no interest in Indian music.

'Leaving his friend in the drawing room' Jameel continued, 'Bhai went to fetch a cassette from the other room. He was watching the cassette when he felt some uneasiness and lay down on the carpet. It must have taken hardly two minutes. I thought they had arranged to bury him there. We had even finished the mourning rites. Ten days later when I went to Bombay to receive sister-in-law and the children I was astounded to see that she had brought her husband's dead body with her. Once again the old wounds opened, once again we went into mourning.'

'And look at the irony of fate,' Jameel said after a pause. 'All this happened when he was on the point of seeking repatriation to India. When he had come here six months ago, he had said that it was only a matter of months for his service contract to come to an end, after which he would return to India. 'I've no intention of staying there any longer,' he had said with an air of finality. 'One's own country is one's own, he said. He had had a nice house constructed on Shimla Hill and had planned what he would do after settling down in India. He seemed to be very happy. It never occurred to him that he might not be able to live in that house of his, which he had constructed, brick by brick, under his own supervision.

'A strange thing happened last time when I had gone to see him off at the airport. I was suddenly overpowered by a strong impulse to throw my arms around him and hug him warmly, holding him close to my heart. At the last moment I thought it would seem like sheer emotional exhibitionism and desisted from doing so. Thus I lost forever the chance of expressing my feelings for him. Now the sense of regret at having missed an opportunity which turned out to be the last, keeps nagging me all the time. Has it ever occurred to you that due to a mental blind spot or a passing whim or some vague impulse, we blindly act in a manner which suddenly reveals the real man in us?'

Kaneez pushed the plate of betel nuts towards us. I had not noticed that she had come in with the betel. I quietly accepted a betel from her.

Jameel had touched me deep down in the innermost recesses of my heart. It was like squeezing out all the feeling within me. I started staring at the wall in front of me on which 'Allah' was inscribed in calligraphic style. Allah! Allah! Allah!

They showed me Huseen's photographs. Huseen Bhai in the garden with three children. Huseen at the steering wheel while his wife was opening the door of the car. There was another photograph, a comparatively recent one, most probably taken in Bhopal, which figured Huseen only. I picked it up to have a closer look at it. Huseen with his smiling face—but he seemed to be ageing rapidly. And it surprised me a little to note that his face showed no sign of affluence. Instead he appeared to be withering like an old tree. He had become balder than before and his beard had grown longer.

'I reckon this photograph was taken somewhere here,' I said.

'Yes, he was lying here when I quickly pressed the button. It was taken on his last visit.'

'Why is he unshaven?'

'He had started sporting a beard. When did you meet him last?'

'About three years ago...Right here. That time I had come on a visit from Delhi and by a happy coincidence he was still here. In between he visited Delhi twice in connection with his visa. He sent word to me and also called at my house. But unfortunately, I was held up somewhere and could not reach home in time. He had to go away without meeting me.'

I was telling Jameel a blatant lie. The truth was that I was reluctant to meet Huseen and therefore deliberately avoided him. I had no desire to meet him though I could not ascribe any specific reason for it. Now I was holding his photograph in my hand and had been intently looking at it for a long time. My mind seemed to be in a whirl.

'Do you know what the doctors asked me when the attack came?' I said.

Jameel gave me a questioning look. Kaneez had already left the room, leaving the two of us to ourselves.

'The doctor asked me if I could recall any significant event in the two days prior to the attack. Any kind of tension? Any mental shock? Any disturbing news?'

'I told him that I could not recall anything of this nature. It was true that at that time Meerut was in the throes of a communal riot but I had no relative or friend living there. It was equally true that old Delhi was in the grip of tension and curfew had been clamped there. But I was living in New Delhi.

'After thinking for a while I told the doctor that Huseen was no doubt a friend but for the last many years we had been thrown apart. Now I don't whether what I said had any element of truth and if so to what extent. The fact is that after taking all things into consideration I found that Huseen was a frank, forthright and honest man—a noble soul. And I loved him. I loved him most dearly.'

As I said this my voice grew strained, my eyes filled with tears and I found myself crying.

Yes, really crying!

Ram Darash Mishr

The Road

A jeep came hurtling up and stopped outside the tea shop.

'You there! Four cups of tea.' A man got down from the jeep, followed by three others. They sat down on a string-bed in front of the shop and immediately went into a huddle. They were discussing the road under construction.

Water was already boiling in a pot on a charcoal fire. The man owning the shop poured the boiling water into another metal pot, threw a handful of tea leaves into it and, measuring the quantity of sugar and milk with a calculating eye, added them to the concoction. Allowing the concoction to simmer for a while, he poured it into four cups and picking them up with shaking hands he placed them on a teapoy lying alongside the cot, without looking up.

'What rotten tea!' the man grimaced. 'Can't this old buffoon do better?' He threw the cup, contents and all, on the ground. His three companions nodded in agreement but kept sipping the tea from their cups.

The tea seller raised his eyes. The irate visitor, still muttering under his breath, suddenly looked up at the tea shop-owner. 'Oh, is it you, Master Saheb!' he exclaimed in surprise.

Master Chander Bhan Pandey, with a shock of recognition, realized that his customer was none other than Jang Bahadur Yadav, the MLA of his constituency. He lowered his eyes in embarrassment and his gaze remained stuck on the big hole in his own dhoti.

Yadav guffawed. 'So it's you, Masterji,' he said. 'So you have started this business? Good for you. One must keep busy. Money really matters. Please don't hesitate if I can be of service to you.' He laughed loudly and his companions joined in the laughter. One of them said in a sheepish voice, 'Yadavji, it's through your good offices that they have agreed to construct a road in this area. It'll provide a livelihood to many.'

Yadav took a five-rupee not from his pocket and held it out to Masterji.

'I don't have change,' Masterji said.

'Who's asking for change? Keep it.'

'No, I've no right to take money from you. You didn't even drink the tea.'

'I'm not paying you for the tea. It's my homage to a teacher— a token of our traditional teacher-pupil relationship. Keep the money. It'll come in handy.'

Pandeyji seethed with anger. The five-rupee note was burning a hole in his fingers. As if overcome by a tornado of anger, he advanced towards Yadav, his eyes full of hate. He flung the note in his direction. 'Yadavji, I'm not asking for alms!' he cried.

But Yadavji had already got into his jeep. He smiled, his smile flitting from Pandeyji to the currency note lying on the ground. The jeep's engine purred, the vehicle shot forward and started racing, raising a cloud of dust behind in which the note went fluttering and fell at some distance from Pandeyji. He kept looking at it for some time as it came fluttering down in the dust-laden wind. Then he slowly advanced and, picking up the note, brushed the dust from it with his hand. He was in a quandary, not knowing what to do with the note.

Fair, broad forehead, silvery hair, a threadbare white dhoti, a part of which he had flung over his shoulder to cover his torso. He sat down on a bench outside his cottage, looking a picture of gloom. The dust thrown up by the jeep had settled on his wrinkled face.

Yadav had indeed humiliated him. From the very beginning he had had doubts about whether his business would succeed. A Brahmin, an old Congressi, and a retired school teacher at that, was he fated to round off his life by putting up a tea-stall like low class people and selling tea, salted *pakoras*, cheap snacks, and tobacco laced with lime.' But his son Ramesh, would not listen to him. He was determined that his father should put up a tea-stall and many people threw their weight on his side.

'B..r..r..r!' Pandeyji felt outraged. His dhoti had again given way at the haunches. It was already a patched-up affair. This khadi cloth seemed to have conspired to make him naked. But he would keep wearing the dhoti, covering his body sometimes on one side, sometimes on the other. There was not a single place where it did not have a patch, leaving no further scope for manoeuvering. His son, Ramesh, would say, 'Father, give up your fad for *khadi*. A mill-made dhoti is strong and cheap. It does not betray you like a dhoti made of *khadi*.'

Ramesh had been dinning this idea into his head for a long time and at last Pandeyji had conceded the point, thinking that his son might after all be right. But now at the fag end of his life it was too late to change from khadi to a mill-made dhoti. There was no point in breaking a self-imposed rule in old age. But to buy a new *khadi* dhoti was a formidable proposition. He would have to shell out no less than fourteen rupees for a new one. And where was the money for it? Besides, a new cap, a kurta and a towel must go with a new dhoti. He could buy a set of mill-made clothes with the same money and it would last much longer. But he could not bring himself to do so. After all, how long had he to live? But now that he came to think of it, it was not merely a question of reconciling himself to the changed situation. It was six years since he had retired from school and he had only three *bighas* of land to fall back upon. Being in a low lying area it got completely flooded during the rains. Could a family of five or six people live off this land?

After completing his education, his elder son, Mahesh, had found a job in the city and had shifted there with his family. He found it difficult to make both ends meet on his meagre earnings. The younger son, Ramesh, in spite of pushing and prodding, could not pass his eighth class and took to looking after the land. He had three children and they were always half-starved. Under such dire conditions where was the money to come from for a *khadi* dhoti?

There was a little traffic on the road. Going behind his hut, Pandeyji tried to readjust his *dhoti* but there was hardly any scope to cover himself adequately. It made him so angry that he felt like tearing his dhoti into shreds and standing naked before the public. For that matter it would have hardly made much difference for he was already as good as naked. The tea-shop had totally exposed him. People gave him amused looks and asked him awkward questions. And to cap it all, this man Yadav had gloated over humiliating him publicly. If only those days could return! He would have made the fellow stand on the bench and caned him on his buttocks. But now he was an MLA and not a pupil. His only satisfaction was that when he was a pupil he had often caned him and he must still be carrying those cane marks on his buttocks. Those school days flitted past his eyes. Who would have thought that this yokel would become Shri Jang Bahadur Yadav, MLA? He was considered the dunce of the class and came in for a thrashing almost every day. He was even in the habit of stealing his class-fellows' pencils and penknives. One day he had torn out Gandhiji's picture from a class-mate's book and pissed on it. In consequence, he had been rusticated from the school. It was only at the intervention of some respectable people of the village that he was taken back. And now the same loafer had become a political leader! It was indeed a veritable miracle. Anything could happen in this country! People had made good in life while he had remained stuck in the same place, threadbare *khadi* dhoti and all!

When Ramesh returned in the evening, they closed the shop for the day and brought all the paraphernalia to the house for safe keeping.

Pandeyji sat silent for a while and then said in a drained-out voice. 'I can't manage it.'

'Why, Father?'

'They all look down upon me. I can't stand their contemptuous looks any longer.'

'Yes, Father, a man's looks can be more devastating than hunger. Well, I agree with you we should rather go hungry than stand their stares.'

A long silence yawned between them.

'I could have looked after the tea-stall and nobody would have dared bandy looks with me. I tell you, I would have put all of them in their proper places. But then our land would have remained neglected.'

Pandeyji was silent.

'Did you earn anything, Father?'

'Yes, two rupees from the sale of tea and five rupees as a votive offering from and old pupil.'

'What kind of votive offering?'

Pandeyji told Ramesh what had transpired between him and Yadavji.

'Why should you feel so bad about it, Father?' If he can wheedle hundreds of rupees from us by unfair means what if he gives back five rupees to us?'

Pandeyji looked at Ramesh like one chastised. His son was laughing.

When Pandeyji retired for the night he was feeling very listless. He kept brooding over his fate. 'You idealist Congress worker!' he said to himself.' You hard-boiled teacher, you enemy of the boozers—is this how you have been rewarded for your services to the country? Your students, whom all your life you had fed on the nectar of learning, now must you kow-tow to them and serve cheap tea? Must you live to measure out chewing tobacco to those very people against whom you had thundered for boozing? No, no, you must not submit to such inequity.'

No one knew better than he that there was a dire need for a road in this backward area. He along with others had been pressing for it for a long time. But all along the government had turned a blind eye to the needs of the people. There are many roads, but to have a road in one's own area has a charm of its own. It is indeed not a pleasant experience to go jumping over ravines, streams and pits. A road added to one's comfort in many ways. But at that time it had not occurred to Pandeyji that a road could also be a curse.

And now Pandeyji's dream had become a reality. The road was in the final stage of construction and was being paved. Ramesh said to his father, 'I feel pleased with it. The road runs along our field. There is a proposal to build a bus stand very near our field. We would do well to open a tea-shop there. We can also stock some items of daily use such as chewing tobacco and the life. Even now, when the road is under construction, there are a lot of gangmen working on it. They will come to us for a quick cup of tea and snacks.'

'Well, time enough to think about it,' Pandeyji said in an evasive tone.

'There's no time for delay,' Ramesh said. 'The same idea may occur to others and they may steal a march over us.'

Pandey was silent.

'In your old age you have to look after the land and harvest gather the crops,' he said. 'It will be a good idea for you to look after the shop—a cushy job. And it will bring you some money.'

'How you talk! You mean you want me to run a shop? At my age?' Pandeyji got up in a huff. A big tear appeared in his dhoti.

Father and son used to have a regular squabble over it. One day, out of sheer desperation, Pandeyji agreed. A small hut was built on his own land at the edge of the road. The paraphernalia required to set up the shop was bought. Today was Pandeyji's first day at the shop.

He had decided that he would not go to the shop the next day. The very thought of sitting in the shop was abhorrent to him. What if he was poor? he was not going to be disgraced in his old age. As he turned on his side his dhoti again ripped under the pressure. He could stay half-naked in the house. But to go out in that state! His mind boggled at the thought.

In the morning Ramesh was ready with the materials for the shop. But Pandeyji made no move to get up from his bed he just kept lying there half-naked, feigning sleep.

'Father, aren't you going to the shop?'

Pandeyji very much wanted to blurt out a loud 'no'. But he could not bring himself to do so.

'You mean I should go naked?' he at last said in a painful voice.

Ramesh put down the things on the floor. 'But there's nothing we can do about it,' he said in a heavy voice. 'As soon as I am able to put by some money I'll buy a *khadi* dhoti for you. *Khadi* has become so costly these days, you know.'

Pandeyji saw Ramesh's children going to school in threadbare nickers. The sight wrenched at his heart. Must he have a dhoti of *khadi* at the cost of his grand children? That was what he had been doing all the time. Why didn't he realize that there was a difference between *khadi* and *khadi*? There was the *khadi* worn by Yadav and there was the *khadi* worn by him. Only Yadav had the right to wear *khadi* because it was on his body that *khadi* had evolved. On Pandey's body it had always been reduced to tatters.

Ramesh was going back into the hut, carrying the packets of material in his arms when Pandeyji called him.

'Yes, Father?'

'Have you got a spare dhoti.'

'Then bring it for me, son.'

Ramesh gave his father a look compounded of pain, surprise and pleasure. But his father had turned away his face.

After a while Ramesh was seen going to the shop with Pandeyji in tow. He was wearing Ramesh's dhoti.

Gyanranjan

The Gong

Patrola was located fairly deep in the heart of the city. To get there one had to walk past the tailor's shop, the cycle-stand and the bus stop. A rather unfamiliar place, it was well-known to the police. We had made this inaccessible place our haunt. The peace and freedom we had here was unavailable in other places; we were fully at ease here. In short, it was the kind of place with which the ordinary citizen had nothing to do. As for ourselves our citizenship remains like a thin layer of skin. Being rootless we were supposedly most with the times but the fact was that we only sat together, hissing but not stirring. Our bodies have become phlegmatic as if made of dead tissues. Our intoxication builds up a sort of anger in us, which, after squabbling, vanishes into the sky above. In this intoxicated state we sometimes feel alive. Our consciousness gets heightened and we think that our hour of redemption has come. That, having seen through the smoke-screen of hypocrisy and cant, we are on the point of shaking off servility for good. We forgot for a moment that Sant Malik Das had taken such powerful hold of our minds that we could not but toe the line. We felt it was impossible to get out of the life-pattern of Patrola. This place had become our 'retreat'. However, getting out of Patrola when we trudged back to rooms in the city we perceived the framework better than we. My companions had hardly any links with their wives and children, with society, the country or the world at large. They were 'anti', naturally.

I was the only one among my companions about whom life had not yet taken a final decision and who still sometimes tried to examine and understand things in this world of many temptations. It is highly probable that I have become for good a clever person of sorts—but I can't say this for certain yet.

It often happens that when my health is at a low ebb my sleeplessness exceeds all limits. Mercifully, it does not corrode my respectability. On the other hand in enhances it. I sleep for long hours and go out window-shopping, drink Coca-Cola and say 'hello, hello' all round. I give the slip to Patrola. My companions quite likely know about it to some extent but they don't care. I have some clothes which go ill with my person and my past way of life. I look like someone in disguise when I wear them. I put them on when I wish to turn my face against Patrola. I am a little ashamed of these 'period pieces' but I have not thrown them away. I have not worn them for years yet I have preserved them with care.

One day I went to the *paan* shop outside Patrola and there I ran into Nem. It was quite late at night. Since becoming an insurance agent he has begun to look handsome. At one time Nem had reached a stage in his life when he seemed ripe for the Patrola gang. But he was saved by a hair's breadth. Even now, after attaining happiness and security, when he meets us he feels tempted by the life at Patrola. He says, I got trapped in this insurance business. To be with you in Patrola—oh, it would have been such fun! Now where's the chance?' I think he has made a neat pile and has gained all the comforts of life. Within hardly a couple of minutes of our meeting Nem began talking about Kundan Sarkar. I knew he never failed to talk about Kundan Sarkar. And in spite of his haste I was ready for him to broach this subject. Whenever he met me he would bend over backward in his effort to introduce me to Kundan Sarkar. Obviously, he got a special pleasure from this. Perhaps he wanted to show me that their friendship was intact, that time had not effaced it.

The story of Kundan Sarkar had held the centre stage for years and had not yet receded into the background. This time Nem told me in sibilant whispers, smiling, that Kundan Sarkar would entertain me with excellent liquor. He stressed that with Kundan Sarkar I would not feel bored. 'You are a writer and he is an intellectual. Both of you will hit it off nicely.' The truth was that I had parted company from literature years ago. Some vestiges perhaps clung to me yet. But I kept it from Nem. I knew that to get entangled in argument with him was a sheer waste of time. That way he is like a leech. He goes on and on and sucks you dry. While going he gave me a parting shot, 'So, don't forget. Don't go back on your word. It's not every day that you meet a man who gives a damn to status and position. A friendly sort and refreshingly lively. What more do you want, brother?' He stopped and added, somewhat worked up, 'He won't mind going to that abominable place for a booze. He would go there without turning up his nose or brushing down his clothes afterwards. Remember then, tomorrow.'

I was prepared for all eventualities, booze being the main attraction. With Sarkar uppermost in my mind I returned to Patrola.

Kundan Sarkar was something of a sensation. All the local writers and intellectuals had access to him. Most of them middle class writers. They ate at his table and sang his praises. His very name made their bodies tingle. They would have wagged their tails had not the Theory of Evolution accounted for its disappearance from their bodies. Still their behinds tingled at the sight of him. There was a large body of onlookers who watched the interaction between Kundan Sarkar and the intellectuals with morbid interest, and had carried his name to all the literary centres of the city. I did not tell my companions about my impending visit to Kundan Sarkar and avoided them for sometime. I could not tell them of my greed. The majority of my companions at Patrola were the sort that kept people like Kundan Sarkar in their proper place; they were fully alienated. I was the only one with his heart in its right place, who was still stirred by considerations of reputation, status, money, society and country.

Kundan Sarkar was in a position from which contact with ordinary people was not possible. Despite this he was very sociable. No one knew how he had managed to befool the government. He was keen to cultivate literary persons, art lovers, intellectuals, mix with them and entertain them with drinks and food. The city boasted of a horde of writers and artists but Kundan Sarkar could hold his own against them. He always kept one close to him. One at a time. It was in the nature of an experiment. The person on whom he bestowed his favour was known as 'his gong.'

In those days I happened to be his 'gong.' He didn't wince the least at me despite my being so slovenly. Entering his house in my dishevelled state I thought this place couldn't possibly be the right or congenial place for me. But greed knows no limits. Drink had become the moving spirit of my life. Drinking at other's expense was to me the height of cunning. That was how matters stood.

Initially, he gave me the less expensive booze although I knew that he had the choicest liquors in stock. He wanted to size me up as an intellectual. In the second place I was almost a pauper. Had I been a well-to-do intellectual his behaviour would have been very different. Kundan Sarkar did not lay open his treasure. Under my tutelage he opted for cheap joints to savour their sordid life. But I knew none of these disreputable places.

With me, when tired after walking the roads, he would refuse to hire a rickshaw even though he knew we were on our last legs. Many days we subsisted on tea and coffee and nothing more substantial. He would borrow my *bidis* and finish off the entire bundle while expensive imported cigarettes were in his pocket all the time. What could I gain from all this? Yet I don't know why I kept waiting for something to turn up. But for Kundan Sarkar these experiences were full of fun and fulfillment. Was it for this kind of folly that I had given the go-by to my companions? But Kundan Sarkar would gleefully confess to me, 'Pal, the thrill of a free life! I had never savoured such fun before.'

The time of my life, my foot! I would silently fume, 'You son of a bitch, is this what you have come to me for?' I felt like tearing apart this life of sham—his and mine. I was also tormented by shame. I had ditched my friends, kept them in the dark and had come here in search of pleasure and drinking orgies. Although my companions believed in living dangerously they had never wavered from the right path. They were made of sterner stuff and not given to self-pity. But I was unhappy with myself for playing the lackey to Kundan Sarkar. I was deluding myself, befooling myself. I decided to put an end to this situation in which I could neither throw up nor digest my chicanery. The moment of truth is near, I told myself, and the end was not far away.

Soon I realized that it was difficult to keep pace with Kundan Sarkar and also unnecessary. If you have the stamina to discuss literature with him for two hours every day you can get along with him. I didn't know this was his chronic state. Literature agitated him like bleeding piles. However grave the situation and whatever the topic of discussion, he could give it a literary turn in no time—just the time it takes to change gear. I didn't have this kind of dexterity. I cracked under the strain. In spite of biting off more than I could chew, the moment of truth finally arrived.

One day Kundan Sarkar had explained to me in great detail that an artist should lead a death-oriented life. Only then could his coffers be filled with experience. He knew countless names who, drawing sustenance from bare experience, had disarmed contemporary rivals. His pronouncements on literature were so strange that I used to feel like beating my head. He maintained for instance, 'society is epitomised in the field, life is manure, the writer is the tiller and literature the crop, just as woman epitomises the earth, man the plough and progeny the fruit.'

I had perforce to speak. Silence was impossible. If he had guessed that I was fed-up, he would have shown me the door before I could decide to make an exit. So I went on biting into the straw pretending that it was sweet juice. 'You have the gift of language,' I would say. 'There is magic in it.' He would flare up. 'Magic! Do you call reality magical? Great!'

He told me again and again that he was a devotee of truth. 'You see, I can afford to drink Scotch and yet I go in for raw country liquor. Why do I smoke *biris*? Why do I loaf around in the streets? Why do I wear *khadi*? Why do I go on foot though I have a car? When I am no writer? I'm just an intellectual. The fact is that I find truth beautiful and I am collecting nuggets of truth.'

Somehow the last day arrived. A cold had sapped me. My nose was running like a tap. A strange irritation clawed at me. The cold confirmed the hour of good-bye. By a funny coincidence, on that fateful day, his pocket was bursting at the seams. He spent lavishly on me that day. From morning to evening we went around boozing. I said to myself that I must fleece him to the bones. I wouldn't have another day with that bastard. In the evening when the lights came on he took me to the kind of restaurant to which I had never been before. It was too respectable a place for me to venture there. The question of money apart, I find respectable places insufferable and I feel like throwing up. But that evening seemed different. My body was filled with intoxication like a honeycomb with honey, and I swayed like a tree without falling.

The restaurant was crammed with people. The lights were subdued and men and women seemed in equal numbers. The place was permeated with scents which changed their character at the slightest motion. We got a table for two. A half pint bottle of gin was tucked in Kundan Sarkar's pocket. As soon as he settled down his eyes roved around as if he were throwing a bait to attract a catch. I felt uneasy as if I had been trapped. Gradually my breathing eased and I looked around to familiarize myself with the place. I had never before seen so many elegant men and women gathered together. My cold and the liquor had soaked my brain, making it turgid. Yet it was intact somehow. For some time I kept thinking of my land—my India.

Kundan Sarkar told me that this restaurant was mostly patronized by army officers, their families and friends. I had no difficulty in believing that the people sitting there could only be army officers. The place seemed to have no links with the outside world. Here nobody looked sad, angry or grave. All the faces were healthy, smooth and shiny. Kundan Sarkar also looked like a member of this fraternity. Could he be disowned by this fraternity simply because he was entertaining a destitute?

I noticed that there were two types of women in the hall. Some looked feather-weights and there were others who looked as if they must be shitting bucketsfull. The fat women were behaving most coquettishly with the men. The men did not lag behind either. As they ate they delicately licked the wives of others. It seemed as if others had no existence for them. They seemed to be under the happy delusion that this place had been created exclusively for their benefit and this world solely existed to set them off. Mother... I swore under my breath and my mind suddenly tautened. How long would people remain slaves?

By now Kundan Sarkar had uncorked the bottle of gin and poured its contents in glasses half filled with water. The gin could pass for water. He sipped it slowly as a sophisticated man would. Just then the orchestra on the dais struck up. The music was like jackals howling and ended in murderous screams. I don't know whether it was the effect of the gin or a manifestation of my own self but the sounds of the music made me nauseous. I felt I must do something desperate before the bitter taste in my mouth changed into pleasurable flavours. A slight let-up, the slightest sign of sluggishness, and the world forces itself down your throat. I didn't want to swallow. I wanted to spit. The liquor in the end had saved me for I suddenly felt light in the head. Otherwise I would have mouthed a few abuses and hit the floor. My mind was filled with a rebellious euphoria.

I noticed that the situation had improved. Before, I just smiled at the world as if it were inhabited by nincompoops and I had seen through it. A stage had come when I was being taken for a dud because of the smile. This smile did no harm to the establishment. A compelling smile comes only to a king, a priest, a woman and those rich guys who feel secure in their self-made paradise. The smile gone, nausea had taken its place. I am in a smashing-up mood. I could make a nuisance of myself. I wish it could be so for ever. The lure of democracy and civic sense have been so rammed into us that the desire to smash up becomes marginal and all that remains is a tepid ferment. A vague feeling of general disaffection keeps simmering in the mind.

I quickly emptied my glass. I feared lest my nausea and anxiety should vanish, giving place to that perennial anaemic smile. I must pluck out the smile, root and branch. I looked at Kundan Sarkar. This was my last day with him. After today I will not be your lackey. But Kundan Sarkar was blissfully ignorant about what was passing in my mind. He sat there drinking with smug satisfaction. There were still many in the city waiting to be his lackeys.

He looked at his watch and asked the bearer to bring something to eat. Then, turning to me, he said in a low voice, 'Time for the wench to come up and sing.'

'Very, well, let the wench come,' I said nonchalantly.

Kundan Sarkar poured the remnants of the bottle into his glass while I set my chair in the direction of the dais as if a film show was going to begin. My view was obstructed by the solid black head of a woman, as big as a flower pot, forcing me to re-adjust my chair. In the meanwhile some hefty and handsome goons came up and after fully circling the hall disappeared somewhere inside. Presumably they were the security men. At first I thought they were looking for girls or maybe for smugglers. But no, I was wrong. They left after making their presence felt like an army doing a road march with a special objective.

The girl breezed into the hall. She did not seem to be walking. She seemed to be swimming in the air. Before stepping on the dais, she gyrated in all directions, blowing kisses like children stabbing the air with their paper planes. The girl looked very fresh and young. On her body was a one and a half foot long, very tight, gold coloured kurta. She started singing, swaying her hips and moving on teetery steps. Her eyes and her bosom proclaimed that she was game. While singing, she would provocatively raise her shoulders, like birds flapping their wings, and bounce, swinging her breasts. This seemed to be a clever device to bring the lines of her song into relief. She made dramatic pauses, joining her hands together as if she were trying to remember the next lines, and would then start singing again. She did not in the least look concerned about her profession and the waxing night. From time to time she gestured to the orchestra, as if giving it the cue.

The restaurant seemed to be simmering with carnal passion. People sunk in sofas exchanged notes in hushed voices. I don't think they opened their mouths bigger than a goat's anus. The men thought the singing girl was a prostitute, worth four annas and their wives were not prostitutes. In their eyes shone bedroom scenes. They seemed to be telling their wives, 'There are other women apart from you who can be had easily. Their women also refused to take the jibe lying down. 'Look at the left hand corner table. Look how smart the man sitting alongside the blue georgette looks, darling.' 'He is not a squadron leader yet. He is junior to me.' 'So what? He's smart and handsome. Wait till be becomes a squadron leader. He'll become smarter still.'

A little away from us, at the third table, there sat a middle-aged man, sporting a long, needle-sharp moustache. Every now and then he slyly grazed his moustache against the cheek of the woman sitting beside him. While doing this he would gaze at the dais as if the game of moustache and cheek was an accident.

As I sat watching something extraordinary happened. The salwar cord of the girl who was accompanying the singing loosened either because of the continuous swaying of hips or in the hurry of changing and came down dangling between her legs. It looked slightly soiled compared to her costume above and below. With the music the cord also shook. I burst out laughing. It issued from the region of the heart and was absolutely uncontrollable. It could sound boorish and jarring to sophisticated ears. Kundan Sarkar was startled. He had been drinking heavily but he was still conscious of his surroundings and he found my laughter uncouth. This kind of consciousness is something that keeps a man insulated against accidents. Kundan Sarkar scolded me roundly. 'Behave yourself. It's an elite place. Have you seen anyone except you laughing at the dangling cord? The people sitting here are civilized enough to realize that this could happen to anyone?' Then he fired another shot at me. 'Perhaps you think you are sitting in Patrola.'

'Shut up, you!' I got to my feet. I could not bear to hear the name of Patrola from him. I had a Coca Cola bottle in my hand. He immediately softened.

'My friend, you are drunk. Wait, I'll call for fresh lemon for you,' He cajoled me back into my chair. For the first time he disclosed his elitism by speaking the language of his class in my presence. He had scotched my priceless laughter.

I had not fully regained my composure. My mood had changed drastically. But I kept sitting there holding both ghee and water for the fire that was raging in my heart. I was still undecided whether to quench the fire or to fan the flame. I sat on as if I were alone and Kundan Sarkar in front of me was nothing but an empty chair. His bullying language had deeply hurt me. I had gone to him for booze, not to cower under his bullying ways or to mourn for literature or to get brainwashed. Kundan Sarkar needed a shameless pimp.

A cocktail of remorse and anger befuddled my brain. All around me were the goody-goody spineless gentry spread out like rubble and I did not know where I had lost my earthy vigour and zest for life. All that remained was sham and at the most an impotent contempt. Darkness was growling and enveloping me. A clangour went on in my head. Suddenly I started addressing the people gathered there: 'You army mosquitoes and delicate women,' I began. 'The time is not far when civilization will make a volte face and give you such a kick that your shit will dry up. You will hop around holding your behinds. These rifles which you have and which give you bread will be snatched away from you. Run! Run! Rifles are not meant for filling bellies!'

Yes, ten years of my life have gone to waste. Sometimes nausea, sometimes smiles, sometimes smiles. What a bloody sequence! Those people who pocketed fat salaries in the name of patriotism and this whore from the red light district parading as music queen. What do they care. They think the whole country is waiting to be stuffed up the one centimetre space between a woman's legs. As I cooled down a little I realized that hundreds of healthy youths, who had given up everything, were sitting in dingy wayside hovels, blowing out *ganja* smoke. Ah, the road of *ganja* will never end.

There is commotion in the hall. The people are getting restive. I felt elated as if I were sinking into a deep dream. The blood pulsated through my veins as if it feared nothing. The orchestra sounded sluggish and wheezing. The girl seemed to be drowning in the rhythm of her own tune. In my mind an unknown and clandestine strategy was unfolding itself.

Andro must have called. This was my last chance. If I let slip this chance, my life would again settle into its old groove, becoming dull and humdrum. Suddenly my fists clenched of themselves. I was getting beside myself. Kundan Sarkar deftly grabbed my arm. He must have been watching me intently. By then the bottle of Coca-Cola had gone out of my fist with a sharp tintinabulation. The glass wall in front came crashing down. As if coming out of my reverie I saw that the girl on the dais had panicked and was fleeing, yelling, 'Police! Police!' She fell straight into the hands of a goon coming from the green room.

I gave my table a vicious kick, upended it and stood erect, facing the people like a military officer in command. 'Get out of here! Or you'll be kicked out...' And I don't know what else.

When I came to I was being bashed up. Some goons had surrounded and were kicking me around. One of the goons was yelling at the onlookers, asking them to resume their seats. Another goon escorted the frightened singer on to the dais and kept guard over her like a watchman. He picked up the girl's trailing cord and she thrust it into her clothing. The man who was supervising my beating seemed to go by the name of Kallu Guru. Just as the debris of a wreckage is cleared up swiftly, in the same way the splintered glass and I were being cleared up. Kallu Guru gave a powerful kick in my behind sending me stumbling up to the stairway. My eyes searched for Kundan Sarkar but he had slipped out of sight. I even shouted, 'Kundan! Kundan!' and Kallu Guru gave me a powerful blow on my jaw in the name of Kundan, drawing blood. Blood dripped from my jaw. I found a man near the table whose leg I had clutched to rise. A decent man, he looked scared as if waiting for peace to be restored. He whispered to a woman sitting by his side, 'He looks like a loafer!' It made no difference to me. She kept faintly smiling at me.

I was in no condition to receive a second kick on my bottom. I got up quickly and climbed down the stairs. I clearly remember I was just half way down the stairs when the orchestra above struck up again. In just a couple of minutes sanity had returned to the restaurant. The gate-man opened the door for me. How was he to know that the man whom he saluted was not worthy of it?

In this way the lackey of Kundan Sarkar fell on the road. I was like a cyclist on a jam-packed street who rarely gets hurt on falling from his bicycle. Brushing myself down I came onto the road which was fairly deserted. My revolutionary fervour was gone. My nose had started running. I made for Patrola where I met my old companions in our old haunt. On seeing me they laughed mildly. Beyond this they did not misbehave in any other way with me.

Mudrarakshash

Encounter

How endless and sharp a beating is, whether from the policeman or the weather! Like the scream of a kite, fluttering in mid-flight, Rajjan's cry of pain was heard... 'Oh, Maaaa...

Nathu's grip on the cloth bag tied round his waist slackened—so that if it hadn't been secured as if it was a part of his body, it would have slipped. The cry, like a bamboo being split apart, was not too long, actually, but it travelled far and deep into Nathu's veins like a line etching itself.

How endless and sharp a beating is, whether from the policeman or the weather!

In the blistering heat of June, when the sun soundlessly raged like high fever, the spot where Nathu had halted, was just a few steps away from the back wall of his house. White, shell-like eruptions had appeared on the wall of raw earth, in such a way that they looked encrusted and decorated. The track of baked mud and earth down the ornamented wall made it evident that at the next lashing of the weather, it would crumble down. Perhaps the crumbling of the wall too would be accompanied by the kind of horrifying and stork shriek which had just escaped Rajjan's lips. Nathu had stopped in his tracks, maybe because he was waiting for the next shriek, or maybe to assimilate into his being the shriek he had heard. But Rajjan did not shriek again. Like the wall peeled under the assaults of the weather, perhaps with just one more charge of the lathi, he too had fallen, a wall made of the brown-black mud of the river bank.

Nathu re-secured his grip on the bundle. In it were lentil pods of which he had plucked a fair quantity. Boiled with their husks, and eaten with a little salt, they made a tasty meal. In matters of food, this season was more or less the season of plenty. It is not easy for everyone to know what the tastiest food in the world is, but certainly Nathu knew that next to mahua flowers, dripping with juice between mud and rotting leaves, boiled lentils made the most flavoursome meal. *Arhar* lentils are such a shameless crop that without water or manure, without proper tending, it crowds the fields untidily, and stands so long, that it looks as if it will be around forever. Not only those who keep watch on the fields, but even marauding animals turn away from it. This being the case, to pluck half a kilo of *arhar* which stood like old men rustling in the heat of the sun, was not of such consequence as to attract attention.

After that flailing shriek of Rajjanlal's, everything became quiet. Only the call of a certain bird was heard, about which not only Nathu but everyone in the village had heard a gory and horrifying story. Whenever one collected juicy mahua flowers the bird called without fail, and re-invoked the story. It was said that an old woman had spread manure outside her hut to dry, and, going out to collect fuel wood, asked her grandson to keep an eye on the mahua. Under the blazing sun the mahua shrank and looked greatly reduced. When the old woman returned from the jungle she thought the grandson had eaten them. Enraged, she hit the child with the stone on which she pounded spices. The child died. People told the old woman that the child had not eaten the mahuas, but that they had shrunk under the heat of the sun. After that the old woman changed into a bird, and every afternoon called, 'Get up, son, son, son, son...'

They had taken away Rajjan at about eight in the morning. One of them was a police sub-inspector, the rest, constables. What they wanted from him, no one knew.

When the police took away Rajjan a crowd of children had followed him, but not a single adult man or woman. The children lingered around for a long time. Skirting the village head-man's fields, and the place where they stored the harvested crop, and passing behind the one-roomed school, the path led to a misshapen mound, taking in some disorderly graves on its course. On the mound grew wild bushes covered with the pollen of the palash flower, and high dry grass on which grew flowers like spiders' webs.

Among the people watching Rajjan and the children was Nathu too. For some reason he felt that he should not be seen there at that time. Perhaps it was the same indefinable sense of danger that made him think that he should spend more time plucking beans, and as far as possible not take the straight road home.

After a detour as he approached, the village he had heard this long drawn, horrendous sound. It was Rajjan's voice. Somewhat like a fish caught in the mire, being bored with a sharp pointed stick. Along with his cry came from among the thin, shapeless babool trees, the bird's voice, 'Get up, son, son, son, son.' As if it was saying, 'Son, get up. The mahuas have not decreased in number, they are all here.' When this bird began calling, it went on and on, in a sharp, poignant voice, often for hours—'Get up, son, son, son, son.'

As Rajjan's cry went up in the air the gang of children ran to the ramshackle so-called school. Perhaps the police had threatened them and driven them away. Among the gang was Rajjan's son too. Stopping near the school the children looked at him. There was neither curiosity in their eyes nor compassion. Staring at him they were also thinking out some plan of action to quell their agitation. Rajjan's son had been quite composed till now, but at the sound of the shriek he suddenly looked weak and ill. His brown face looked as if under a coating of ash. Slowly he sat down on a heap of dry cow-dung. It did not take the other children long to find a diversion for themselves. They began flinging stones and clods of earth at the topmost branch of an aged mango tree, to bring down a withered mango hanging on it.

The mango, perhaps, had been there for many days. Or maybe, when it came down, another mango as decrepit had taken its place. The children had been throwing stones at mangoes for a long time. Nobody knew whether any mango had ever fallen. But yes, the tin roof of the school always resounded as stray stones fell on it. After a lot of stones had hit the roof, the voice of the lone teacher of the school would be heard, 'Wait, you rascals!'

The threat usually worked, for the children would stop pelting stones and get busy in some other equally engaging pastime.

The boys had cast only two or three stones at the mango, when instead of the teacher's voice from within the school they saw the teacher himself coming out in person. This was something unusual. They froze.

'Run off!' Kishan Babu said in his heavy voice. The children scampered off. Kishan Babu did not go back into the school. Fixing his eye at the horizon that was yellow like a jaundice patient in the heat and dust, he steadily gazed in the direction from which Rajjan's shrieks had come. Now they were not like sounds of shrieks, but like sounds disgorged straight from the lungs.

Silence reigned around the school. That it was a school few could believe. With unpaved floor and tin roof, the longish room had classes from the second to the fourth, going on simultaneously in three of its corners. In the fourth corner sat Kishan Babu behind a table. He was the teacher of the school, and the postmaster of the village too. After impaling the boys with some writing work and a shower of abuses, he would go to sleep. Sometimes, irritatedly, he would wake to give a postcard to a customer or to write a letter for someone.

On waking Kishan Babu would be stormily angry. But for a very short while. The man waking him would laugh instead of being angered at his ill temper. It was a peculiarity of his personality that he was known both as school teacher and post-office. The word post master was not easy to pronounce anyway, but because of his nature people liked to call him post-office. There was good reason for it, a good and mischievous reason. The village people believed firmly that what was told to Kishan Babu travelled faster the not only a letter, but even a telegram. That was why he was considered a post-office, and not the clerk of a post-office. But this was not Kishan Babu's fault, really. He had never in his life gone to a place of entertainment. To keep his spirits up, along with growing age, he had hit upon a device that in crude language is known as back-biting.

In that small village this was the least expensive and most popular entertainment. The special feature of this entertainment was that it could keep you diverted for days on end. In the neighbouring village there would be nautanki shows. A small town lay beyond the village which boasted of a cinema hall. But both these forms of entertainment went so far, and no further. Frequently, the nautanki watchers and the cinema goers, to keep up the fun, had to take recourse to white lies, which were often found out. For instance, Pandit Radhey Shyam once went to see a film and returning, said that it was a very dirty film in which men and women did things openly.

'Do things openly?' his listeners' ears perked up.

'They are very dirty. Don't make me talk.' He even spat.

'But what exactly happens?' Imaginations whirred.

'Arrey, what doesn't happen, you should ask. Just prostitutes they are. They can do anything.'

'You mean take off their clothes and all?'

'Listen to this fool!'

Everyone was convinced that Pandit Radhey Shyam had seen something rare and out of this world, and that too, among people beautiful and well-got-up.

Without letting each other know, the next day, a lot of them disappeared from the village and on returning cursed Pandit Radhey Shyam even more. They had certainly seen the hero and the heroine in the film taking off their clothes, but nothing more. Seeing their clothes lying heaped on the floor, they had held their breath in the hope of seeing the hero and the heroine in bed together. But there was a black out on the screen, and when it was light again, they just saw a lot of people crowding round the heroine's father, making complaints.

In such conditions, Kishan Babu could easily be champion entertainer.

'Have you heard? No? All right, leave it, then. What's the use of telling you?'

These opening lines from Kishan Babu would shame the listener more than whet his curiosity, for immediately afterwards, Kishan Babu would add: 'The whole village knows. How are you in the dark? I'm late for school'.

After this Kishan Babu would even take a few steps in the direction of his school. The listener would be left with the uncomfortable feeling that he was being deprived of participation in some choice happening. He would either become suppliant or crafty. Eyes gleaming with curiosity, he would come very close to Kishan Babu. 'I'm telling you, Post office Babu, I have been so swamped with work, I can't tell you...'

'Then remain swamped with work, stupid. I don't go around poking my nose. The whole village knows about Nandu's wife...'

After this Kishan Babu would not wait. By the next day the whole village—men, women and children—would become Kishan Babu, each anxious to prove that it was he or she who had broken the story about Nandu's wife. In the telling the story would snowball into something fantastic. It would become a subject of gossip for days together, assuming different forms at no cost to anyone.

This kind of entertainment was a potent and powerful source of entertainment, but it was also the root of much confusion. For instance, there might be confusion about Radhey's sister-in-law, but the name bandied about would be Raghunandan's wife's, and the quarrels that arouse from this change of names were usually very entertaining. By the time the cycle of mirth had run its full course it would transpire that Raghunandan had beaten up Mansa, and Mansa in turn had abused Nandu, and the latter had taken it out on Radhey by hurling a stone at him. This kind of quarrel was not allowed to end soon, for if it did, a whole platform of entertainment collapsed.

When Nandu hurled a stone at Radhey, Radhey laid bare Gopal's aunt's secret, while Mansa, who had come in for a beating at the hands of Raghunandan, unveiled the affairs of Tingu's home. Thus, so long as squabbles lasted the possibilities of fun increased manifold. That was why, while they pacified two contending parties on the one hand, simultaneously they also sowed seeds of discord among four others, so that by the evening a fresh squabble raged in the village. This game, which the village played with such recklessness, but with such interest, seemed to have some mysterious power which made it look as if it was the game that was playing the village, not vice versa—like a pulley which glided down swiftly, uncoiling the line and could as swiftly glide up, coiling it up again.

A day in a village, in spite of its higgledy-piggledy quality, is not such a bad proposition as is generally thought. There is something in a village day, which draws one towards itself, even if it is nothing more than a bundle of jute lowered into the pond to rot, or a tobacco plant asking for water. But night in a village is different. A village night brings with it an unknown terror. In the dark, one's hair stands up in a hard terror, like a man-eater sniffing its quarry. In such circumstances people either spend the night sitting around a fire, like primeval nomads, or stay couched in the cavernous interior of their mud houses.

Like day and night, this entertainment too had two aspects. One was enjoyment, and the other, the problems it brought in its wake. Unwittingly, the problems would knot themselves up so hard that like a running sore they could also take their toll of a few lives.

For the last few years several such running sores had brought great pain and tension to village Nauban. When and how these running sores of relationships became fatal, nobody could tell, but in the severe winter of last year the ant-ridden corpse of Nanhe gave rise to quite a commotion. How and why the stench of these running sores had got attached to Nathu and Rajjan is as inexplicable as the agitation that arose around Nanhe's corpse.

Somebody said that behind Nanhe's murder was some story about Horilal's younger sister. Nanhe had been murdered, they said. Horilal had said nothing, but his younger brother had soundly beaten up Santoo with a lathi because he thought that Santoo was the one who had spread the story. Santu did not regain consciousness. Since Horilal's brother had killed him all by himself, under cover of darkness, it had not been possible to establish the identity of the murderer or murderers. But one detail gained or was given currency. Someone said that Santoo was a dacoit, and so, Madanlal's gang would avenge him.

Possibly, Kishan Babu had spread this story, but it was compounded by the fact that Madanlal was Barsati Ram's enemy. Undoubtedly, Madan Lal, with his gang would attack Lala Barsati Ram.

With these events as backdrop and context, Nathu and Rajjan came into the picture. They fitted into the setting so smoothly that it seemed as if they had always had a stake in it.

It would have been very surprising indeed, if they hadn't seemed part of it all.

Nathu and Rajjan were special characters of village Nauban. Both were informers. They were real brothers but were sworn enemies. Rajjan spied for the dacoits' gangs, while Nathu for the police. So people thought. But Nathu, somewhat more clever, was informer for the dacoits too. After informing the police of the presence of dacoits somewhere, he would, with equal briskness, put the dacoits wise about the police being wise to them. Since the information more often than not proved correct, Nathu was the more successful of the two in the work of informing. In the beginning it was frightening work for Nathu. For Rajjan too. He knew that this fascinating entertainment of the world in which he lived, tale-carrying, was an instrument that could open private lives to a dangerous degree. All too soon the people of Nauban came to know who had done what and where. The first time, when Rajjan carried the news of the gold jewellery at the Mirpur wedding to Madanlal, he was in a state of terror on his way back. But soon enough he came to know that since his name was associated with Madanlal's gang people would live in as much awe of him as of Madanlal.

Nathu had taken to spying for the police partly out of spite against Rajjan. One day he was returning from the jungle with a heap of prickly beans, contact with which caused the skin to itch severely. He was carrying the prickly beans for pure fun. Just then he saw Rajjan in a totally new situation. He was dead drunk, and had a big slab of *gur* mixed with gram, tied in his upper cloth, a corner of which, peeped out of the cloth like a living advertisement. Rajjan had earned well that day. Even though it hadn't been easy to earn the money, he was still very happy.

The enterprise had started only three days ago. He was returning from a friend's marriage. He had borrowed a vest from Radhey, and had washed his dhoti and kurta. His shoes were hob-nailed like horse shoes, which made a royal sound as he walked. Putting a cap on his head he had picked up a lathi too. Walking thus, he felt a man of substance, a man of consequence.

The night was far advanced by the time he came back to Nauban. Filtering through the dark trees on both sides of the road, the moonlight scattered small and big daubs far onto the road. As he walked on the road, crushing the shadows of moonlight under his nailed shoes, he began singing to the beat of his boots and lathi. His bliss ended cruelly. Heckling with shocking rudeness, the dozen masked men who surrounded him, not only hurled abuses at him, one of them also struck a blow at his waist with his lathi. More than the injury it was the humiliation that made him cry out.

His assailants were dacoits. After disclosing their standing they beat him some more and, satisfied with their handiwork, told him to surrender everything he had, without a fuss.

His surrenderable goods consisted of one and half rupees. There were some sweets too.

The booty made the dacoits more furious, and Rajjan came in for another round of beating. 'Kill the swine, dump him in the ditch,' one of them cried.

Amidst tears, Rajjan said, 'What will you get by killing me, Dada?'

'Then whom shall we kill to get something, eh?'

This dialogue opened up a new avenue for Rajjan. He told them about Munna, the money-lender, and informed them that the jewellery Munna took as mortgage was kept in the room where he stocked fodder.

'Sala, if we return empty-handed we shall cut you into pieces,' they warned Rajjan and gave him a few more slaps.

Beyond doubt, they had made a rich haul at the money lender's, for just a little while later two of them sought out Rajjan again. He had just braced himself for another beating when they made him an offer.

If he game them accurate information, and substantial profits resulted from the information, he would be given twenty rupees, along with country liquor and good food.

Soon, all this cushy living, all the subtleties of the new job became an open secret for every man in Nauban. And thus it was, that seized by pique at all this, Nathu one day decided to enlighten the police about the goings-on.

On reaching the police station after a long detour, Nathu felt he had made a mistake coming there. To think of going to the police was easy, but on facing the police he lost his nerve. He felt he was Rajjan, and had come there to give himself up. The sub-inspector stood right in front of him. He had just finished his meal, and after picking his teeth, was getting ready to stretch out for a nap on the string bed under the tree. At the sight of him Nathu's face shrivelled like a criminal's, and his throat dried up.

'Who's that? What are you doing here?' the sub-inspector spat out the particle of spinach he had prised out from between his teeth.

'Huzoor, I humbly seek to serve you,' Nathu stammered.

The sub-inspector gave Nathu a sharp look, then barked at the constable sprinkling water on the earth: 'Take this thing away, and find out what stuff it is made of. Looks special.'

The constant glared at Nathu. After grilling him with some questions he dug his nails into the back of Nathu's arm and pushed him inside. And once inside, immediately, before Nathu had said anything, he turned him around like a puppet and gave him a blow in the middle of his chest without any expression on his face, as if he were practising boxing on a sand-bag. Simultaneously, with his left hand he gave him a slap at the back of his ear. Nathu sagged a little, but as soon as the slap fell he turned about and crashed into the wall.

Not only Nathu and Rajjan, but every last man in Nauban knew that a dialogue with the powers-that-be usually started this way. Therefore Nathu soon brought his terror under control, after the first blow. 'Hazoor, Inspector Saab, I had come to give you some vital information.'

At this the constable hesitated a bit, but asked immediately after giving him another hefty blow. 'Sala, so you've come to give us information? What information? Eh?'

'Hazoor, those dacoits...'

'Dacoits? Which dacoits?'

'Hazoor, dacoit Hariram is going to commit a dacoity tomorrow.'

'Listen to this twit,' the constable said as if speaking to the wall. 'What kind of wealth is bulging from your pockets, Sala, that Hariram should come to loot you? Up to your tricks, eh? Sala, want to trap some innocent person? Your...'

The constable beat Nathu some more.

'But just listen to me, Hazoor! Afterwards you can hang me. Hariram will loot Kundan.' Nathu brought out the words somehow. This information he had gathered from a keen study of Rajjan's movements.

This time the constable didn't beat him, just showered some choice abuses, and pushed him over to the sub-inspector sprawled on the bed under the tree.

'What's up now?' the sub-inspector growled in irritation.

'This swine says that Hariram is going to commit a dacoity at Kundan's house tomorrow,' the constable said.

'Beat the fellow and lock him up,' the sub-inspector ordered.

Nathu was beaten up a little more, and kept in custody. But the second night, the dacoity did take place, and it was a big one. Kundan's brother-in-law was in the house that night. He was a clerk at the Khampur police station. He tried some swagger with the dacoits on the strength of his police contacts. He even roughed up one of Hariram's men. After this Hariram zoomed in like a filmi dacoit. He not only looted the house, but also lined up four inmates of the house, Kundan's brother-in-law among them, and shot them dead.

As soon as the news reached the police station, Nathu was released. He had become a trustworthy police informer. Since among those killed was one who was a clerk of the police, the police soon established contact with Nathu. From here on, the game took a new turn. Somewhere, it junctioned with the lives of both Nathu and Rajjan. Although the work did not bring in any handsome income, at least it kept them going. And the main thing was that they felt important.

Even though the job of informing had had its origin in the feud between Rajjan and Nathu its further development brought the two so close to one another that they became, to a large extent, supplementary and complementary to one another. Most of Nathu's information for the police desk came from Rajjan himself, and Rajjan began to gather from Nathu information about police movements for the benefit of the dacoits.

Another interesting feature was that it was not only the informers who were happy with this machine-like smoothness of the operations, but also the police and the dacoits. Because of these informers both found their work facilitated greatly. The police and the dacoits both knew who, where and when. The dacoits would come in with confidence, carry out their task, and go away. Then the police would storm in. They would swoop down on the very places from where the dacoits had already fled. They would collect empty liquor bottles and half-burnt cigarettes, seal the place, and depart. Neither party's play-acting ever failed.

But amidst all this, one day, a major confusion occurred. The brother of a minister was one night returning in his car with his family after a hunting trip. Some dacoits stopped the car, killed them all, and went off with whatever they could lay hands on. This was a serious happening, and not only the police and the dacoits, but Nathu and Rajjan too realised that this time there was no easy way out.

Nathu wanted to hand over the bundle of lentils to his wife, and disappear from the village before the police went into action. He was about to gently tap on the back door of his house, when he realised that there was someone inside. Was it the police?

Gathering himself he decided to peep in through the gap in the door. This was circumspect. He knew that the back door squeaked, and would make an abominable racket at the slightest touch. The sounds from within were clearly audible, and they were funny.

With great caution he peeped in. The uniforms were familiar, undoubtedly the kind that the police wore, but surely he was not mistaken in recognising Madanlal among them? Strange, the uniforms of both were the same, but informing was separate and exclusive.

He didn't get much time to think, for what he saw happening on the bed near the wall drained the blood from his face.

Sitting on the floor Madanlal with his companions was gorging something in big mouthfuls. On the bed, lay his wife without a stitch of clothing, like the rag doll they put up at road crossings during rain festivals, and which they beat with sticks till it tore.

He drew back from the door. The voices coming from within rang cacophonously in his ears.

Bending, he put the bundle of lentils in the sun and turned back.

This time it was no game, but the real thing. These people were there and would be there for some time: Madanlal with his full gang of dacoits. Never mind if the police came, and seeing his wife thus, shared in the fun. But the police had to come, they had to.

Without wavering he made straight for the mound off the village.

Rajjan's shrieks were heard again, but this time they were partly drowned in the lesson on Mahatma Gandhi which

Kishan Babu told the children to recite at the top of their voices. It was a long time since he had taught them with such urgency.

In the fever-like heat which set the earth and sky quivering, when Nathu descended on the other side of the mound, through the quivering haze of the hot air which settled on his eyelids, he saw Rajjan later, while the police saw him first. Rajjan was on the ground, either lying or writhing, and every now and again, a policeman thrust a stick between his thighs, as if gauging the level of water there.

As soon as their eyes landed on Nathu everything suddenly came to a stop. Speeding up a little, Nathu came to them and without meeting their gaze whispered in the ear of one policeman: 'Madanlal with his entire gang is hiding in my house. Please hurry, huzoor.'

'Who called this bastard here?' The police inspector asked from a distance.

Running up to him the policeman told him what Nathu had said. For a moment the Inspector stood in complete bewilderment, as if preparing for a tricky scene. Then he stood up. He shouted to the jeep driver and said to the constable, 'Put this accused in the jeep. And take this other fellow too. Hurry up,' he said, pointing at Nathu.

Nathu ordinarily would have smelt a rat at such an order. But after what he had seen just now in his hut he had no hesitation in going up to the gang even though he was unarmed. He climbed into the back seat of the jeep on his own. Rajjan was flung between the seats and the policemen got in smartly.

'Go by the longer route. Drive along the babool forest there.'

The jeep turned back all right, but did not turn into Nauban. Instead it went past some distance. Nathu noted this, but thought the police would encircle the dacoits in their own way.

Just then the Inspector shouted 'Stop!' The jeep halted.

Pressing the point of his boot into Rajjan's ribs, the Inspector said, 'Tell this piece of dirt to get down. If he resists, throw him out'.

Perhaps a man dealt with in this manner suddenly becomes strong. For, with a little effort by the police, Rajjan not only tumbled out, but also shakily rose to his feet.

'You too. Get down,' the Inspector barked at Nathu. A little insulted at this uncivil manner Nathu got down from the jeep.

The moment he stepped down, the Inspector screamed, 'Run! Run immediately!'

Nathu could not understand.

'Will you bastard run or not? Want a beating?'

Nathu fell back a little at first, and then started running at a very slow pace. Now, because his back was towards the jeep he could not see anything. He only heard Rajjan's piteous cries as if begging for mercy. And before he could turn his head to look he heard the ear-splitting sound of a gunshot. He wanted to turn his head and look but just then he felt if someone pushed him savagely from behind, and a slab of meat swung out in front of his chest. He wavered and fell. Birds flew and started twittering shrilly. After falling Nathu's pain somehow miraculously ceased.

The jeep backed and drove away. Bot the corpses lay there. Nobody knew when a policeman threw a rusty pistol near them. The birds became silent after a while. But the call of that sad bird kept ringing: 'Get up, son, son, son...'

Ramakant

Disturbance

Off and on mother would say, 'We are in for bad times.'

We would put two and two together. Mother must have told Father to bring vegetables or some other household article from the bazaar for the evening and the next morning.

'Oh, yes, of course,' Father would have said. 'Hand me my bag and the money.' Mother would have placed both by his side but father would have shown no sign of getting up. 'I've given you the money and the bag,' Mother would have reminded him. 'Can't you see them lying there?' 'Oh, yes, I'm leaving in a minute,' Father would reply. 'Just let me rush through this news item.' Don't you see the fire in the stove going waste?' There would have been an edge to her voice. 'Why don't you go? The news can wait.' Father would have suggested: 'Why allow the fire to go waste? Make the *rotis* in the meanwhile.' The *rotis* would have been made. And, Father, his eyes still glued to the newspaper, would have said. '*Arre*, the *rotis* are done! Don't you have some pickles or chutney? That will do.'

'It may, for you. But Mallu and Gullu have to go to school early. There is never any milk or butter for them. With some vegetables they would at least eat a couple of *rotis* each and carry on till afternoon.'

'Then send one of them to get the vegetables.'

'No, that's out of the question,' Mother would have overruled him. 'The bazaar is not nearby. And how risky walking on those reads is. Rickshaws, tongas, cars—all speeding along. And those boys of the *mohalla*, are menaces ever ready for brawl. If you can't go, why don't you say so? I'll take over the job of rushing around too, and you can read your newspaper in peace. Oh, this wretched life of mine...'

'All right, all right, stop bickering.' Father would have carefully folded the newspaper and put it away and then picked up the money and the bag and left for the bazaar.

This was practically the daily routine. On his way back from office, Father would bring a book to read at home. They were generally old books picked up at junk shops. Some were without binding and some with their pages falling apart. His bed was in a corner of the room. Reclining on it, he would spend a long time arranging and putting together the pages of the book and then get down to reading it. That was when Mother would descend on him, nagging him to go to the bazaar.

One day this sequence changed.

That year the winter had set in early. In other years there was plenty of time to remove the quilt covers, have them washed and their padded cotton threshed anew. But that winter there was no time for this renovation. We had to use old quilts. Their cotton padding had become loose and shifted in places, but to set it right now was out of the question.

My coat had become tight and my sweater had sprung holes. I would wear it over a shirt and then cover it with another shirt.

It was intensely cold that day. When I placed a cup of tea before Father my teeth were chattering.

'Why don't you put on your coat?' Father asked me.

'It has become a size too small for me.' I replied. 'It fits Mallu all right but not me. Please have a new coat made for me.'

'You mean it's too tight for you?'

I took my coat from Mallu and wore it to show him. The sleeves were four inches above the wrists, and the whole thing was so tight that I could not button it up.

'You are growing up fine,' Father patted me on my back, while scrutinizing me carefully. The laugh lurking in the corners of his moth broke out. I had never seen him laugh. Even his eyes seemed to be laughing. But only for a moment. The next moment they were sad again. The haunting sadness habitual to them spread again.

That day he did not read a newspaper or a book. He placed the newspaper and book on the shelf above his bed, and resting the nape of his head on his palm kept staring at the ceiling a long time. When Mother asked him to go for the vegetables, he did not hem and haw at all. He picked up the money and the bag and went out quietly. After that for many days he did not bring any newspaper nor any book from the junk shop.

We came to know about it many days later. One afternoon when we returned from school we found Father sitting on a stool near the window and poring over something. Raising his head he glanced at us and then returned to his poring. As though his gaze would be stilled there for ever. For us there were always the morning's left-over *chapatis* to eat in the afternoon. But that afternoon we did not get them. Unlike other evenings Mother did not ask Father to go to the bazaar either. At night Mother placed two *chapatis* each before us with salt and water to wash them down with, and started sobbing.

Still crying she told us—Father had lost his job two months ago.

We again put together the sequence of events.

Every morning Father would go out in search of a job. He would leave home even before we set out for school and would return late in the evening. He would enter the house very tired, and going limp, sit on his bed for a long time, holding his head between his hands. In the other corner of the room we boys would sit studying. We would try to look unaware of what was going on. Mother would pull up a stool before Father and place some food on it for him. We noticed that the quantity of food kept decreasing day by day. We feared that a day might come when there would be nothing on the plate. Father would eat one *chapati* and then get up saying, 'I'm not hungry.' Soon we all started doing the same. We would take a bite or two of the food, gulp down a huge quantity of water and declare, 'Not hungry.'

In the beginning it was a pretence, but soon it became real and a habit. Our hunger really decreased.

Mother began living in a state of fear. Her fear-ridden self was strange, unfamiliar. Now she did not speak strongly about anything. She did not go on at Father for reading. But Father did not give her occasion, for he had almost given up reading. He did try to read, lying down, but he would soon put away the book, turn off the light and go to sleep. Seeing his changed habits, Mother would get even more frightened.

One day a man came with Father. We knew the man. He ran a junk shop by the road-crossing.

Mother went about collecting a lot of things from remote corners of the house and heaped them in the middle of the room. Last of all she brought out her sewing machine. We felt she might collapse while placing it on the floor. The man gave her a hand with it. Our fear was baseless. Carefully she put the machine on the floor, wiped her hands on her sari end with finesse and detail, bargained over every item.

That evening, after many days, Mother urged Father to go to the bazaar. That evening we too did not complain of lack of appetite.

But this did not last long.

Mother said to Father, 'Why don't I look for work?'

'You?' Father said. 'What will you do?'

'How do I know? That's why I'm asking you?'

'And I am telling you forget about it... Just for a few days the going will be hard, it'll get all right soon.'

The 'few days' passed rapidly. Our troubles did not pass. Mother did not talk about work to Father again. But yes, one day she went out somewhere with two or three women of the neighbourhood and brought back a lot of cloth. Immediately she set to work cutting the cloth. By the evening she had cut many petticoats and blouses and had tacked them by hand.

Father came home in the evening, and saw the job she had done. Surprised he started to say something but then kept quiet.

Mother went out every third or fourth day. She brought cloth, cut and tacked. Then one of the women going to the bazaar would complete the stitching and take them to the shopkeeper. But she could not bring cloth every day. Sometimes there was no work and she had to come home empty-handed.

Father had given up reading. One evening when he returned home there was a stranger with him.

Father made him sit down, went to his cupboard, and one by one, drew out the books and spread them on the floor. The man was a dealer in waste paper. He examined each book carefully, consigning it to its special lot, according to its state.

When he had classified all the books in this manner, he made some calculations. 'Babuji, I'll pay twenty rupees for the whole lot,' he said at last.

Mother was silently watching the goings-on. Hearing the amount proposed, she stepped forward, forestalling Father's reply.

'Leave them alone. We are not going to sell the books.'

Caught in a quandary, the dealer looked at Father.

'*Bhai*, don't pay attention to her,' Father said.' But I must say that you are offering a very low price.'

'No, no,' Mother said in a firm voice. 'Even if you give a hundred rupees we are not going to part with them.'

'They are of no use to me any more,' Father said. 'I'll sell them off and buy new books with the money.'

After some haggling the bargain was ultimately struck at twenty-five rupees. The dealer tied the books into bundles and carried them off. Handing over the money to Mother, Father said, 'You worry for nothing, Our bad times are not yet over—it's just that.'

'But you said that you were selling them to buy new books,' Mother said. 'You swear by all of us that you will use the money only for what you said.'

That day again Mother could not control herself and kept crying for a long time.

The next week Father got a job. When he returned he did not look fagged out as on other days. He did not throw himself on his bed either. As soon as he stepped into the house, he washed his hands and face and asked for food. In the midst of eating he announced the good news.

'There you are!' Mother said triumphantly. 'I knew something would turn up. Didn't I say so all along?'

'They will pay me ten rupees less. But still I've accepted it. It's better than no work.'

Mallu had long since given up squabbling with me. Today, after many days he pinched me. I thumped him on the back. He ran up to Mother whimpering and complained about me. Mother scolded both of us but her eyes twinkled with laughter. It appeared as if we were seeing Mother and Father after many years. Mother picked up Mallu and caressed him. She also said some nice words to me and made me sit by her side.

When father received his first pay he had new clothes made for us and bought us new canvas shoes. He went back to bringing second-hand books in the evening when he came home, and Mother, as unsuccessful as ever in making him budge to get the vegetables, began be-moaning her lot again.

One day Father again did not bring any newspaper or book with him.

That day I had put Mallu's ball in my school bag and he had bickered with me the whole day. But now he forgot the ball.

Father sat on the bed, holding his head between his hands. Mother made tea and put it before him. For a long time he did not even look at it. Mother was feeling shaky within. 'Drink your tea. It's getting cold.'

'Yes, will.'

'What's happened today, why're you sitting like this? Have you been fired from your job?'

'No, they haven't told me to go.'

'Then why are you sitting like this? Are you ill?'

'No.'

'Then?'

'I don't know whether I'll be up to this job. That's what is worrying me.'

'What makes you say that?'

Father did not speak for some time.

'Why don't you speak? If you've not lost your job then what's worrying you?' Mother said, feeling a little reassured.

'It's more dreadful than losing my job,' Father said.

Mother was fanning the fire in the stove. Her hand remained arrested in the air.

'Yes, more dreadful than losing my job,' Father repeated as if soliloquising. 'Understand?'

'But didn't you know before?' Mother asked.

'I knew of it all right. Some of us were employed to fill the places of those who had gone on strike. Today they came in procession and staged a demonstration. There were about twenty-five or thirty of them. Their women and children were with them. And then the police swooped on them. They were carried away in trucks.'

'What about the others? Have they also decided to quit?'

'I don't know about the others,' Father said. 'But will it be right to stick to this job?'

Mother did not say anything.

Father too remained silent for a while. Then he said, 'You haven't told me. What do you think? Will it be right to work there?'

'What do you want me to say? If you don't want to work, who am I to force you?'

The fire had died in the stove Mother did not seem to have the strength to fan the fire and we all felt that the fire would never kindle again in the stove.

Father flopped on the string bed. His glance fell on us.

'What are you standing around for? Go and play,' he shouted at us.

We pretended not to have heard him.

He shouted again, 'Go out and play. Go out! At least at this moment, don't stand before me.'

Scared, we huddled together in a corner. But why was he shouting at us like this? We could not put two and two together and come to any conclusion this time.

Govind Mishra

The Splinter

The night was young but winter darkness had descended on the village. At its lower level a sheet of bluish smoke had thickened into an opaque blackness. Today was market day at Rampura. On this day people from here and the villages around came to buy and sell and lay in stock for the week. They returned home only in time for the evening. They came home on foot, or on bicycles or in bullock carts.

They were two. Tough, lively youths, within them an elastic tension, like a savagely growling dog held in leash, absolutely taut... They stopped at the door. Then, with hands that seemed to know their job, they rattled the door chain and put their ears to the door. They were right. Only Paltu and his mother were inside. Paltu's mother's voice rose from some corner of the house and advanced towards them.

'Have your father and mother given you no name—why don't you tell your name?' Paltu's mother muttered angrily.

'Sister-in-law, I'm Jaggu. Paltu's father met us at the market. He told us to come here, and said, he would follow close at our heels. Something important to talk with him.'

Paltu's mother crept right up to the door and they thought it was the right time to dole out the information to her to set her mind at rest. She opened the door and led them in, spread a cot for them in the courtyard and watched them settling down.

'What's it, brother? Where are you from? Never seen you before.'

'We live in the city—both of us.'

Not a very big lie. They were runaways to the city in search of jobs. The city gave them no job but it initiated them into night life such as seeing late cinema shows which sharpened their wits and made their fingers nimble. This had set them dreaming—the dream of this century—the dream of becoming rich. They hadn't yet become hardened city sharks.

'So you are city people. Bhaiyya, earlier the man who wore pants stood out from others. But now anyone you set your eyes on is seen going about in pants... All right, brother, make yourselves comfortable. I've my kitchen to see to.'

As soon as Paltu's mother disappeared into the kitchen they looked around. One of them gestured to his companion and the other muttering, 'Oh, how cold! Oh, how cold!' went to the door, and fastened the door chain and sharply looked around. The first one moved to the kitchen door to mount guard.

'Sister-in-law, where's the brazier? We want to warm our hands. It's very cold. Just tell us where. We'll light it ourselves.'

'It's lying near the cot. The cow-dung cakes are also lying nearby. See if some embers are still left in the ash. If not, bring the brazier here. I'll give you a live charcoal or two.'

He ran and brought the brazier and then fetched some cow-dung cakes which he placed near the kitchen door. Breaking them into small pieces he placed them on the brazier. Some fire still smouldered under the ash. As it ignited, smoke billowed and a smoke screen rose between the kitchen and the courtyard. He sat down in such a way as to make it seem that his companion on the other side of the screen was also warming himself at the fire, while the fact was that his companion had already gone into the inner room and seemed to have got the hang of affairs there.

'The weekly market has lost its old charm,' he said pressing his calves with his palms.

'Well, son, prices have gone so high that one just doesn't know what to eat and what to wear. In my father's time every two years or so we saw a new pair of calves tethered outside our door...'

Paltu's mother was set now, wound up like a mechanical toy, she went on and on without getting derailed. As for the young visitor he seemed to have nothing to do in this world but to bask before the fire. Paltu's mother kept at her chores, to the accompaniment of a patter of talk, beside throwing in a word or two at Paltu who was sitting at her side eating his food.

Thin slivers of wood were burning in the stove, making a crackling sound. The cow-dung cakes had started blazing in the brazier, particles of hard ash falling from them. A flame would dark from the brazier and suddenly die out. Time crawled. That's the trouble in villages. In the city you never had to count the hours. Here time planted itself on your brow and stayed put there in a vicious manner. How long would Paltu's mother go on jabbering? What was he to say to keep up the conversation?

'Sister-in-law, which village do you come from?' he fired the question at her the moment she paused.

'Biraura... And you brother?'

'I... I'm also from Biraura.'

'Oh, you should have told me before. So we are brother and sister, so to say. How odd—I'm your sister and you've been calling me sister-in-law all this time! Paltu, look who is sitting here. Your maternal uncle.'

The visitor's heart stirred a bit. But he knew that in these villages around, everybody was somebody's maternal or paternal uncle or aunt. Even Harijans were addressed in these terms. Relationships were forged between one village and another on these terms. If a girl of one village was married into another village the elders of the girl's village would not drink water from the well in her in-laws' village. The entire village was regarded as the girl's husband's home. All this seemed farcical to him. Would they eat with the Harijans they addressed as uncle and aunt?

'So, brother, whose house in Biraura?'

He started as if a cow had suddenly kicked him and its hoof had hurt him. He became tense. He had said it on the spur of the moment but it was creating problems. He tried to get a grip on the situation.

'Now how do I know... My great-grandfather left the village and settled down in Kanpur. Then from generation to generation we kept hearing that we originally belonged to Biraura.'

'So what, brother? We may settle down anywhere but we still belong to Biraura. Call me sister, I'll serve you food. Yes, both of you sit down to eat. This good fortune does not come a sister's way every day—to feed a brother in her in-law's home.'

A small ball of emptiness rolled down his throat and into his gullet. He suddenly lost his tongue. His brain was quite fertile and he could talk engagingly but it was clear that the more he talked here the more he would sink into a morass. There was something in Paltu's mother's soft-spoken words which wove a spidery gossamer thin web around him. He must stay away from this web of illusion. He must just do his job and scurry off. He tried to appear calm to Paltu's mother but a storm raged inside him. His partner should have emerged by now. But he was still in that back room, tinkering around. Outside, in the lane, every once in a while the sound of shoes creaking along and the buzz of conversation rose in bursts, adding to his unease. People had started returning from the market. Paltu's father could show up any moment. Or a chance visitor could drop in.

'So brother may I serve you food?'

'Oh sister, where's the hurry?'

'Oh, you want to eat with your brother-in-law?'

'Yes...'

'Don't wait for him. He may turn up right now or he may not come till midnight.'

'The fact is we have eaten our fill at the market.'

He said it with an air of finality as if he were slashing down a wild bush with one stroke of the knife. Paltu's mother's persistence irked him. And that fellow in the back room—quite safe and secure, while he was being grilled here. He did not hear what Paltu's mother said to him in reply. He only saw her pulling out the faggots from the hearth and dousing them with water. Steam mixed with smoke rose in the air. Paltu had finished eating.

He coughed loudly as a warning to his companion to finish his job quickly. Paltu's mother could emerge from the kitchen any moment. As soon as she made a move to come out of the kitchen he would bang shut the kitchen door and bolt it from outside. She would raise an alarm, without doubt. But they must escape before the neighbours heard her cries. If she came out and saw them in their true colours that was the end. The women of this village were a fierce lot. They were the loving kind, no doubt, but it was said that they were capable of rushing out alone into the darkness to chase a thief.

Paltu's mother had tidied up the kitchen and pushed the used utensils to one side. Then she put Paltu astride her waist, and picking up the lantern in the other hand, started to come out of the kitchen. This was his chance. Pounce before she could come out, gag mother and child, tie them up, and bolt the kitchen door from outside. That would give them a little more time to make their escape.

But he just kept sitting there without stirring. Something inside him had suddenly wilted. As if he could not do this to Paltu's mother. There was something in this woman that curbed violence. He began brooding and then his blood cooled down. He felt that he was betraying his partner and could put him in trouble. It was his job to keep Paltu's mother occupied. And he had already made a hash of the whole thing. But why blame him alone? Why couldn't that idiot get over with it fast? He felt a like grumbling—partly at his helplessness and partly at the situation. But he must take hold of himself and keep Paltu's mother at bay as he had done hitherto.

She had now come into the courtyard and he followed her there, carrying the brazier with him.

'Come sister, warm your hands at the fire.'

'Where's the other brother gone?'

'He is a tobacco addict. He's gone out to buy it.'

'What kind of brother is he? He should have told me before going. I've lots of tobacco in the house. Haven't you seen Paltu's father eating it all the time?'

Paltu's mother put the lantern down and sat Paltu near the brazier. She again picked up the lantern and moved towards the kitchen.

'There's a wretched black cat around here. Even if I doze off for a minute that queen steals into the kitchen and eats everything she finds.'

Muttering, she poked into every corner of the kitchen. It could be lurking anywhere—behind a pot, or under a shelf. Now was his chance. Follow the woman into the kitchen, tie her up and then Paltu in the courtyard... No, he would cry out and as every one knows a woman becomes ferocious as a lioness where her child is concerned... Thinking again! Since when had he given himself up to so much thinking?

Just then his partner came walking limply and sat down by his side. He had heard every word of what was spoken in the courtyard, like oil falling drop by drop from a wad of cotton. Stretching out both hands he held them before the fire in the brazier, more or less in the position of 'hands up.'

'Well?' he whispered loudly.

His partner was silent. A stale coldness lay over his face.

'Nothing?' he probed his partner again. The partner raised his eyes and lowered them again. His face looked worn with helplessness. He licked his lips and swallowed the saliva gathered in his mouth.

Both seemed to have gone to pieces. How things had taken such a turn was beyond their comprehension. The strategy they had drawn up would certainly have flopped in the city. People would have looked out of the peep-hole and refused to open the door. But here it was new. It had every chance of success. But here they had got involved in a new kind of trouble. There was no obstacle before them which could be removed but there was something invisible which gradually spread around them and then pierced into them.

'Sister, we must be going.'

'Why? Tired?'

'Yes, so it seems.'

'If there's something I can give you, tell me.' I've heard one always falls short of money in the city...'

They couldn't keep sitting there. They got up—completely shattered. He pulled out a five rupee note for his pocket and held it out to Paltu's mother.

'Sister, buy sweets for Paltu on our behalf.'

Paltu and Paltu's mother came out to see them off.

'Paltu is asking when you will come again.'

Their eyes were lowered. Without looking up, they turned and gradually merged into the darkness.

Kashinath Singh

Go Your Way, Baba!

Devnath had stopped to buy a packet of Wills Filter from Mewalal's shop when he heard someone at the next shop asking the way to the lane in which he lived.

Devnath was not the only one living in that lane. There were hundreds of others there and the man could be bound for any of the houses in the lane. But the man's voice, however, had a familiar ring. Devnath felt curious but dared not look that way; he kept looking the other way. Instead of taking the straight route, he decided to go home by a circuitous route.

In winter the night descends as soon as the sun sets and it becomes very cold.

Even before he entered the house, he saw that his two children were as usual playing noisily in the inner room and his wife Asha, was enjoying their pranks. Devnath was feeling a bit out of sorts. He reproved the children and after driving them upstairs, told Asha that he had a splitting headache and was going to lie down for a while. He added that if a visitor called she should tell him that he was not well. 'And look, there's no need for you to go down. Just convey the message through the railing.'

Asha gave her husband an anxious look and felt his forehead. It seemed to be slightly hot. But what really puzzled her was that only a few minutes ago when he had gone down to buy cigarettes he looked all right. She offered to massage his forehead with oil. At this he suddenly flared up. 'Do as I tell you,' he said.

Asha quietly proceeded towards the stairs.

Devnath closed the door, pulled the quilt over his face and then sank his head into the middle of the pillow which was stuffed with silk cotton, in order to cover his ears with the raise ends.

Then he abruptly pushed away his quilt and ran towards the stairs. 'Don't tell him that I'm ill,' he called out to his wife. 'Tell him that I'm out of town.'

Having thus guarded himself against all possible eventualities, he again lay down. He kept thinking of the impending danger and tried to take his mind off it. He would have liked to think of something which should be both interesting and profitable. It would help induce sleep and he tried to concentrate his mind on something really pleasant. He decided that the house that he would build for himself in Manas Nagar would have Ashoka trees at its four corners. There would be a beautiful lawn in front and its guest room would be so beautiful and well-furnished that the Commissioner Saheb when he came on tour would prefer to say here than at the government Circuit House. By that time he too would have been elevated to the position of an 'A' class officer and the Commissioner would have no hesitation in putting up with him. What would his guest room look like? Why, he would pattern it after the cottages he had seen in Mussoorie and Nainital.

He heard a sound outside and Asha opened the door. Is someone by the name of Deo living somewhere around here?'

Devnath looked at his wife and beat his head in despair.

'I have been telling the old man—he looks like a villager—to go away but he insists that someone answering to this name lives here.' Asha came out with an explanation, clarifying that she was not to blame.

Devnath sat up in bed. Throwing away his quilt he slipped his feet into his slippers. Why was his wife so stupid. A hint is enough for the wise but... He was seething with anger. Without exchanging another word with his wife, he walked through the drawing room and came out.

'*Arre*, Bechu Baba! Is it you?' He rubbed his eyes and looked at the old man. 'Where have you come from? I hope you did not have much trouble finding the house.'

Bechu Baba was carrying a jar on his head. Panting, he took the jar down and carried it into the drawing room. Then he removed the rough woollen blanket from his body and placed it on the arm of the sofa. Taking off his turban he rubbed its end on his thick moustache and grizzly beard, and stood his staff in a corner of the room. His gaze travelled round the room and at last came to rest on Devnath who was sitting on the other side of the glass-toped centre-table. Baba blinked and smiled.

He kept smiling for a while. Then he got up and went over to Devnath, felt his head, jaws, shoulders, arms and knees with his hands. Bringing his eyes near his face he said in a voice thick with emotion, 'Child, Devu, it is you, isn't it? You have become like a dream to me. You have your house, your village, the sign of your forefathers. You are not living too far away. You must come sometimes. Why don't you? That's what's going to stand you in good stead. In the end you'll come back to us, I'm telling you that.'

True to style Baba was talking in a loud voice as if Devnath was deaf. Devnath's children had come to the door and were looking at Baba with curiosity and fear. They would peer at him and then look at each other.

Standing at the door against the light they cast a shadows which did not escape Baba's notice. 'Our grandchildren?' he asked Devnath. Devnath nodded. Baba stood up and stretched out his hands. 'Come here, children. Do you recognise your Baba?' he said thumping his chest.

Seeing Baba advancing, the children fell back and then bolted.

'No, they don't recognize me. How can they?' Baba looked at Devnath and laughed. 'See, how they have grown!' he said resuming his seat. Time flies. When I last saw them they were so small.'

Devnath nodded but did not join in his laughter. He placed a glass and jug of water on the side table and went up to fetch something to eat.

Asha was boiling water on the gas for tea while the children stood by her side narrating to her what they had seen downstairs. Tugging at her house coat the younger boy was excitedly describing Baba.

'Just a cup of tea will not do,' Devnath said as he stood at the kitchen door.

'Who's this village yokel, anyway?' Asha asked.

Devnath explained: 'Didn't you know Sudama who was our neighbour in the village. He is his father.'

'Devu!' the elder boy said in mimicry, and ran out clapping his hands. Devnath pretended to chase him and they all started laughing.

Asha suddenly turned grave. She was trying to decide what to offer the old man to eat. Then she had a brain wave. She went into the back room and returned with two sweets on a plate.

Devnath smelt them and made a face. 'This looks stale and stinks' he said. 'How old is it?'

'Agarwal brought these sweets for us only a week ago. Nobody would touch it. Ultimately the maid-servant took away the whole lot. Only these two pieces were left—lucky for him.' She put down the plate and began to pour out the tea.

'And what about the sweets Shamlal brought for us yesterday?'

Stop carping now. Must you pick holes in everything? Any kind of sweets would seem good to him. Sweets are so scarce in a village.' Asha placed the cup of tea in the tray next to the sweets.

Devnath felt sorry for Baba. He knew that the old man probably could not discriminate between good and not good, and might enjoy the sweets. But he did not quite like the tone in which Asha had spoken.

He picked up plate and cup and went downstairs. But he was taken aback as he entered the drawing room. He had not expected it to be in such a mess. Fortunately he had removed the carpet a few days ago. Right from the door up to the centre-table and the sofa the floor was wet. It was evident that Baba had washed his hands and feet and even rinsed his mouth in the drawing room. His staff was still standing in a corner against the wall but his other things had travelled into the inner room with him.

His wet foot-marks led in the direction of the threshold. 'Oh, he has ruined everything!' Devnath groaned. A fear seized his heart. 'Baba!' he called out, and entered the bed room. Baba was lying stretched out on his bed, one foot resting upon the other, their soles cracked and caked with dust. Devnath noticed three or four grey stains on his milk-white bed-sheet and his heart sank. He felt bad but then realized that the fault lay with him. He should have shown him the bathroom and explained to him how to use it. But Baba could have asked, he added to himself.

'Here, please have tea,' Devnath said, placing the plate and the cup of tea on the table.

Baba got up with a groan and picking up a sweet from the plate examined it closely and then bit at it with the few teeth that were still intact in his mouth. He looked at Devnath and opening his mouth wide popped the piece into his mouth. Sweets really are a scarce commodity in a village.

After finishing the sweets, Baba picked up the cup of tea, blew on it three or four times and then drank it noisily. The very first sip burnt his tongue and he promptly put down the cup.

'Is this terrace ours too?' he asked, pointing towards the roof. Then he asked in detail about everything in the room—the photographs, paintings, the clay and metal statues, toys, two-in-one, the cassette stand, the drawing room sofa set and carpet. He would touch each article and fire a question. Most of the explanations went over his head. The cost of many things astounded him. He said that with the same money one could have bought a bullock, a buffalo or a sugarcane crushing machine. The photographs were hanging a little high up on the wall, slightly out of the range of his vision and he touched them with the tip of his lathi. But what surprised him most were the roses in the flower vase, leaves and all. What kind of flowers were these that neither withered nor grew and that needed no manure or soil; they were only dipped in water and yet they looked so fresh.

Devnath was getting impatient, following close at Baba's heels. But he was pleased too. On returning to the village, Baba would surely tell everyone about his affluence.

'They are made of plastic,' he explained in a loud voice and laughed.

'Hm! That's why.' Baba picked up the flower vase and took it close to his nose. He rubbed the flower leaves and petals between his fingers and put the flower vase down where he had picked it up.

'I feel so happy, son,' he beamed at Devnath. 'People earn money right and left. But there are only a few who earn prestige and honour along with the money. May God enhance your prestige.'

Standing behind him, Devnath twiddled his fingers modestly.

'Well, tell me did you buy all these things or get them as dowry?' he asked sitting down on the bed. He also asked him about his salary and how much he made under the table.

Satisfied, he thumped his chest with pride and gulped down his tea. Then he went to the window which was covered with wire mesh. Standing against the window, he pressed his right nostril with his thumb and drawing in his breath blew his nose noisily. 'You've done so well, Dau. You lack only one thing—a cow. If you buy a cow you won't have to worry about providing milk to the children Devnath,' he came back and settled down on the bed. 'I was about to leave the village when I suddenly remembered how you used to love cane juice. You would roam around the Siwan for hours sucking sugar cane. It came to me, that you must be going without sugar cane juice and your wife and children must be pining for it. You can get everything in the city but not that kind of fresh cane juice. Sudama did not think much of my suggestion and he kept muttering under his breath. But I put my foot down. I said, no, I won't go to my son empty-handed. I had green peas plucked from Kharpat's field—you know the place. It's where the neem is standing. I also obtained oven-hot parched gram and finally a jar of sugarcane juice from the sugarcane press. Just have a look!' Baba removed the mango leaf covering the mouth of the jar, spilling some cane juice on the floor in the process. 'And look!' he proceeded to untie a bundle. Devnath's heart sank. He feared that Baba would unload handful after handful of parched gram on the bed, spoiling the entire bed-sheet. But mercifully, Baba again tied the knot of the bundle. 'Well, here they are. You couldn't be getting these things.

Devnath looked at the drops of cane juice Baba had spilled on the floor. It would not be long before ants and other insects invaded the room. The floor had already become quite sticky and he must have it swept and washed.

'You haven't told me the purpose of your visit,' Devnath said.

'Purpose?' Baba found the question very odd. 'So you want to know the purpose of my visit?' Baba gave Devnath a withering look. 'With what purpose does a father visit his son?'

Devnath immediately realized that he had been tactless. 'No, Baba, I was just asking what has brought you here?'

'Then say that,' Baba heaved a sigh of relief. 'Son, I want to get admitted into a hospital. Any hospital you life. I can't bear it any longer. Sometimes I get such excruciating pain in my stomach. It becomes unbearable. I feel as if I'm going to faint. I have been having this trouble for the last three years. But now its frequency has increased.'

Devnath listened gloomily as Baba spoke about his urine, stools, appetite, breathing trouble, and the pain in his chest, his knees and the small of his back. The conclusion was that he must get admitted into a hospital. Devnath was a big shot and he commanded great influence. All the city doctors, hakims and vaids must be his friends. He could easily get him admitted in a hospital and arrange for his treatment. 'Well,' Baba pulled up his vest and pointed towards the fold of his dhoti, 'Don't worry I've pinched some money from Sudama. But first take this jar of cane juice and the bundle of parched gram upstairs. The children must be keen to know what Baba was brought for them.'

Devnath was either not listening at all or listening very attentively. He was looking at the floor where ants had already appeared and were forming themselves in a line. There was a frown on Devnath's face, because Baba's demeanour and bearing gave no indication of illness. Devnath kept looking at the ants, the frown deepening on his face.

'What's there to worry, silly fellow!' Baba got up and thumped Devnath's back, thinking that he was worrying about him. Holding him by his arm he made him rise to his feet. 'Get up. Take these things upstairs.' Devnath put on the light and went upstairs.

Sitting in the dining hall, the children were engrossed in their studies. They were reading from a book: 'It was summer. A starling sat on a tree.' Seeing the jar they put aside their books and ran towards Devnath. The elder boy shoved his hand into the bundle and the younger one put his hand into the jar. Seeing the cow-dung, on the jar, one shouted: 'Mummy, didn't we tell you? The old man looked very dirty.'

Asha was sitting in a chair, peeling vegetables. She looked at Devnath as he pulled up another chair and sat down by her side.

'Is he going to stay the night?' she asked Devnath.

He gave her a scornful look. 'Now you will rue it,' he said testily. 'Didn't I tell you to say I was not at home?'

'Don't you have any sense? Now that he had come all the way to the city would he have gone away without finding you? But...'

'Don't try to evade the point. He had once told me that one Buddhu Gaur from our village lives in the square here. He could have gone to stay with him. Who knows if he hadn't found me, he might even have gone back to the village.'

Asha kept quiet and started peeling potatoes.

'He has come to seek admission in hospital. It's a hell of a job. After getting admission he will expect me to look after him, buy medicines for him and get him the diet prescribed by the doctor.'

'Why don't you tell him you're too busy, and be done with it?'

'You don't know the ways of the village. He is father's older brother. They started living separately only ten years ago. He has always cared for me more than for his own son. If I turn him away everyone will taunt him: 'Well, what happened? You had great faith in your son! Now your understand the ways of the world!'

'Why hasn't he brought his son with him?'

'You mean Sudama? How could he? His crops would have been ruined in his absence. He is the only son. Besides, the son doesn't much care for him. *Arre!...*'

Devnath leapt forward. The children had dragged the jar towards the drain and were emptying out all the juice. By the time he stopped them the jar was empty. He shook it—only half a pitcherful of juice remained. He got hold of the older boy's ear and dragged him away.

'Oh, how it smelled, Papa!', the elder boy said

'Leave it there,' Asha said. 'We shall give it to the sweeper-woman in the morning.'

Devnath sat down holding his head between his hands. His mind seemed to have stopped working. Looking very grave, Asha got busy cleaning the rice, scanning her husband's face in between. Her eyes met his. 'I'm telling you,' she said seething with anger, 'I won't be able to cook food for him every day. Better engage a servant. Do as you please I would have managed it had it been a matter of two or three days. He is your Baba, not mine. He is nothing to me. He can call his daughter-in-law here, take a room on rent, or live in a dharamsala, cook there and eat. I don't want to get involved in this rigmarole.'

Looking very adult, the children were intently listening to the discussion between Papa and Mummy. When Mummy talked they would look at Papa's face to gauge his reaction and when it was Papa's turn they would scan Mummy's face.

Going by Devnath's expression, it appeared he was not paying much heed to what his wife was saying. He kept puffing away at his cigarette and scratching his head or leg.

'There's one more problem to reckon with,' Devnath said. 'If we get him into hospital and look after him, he will go back to the village and sing my praises to all and sundry. Then we'll be done for. As soon as anyone gets a cold, he'll come to the city for a holiday, to see the circus or have a change of climate. Let alone all those who are really sick or dying.'

Asha pulled a long face, turned on the gas and put a pot on the ring. Devnath threw away his cigarette and went down.

Baba was lying on the bed, snoring heavily. His eyes were slightly open and his lips trembled rhythmically, making a hissing sound. Saliva trickling from the left corner of his mouth had wetted the pillow. Worst of all, flies had invaded the room in swarms and were buzzing around his face and neck.

Devnath immediately put on his suit and carefully adjusted the knot of his tie. Then waking up Baba he took him out and started his scooter. Seeing the *lathi* in Baba's hand, he stopped the engine. 'There's no need for the *lathi*,' he said in a loud voice. 'We are going to the doctor—to consult him.' Taking away the *lathi* from Baba he stood it against the wall of his room and came out. He was taking Baba to his friend Dr Garg who lived at the other end of the city, and who had visited them for some work a few days ago. He would serve the turn even though it meant some expenditure on petrol. Devnath decided to incur this expenditure, and soon they were flying through the city.

Sitting on the pillion, Baba was enjoying the ride but also feeling somewhat scared. Holding Devnath's seat firmly from behind, he kept looking right and left at the brightly lit shops. When he looked to the right, he missed the shops on the left and when he looked to the left he had to skip the shops on the right. And at times, out of fear, he missed the shops on both sides. He marvelled at the dexterity with which Devnath manouvered the scooter through the thick traffic. 'Wonderful' he would exclaim at Devnath's driving skill. As the scooter came out on the open road, he felt a little chilly and was about to pull his turban down over his ears when the scooter suddenly stopped with a jerk in front of a big building. The scooter barely escaped capsizing when Baba jumped down from his seat. Glancing at the shops flanking the building he followed Devnath into the doctor's clinic. As he looked at the number of patients in the waiting room he felt reassured that Devnath had brought him to no ordinary doctor. Without waiting for his turn, Devnath straightaway entered the doctor's clinic. 'My son!' Baba said with pride as he sat down on the bench and looked around at the waiting patients. 'He's a big man. Then a man came out and led him into the doctor's clinic.

Though the doctor looked young yet he appeared to be experienced and capable. Like Devnath, he also addressed him as Baba and tried to put him at ease. He asked him about his village, his land and his farming. Baba became sceptical about him. What kind of doctor had Devnath brought him to? Then the doctor took charge of him. He turned Baba's eyelids and examined his eyes. He examined his tongue, thumped his back and asked him to flex his knees. He applied his stethoscope to Baba's chest and measured his blood pressure. He asked Baba many questions, to which Baba replied in great detail.

After that the doctor laid Baba down on a narrow bed behind a curtain. Asking him to strip, he pressed his stomach and asked him questions about his stools, urine, his appetite and the kind of aches he suffered from. The examination over, he asked Baba to put on his clothes and come out.

The doctor expressed his suspicions to Devnath and said, 'I think it's just the initial stage. X-rays and investigations and a biopsy will have to be done. There's nothing to worry. I'm sure he will get well.'

Baba had heard the doctor's last sentence and he came up and stood next to Devnath. But now the doctor started talking to Devnath in English which was beyond Baba's comprehension.

Baba looked at the doctor inquisitively.

'I've explained everything to Mr Devnath,' the doctor said. 'There's nothing wrong with you.'

Gazing at the stethoscope and other instruments, Baba folded his hands.

'My God grant you long life, Sarkar,' he said gratefully.

No sooner had the words of blessing escaped his lips when Baba was overcome by embarrassment. 'Force of habit, you know,' he said to Devnath as they came out, 'We address the tehsil officials as sarkar. I hope the doctor did not feel offended.'

Devnath's reply was drowned in the roar of the scooter. Baba was bubbling with joy. 'Son, I feel so relieved,' he said. 'I'm so happy. But why are you looking so sad?'

Devnath was not sad but he was certainly worried. The harassment he was trying to avoid now seemed to have got him by th neck. True, he did not wish to take upon himself the responsibility of Baba's hospitalisation but somewhere in his heart he still had the feeling that all was not lost and he would get well. Baba was no stranger but a member of his family. They were one family till the brothers started living separately.

Devnath's mind was working on another plan but this too bristled with difficulties. Maybe he could take Baba's son, Sudama, into his confidence. What if he as an older cousin scolded Sudama for his neglect of Baba? But Sudama was a blockhead. At best he would turn up perhaps with his whole family. Sudama who had to take care of the land and could not afford to absent himself from the village for long might return after dumping his family here, leaving Devnath to look after the whole jingbang lot.

After doing some hard thinking, Devnath at last decided that for the time being he would keep the whole thing to himself.

As Baba got down from the scooter, he asked Devnath if he had the doctor's papers with him.

'What have you got to do with them?' Devnath asked in mock anger. 'Please go in and have your food. I'll be back in a minute.'

Devnath could have conveniently bought the prescribed medicines on the way back home. But in that case Baba would have kept an eye on him, plied him with unnecessary questions and asked what these medicines were meant for. He would also make a mental note of the cost of the medicines. Devnath bought 100 capsules of B complex, 50 tables of Liv 52 for five paise each and ten tablets of a pain killer. He was relived that it all cost him less than ten rupees.

Back home, he was breathing deeply as he sat before Baba and in spite of Baba's asking he could not tell him why he was panting so hard, for even speaking strained him.

Baba had finished his meal. He was in good spirits. He had covered his body with his blanket and was massaging his bald pate and smiling happily. From its smell, Devnath could easily make out that what he was applying to his head was not hair oil but Dettol which Baba had seen lying on Devnath's dressing table alongside his shaving kit. Baba too seemed to suspect it because he kept sniffing at his palms. Devnath felt no exasperation or anger because he was trying to appear normal.

'Here are your medicines,' he said, placing all the phials before Baba. He gave him directions as to which medicine was to be taken at what time and in what quantity.

Baba did not look at the medicine. Just kept gazing at Devnath. Then his grey eyebrows drooped over his eyelids. 'Have you eaten?' he asked in a feeble voice.

'No, not yet. I'm in no hurry.'

Suddenly Baba's eyelids fluttered and he started sobbing. 'For three months I've been asking Sudama to take me to the hospital: Please set apart a day for it, I told him. You must come with me.' But he had no time for me. And his wife is so foulmouthed that many times I leave the kitchen without eating. Today when I went to buy cane juice Sudama stopped me on the way. He said it would not be possible for me to travel so far, carrying a big jar on my head. I asked him to tell the servant Kharpu to carry the jar for me up to the bus stand. Sudama said that he could not spare the man as he had other work to do. But actually what upset him was that he could have made some jaggery from that cane juice. I asked his wife to give me some gram and then... But son, to whom am I to recount my woes?'

He started crying. 'And you? How different you are. When I set out from home the whole village mocked me. They thought you would teach me a lesson. But you have been running around for me all day at the cost of your own work. And for whom? You haven't once asked me where's the money for all these medicines going to come from?'

He kept talking between sobs and wiping his nose. 'When you were very small I used to carry you on my shoulders while ploughing the land. I used to carry you all round the village—even to the country fair. Yes, I did beat you—but only once. I gave you a very severe beating that time. It was because of your father. He was alive then. He blamed me for spoiling his son. Of course, you were also at fault. At somebody's instigation you threw Algu into the river, cot and all, while he was asleep at night.'

He narrated the whole story with gusto and began to laugh, while still crying. 'You had only one bad habit,' he added. 'You used to piss while perched on my shoulders. You...'

Laughter prevented his from completing his sentence. Then wiping the white hairs on his face he asked Devnath to come closer to him. Gathering his blanket he made room for him to sit by his side, fondled his head and secretively peeped into his eyes. 'The doctor told you too that there's nothing the matter with me didn't he?' he asked.

'Yes, he did. You must have heard him.' Devnath felt a bit scared at Baba's tone. But soon he controlled himself.

'That's what I wanted to make sure of,' Baba said happily, patting Devnath's back. 'Go. Eat and go to sleep. I'll leave early tomorrow morning.'

'How can you go tomorrow? You've just come.'

'But you've already done all you had to. Go and eat.'

Slowly climbing up the stairs, Devnath came to the dining hall door and stopped. This inner room was dark but they were still awake. Asha was telling the children about the old man, about his outlandish ways of eating and the way he had messed up the room, how boorish and backward and crude were the people of Papa's village. And how loudly they talk, yelling at the top of this voices.

'Mummy, Papa has locked the outer door,' one of the children said in a sleepy voice. Then Asha and the children stopped talking. Perhaps they had fallen asleep.

Devnath stood outside the door for a while. He could see the kitchen from where he was standing. He did not feel hungry. His eyes went to the jar which had travelled sixty miles by bus and part of the way on Baba's head in order to reach this drain pipe. His eyes grew moist.

He walked up to the railing on stealthy steps and sat down on the threshold. Outside, it was cold and still. In his imagination Devnath saw his dear little village—its orchards, the stirring of the leaves and the mangoes falling in the heavy wind, the planting of sugar cane and the fishes frolicking in the ponds. How they went fishing and stole water-chestnuts and how they went swimming in the tank. How many years had passed since then? Everything had vanished into thin air in the twinkling of an eye. He too must have once been as simple and naive as Baba. And now Baba was departing not for tomorrow but for ever. He could stop him. But no...

Suddenly he felt hungry. But the memory of the jar inhibited him from going to the dining room. He lit a cigarette and blew out the smoke.

'Forget it,' he said to himself. 'Let's go.' He got up and brushed the seat of his pants. 'Your whole life, the whole world and the era lie before you and you sit here getting sentimental about an insignificant old man!'

Asghar Wajahat

Cake

He brought his fist down hard on the table, and the table shook for a long time. 'I say that unless we shoot five hundred people at a time things will never be right!' After expending considerable lung power he started painting. Then he pressed his upper lip hard with his lower, and glared at me. He surmised correctly that I was smiling. Then he ceased staring and got busy with his plate.

Every day our talk at table was about politics. The lowly work of proof reading from two in the afternoon till eight at night generally put him in a cranky mood.

'Have you included yourself in the five hundred?' I asked.

'Why should I! Am I a crooked politician or a smuggler or a black marketeer raking in crores of rupees?'

He again glared at me, at which I laughed. He began staring at his plate.

'You people don't take anything seriously.'

After finishing his food he picked up the used plates and went into the kitchen. Mrs D'Souza, still seated in her chair, said, 'David, get me some water please.'

David returned with a jugful of water. After giving Mrs D'Souza a glass, he said to me, 'Drink water, mister, drink water.'

On my declining, he gave me a pitying look. 'Thanks to God, there's water the whole day here. If you lived in Indrapuri you would have known different. Well, if you don't want to drink water I do and will.' He drank off three glasses.

After the meal David Saheb begins work at the same table. Today too he sat down with his pile of proofs, after cleaning the table. He steadied the bricks under a leg of the table to keep it from wobbling. He sat on the broken chair, then he suddenly stiffened, and adjusted the glasses on his nose as though he were loading a gun. he pressed his lips in a special way. he began comparing the proofs with the manuscripts. The gun had started firing. In this manner Mr David kept reading proofs till midnight. While at it he would remove his glasses and put them on again at least fifty times. Something is wrong with the gun. Five years ago he had his eyes tested and bought a pair of glasses. His eyesight has deteriorated since then, but he has not changed his glasses. On the fifteenth of every month he talks about buying a new pair. But the cost of guns has risen steeply. In the midst of proof reading if he drinks water he cries 'Victory to Basu!' Basu is his boss against whom he has dozens of complaints. As far as I can see, all are legitimate. I too have the same kind of complaints—about three dozen—against my boss. Such grievances are the hallmarks of all low grade workers.

A soul killing job, Sir,' he tells me, raising his head. I mumble yes to prevent the talk from continuing. But he won't be quiet. Removing his glasses he rubs his eyes. These are days of high level bungling. Nobody bats an eyelid at small-scale corruption. The whole machinery has become rotten. These are not men, they are dogs... Before Independence I too was a staunch supporter of Mahatma Gandhi and thought nonviolence was the best policy. But now I think it is idiocy. Violence is the best policy. Hang five hundred people at the gallows. I tell you, these people should face a public trial, a public trial.'

'Who will conduct the public trial, Mr David?' I lost my temper. He's been talking this nonsense much too long.

He sits back, holding his head between his hands. 'If the left forces among the masses...' he keeps mumbling for a long time.

I once again save the hero of my detective novel from a hail of bullets.

'Why do you write these pot boilers for the sake of two or three hundred rupees?' he asks.

I smile and glance at his bundle of proofs, and he falls silent. He becomes grave.

'I think, sometimes, brother, are you and I to correct proofs and write cheap detective novels all our lives? Just think! How big the world is! We know how well life can be lived. How much comfort and peace there can be in life, how much beauty...'

'The problem is mine more than yours, David. You can do many things. Start a poultry farm, start a bakery...'

Closing his eyes he laughs, a cynical laugh, striking against every solid object in the room the laugh returns to the confines of his mouth.

After dinner he often strikes up thus. He can't put his mind to the work, and time hangs heavy on him. I feel like entering a fashionable colony, with a big iron rod in hand. David Sahib would of course be ready to go with me. There he starts raving and his pet words 'bitch', 'crook', 'nonsense', 'bungling', 'public trial', 'exploitation', 'class struggle' are heard again and again. In between he lets loose a barrage of Hindi abuses.

'What can be done now? After twenty five years of proof-reading what else can I do? I came to Delhi in 1948. My friend I've seen land in Defence Colony sell at three rupees a square yard, and now its value is four hundred rupees. From Nizamuddin to Okhla it was just jungle. No decent man was ready to live there. If I had bought land in Nizamuddin at that time I would have been a millionaire today. But at that time I didn't have the money, and today... There was a fellow, Potty, with me in Senior Cambridge. If you look at him today you would not believe that I was his class fellow. White as milk,

A-class health, a jeep, an Ambassador and a tractor, all this he owns. Has farms near Mirzapur. He bought that land at that time for ten rupees a *bigha*. He pressed me, 'You too buy, brother David, some four or five hundred *bighas*. Just facing his land was a plot of five hundred *bighas*. A-class fertile land. But in those days I was a different sort'. He gave a hollow laugh. 'Today his income is three lakhs a year. He has his own poultry farm, his own dairy, lives in style...' Mr David suddenly looked cheerful as if all that he described belonged to him. Putting aside the bundle of proofs, he said, 'I was destined to become Mrs D'Souza's tenant in this beautiful room.'

Pay Mrs D'Souza fifty rupees and you get a room. Pay twenty-five more and you get breakfast. Thirty rupees more, and you get dinner too, what Mrs D'Souza calls 'English food.' No tenant is allowed to remove the photographs, the walls mostly of Mrs D'Souza in her young days. In some photographs she is seen reading a book by candle light. In others her hair hangs down to her lap as she tries to look into space. Mrs D'Souza introduces some males in the photographs as British army officers, although they all look Indian. There is one photograph of her daughter, which stands on Mr David's table. The girl looks a tart. Tartishness oozes from her face so thickly that if you place a bowl under the photograph you would have to empty it ten times a day. The sight of her would drive anyone crazy. Some neighbours allege that it is the repeated exposure to this photograph that robbed Mr David of the urge to marry and the capacity to produce children. Mrs D'Souza has looked out for several Indian Christian girls for him. But to no avail. He has been reduced to ash by a charge of two hundred and fifty volt. And one day, driven to despair, Mrs D'Souza proclaimed him impotent in the neighbourhood, and took to changing her clothes in front of him.

Morning's second name is hurry. Hurried cups of tea without milk. Hurried ironing of clothes washed at night. Hurriedly polished shoes. A quick massage of the eyes to brace them for day-long proof reading. Bundles of proofs. Those corrected and those just come from the press, and again, those corrected and those come from the press, ad nauseam. The wretch of a chief compositor flings the galleys wham! Almost in his face. 'Look through them fast, babu, do it fast. The big boss wants to look through his column.' All life has become a proof on cheap galley paper, which we continuously correct.

Stepping out of the house and rushing to the bus stop, as though in pursuit of someone, we jump on the same bus. On the way, everyday, Mr David talks about the same things—the benefits of eating green vegetable, the starch content of each vegetable, and how, if you regularly eat chicken and eggs you can produce a son even at eighty. He knows very well the subtle differences between mutton and buffalo meat. His information about English food is encyclopaedic. How much flour is needed for a cake. How many eggs. How to mix the jelly and the fruit. How long to whip the milk. He has his own, special opinions about baking a cake. He has hundreds of formulae for creaming and glacing which no one in India knows now. Sometimes he says, these dhoti flapping people, how can they know anything of the arts of cooking and eating? Buy an enormous quantity of vegetables, put them in oil, and swallow them down that's all. The arts of cooking and eating are known only to the British and the Muslims. The British have departed, and as for the Muslims, they have grown dull by feeding on buffalo meat. Eat buffalo meat and your brain will become dull like that of a buffalo and you will be harnessed to an oil mill like a buffalo. At night you will fall upon your wife like a buffalo.'

Today again he reverted to his favourite topic. 'Breakfast of course, should be heavy.'

I nodded. Only a fool could disagree with this.

'Heavy and energy-giving.' He stopped in his tracks. Looking at a house being built he said: 'Looks like a blackmarketeer's house.' Then, with military stiffness he took out his glasses from his pocket, adjusted them on his nose and carefully surveyed the building. Gunfire blasted with a terrific explosion and the house came tumbling down.

'Just one glass of milk, four toasts, and butter, porridge and two eggs.' He sighed deeply like air escaping from a balloon.

'No, I don't agree with you. Fruit juice is a must. Without...'

'Fruit juice? If you have milk, fruit juice is not necessary'.

'What about a breakfast of *parathas* and eggs?'

'Very good! But the *parathas* must be light and soft'.

'And what if you have cake for breakfast?'

He laughed, a flat and bleak laugh.

It was many years ago. Around the time I first came to Delhi. David Saheb had got a cake made on his birthday. The budget had been carefully drawn up in advance. It added up to seventy rupees. On the first of the month David Saheb went to Khari Baoli to buy flour, sugar and dry fruits. All the stuff was re-weighed at home. Then he made enquiries about a good baker. Many of David Saheb's friends spoke highly of a baker in Daryaganj, so he went to him one day to talk it over, exactly like the prime minister of a country going to discuss matters of grave importance with the prime minister of another country. Mr David put him a question to which he had no answer. 'If you don't put all the materials in the cake and keep something back how will I come to know?' He himself came up with a solution to this problem. A man must sit with the baker till he had finished making the cake. Mrs D'Souza offered her services for this job. But actually Mr David did not trust Mrs D'Souza either. She could well join hands with the baker and conspire against him. Since a trustworthy man could not be found in the whole of Delhi he took leave for a day. I had shown no interest in this work, so he was grumpy with me for many days, and behind my back told Mrs D'Souza that I hadn't any idea what a cake was. I knew that after the cake was made I could return him to good humour by bringing up the topic of opening a poultry farm, or I could enthuse him by talking about the lifestyle of his friend who owned a big farm near Mirzapur.

The cake came home a day before the birthday. Now there was the problem of where to keep it. Mrs D'Souza's house had more rats than were strictly necessary. I came to his rescue in this hour of crisis. I emptied my tin box of all my clothes, wrapped them in a towel, and the cake was put in the tin box.

Even now all of us talk with gusto about that cake. David Saheb regards it as his greatest achievement. And I regard my emptying my tin box as contribution of no mean order. Since then we have formulated many programmes to have another cake baked. Mr David now lays down the condition that everybody should share the cost. When he is in a good mood he agrees to bear half the cost.

According to him, since childhood, he has been attached to two things—Julie and cake. Julie married a captain and in course of time he forgot her. But cake he still loves. Who can marry a cake? But after making many rounds of Khari Baoli he realised that even a cake could get married. Yet he could not stop liking it.

On returning from office my whole body was aching as if I had been badly beaten up. Mrs D'Souza came to open the front door. Perhaps she had been dozing in her hammock in the kitchen. Her private garments were drying in the courtyard. The words 'private garments' made me laugh. What part of the body has remained private? Climbing into and out of DTC buses has been an education to me on the geography of private parts. I have gained considerable expertise on their warmth, softness, roughness, dirtiness and allure.

'You are early today', Mrs D'Souza began taking down her 'private' garments from the line. 'Will you have tea'? I haven't had tea yet.' 'Yes, certainly.' Of course, if the mean thing had already had tea she wouldn't have offered me any.

I went in. Under the stone ceiling the dining table lay. One leg consists of a column of bricks. The other legs are secured with strips of tin and nails driven in. Propped up with the support of string, tin and iron strips, wire and bricks, the table looks at first glance like a primitive machine. Mrs D'Souza's sewing machine is one on the table. At dinner time the machine is taken off the table and placed on the ground. Dinner over, the machine is put back. At night, Mr David reads his proofs at this table. He drinks several glasses of water and when he gets up at one o'clock, the room is left to itself. I become a part of the room like the table or the sewing machine.

'Here's your tea. It's Green Label.' She puts the cup before me. She uses English terms for all foods. Roti is bread, for some reason she calls lentils soup. Vegetables are 'Boiled vegetables.' She calls bitter gourds a 'hot dish'! Mrs D'Souza can also speak a bit of Queen's English which impresses the people of the neighbourhood. I took the tea, Mrs D'Souza began comparing the present era with the past. She remembers the prices of things forty years ago. Her second favourite topic of conversation is her house, the purpose of which clearly is to brag and impress us. She forgets that having let out two rooms she herself has to sleep in the kitchen.

Fed up with her idiotic talk I went into the bathroom. It would have been nice if David Saheb had been around. She would have sat there with gaping mouth, listening to the finer points of running a poultry farm.

'You don't need much. Work can start with just two thousand rupees. A grand start can be made with four hundred birds. Four hundred eggs per day means a minimum of one hundred rupees a day. Three thousand rupees a month and thirty six thousand year.

'Auntie, I am definitely going to do this business some day in my life. Profit? I tell you, you become a millionaire in four years. Its profit all the way. Then the pleasure of eggs and chicken every day. Kill a bloody chicken every day and make a pudding with twenty eggs. Then you leave this place, Auntie. Is this a place for human beings? You'll have a bungalow built in Maharani Bagh or Vasant Vihar. Buy a car too.'

For a short spell both of them would find themselves in Vasant Vihar. On the right side of the gate of a palatial house would hang a brass name plate with 'Eric David' and 'Mrs J. D'Souza' in letters scintillating like miniature suns.

When I came out of the bathroom David Saheb was there. He had changed his clothes and was sitting in the courtyard, showering abuses wholesale on Basu. Mrs D'Souza was busy preparing a 'hot dish'. Mr David was saying, 'This wretch Basu Saheb is fit for a public trial.' There was hatred and disgust in his eyes. His glasses had slipped down his nose. Stiffening his neck, he readjusted his glasses. I saw Basu's body swinging from a tree near Tilak Bridge, a huge, surging crowd round it. After, a few minutes I saw David Saheb locked in a small hen cage, wire mesh covering its four sides, and David Saheb pecking grain along with two hundred other hens. He bends his head to drink water and lays eggs. He is sitting on a heap of eggs. Outside, through the wire mesh Vasant Vihar can clearly be seen.

I said, 'Why are you fretting David Saheb? Give a kick to this bloody job of yours and set up a poultry farm. And then build a house in Vasant Vihar.'

'No, no. I won't build a house in Vasant Vihar. Basu is building his house there. Brother, this is the bane of this country. Nobody can live like a human being here unless he is a crook. To live like a human being you have to do black-marketing and exploit others. Now tell me do I work less than others? An eight hour stint every day at the office, and two hours waiting for the bus.'

'You're very abusive,' Mrs D'Souza said.

'I can't help it Auntie. Do you expect me to pray to Lord Jesus Christ who has played such a cruel joke at least on me?'

'Forget it, David Saheb. Talk of something else. Did you get too may proofs to read or what?'

'That's right, forget it. You have been in Delhi only three years! And it's to do with your youth too. Perhaps you haven't yet seen the razzle-dazzle of Delhi? Aren't we ever to have a share in it? Have you seen the money flowing in Connaught Place? He waved his hands in the air to show the flow of money. 'Lakhs and crores are burnt there. Money flows down the bodies of women, or swims around in the shape of cars.' He was getting worked up. Taking out his glasses from his pocket he stiffened his neck and adjusted the glasses on his nose.

I felt uneasy. My spirits plummeted, as if my youth had collapsed to my feet. I had trouble breathing. The room suddenly started looking barred like a poultry cage, filled with stench. Mrs D'Souza has several times forecast that one day Mr David will get all of us arrested. And Mr David says he will welcome that day.

His lower lip has become quite thick by being pressed by his upper lip in anger all the time. Three lines form on his face. In childhood we used to hear that one who had three lines on the forehead would become a king.

In a short while he became tranquil. At the dining table he shouted, 'Basu ki Jai', and gulped down two glasses of water.

Mrs D'Souza's 'hot dish', 'soup' and 'bread' were ready.

'Cooking bitter gourd is an art, Saheb,' Mr David said, working his jaws rapidly.

'This one dish takes as much time as three others,' she said, to put her boarders under an obligation to her.

Ignoring her remark, David said, 'The real joy of eating bitter gourd was in Sitapur, Auntie. In the kitchen garden behind our bungalow Daddy grew a large variety of vegetables. If you stuff gourds with mincemeat and a lot of onions and cook it, it makes a wonderful dish.

We knew now Mr David would reminisce about his childhood. And along with these stories, would also be the one about his governess Naseeban, who on her salary of one rupee a month was always happy, and whose main job was to look after David Baba. She was corrected a thousand times, but Naseeban always called David Deepak Baba. This was also the context for bringing up the event of the picnic in which he had driven his father's car over the slope of a bank on the Jamuna. The loyal and experienced driver, Ismail Khan, had started sweating. David Baba had scolded him and got him out of the car. All the boys and girls had got down. The English boys had lost their nerve. But Julie had refused to get off. David Baba thought for two minutes, started the car. He changed gear, pressed the accelerator, and in one bound the car ascended the slope. Ismail Khan came up and kissed David Baba's hand. He had seen high-up British officers drive. But David Baba had excelled them all. That day Julie had promised David baba a kiss.

While narrating these stories Mr David's bitterness evaporates. He does not look like David Salteb but Deepak Baba. A thin cloud of dust floats up and the 1930 vintage Ford enters the gate of a bungalow in Civil Lines, Sitapur. On a pillar at the gate is written in distinct letters, 'Peter J. David, Deputy Collector'. The bungalow has a tiled roof. Round it is a large compound of several *bighas*. At the back are mango and orange groves. To the right is a tennis court, and to the left a big kitchen garden. Under the high-ceilinged verandah a liveried peon can be seen dozing fitfully. In the hall inside is Victorian furniture, with a hand-pulled fan. In the afternoon the coolie who pulls the fan dozes off while pulling the fan. Mr Peter. J. David, with kicks from his English boots, makes blue flowers bloom on his black body.

The children sit at the dining table, wearing ties, and drink soup. They round off the dinner with ice cream after which they bid good night to Mummy and Daddy, and retire to their rooms. At about nine thirty, the 1930 vintage Ford sets off again with Peter. J. David and his wife, in the direction of the club. Or it goes to the house of a native aristocrat and returns wobbling at midnight.

The lights of Delhi can be seen from Mrs D'Souza's roof. The blinking eyes of thousands of wild animals shine in the might. I come down for drink of water. I find David Saheb at his proofs. He smiles, seeing me covers his pen and asks me to sit down. His eyes are heavy with sleep. Softly he explains things to me. I am fed up with his explanations. In the beginning I thought him naive, but later on, I don't know why, his words began to affect me. 'Run away from this city. Run away as fast as you can. Like you, I too came here straight from college, to win the great capital city. But you can see what has become of me, there is nothing in this city, nothing. Never mind me. Where can I go? The city has got into me through my arse.'

'But how long will nothing happen, Mr David?'

'As long as you have nothing to offer. And I know you have none of the things which can be given to people.'

I return to my room. What have I got to offer? Stately chairs of office? English etiquette? Cocktail parties? Huge lawns? Suits and ties, girls, cars, shopping? Then who are these people who make promises to me in narrow corridors and smile? I'll have to think it all over again. And for a long time I keep trying to muster the courage to think again. But my courage keeps receding till I hold it by its arm and pull it forward. But like a stubborn mule it breaks its rope and escapes.

I come down again for water. He is asleep, with his head on the table. The sheaf of proofs lies in front of him. I shake him by the shoulder. 'Go to bed now. Tomorrow you have to go to the site.' A faint smile plays across his face. The next day he has to examine a site for his poultry farm. We have gone to many sites before. My David gets up and has a drink of water. Then he tumbles into his bed as if he has fallen at the feet of the great capital city.

I go upstairs and lie down. 'Why did I study so much in college? No, it is not a question of how much or how little I studied. I shouldn't have been in college at all, and now two years working at a two hundred and fifty rupee job, what can be done? Why did I stay smiling and patient? After skipping lunch for two years what have I gained? From below comes the sound of the buffalo dropping dung. A familiar odour spreads. It reminds me of the smell of that mofussil town I consider my home. Where very few people know me. If I get down at its small station people stare at me after the train leaves. Even the couple of ekka drivers would be frightened to speak to me. To reassure them I have to tell them my father's name. Only then would a smile come to their faces and would they offer me a seat in the ekka. A ten minute run would take me through the entire settlement. On the other side are the fields which means, simply, that on the other side is poverty. They are used to poverty. The police are all-powerful for them and even their cleverest moves are stupid... From the sky overhead comes the symphonic drone of an aeroplane flying towards Palam Airport. Below, on the road passes a truck carrying sand. Labourers sleep on the loaded sand, who sometimes dream of becoming farmers, talk about their villages, talk about the fields there which were once theirs. From the Okhla turning the truck will turn into Mathura Road at great speed. Passing Friends Colony and Ashram, it will whizz past Rajdoot Hotel where ads for all-night cabarets, and for the restaurant go on and off in blinking neon lights. Facing the hotel on the footpath are shrivelled dark men fast asleep, undisturbed by even the grating noise of the truck. In the blaze of the street lights the parts of their bodies seem dismembered. I often wonder why they do not put up roofs over this wide footpath. Walls, even if only of mud, can be raised. But passing thoughts like these lead nowhere. Thoughts filled with stupidity and sentimentality. One who lands on the footpath like an insect, understands everything.

The days pass like a lame man walking. And then the sense of extreme insignificance and helplessness in this metropolitan city makes a man put up with anything. Insults which people in the metropolis casually inflict, do not hurt as they did at first. In the office, the boss, Mr Tiwari's dirty, pig-like face. He is a socialist and a pro-American at the same time. His healthy body, fed on graft, bursts from his tight bush-shirt, and his socialist pen scores out every second line of a draft simply because it has been written by someone else. His arrogance, measured laughter, scheming smile, and at his table four helpless creatures of his empire who know nothing but to keep driving their pens. All around them, the rattling of typewriters. I feel like crushing all these things in my fists. And when I feel hungry I feel hungry enough to eat up all the food in the city. To begin with, the stomach rumbles. If David Saheb were around, he would straightaway contradict me. 'You are wrong. When one feels very hungry it is like two cats fighting. Then a vague ache in the stomach beings which is sweet at first. Then it becomes acuter. If, right then, you drink three or four glasses of water, the stomach feels some relief and you can peacefully work for another hour or two.'

After all this he would without fail advise that instead of starving in the metropolis I would do well to return where I came from. But to go there is to go from one poverty and hunger to another. Thoughts of this kind romp in my head. Fed up at such moments, I ask Mr David if he would like to go to the Greater Kailash market. He smiles and says, 'Wait, let me get ready.' I know he will take a long time to get ready. I polish my shoes and scrub them till they shine so I can see my face in them. Spruced up, I asked Mr David, 'Ready?'

As we go towards the bus stop we look at one another's shoes and derive a strange kind of courage from the sight.

On getting down from the bus we go to the public toilet and groom our hair. He glances at me. Two shiny pairs of shoes trot along in the arcades. I stop in front of a furniture shop, and gaze for some time. Mr David tells me to go in, and, gathering all my courage I step into the shop. The assistants here are very civilized. They mouth two 'sirs' to a sentence. The shiny shoes stroll into the shop. Mr David speaks wonderful English here, shrugging his shoulders and rolling his eyes as if to the manor born. He looks at the things as if they are of very poor quality. Seeing him I am impressed, and try to behave like him.

He lingers at the confectionery shop. Everything is displayed in the show window. At first sight everything looks artificial, made of clay. But of course it is not so.

'Let's go. The rascal is smiling at us.'

'Who?' Mr David asks, and I indicate the shop interior with my eyes. He suddenly enters the shop. Alarmed I move away from the entrance. 'Caught, son,' I mutter. 'Masquerading as the scion of a lat saheb. When a ten paise bus ticket and sixty paise in cash come out of his pocket everyone will laugh at him and he'll have to run away.' Gathering courage I enter the shop. Mr David is speaking in rapid, racy English to the shop keeper who, poor man, is out of his depth. I am pleased. 'So, Smarty, Mr David has floored you all right. Smiling away, you were.' Mr David was asking for a kind of cake of which the shop owners' father, grandfather, or even great grandfather, could not have heard of.

Coming out Mr David puts his hand on my shoulder.

As usual, fine English fare covers the dinner table from end to end. Mrs D'Souza is not in a good mood. The only reason is that I have not been able to pay her on the first of the month. She will look sour for a day or two. And then she will start whining about the high prices of things. Listening to her we will be driven crazy.

The silence is getting oppressive....

'Weren't you to go to Defence Colony this afternoon?' Mrs D'Souza asked, breaking the silence.

'I couldn't go,' David said, raising his face from his plate.

'Then how will you get your things?' Mrs D'Souza muttered. 'Your sister, Cathy, poor thing, has sent them with such love.'

'Love, Auntie?' David Saheb was roused. 'Auntie, her husband earns two thousand rupees a month. Cathy must have drifted to the market one day. She must have lazily picked up a wrist watch and two shirts for one hundred and twenty five rupees. And then she sent them to Delhi through Deenu. Where does love come into this?'

'But go and fetch them, at least.'

'Deenu can bring them here.'

Deenu has his own house in Defence Colony. He has a car. He is David Saheb's childhood friend. He was also a member of the hunting party in which David Saheb brought down four birds with one flying shot.

'It's a long way from Defence Colony to here. And he is a busy man.'

'Am I not a busy proof reader?' He laughed. 'And he can come in his car while I'll have to change two buses.' He was eating his lentils and rice as if masturbating to the fantasy of a cake.

'As you please.'

After dinner we talked for some time. Mrs D'Souza launched forth on the story of the big zamindar who in her younger days had fallen head over heels in love with her, and later on had come to Delhi after getting her address somehow. That was the first time a second hand Ambassador car was parked outside Mrs D'Souza's house. And Mr David had had to sleep in the kitchen. Mr David liked to hear of that zamindar. I immediately put myself in place of the zamindar and get the full thrill of the situation.

After rambling a bit the talk again veered round to food. David Saheb began on recipes for noodles. Then everybody dwelt at length on his or her favourite dish. David Saheb was the first to speak. After we had exhausted the subject of food I said to Mr David, 'Yaar, David, sometimes, I sight a girl in this lane who makes my legs tremble.'

'What was she like? Tell me! Must be Chhidu's wife...'

'Enough, David, don't talk about girls. What a beautiful girl I had fixed your engagement with!'

'What beauty are you talking of, Auntie if you had seen Julie...'

'Julie? Well, I haven't seen her. If you had been my daughter...' Mrs D'Souza's eyes brimmed with tears. 'But that Haji...' She said after a while, 'If she had been here I wouldn't have fallen on these bad days. I would have married her off to some army officer. Any body would have asked for her hand'.

'How can I marry, Auntie? I can't fill even my own belly on two hundred and seventy five rupees and twenty one paise. What's the point of ruining one more life, Auntie? I don't want to leave behind a poverty-stricken woman and a couple of proof readers who would sit night and day in the midst of ear-splitting machines and destroy their eyes. He paused. 'That's what I keep telling him,' he pointed at me. 'This man has some land in his village on which he raises wheat and some rice. He should build a mud house near his land, and grow a pumpkin vine on the thatched roof. He can conveniently keep a buffalo in the village. After sometime he can start a poultry farm. He won't have to worry about food and will have a roof over his head. He can work and eat in peace, like a gentleman.'

'After that you come over, and a cake will be baked. With a lot of eggs,' I joked.

Deepak Baba began to laugh, a totally innocent, childlike laugh.

Mithileshwar

The Return of the Assassins

It is twelve at night. Tega, Sigu and Ganpat, walk along stealthily. They have crossed the city's main road where traffic flows ceaselessly all night. They have also left behind these colonies of the city where night never descends and where all sorts of weird activities are carried on under the milky glow of street lamp posts. Now they have come to the western part of the city, to the most forsaken colony of the city. There is no light in its unpaved, uneven lanes flanked by tumbledown houses interspersed by thatched, decrepit huts. The lanes are always damp and slushy and an open drain running along the edge of one of the lanes stinks to the skies. In this colony live manual labourers, sweepers, rickshaw-pullers and those small ill-paid jobs. They don't have the means to pay the higher rents in other parts of the city.

Ganpat came to this colony yesterday afternoon. With him was a man employed by Haji Seth. The man showed Ganpat a particular spot and pointed out to him an individual. What he is required to do next had been explained to him by Haji Seth himself. As a rule Ganpat asks Tega and Sigu to join hands with him on such missions. The fact is that Ganpat negotiates such deals, settles the terms and draws up the plans. But the actual job is done by Tega and Sigu.

Ganpat has a very perfunctory idea about the man pointed out to him. At first glance he looks to Ganpat a most ordinary sort. But from Haji Seth's talk it seems that this man has become a cause of great anxiety for Haji and his family. Haji Seth, as it transpires, is putting up a new factory in this area and this man is an impediment in his way. Ganpat doesn't have a ghost of an idea as to why this man comes in Haji Seth's way and why he is taking up cudgels against him. In fact Ganpat has never tried to probe into Haji's affairs. All he cares for is the job, for which Haji Seth remunerates him handsomely. He never thinks of the whys and wherefores. He implicitly follows Haji's instructions and that is that.

Ganpat walk along swiftly with his companions. Everyone in the area has gone to sleep. The doors and windows of all the houses are closed. Ganpat likes the stillness of the night and the deserted look of the colony. It makes his job that much easier.

When Ganpat has to work in well-lit and bustling colonies he finds it a severe trial. Sometimes it takes him as a much as a month to accomplish a job for which he has to think of many strategies and work out many schemes. But in this colony he can notch up a job in the twinkling of an eye. For Ganpat, a colony like this is a sort of village in the city—unlit, insecure and without resources.

Ganpat reaches the place of action with his companions. The room in which that person lives is only a few yards away from here. He lives there alone. His family is not with him. Is he married or a bachelor? Where does he come from? No, Ganpat knows nothing. Where the person is from is of no concern to Ganpat. All he is concerned with is to finish his job, make money and booze. He will have a hearty meal and a good time with Hirabai in bed. What else?

Ganpat and his companions are surprised to find the door of the room open. There is a lantern burning in the room and the man sitting at a table is busy writing, the light from the lantern falling directly on his face. His face is clearly visible to them.

In this colony where all the doors are kept bolted, this man is writing with the door ajar. Even though he has had a brush with Haji Seth he does not seem to be afraid. For an instant Ganpat and his companions' enthusiasm cools. At a loss, they stand in a corner of the lane and silently watch the man from there. Then, gesturing to his companions to follow him, Ganpat steps forward and, going into a side lane, advises his companions to hide themselves behind the rubble of a crumbling house. The rubble lies heaped up in front of them. Then he joins them and together they watch the man in the shack. He is clearly visible to them from where they are hiding. Tega thinks he has seen the man somewhere before. He taxes his memory in an effort to place the man.

Whenever Tega goes out on a job of this sort he gets blind drunk. Ganpat and Sigu also drink, but not as much. Tega knows that if he does not get heavily drunk he will not be able to do these jobs. Such jobs cannot be done in one's senses.

Ganpat will whisper under his breath. The three of them together will rush into the shack. Sigu will hold the man's hands. Ganpat will gag his mouth and Tega will do the job. But Tega must be extra cautious, Ganpat warns him. It requires dexterity of hand. They must make a clean job of it without messing up anything.

Tega says, 'Wait a minute!' He is still trying to remember where he has seen this man before.

After watching the man steadily for sometime Sigu says: 'He looks like a decent man. A studious type. Why does Haji want to finish him? I don't see anything bad about this man.'

'How are we concerned?' Ganpat retorts. 'Good or bad, Haji has paid us three thousand rupees. A thousand rupees each. It's no small amount.'

Sigu falls silent. Ganpat too is quiet. Tega is still lost in thought. Through his intoxication a picture emerges. Yes, now he remembers. Last year an epidemic of cholera had broken out in Tega's village. Tega's village is very close to this city—

only five kilometres away. But no measures were taken by the city authorities to control the epidemic. Only that man—the one sitting in the shack—had suddenly emerged from somewhere. With him were some raw youths. They ran to and fro between city and village. After much agitation and noise making they managed to gather a sizeable quantity of medicines and had dragged some doctors from the city to the village. If that man had not come in time Tega's nephew would have died.

Tega keeps staring at the man in the room till his eyes bulge under the strain. He has recognised him for sure. What is his name? He doesn't know. The boys of the village used to address him as Brother.

Now Tega murmurs, 'Ganpat, I recognize this man. A cholera epidemic broke out in my village last year and this man came and saved many lives. He is a very good man. Tell Haji to talk to him and reach a compromise.'

'Don't forget Haji has given us three thousand rupees,' Ganpat persuades Tega.' We have already spent more than half the money. How will we return it to him? It's a lot of money.'

Tega says: 'Tell Haji we shall do some other job for him to make up for this.'

Before Ganpat can say anything further six or seven very young boys come through the lane and swiftly enter the man's room.

Ganpat and his companion can clearly hear their voices. They are panting. They look very angry.

'Brother, at ten o'clock last night Haji Seth's truck came loaded with bricks. We did not allow the truck driver to unload the bricks there. We had a big tussle with Haji Seth's men. They went to the nearby police station to seek help. We also followed them there and told the Station Officer clearly,' Sir, you know that for many generations the children of this colony have been studying under the shade of the mango tree. Now we have raised funds to lay the foundation stone of a school for the children. This land does not belong to Haji Seth. It belongs to the Municipality. The previous Chairman had sanctioned the construction of a school building here. Haji Seth wants to secure this land with the connivance of the present Chairman. Sir, you remember that Brother had taken out a procession in the town against the new Chairman. Until a proper decision is taken, you must not support Haji Seth. Otherwise, Brother will take out a procession against the police too.' And Brother, when we threatened the Police Inspector that you would lead a procession against him, the Police Inspector relented. He restrained his constables from hobnobbing with Haji Seth till we forced the truck to move on.'

After listening to them, the man said, rising from his chair,' You did the right thing. Keep a vigil at that plot of land. Tomorrow we shall meet the Collector, the SP and the Municipal Chairman. We shall rouse public opinion in support of our cause. For years, our children have been studying on this plot of land. This land is not Haji's private property.'

They kept on discussing this subject among themselves. But the talk aroused a fierce response in Ganpat and his companions. Fear of the police often sent Ganpat and his companions into hiding for months together. But the same police were afraid of this man. They whispered into each other's ears. 'This wretch Haji has sent us to the wrong place. We must back out.'

It is morning. Ganpat and his companions are in Haji Seth's room. Haji Seth is angry that his task has not been accomplished. He wants to rebuke Ganpat for his lack of enterprise but recants in the presence of his companions. Ganpat generally talks to Haji privately either before or after the job. But today his companions have also accompanied him to Haji Seth's place. This makes Haji Seth think that something serious must have happened and his plan must have misfired.

'What great obstruction came in your way?' he asks. 'Why hasn't the job been done?'

Before Ganpat can speak Tega butts in. 'Sethji, he is not a bad man,' he says. 'We won't kill him. You talk and come to terms with him. Don't wipe him out.'

For an instant Haji Seth is taken aback at Tega's words. He feels as if he has come hurtling down from the top most peak of a mountain. He could never dream that Ganpat and his companions would ever talk about a man's being good or bad. He cannot understand what magic that weak and thin young fellow has wrought on them that they have started talking in this way.

Haji Seth thinks for some time and then he takes the three of them into an inner room. He opens a cupboard bringing into view an assortment of coloured bottles. A servant comes in with plates of *kababs* and cashewnuts.

Ganpat and his companions have never had such choice liquor in their lives. Nor *kababs* and cashewnuts. Sitting comfortably on Dunlopillo mattresses they drink and eat. Haji Seth begins talking. He must drive home his point.

'This man is a regular bad character, a rogue. He misleads people from dirty slums and turns them into agitators. He creates brawls and gets them beaten up. He even has people clapped into jail. He takes fledgling youths as disciples and passes off as their self-styled leader. I told him that I would get him a decent job and it was time he gave up his nefarious activities. But he has not relented. I tempted him with money too. I told him to take two thousand rupees. Four thousand rupees. Five thousand rupees. But he poses as a Mahatma. How can he directly accept money?'

Before the Seth had completed his story Tega interrupted him, 'Sethji, he himself lives in filthy slums. If he were cheating people he would live in a nice clean place. Cholera broke out in my village and he saved many lives, risking his own life. He did not ask for money from anyone.'

'You'll never understand, Tega. It will take you time to understand people of this mould. I ask you what is his purpose in doing all this? If I do something it is for wealth. Everyone in this world works only to make money. Then why should he alone work for nothing? It's too big a mystery. You can't understand it.'

Tega falls silent. Sethji has rendered him speechless. He is in a quandary. Still he says, 'You may be right, Sethji. But don't finish him. Get him out of the way through persuasion.'

'I've tried all possible means, Tega. Finally, I've come to this decision. You may try to reason with him. He will readily agree with all that you say. But when it comes to clinching matters he will cleverly back out. He will just turn a deaf ear to you.'

Haji Seth goes on for a long time, belittling the man, calling him a rogue, mean, crafty, wily and what not. Slowly the liquor starts working on Tega and his companions, bestirring their propensity for violence. The Seth feels pleased. Studying their changed expression, he opens another cupboard. Bundles of green and yellow notes flash into view, 'Ganpat, I gave you three thousand rupees, didn't I?'

'Yes,'

'Well, here's another six thousand. My job must be done tonight.'

Ganpat and his companions have never seen so much money at one time. They hid the money somewhere in their clothes. The liquor has taken full effect. They had never realized that liquor could be so wonderfully intoxicating.

The next night Ganpat and his companions are once again at the same place. Hiding behind the rubble heap they look in as they did last night. But tonight the door is closed. On examination they find that it is not closed from inside but from outside. An open lock hangs from the door. Sigu feels that the man has gone away. He says that they should not take any risk tonight.

Maybe he has come to know about their design and has disappeared in order to save his life.

'I don't think so,' Ganpat says. 'No, how could he know? No one else knows except the three of us. As for Haji Seth, he is an extremely careful man. The man may be coming. He is in the habit of keeping late hours. Yesterday too he kept reading late into the night.

Tega keeps yawning in intoxication. After a while he says, 'Ganpat we will not attack the man straightaway. We shall explain things to him. We shall bait him with money The man does not deserve to be killed.'

Ganpat and Sigu reason with Tega. Come what may, they must finish the fellow tonight. No one else would pay the amount Haji has paid them.

Tega says, 'All right but I will not kill him treacherously. I'll explain to him, make him come round. If he is adamant and comes to blows I'll not hesitate to do him in.'

Ganpat finds Tega's plan a little odd. They have never acted in this manner before. But Sigu is inclined to agree with Tega. Ganpat cannot oppose them. He knows he cannot do without Tega.

At about one o'clock in the night the man returns to his room. He unlocks the door and enters. He lights the lantern. He changes his clothes. Then he picks up a pitcher of water and comes out. He washes his hands and feet, rinses his mouth and goes in again.

Now Tega, Sigu and Ganpat get up from behind the rubble heap. On jobs like these Tega usually takes the lead. He walks alertly, looking right and left. But this time he goes along fearlessly. Nobody would suspect that there is murder in his heart.

Standing at the door, Tega addresses the man sitting inside, 'Bhai Saheb, we want to talk to you about something.'

Tega and his companions think that the man will get frightened on seeing unknown people at this time of night. But to their surprise the man is not in the least frightened. 'Please come in,' he says.

Tega and his companions enter the room. The room is very small and quite bare except for a table and a chair. Half the space is filled with books. Tega and his companions have never before seen so many books owned by one man. They look with fascination at the books ranged one upon the other. Near the books lies a mat partially covered with a rug. Perhaps he sleeps on this.

The man gestures to Tega and his companions to sit on the rug and they do so. Leaving his chair he also sits down on the rug by their side. 'You sit on the chair,' Tega says.

The man replies, 'You are older than me. You are like elder brothers to me. I won't sit on the chair in your presence. We shall all sit together on the rug.'

The man's words sink deep into Tega's being. He stares fixedly at the man's face. Ganpat and Sigu also look at him keenly.

Suddenly Sigu recognises the man. Sigu was once in jail on account of a dacoity and it was that there he had seen this man. Perhaps he had been there before him and had been consigned to a different ward. In the jail too he commanded great respect. He used to complain against the maltreatment of fellow prisoners by the jail staff. Sigu's mind is filled with respect when be recognizes him. He remembers that while in jail he used to regard him as sublime. He mentally resolves there and then that he will not allow anyone to raise his hand against this man.

The man asks, 'Do tell me what brings you here?'

Sigu gives Ganpat a meaningful look and Ganpat at Tega. For a moment none of them is able to speak. Then Tega says, 'Haji Seth wants to set up a factory in the Bhimpatti area but you are not allowing it.'

Before Tega can say anything more, the man interrupts him. 'No, that's not true. This charge should not be laid against me alone. I put it to you that you also come in his way. I am not fighting Haji Seth to construct a house for myself on the plot of land. My children, your children, will study on that plot of land. You know very well that that colony is worse than this one. It lacks even the basic amenities of life. If Haji Seth usurps that piece of land then there will be no other place where poor children can study. How can these poor children afford to go to expensive schools far off from their homes? I know you are inhabitants of the same kind of colonies. You don't live in colonies like Haji Seth's. Maybe Haji Seth wants you to be instrumental in destroying your own houses. Just think of it, where will the children of your colonies go to study in that case? Haji Seth's son studies in a foreign land. New schools are being opened every day for rich people's children. But who cares for the needs of people lie you and me? We are dying of poverty, hunger and disease. People like Haji Seth will never let us live like human beings. They treat us like cattle. Today Haji Seth is trying to usurp that plot of land meant for a school. Tomorrow he may raze your houses to get his bungalow built there. We will then become beggars to live and die by the roadside. You must have seen the beggars moaning and writhing at the railway station. They do not come from families like the Seth's but from families like ours. I swear to you, if you do not wish to get a school built at this place it will never get built. Who am I to stick my neck out? You go to that colony and verify things for yourself. Every single child of that colony is ready to stop Haji Seth from swallowing up that piece of land. Tomorrow morning we are going to hold a public meeting. You will see for yourselves that it will be your own children who will publicly defy Haji Seth. I tell you, he will not have the guts to set foot there.'

The man stands up. As he speaks, his face turns red. Pacing the room, he continues talking. 'Haji Seth is a fool. I have come to know that he wants to eliminate me. He thinks that with me out of the way there will be no one to oppose him. But little does he know that the entire colony has awakened. How many people can he eliminate? I don't care if Haji Seth gets me killed. After all, we have all to die one day.'

He keeps talking for a long time. Tega, Sigu and Ganpat listen to him with bowed heads. His talk has transported them to a strange world of which they had never known. Nor had they realized that men like him exist in this world. They only know what Haji Seth had told them—that man is prepared to go to any length to amass wealth, that every man toils only for wealth. But this man has given them a new vision of life. Tega was feeling penitent—why had he come here? This rascal Haji was using them to kill their own kind. Sigu's eyes filled with tears. If only he had known all this earlier. Ganpat feels that his plan has already gone awry. In the end he will have to return the money to Haji Seth. So much money!

The man asks, 'Why are you all quiet? Please speak. Unless I know your minds I will not go to that piece of land tomorrow.'

Tega raises his head. In all his life tears have never risen to his eyes. But today where have these tears come from? Tega says in a strained voice, 'Please forgive us. We did not know all this. We came here out of ignorance.'

Sigu, unable to hold back his tears, wipes his eyes. For the first time Ganpat also becomes emotional. Deeply touched, that man embraces them one by one.

By now it is almost three in the morning. The man says, 'I've not eaten yet. I think you haven't eaten either. My food is lying wrapped up in that cloth there. We shall share it.'

In spite of remonstrance from Tega and his companions he brings the food from a corner of the room. Six coarse *chapatis*, made in the day, and gone dry. He unfolds a piece of paper. It holds some salt, a green chilli and a slice of onion.

The man places the food in the centre, bidding them eat. They start eating. While eating they are reminded of Haji Seth.

The Haji—what a great liar he is! He had told them that this man misled poor people to secure his nefarious ends and was now having the time of his life. They saw no evidence of it. Haji was indeed a liar, a rogue, a crook.

After eating the man urges upon them not to go out anywhere at that hour. They could as well sleep there and leave in the morning.

The lantern is put out and they lie down on the rug. None of them speak. But there is a dialogue going on in the mind of each one of them. With closed eyes, they encounter this new reality.

Very early in the morning the three depart, leaving him asleep. They walk across the colony and come on to the main road. From a distance they can see Haji Seth pacing the balcony of his house. He is waiting for them. They go straight to him. One look at their faces and Haji Seth feels that the job has not been done today. Before Haji Seth can speak, Tega throws the bundle of notes at him. 'Haji Seth, I've come to warn you. If anything happens to that man I won't leave you alive!'

Haji Seth looks at him startled. 'What's happened? What's the matter?'

But all three go away. None replies. One of them only turns to give Haji a disdainful look.

Haji Seth calls, 'Stop!... Just a moment... Here, give me back my goods.'

But no one stops—not even Ganpat. Haji Seth suddenly gets jittery. He had given them his imported revolver. Cannot rely on country made weapons. But what's going on here? They are walking away without returning his precious revolver.

Haji Seth cannot understand how all this has happened. Never before has he missed his mark. And he has thrown away so much money at one go without achieving his end. What kind of man is this? What kind of magic has be wrought on these people? And his precious weapon gone into the bargain! He is too confused to get at the heart of the matter.

Utterly confused, Haji Seth keeps pacing his balcony. Just then he sees a man coming in his direction. he looks at him closely. Yes, he is coming to his house. Approaching Haji Seth, the man takes out Haji Seth's revolver from his bag and, giving it to him, says, 'Sethji, your men left your weapon in my room. I thought I would restore it to you.'

Haji Seth takes back the revolver. But even in the chill of the morning beads of perspiration throb on his forehead. His hands start shaking. He cannot keep his grip on the revolver and puts it on a nearby chair.

The man is about to go when Haji Seth breaks into speech, 'Forgive me,' he says. 'I'm ashamed of myself. Come, have tea with me.'

'Sethji, I don't have time. They are holding a public meeting on that plot of land. I'm going there.'

The Seth says, 'Just a minute. Don't hold a public meeting there. There is no need for it. I've made up my mind. I have nothing to do with that piece of land. I will not step on it. I deeply regret my mistake.'

The man turns round and looks at the Seth. The Seth is drenched in sweat from head to foot.

He looks with distended eyes at the man he had thought weak and contemptible. The Seth had thought that he had the power to crush this man between his fingers but today despite his mansion and wealth he feels dwarfed before him. He starts shaking with an unknown fear. Seeing the Seth's condition a faint smile appears on the man's face.

Contributors

Phaneshwar Nath 'Renu' (1921–1977)

Born in a village in Bihar, he was at a very early age caught in the maelstrom of politics and played an important role in the 'Quit India' movement. Though he was imprisoned and suffered from physical disabilities, he relentlessly carried on with his literary activities. He was the leading light of the generation of 'Nai Kahani' and shot into fame with his first novel *Maila Anchal* in 1954 which broke new ground in Hindi fiction. In his fiction he made deft use of local dialect superimposing it on chaste and virile Hindi with all its overtones and undertones. One of his stories *Teesri Kasam* (The Third Vow) was filmed.

His next novel *Parti Parikatha* appeared in 1957 followed by another novel *Dirghtapa*. His more prominent stories were published in three separate collections.

Mohan Rakesh (1925–1972)

An outstanding name in Hindi fiction, he initiated the 'New Story' movement in Hindi. After some teaching stints in various colleges in Bombay, Delhi and Jullundur, he adopted writing as his main profession and devoted all his time to it. For a year he also edited *Sarika*. His writings include six collections of short stories, three novels and three plays. He reached his pinnacle of glory with his plays *Ashar Ka Ek Din* and *Adhe Adhure*. He was the recipient of the Sangeet Natak

Akademi Award and was also awarded the Jawaharlal Nehru Fellowship.

Amrit Lal Nagar (1916–1990)

Born in 1916 at Agra in a Gujarati family settled in Uttar Pradesh, he had to struggle his way up in life. A writer with a social conscience and a humanistic vision, he has thirteen novels, ten collections of stories, thirty plays, besides other works to his credit. In recognition of his outstanding contribution to Hindi literature he was honoured with the Soviet Land Nehru Award, the U.P. Sangeet Natak Academy Award, the Bhartiya Bhasha Parishad Award, and the Sahitya Akademi Award and was also honoured by the President of India with the Padmabhushan and the Sahitya Akademi Fellowship.

Hari Shankar Parsai (b. 1924)

Born in a village in Hoshangabad district of Madhya Pradesh, Parsai did his M.A. in Hindi from the Nagpur University. After a short stint in the Forest Department at the age of 18, after completing his education he adopted teaching as his career but gave it up in 1957 to devote all his time to writing. He also started a literary magazine with his own financial recourses but had to abandon it due to recurring losses. For several years he wrote regular columns in prestigious journals such as *Nai Duniya*, *Nai Kahani*, *Kalpana* and later on *Ganga*. He has two collections of stories, two novels and several volumes of literary essays to his credit. He won the Sahitya Akademi Award in Hindi for his book *Viklang Shradha Ka Daur*.

Parsai appeared on the literary horizon as a humorist. His humour has a strong social content and is replete with biting satire matched by no other writer.

Amrit Rai (b. 1921)

He did his M.A. in English Literature from the Allahabad University. During his student days he was attracted towards Marxism which he viewed with an open mind maintaining that no philosophy can be greater than life. His published works include seven novels, eight collections of short stories, three plays, and a number of volumes on humour and literary criticism. One of his most outstanding books, *Kalam Ka Sipahi*, Premchand's biography, won him the Sahitya Akademi Award in Hindi. He also edited *Hans*, the magazine founded by his father, Premchand, for ten years. He was conferred the Jawaharlal Nehru Fellowship. He is also a recipient of the Soviet Land Nehru Award and the Dwivageesh Samman.

Amarkant (b. 1925)

Born in Ballia district of Uttar Pradesh in 1925, Amarkant was educated at the Allahabad University. His stories are marked by deep insight, compassion and a tantalising streak of satire. With five collections of short stories and half a dozen novels, he has carved a permanent place for himself in Hindi fiction. He has also been a regular contributor to Hindi journals.

Bhisham Sahni (b. 1915)

Born in Rawalpindi (now in Pakistan), Bhisham Sahni was educated at Government College, Lahore from where he took his Master's degree in English Literature. After coming to Delhi he taught in a college. He worked as a translator at the Foreign Languages Publishing House in Moscow for about seven years and on returning to India resumed teaching. So far he has published eight collections of short stories, four novels, three plays, a biography of his brother Balraj Sahni and several translations. He won the Sahitya Akademi Award for his novel *Tamas*.

Kamleshwar (b. 1932)

Born in Mainpuri in Uttar Pradesh, he holds a place of eminence in Hindi literature having distinguished himself as a short story writer and novelist. He has also been associated with films. He was the first editor of the Hindi magazine *Nai Kahaniyan* and subsequently also edited *Sarika, Katha Yatra, Ganga* and the daily *Jagaran*. He also held the position of the Additional Director General of Doordarshan.

Rajendra Yadav (b. 1929)

Born in Agra, Rajendra Yadav graduated from the Agra College in 1951. Along with Mohan Rakesh and Kamleshwar he had a big hand in introducing the modern sensibility in Hindi fiction. His works comprise a dozen collections of short stories and seven novels. One of his novels, *Sara Akash*, was made into a film. He has also published a book of poetry, an anthology of Hindi short stories, and a book of literary criticism besides translating Chekhov and Camus in Hindi. He is associated with a publishing house and is the editor of *Hans*.

Ram Kumar (b. 1924)

Born in Shimla he did his M.A. in Economics from the Delhi University. He has distinguished himself as a writer and a painter. He lived for a long period in Paris and later in America. He has held several exhibitions in London, New York and Sao Paolo. Recipient of the Lalit Kala Akademi Award, and author of two novels, five volumes of short stories and a travelogue, his writing is marked by sophistication and a quiet charm where even a small detail has a telling effect as a brush stroke on canvas. His volume of short stories in English translation was published by the Writers Workshop, Calcutta.

Shekhar Joshi (b. 1934)

Born in Almora, he was educated at Ajmer and Dehradun and worked in a Defence Workshop from where he was since retired and now lives in Allahabad. His first story appeared in *Dharmayug* in 1955 which set him out on the course of writing, marked by a steady output that has claimed wide attention. He has five collections of stories to his credit, besides numerous other writings.

Markandaya (b. 1932)

Born in Keravat, in the Jaunpur district of Uttar Pradesh, he has made his mark as a short story writer. His outstanding collections of stories include: *Pan aur Phool* (1954), *Hansa Jaie Akela* (1960), *Bhudan* (1961), *Sahaj aur Shubh* (1964), *Mahue ka Ped, Mahi*, and *Dana Bhusa Tatha Anya Kahanian* (1980). His novel *Agnibeej* appeared in 1981. He has also a collection of one-act plays, *Patthar aur Parchain*.

Krishan Baldev Vaid (b. 1927)

Born in Dinga, Punjab, (now in Pakistan), he did his M.A. in English Literature from Camp College, New Delhi, having migrated to India after partition. He studied at Harvard on a Fullbright and Rockfeller Foundation Grant and received his Ph. D from Harvard in 1961. Later he taught at the Punjab University, Chandigarh. He was also the Visiting Professor at Brandes University and Chairman of the Dept. of English, State University of New York at Potsdam. With a subtle psychological slant in his stories and high literary virtuosity, Vaid had carved a niche for himself in contemporary Hindi fiction. His published works include six novels and six collections of short stories many of which including two novels having been translated into English and other languages. He has recently been published by Penguin India.

Shailesh Matiyani (b. 1931)

Born in 1931 in a village near Almora, he is a leading novelist and a story writer, having published a dozen novels, ten collections of stories, and a critical work, *Janta aur Sahitya* (The People and Literature). His works vividly describe the problems faced by the unprivileged sections of society. He also edits a journal published from Allahabad where he now lives.

Shivprasad Singh (b. 1928)

Born in Jalalpur village in the Varanasi district of Uttar Pradesh, he did his M.A. and Ph.D from the Banaras Hindu University, where he began to teach Hindi, retiring in 1988 as Professor and Head of the Department. He is now a freelance writer and edits the literary journal, *Sarokar*.

He has published six collections of stories, five novels, five volumes of essays and four volumes of literary criticism beside a biography of Sri Aurobindo. His novel, *Neela Chand* won him the Sahitya Akademi Award for 1990.

Krishna Sobti (b. 1925)

Born in Gujarat (now in Pakistan) in 1925, she was educated at Shimla, Lahore and Delhi. Her forte is the short story though she has equally distinguished herself in her novels which are marked by a virile diction and a bold approach characteristically her own. She has written eight novels and a collection of short stories. Her work *Zindaginama* won her the Sahitya Akademi Award in 1980. She is also the recipient of the Sahitya Shiromani Award.

Nirmal Verma (b. 1929)

Born in Shimla in 1929, he took his Master's degree in History from St. Stephen's College, Delhi. Between 1959 and 1968 he lived in Prague studying and translating Czech literature into

Hindi. He left after the Soviet invasion of Czechoslovakia and returned to India. Acknowledged as the master of the short story in Hindi, his work, like Chekhov's allows the flow of life to find its own form in art. He has published four novels, five collections of short stories and several volumes of travelogue and essays. His collections of stories *World Elsewhere* and *The Crows of Deliverance* were recently published in England. He is also a recipient of the Sahitya Akademi Award.

Mannu Bhandari (b. 1931)

She obtained her Master's degree in Hindi from the Banaras Hindu University. She is now among the leading Hindi writers. Two of her stories have been made into successful films and a play based on her novel *Mahabhoj* has achieved notable success. She has eight collections of stories, four novels and some books for children to her credit. She has recently retired from the Miranda House, Delhi University, where she had been teaching Hindi.

Usha Priyamvada (b. 1932)

Born in Kanpur, Uttar Pradesh, she did her post-graduate in English from the Allahabad University. After a brief teaching stint at the University of Allahabad and Lady Shriram College, University of Delhi, she did her post-doctoral research at Indiana University, USA, as a Fullbright scholar. Currently she is a Professor at the University of Wisconsin. Her publications include three novels, four collections of stories and two biographies. She writes in Hindi and English.

Giriraj Kishore (b. 1936)

Born in Muzaffarnagar in Uttar Pradesh, and educated at Agra, he started writing right from his school days. His published works include ten novels, seven collections of stories and half a dozen plays. At present, he is the Head of the Centre for Creative Writing and Publications, Indian Institute of Technology, Kanpur.

Hridayesh (b. 1930)

Born in 1930 at Shahjahanpur in Uttar Pradesh, Hridayesh is working at the District Court, Shahjahanpur. Ploughing a lonely furrow he has carved his way in the field of Hindi literature, maintaining a steady output. His first story was published in 1951 and since then he has published five novels and five collections of stories.

Shaani (b. 1923)

Gulsher Khan Shaani was born in Bastar, Madhya Pradesh. He began writing at the age of 20 and has so far published ten collections of short stories, four novels and a socio-anthropological travelogue on Bastar. His novel *Kala Jal* has been translated into English, Russian and Lithuanian. Recipient of the Shikhar Samman, he has for a number of years edited *Samkaleen Bhartiya Sahitya,* the Hindi journal published by the Sahitya Akademi.

Ramakant

He did his M.A. in Hindi and after working with the Soviet Information Services for a number of years he relinquished his job to devote all his time to writing. His chief works are *Doshi*, (1979), *Teesra Desh* (1981) and *Koi Aur Baat*. His collections of short stories include *Bhai Mukti* and *Ghar Ki Vitto*. He was honoured with the Soviet Land Nehru Award for his contribution to literature

Ram Darash Mishra (b. 1924)

Born in Dumri in the Gorakhpur district of Uttar Pradesh, he did M.A. and Ph.D in Hindi Literature from the Banaras Hindu University. He was Professor of Hindi at the Delhi University for several years. His published works include ten novels, seven collections of short stories, seven volumes of poetry, a volume of belle lettres, a number of books on literary criticism and an autobiography in four volumes besides a travelogue on Korea.

Gyanranjan (b. 1936)

He attracted wide notice with his provocative short stories, particularly his collection, *Fence Ke Idhar Udhar*, published in 1967 and followed by *Yatri* and *Kshu ijivi*. Currently, he devotes all his time to *Pahal*, a literary magazine published by him.

Mudrarakshash (b. 1932)

Subhash Chander, who writes under the pen name Mudrarakshash, was born in a village near Lucknow. He did his M.A. in Philosophy from the Lucknow University whereafter he acted as the Assistant Editor of a prestigious Hindi literary magazine published from Calcutta. Later he joined the All India Radio at Delhi where he simultaneously wrote and acted in plays. He is known for his quaint experiments in poetry and daring incongruities on the stage. *Tendua* (The Leopard) and *Gufaen* (The Caves) are his two well known plays. He has also made his mark as a short story writer, having three collections of stories and two novels.

Govind Mishra (b. 1939)

Born at Banda in Uttar Pradesh, he did his M.A. in English literature from the Allahabad University and joined the Indian

Revenue Service. He has published six novels, an equal number of collections of stories besides a travelogue and a volume of literary essays.

Kashinath Singh (b. 1936)

Born in Jeanpur near Banaras, he passed his Matriculation from the village school and did his M.A. and Ph.D. in Hindi literature from the Hindu University, Banaras where he subsequently held a position in the Hindi Faculty. He started writing in 1960 and has since published six collections of short stories, a novel and a play. Having Marxist leanings in politics he has also translated Polish, and Japanese writings into Hindi.

Asghar Wajahat (b. 1946)

Born at Fatehpur in Uttar Pradesh, he did his M.A. and Ph.D. in Hindi Literature from the Aligarh University. He has published four collections of short stories, a number of plays and a novel, besides an anthology of progressive poetry. Currently, he is teaching Hindi at the Jamia Millia Islamia, Delhi.

Mithileshwar (b. 1950)

He was born in Arrah in Bihar. Author of more than eight collections of stories he has carved a niche for himself as a short story writer in Hindi. His important collections include *Meghnad Ka Nirney, Gaon Ke Log, Dusra Mahabharat, Band Raston Ke Beech* and *Chhah Mahilayen*. He has also written a novel, *Yudha sthal* which was published in 1981.

Jai Ratan (b. 1917)

Jai Ratan was born in Ludhiana in 1917 and now lives in Delhi. He retired as a senior executive from a known business house of India. He was educated at the Forman Christian College, Lahore, from where he took a Master's degree in English literature. He is a founder member of Writers Workshop, Calcutta.

Apart from writings of his own, he has translated extensively from Hindi, Urdu and Punjabi into English. He has over three dozen translations to his credit. He has also edited and has been published in several anthologies published in India and abroad. He is the recipient of the 'Divagish' Award for 1991 and very recently the Sahitya Akademi Prize for Translation (English) in 1992.